A HYMN FOR JAMIE

RICHARD JOHN THORNTON

A HYMN FOR JAMIE

DEDICATED TO FAMILIES EVERYWHERE

Beware the declarers of undying loyalty.
Such virtue should never be openly discussed.
For what remains unspoken.
Remains unblemished.

PROLOGUE

Nearly twenty-four months had passed since our return to Nottingham. The euphoria we derived from both reunification and relocation is something that cannot be depicted by mere sentiment.

The flush of emancipation entered our bloodstreams and had since remained installed as part and parcel of our genetic make-up.

After all those years of psychological and physical distress, Martin, Bobby, and I were finally feeling freed of the spiritual shackles that had restricted our existence for far too long.

The three of us fully embraced our newfound liberty. It was a thoroughly uplifting experience for us to be able to finally begin selecting our own paths in life, as opposed to the paths that fate had chosen for us.

A pivotal factor in this process was Bobby's open adoration of my brother. They had evidently bonded implicitly amid the years of relentless abuse. Their partnership looked to be rock solid, and this was a major spur for me to finally spread my own wings and plough my own furrow.

Martin of course took everything in his stride as usual and rarely felt inclined to offer commentary or opinion regarding what had transpired in the past.

He certainly never broached the subject of love to me, and I honestly never found reason to openly discuss it with him either.

It was my comforting presumption that he and Bobby Jones were bound together by destiny, and that their compassion for one another didn't require any vocal acknowledgement from anyone.

So much for my theory.

Well, unbeknown to anybody - including *you*, dear reader - my brother had secretly hatched a plan and eventually played his trump card on me, didn't he.

Four days after I had commenced an enticing second year at Swansea University.

You've possibly already guessed.

He went down on one knee to Bobby in the middle of Costa.

Ring ready in hand and grin planted on face, apparently.

The little dark horse.

He never gave me the slightest hint it was coming, so I can only imagine how surprised Bobby was.

It was a bolt from the blue that was eventually alerted to my attention, firstly via a text message from Bobby whilst I was re-arranging my living quarters on campus.

It stated that she needed to talk to me if it was convenient to do so.

I went into panic mode thinking they had run out of milk and couldn't remember where the shop was.

In all seriousness, they were coping without me just fine.

And the same applied to yours truly.

I was relieved that they didn't need babysitting anymore.

Besides, that bungalow was always too cramped for three.

But thankfully, when the buoyant reality of the latest news was eventually conveyed to me through screaming hysteria echoing from the other end of the line, I guessed that the scenario for them both had ultimately played out as they had hoped.

Bobby sounded beyond delighted, as I suppose any woman does when her man pledges himself to her for the rest of his life.

Martin was a little more guarded about his feelings as usual, but did offer me an explanation for the unexpected move when I eventually got Bobby *off* the phone and my brother *on* to it:

'I felt guilty for making her wait any longer, Jamie. Plus, I think she deserves commitment after all the struggles she's had to withstand because of my baggage. I've always known she was the one for me. Forever and ever. And considering everything on balance, I think I'm a pretty good catch for her.'

Not much chance of my brother developing an ego, is there?

Not when he's already got one the size of Nottingham.

And why shouldn't he have?

I would begrudge him nothing.

The truly beauteous aspect of this revelation was that whilst it cemented their relationship for the long-term future, it also gave me a private boost knowing that Martin was immersing himself deeper into the realms of orthodox everyday living.

Doing things that ordinary people are permitted to do, instead of enduring the restrictions that his previous existence employed.

Of being haunted; beaten; tortured; mocked; imprisoned; concealed; excluded; ignored; tolerated…

It's old ground, dear reader.

Apologies. I forgot…you already know the story inside out

After all, you've lived through it with us for long enough.

So anyway, back to the positives and the phone call.

Bobby recalled the electric moment just as it had transpired in the coffee shop.

Martin was in the process of slicing up a Cherry Bakewell into quarters when suddenly he rose from his chair and glanced around the room.

Apparently, the place was crammed full of customers, too.

And without further ado, down he crouched to said knee, removed the little box from his jacket pocket, opened the lid, and did the deed.

No hesitation whatsoever.

He asked for the ultimate honour.

His woman's hand in marriage.

Bobby herself claimed that the dozens of onlookers were transfixed by the entire event. It's a bit of a giveaway what's in store when a guy sinks down onto his knee, isn't it?

Unless he's receiving a Knighthood, of course. And I'd hazard a guess that we've earned one of those too, but there's been no invitation from The Palace yet.

But I give Martin his dues.

He had waited for the perfect moment to strike.

Maximum public spectacle. Attention fully focused on the lady in question. Her broad, ever-striking smile exhibited to the impromptu audience before the onset of jubilant emotion completely ruined her make-up.

Bobby was in raptures, apparently.

Undiluted ecstasy.

Those were *her* words. Not my brother's.

Martin always reacted to anything with automatic control.

He rose back to his feet after his request was eagerly obliged and he duly slipped the engagement ring onto his fiancée's finger.

A diamond solitaire, no less. I still don't know how he found the cash to pay for it but who am I to pry?

He kissed Bobby full on the lips and turned to the naturally appreciative members of the public with a heartfelt message:

'Thank you all for being here. But it was no coincidence. Having guests to spectate has really made it something special for us.'

Typical of my brother.

No big show. No emotive outburst. Just business accomplished as per the plan. Got to love his style, haven't you?

After all, he'd been forced to live by his own judgement his entire life. He'd learned to trust his well-honed instinct on deciphering right from wrong in all matters.

Seeing the correct path through the fog.

Ascertaining risk against reward.

Mistakes were not in his remit.

He knew he loved Bobby, so wisdom dictated that he proved it to her. Can decision making be any more concise?

Any more deliberate and positive and wilful?

I think not.

Bobby laughed at the fact that his cool and collected exterior clashed deliriously with her total loss of composure. She screamed the ceiling down with happiness, allegedly.

No doubt a few swear words were involved, too.

Hysterical with emotion.

Thank the lord she said *yes*, eh?

And whilst sad in origin, my inheritance of the property at number thirty-two, Glenfield Avenue from Henry, had provided concrete foundation for their relationship to bloom properly during the previous couple of years.

A ready-made domestic haven.

A situation that I had the foresight to rubber stamp.

By law it now belonged to all three of us, thanks to my assertion that should anything happen to any one - or any two of us - then the three officially signed wills and testaments would clearly designate the potential benefactors.

We all agreed it was worth doing now that we actually owned something of value, and that we were completely invested in one another as the thriving remnants of the Andrews family.

Inevitably, Martin and Bobby were both grateful and graciously compliant with my suggestion that we proceed with the arrangement, and the legal documentation was procured without delay.

But anyway, enough about those other two for five seconds…

You want to know more about *my* current fortunes, yes?

Of course, you do, dear reader.

Whilst all this razzle-dazzle partying and hanging of bunting had been occurring in Nottingham, I had been establishing myself as resident heart throb for a year in the stimulating confines of Swansea University student campus.

You probably won't be surprised to know that I was in my absolute element.

Living the life that I wanted.

How I wanted.

When I wanted.

Indeed, like my brother and Bobby, I swiftly felt completely untethered as an individual.

Having said that, my departure to Wales encouraged a quite surreal few months apart after battling for so long for the three of us to be back together. But the rewards for our united endeavour were in evidence.

By all accounts, Martin was doing superbly at St. George's Secondary.

His natural flair for all things academic may have rendered him something of an oddity, but the staff were in awe of my brother and the rate at which he had progressed at G.C.S.E. level having missed so much of both his primary and secondary schooling.

His acumen in the classroom had almost gotten to the point whereby his albeit mild autism was quickly relegated to something of a non-existent issue.

But there was a slightly negative consequence to our success.

For me, trips back to the Midlands between terms were a rarity in my inaugural year on campus.

However, frequent phone calls allowed me to retain a careful and appreciative eye over the lives they were making for themselves.

Okay, my bad. I'm back on to *them* again aren't I…

My moment of self-indulgence didn't last long, did it?

But no problem. They deserve all the praise in the world.

Bobby had come a hell of a long way since the days of backstreet pot-washing by the seaside just to pay for her next fix.

No longer the mouthy and overly brazen character from Blackpool, she had gradually transformed herself into a different creature entirely.

No more the short skirt and cowboy boots.

Now she plumped for more fashionable feminine attire - yes, including summer dresses!

At least, I *think* that was her on the photos they sent me…

She became a more responsible, demure, and increasingly refined individual, but still retained the earthy authenticity that struck me on our first meeting in that cess pit of a pub.

Her previous incarnation had evidently been a façade.

An act which allowed her to fit in with the unsavoury surroundings and the even more unsavoury characters. She had her own issues of course. But she willingly entered combat against her demons and had hopefully come through the other side victorious.

I could not hold this woman in any higher possible esteem.

As a trio, we felt like an authentic force to be reckoned with.

Almost akin to two brothers and their newfound adopted sister.

Not quite bonded by blood, but the next best thing.

Even with me being separated from them by two hundred miles for most of the previous twelve months, our intimacy as a family unit and mutually abiding three-way loyalty, was never brought into question.

Swansea was only five hours away by rail. I was always ready to return to my hometown to assist them if I was needed. It told its own story that my presence became less necessary as time went on.

Bobby's ascent at the supermarket with the evergreen John Harrison, and Martin's success at school were anchoring factors for the immediate future. Being generally left to their own very capable devices was a blessing for the three of us.

Routine brought solidity and grounding.

Elements in life that are worth their weight in gold.

The longest time I had spent with them since first departing for Swansea a year ago was for five days over the previous Christmas period. A week of fun and frolic observing two young people enjoying the fact they could host me as *their* guest in *their* little corner of heaven.

The epitome of contentment.

No overriding issues or underlying current of negativity.

Just pure adventure. The visual and tangible definition of bliss.

No black clouds creeping over the horizon.

Nothing seemed to be amiss so far as we could all predict.

But, dear reader, as I can confirm - and as you will readily vouch for - life can take a completely different direction at almost the flick of a switch.

Especially if your surname happens to be Andrews…

I
UNSETTLEMENT

1
AN EXPECTED DEVELOPMENT?

It was now early October. Two Thousand and Six.

I was barely into my middle year at Swansea and enjoying it immensely. Against the odds I had managed to secure a little more time in campus accommodation due to local digs being overfull.

I was very thankful to the Uni authorities that my tardiness in securing lodgings off site over the summer, was an oversight that had been pardoned for the time being.

Not an inconvenience for me, to be truthful.

I *loved* living on campus.

Well, who *wouldn't*?

The droning of my mobile phone awoke me from a light slumber on the sofa bed. I think I had been watching a Tom Cruise film when I fell asleep. It might have been Mission Impossible, but my eyes closed before it could absorb my interest.

Prising the vibrating handset from under my backside, I scrutinised the caller display through blurred vision.

At this early juncture, dear reader, I would anticipate that you are already very impressed with the fact I'm even using a mobile phone at all.

Yes, I know. It took me long enough. Hands up. Guilty as charged.

On with the recap…

It was Bobby on the hotline again. I mumbled a slovenly hello as my eyes adjusted to regaining their function.

I strived to establish the time of day as nearly eight p.m.

My hearing seemed to be off kilter, too.

Her voice was not carrying the usual confidence or sternness that had become customary over the previous months.

Her tone was unusually tremored.

In fact, it barely supported the words she wanted to say.

I strained to compute what she was telling me.

As I listened to her stammered request, I would have gone as far to suggest that she reminded me of the Bobby Jones of old.

Look beyond the bold and sassy front cover and she was presenting herself as quite wary and nervous again.

I might even say…frightened.

When she briefly disclosed the reason for the call, I suppose I was not taken completely by surprise. Although I dared not admit it. Perhaps it was the long-suppressed anticipation that caused me to accommodate a sense of disappointment, as opposed to resultant dread and anger.

The inevitability of the revelation also left me feeling rather empty inside.

Call it supreme naivety, but the way our lives had prospered since departing Blackpool was a process that had perhaps been taken for granted, somewhat.

The three of us presumed quite innocently that we had each turned the corner, and that the bright prospects offered by the future would go the whole hog in managing to erase the untenable and destructive chronicle of our history.

But unbeknown to us, as we wallowed in the newfound oasis of endless pleasure and admired our azure-blue horizon, our little patch of idyllic domesticity was about to be polluted.

The three of us had been tracked down.

A ghost had apparently been following us.

Hiding in the shadows.

Out of sight.

Cowardly, invisible, and soundless.

Presumably awaiting the appropriate time to eventually make its very unwelcome entrance.

How long the phantom had been spying furtively in the wings, nobody was sure.

I listened to Bobby's desperate if trimmed monologue with very little to offer as a retort. My long-held instincts had been proven correct, but I didn't want to add to her gloom by declaring such a fact.

When our exchange had concluded and I had agreed to get the first train back to Nottingham the next morning, one word etched itself at the forefront of my mind.

Destiny.

It was always going to be a matter of time.

Not *if*; but *when.*

So much for being released from the shackles.

The burden we had laid down with such relief was about to be hauled back on our shoulders.

Bobby had been unfortunate in that she had to make the announcement to yours truly.

It was undeniable. The moment had apparently arrived.

I was needed back at Glenfield Avenue.

Because according to Martin, our father was in town.

*****

I had tried to brush the news off with a forced inner stoicism. I was adamant I was not going to let myself descend into the vortex of worry that had enveloped my formative years.

Who was I kidding, though?

I didn't sleep a wink the remainder of that night.

On leaving Swansea the very next morning I was nervous.

And by the time I had made my principal connection at Bristol, I dearly wished I was returning to the East Midlands for any other reason than the one that beckoned me back there that day.

Despite repeatedly trying to convince myself there would be nothing to get overly concerned about, it was whilst travelling through and beyond Birmingham that the stark reality of the scenario successfully overpowered my flimsy self-pretence.

With the nature of the journey being rather un-scheduled, one could supposedly term it as an emergency. After all, emergencies are generally *unscheduled* incidents, aren't they?

But I still knew no specifics concerning Martin's alleged encounter with our father.

I told Bobby with a bracing insistence that she could relay the full story to me face to face. There was no point talking for hours on the phone if I was coming back anyway.

As the train approached Nottingham, my insides squirmed, yet I forcibly ensured that my facial expression remained unruffled. I had spent half a day staring aimlessly at strange landscapes that passed by at fifty miles per hour.

My façade of calm was just about intact.

But it was not a state of panic that clouded my thinking as it seemed to have done Bobby's.

When stripped down to the basics, the situation was hardly terrifying in essence.

So, our father had followed us back to base.

Barely the work of Sherlock Holmes, was it?

I mean to say, where *else* would he begin to start looking if not there?

But the overriding issue for me wasn't so much his success at discovering *where* we were.

The bigger question from my standpoint was, *why* he might be interested in locating us at all?

Perhaps through our deliriously poor judgement, the three of us were guilty of overlooking the potential likelihood that he might ever wish to pursue us back to the Midlands.

After all, on departing his residence on twenty-seven, Joseph Street, just over two years earlier, we presumably left him with a rather painful and distinct calling card.

I personally hoped we had done enough as a trio to bring an end to his very fleeting and inherently twisted curiosity in his offspring.

Surely, he knew he would still be backing a loser by chasing us.

It might stand to reason that the undoubted scar Martin engraved into the top of our father's skull should have been enough of an incentive for him to let sleeping dogs lie. And that if his sons had managed to secure victory once, they were infinitely more than capable of repeating the feat?

However, we could not ignore the wretched possibility that he might be out for revenge.

His mindset was so pathetic, vindictive, and unhinged that it was conceivable he would wait all these months to think of some scheme in which to successfully weave his wrath.

But *he* obviously hadn't learned one vital lesson.

That being, we did not want him anywhere near us.

So far as his offspring were concerned. his minimal, yet perversely influential role in our lives, had ceased long ago.

His unwarranted involvement was, at very best, completely offensive and of no beneficial purpose to either me, Martin, or Bobby.

Nonetheless, he was on the radar once again.

And his renewed interest was already casting a sinister new shadow.

Even with a wilting track record such as his, could Jim Andrews truly be so bloody-minded in insisting on a re-match?

*****

And yet, despite the fragile conviction that all would end well, by the time my train screeched into Nottingham Central, the involuntary trepidation I felt in my gut was relentless.

I was effectively looking over my shoulder even before stepping from the carriage onto the platform.

Yes, dear reader. I willingly confess to you as a trusted confidante, that he had gotten in my head already. Lock, stock, and barrel.

This was the prevailing issue in my conscience as I stood in the foyer at Nottingham station looking aimlessly at the illuminated orange text on the overhead information screens.

But my concentration was shot.

Scrutinising for my next scheduled service was a testing mission.

But at least it allowed my brain to try and divert from the looming negativity for a minute or two.

I even struggled to recall the name of my next destination.

Little Henton. Departure in ten minutes. Platform 6B.

I was three stops away from Glenfield Avenue, and the uncertain reception that awaited.

My final connection was already engaged for departure with a low hum emitting from its underbelly as I approached.

I tentatively climbed aboard with unfeasibly weary legs, even though I had spent most of the day on my backside.

I selected a vacant double seat by the window and for the next few minutes I idly watched through the grease-smeared glass, as a smattering of fellow passengers gradually join me on board.

I retrieved my phone and was about to messaged Bobby that I would be at the front door in thirty minutes.

Then I changed my mind and put the phone away again.

There was no point informing her of my estimated time of arrival.

She would be at work and Martin would be at school.

And we would meet up again soon enough later that day.

Through the grime-laden pane adjacent to my seat, I observed the onrushing figures beyond and their aggrieved faces, as though they had the weight of the world to carry. It was as though catching the train was just another item to add to their ever-lengthening list of woes.

So much angst on display through my single, solitary, tiny portal of dirt-riddled glass.

Dismay etched itself into people's expressions everywhere I looked.

And I was suddenly grateful.

Grateful for the fact that I was supposedly freed of such an affliction. Until today, anyway.

My reservoir of unfounded consternation had supposedly been depleted by life's events.

Or so I'd hoped. Until today, anyway.

Personal endeavour and harsh experience had served to eclipse the recent, horrendous past.

Secondment to Swansea just over a year ago had enabled me to completely turn the page.

A brand-new lease of life for a brand new me.

I shall indulge you, as a brief but timely digression from the dread.

My first terms at Uni had been a wondrous process of sampling the delights on offer.

And before you begin to worry yourself, please don't, dear reader.

The delights I refer to are far removed from the legendary affiliation students have supposedly had with sex, drink, and drugs.

But it was no exaggeration to claim that every social activity that *didn't* require artificial stimulants, I desired to indulge myself in.

In hindsight I'm surprised I managed to find spare time to attend any lectures.

The gymnasium and leisure complex were real draws. State of the art with every modern piece of fitness equipment to hand. I needed the endorphin rush.

That became a drug in itself, and I couldn't get enough of the personal daily fix.

Whether it was weights, the treadmill, or a regular game of racquetball, I didn't care. My physical agility levels were through the roof by the time I first went back for Christmas with Martin and Bobby.

My mental wellbeing had never been in finer fettle, either.

The Uni badminton club was an area of particular interest too, but this was perhaps because the great majority of my opponents happened to be female.

Surprise, Surprise, did I hear you quietly sigh?

With your sarcasm carrying not one iota of surprise?

Yes, that silly playground show-off was still in me somewhere, and despite fluttering the hearts of perhaps half a dozen young ladies from across the net, my prowess with the shuttlecock wasn't quite enough to entice any potential girlfriends to come forward and claim me as their very own.

But I was happy with the company and the attention.

You know me by now, dear reader.

Of course, there were parties galore, and music gigs every night. The local town centre was always thriving with plenty of nubile young bodies who wanted to waste their government grants on getting wasted and maybe bedded into the bargain.

But I steered clear of going anywhere near the whole hog.

Though an entire summer on the beach was a memory that I shall cherish forever. And you can mind your own business on that score.

I was maturing, evidently.

I was in my element, certainly.

And if I am being absolutely honest with the world, the phone call from Bobby that fateful previous evening was not anticipated, and it proved a real wrench to think that I should have to get back on the train just a couple of weeks after university life had begun in earnest once again.

I had found a niche in Swansea that I was very keen to resume.

My ducks were in a row at long last.

Whilst many fellow students held down hours working at local bars and restaurants, I had a part-time job at the local Tesco supermarket and the cash-flow scenario in summer was quite bearable with the overtime they were throwing my way.

I would refer to it as beer money, but I wasn't drinking all that much beer to be fair. I didn't feel the need.

My solace now came from within.

I had no craving to numb pain with alcohol.

Because I had no pain that needed numbing.

It was a pleasant alternative to the previous eighteen years.

I felt cleansed in mind and body.

Whilst many of my peers were enthusiastically pissing their student loans up the wall in the first three terms, they were then left begging their parents for blank cheques or bank transfers to get them through their second year.

Booze wasn't my forte.

I suspect my father's incurable love of the bottle had cured me of any inclination to regularly drink to excess.

Witnessing what fifty years of alcohol abuse had done to *him* would be enough to repel anyone from going through the pub door.

Not for me, thank you.

All facets of my life were healthy, and I was prospering at last.

Mentally, physically, and spiritually, I felt invincible.

And then, along came fate once again.

*****

After what seemed an eternity of sitting and waiting, I finally felt the train grind into its departure from Nottingham station. As it slowly engaged through the gears, the gentle increase in speed was matched by the acceleration of my pulse rate.

I was re-entering very familiar territory for the first time in months, and I can tell you it garnered not a single pang of satisfaction within my soul.

Out of the clawing city walls and into neighbouring districts. Through industrial estates and past a pharmaceutical plant. Flanking the Regional Headquarters of the Inland Revenue. The so-called Castle of Nottingham was now rendered a distant and uninspiring silhouette in the background.

Footbridges and road bridges criss-crossed overhead minutes later, as we came to the first interruption in the last leg of my journey.

Aimlessly staring at the vista beyond the window, I quietly appreciated the quaint wooden décor of the station's fixtures and fittings. Ornate in design, but it needed a lick of paint for sure.

My heartbeat thudded relentlessly now.

Again, my patience was tested as we remained unmoving.

Nobody alighted or boarded.

Eventually after a painfully overlong hiatus, the wheels beneath me squealed into a forward motion once more.

Ten minutes until touchdown.

The carriages shuddered onward, and I was now glad of the fact that no one knew what time to expect me back.

I didn't want the big welcome.

I didn't want to be there at all.

My attention reverted beyond the stained pane. The scene altered pleasantly from urban disarray and decay to rural splendour.

I now observed lakes, canal towpaths, dog walkers, joggers, and churches.

Despite the slate grey October sky, it was still comparatively mild for early Autumn. Coats weren't vital to the arrangement, but it certainly wasn't short sleeve weather, either. And then the penultimate stop was announced by the abrupt re-application of whining brakes.

The locomotive shuddered to a standstill once more. An elderly couple disembarked and a teenager with a bicycle rolled aboard.

More soundless seconds elapsed as my mind hammered home the unwanted reminder that I was now only three miles from base camp.

I felt more than slightly aggrieved by this point.

I so wanted to be back in Swansea.

Crazy as it sounds, I didn't particularly want to see Martin and Bobby.

I loved the new life I had chosen and felt likewise for them.

Such a swell of confusing emotion had engulfed me.

I felt I was again being denied something I had rightfully earned.

Being forced against my will.

As though I was once more conforming to the demands of unseen puppeteers.

Sounds bloody selfish? Yes, I know it does.

But I thought I'd bowed out of the familial charade long ago.

I wanted our separate happy destinies to continue untainted.

Forging our own directions with our own details. We'd been bound by circumstance for far too long. And here we were being pushed back together all over again.

Perhaps my approach was callous. But my brother didn't need minding any longer. He didn't need his hand holding. Certainly not by me, at any rate.

Then again, perhaps I was underestimating the validity of my unplanned return? Maybe the urgent request for my intervention *would* be warranted, after all? Could it have been that I was subconsciously underplaying the potential severity of current developments?

I would find out soon enough.

At long last the hissing engine recommenced its pull. The wheezing rattle along the tracks soon resumed velocity through the folds of peaceful countryside.

A canvas of untouchable glories flashed by.

But I had to make the most of the idyllic exterior.

The distracting tranquillity that I enjoyed within the seclusion of the train compartment would be short-lived.

*****

Back gardens soon honed into view as the neighbourhood of my upbringing opened its arms. Lying in wait.

I always found it to be an amusing aspect of human domesticity that most homeowners genuinely take an authentic pride in how the rear of their properties are developed.

At ground level they might appear manicured, arranged and uniform. Yet to me, when viewed thirty feet higher from a railway embankment, they mostly seem distinctly dishevelled and unkempt.

Ramshackle sheds, rusting swings, and dodgy slides.

Algae filled fishponds and filthy conservatory rooves abound.

Broken fences and overgrown lawns.

And so, my journey begins its end.

The train flirts briefly with the local marina before slowing down to begin its engagement with my port of call.

I might have once fancied the idea of life on a narrowboat.

But I'm fairly convinced that there wouldn't be enough elbow room, that I would keep banging my head on the ceiling and that the beds would be far too small. I'd be useless at working out the canal locks too.

But a willing partner could've helped me, I supposed.

Maybe one day in another life. Perhaps with someone important enough to me that wants to tag along.

Oh, the innocent joys and barbed futility of daydreams.

Why do I bother, dear reader?

Residential estates and connecting roads converged at the hub of the main traffic island junction below, as the train glided overhead atop a sandstone bridge.

The carriages clattered to an unearthly halt at the platform.

I begrudgingly vacated my seat, grabbed my overnight bag, and re-positioned to the sliding door with my finger hovering over the operation button.

The butterflies in my stomach were now beyond being tamed and betrayed my outward air of casual indifference.

Secretly timid as a kitten, I reluctantly ambled off the train and swung my rucksack over my shoulder.

How I so wished I could have stayed on that ride.

To have continued with that soothing trek, up and away into the Derbyshire peaks.

But I couldn't remain within my fantasy.

Because I had been commanded to alight, right there and then.

To tend to other more pressing matters.

And for a place that was so identifiable to me that it was almost ingrained in my DNA, I couldn't for the life of me understand why I should suddenly feel enveloped by utter terror as I departed the railway station grounds at Little Henton.

2
WHERE IT ALL BEGAN

I couldn't be entirely certain why the impulse gripped me.

Having exited the village station, I stood on the kerbside with one destination in mind that unexpectedly prevailed over any other, as needing my imminent attention.

I hadn't thought about number fifteen, Lodge Close ever since being called to extricate Martin from the front of the property and away from the attentions of some irate residents and a couple of confused Police officers.

As you may well recall, dear reader, that incident was months before I first went to Swansea.

Despite the fact my brother narrowly avoided being arrested for affray, that street remained an undeniably pivotal part of our history.

But it had also gradually become a place that no longer bore any relevance to my future and I had subconsciously turned the page.

So why at that precise moment I felt the unquenchable and innate desire to go and revisit the house of my childhood, I have absolutely no grasp.

Apart from suspecting the old Andrews' family chestnut.

A higher calling *ordained* me to be there…

Of course, it did. Give me a break please, *someone*.

Anyone!

From the deepest recesses of my mind, I was receiving a persistent signal that demanded I return to the unreliable nest of my youth.

And so, without further ado, that is where I headed.

As I walked, I felt it only fair to message Bobby and let her know I was back. It was one less thing for her to worry about, I supposed.

And I had little doubt that she was worrying about a hell of a lot of things at that moment.

Meandering casually through the residential estate I found the aura of the place completely unchanged.

The frontages of the buildings gawped at me like faces grimacing at the arrival of an unwanted guest at a party.

Especially as I eventually made my way along Lodge Close.

Number fifteen, whilst far from being a strange domain to me, had also seemed to have adopted a mask of disdain in response to my unannounced re-emergence.

The top floor windows peered down at my wayward presence with disapproving, suspicious eyes.

The front door formed a narrow, drooping pout of unhappiness. This wasn't much of a surprise as it was still coated in that blistering brown paint from many years ago.

The plastic figures denoting the house number were still screwed in crooked.

To the uninitiated, the uninviting exterior offered nothing untoward.

But once I was in position directly opposite, I could only stand there and endure the diluted yet still toxic vibe that it still emitted.

The front lawn was as uncared for as ever.

Except now it had been decorated with various items of refuse including the obligatory mattress, a couple of broken garden gnomes and the neglected frame of a children's bicycle.

The dubious realm of my formative years was a far from welcoming vision to behold, and certainly offered nothing in the way of nostalgia.

So, quite rightly you may shout the question, dear reader:

What the hell was I doing there?

I checked my mobile phone whilst furtively continuing the inspection. Bobby hadn't yet responded to the disclosure of my landing.

Again, I gazed at the dormant structure before me.

The same three tiles on the roof were still slipping ever assuredly toward the guttering ledge. Nothing about the front of the house had altered.

As though it were trapped in time somehow.

Dead outside. No sign of life inside.

With new occupants I perhaps anticipated improvements around and about the place. But no.

It remained just as I remembered.

Unloved and neglected.

Pretty much the same story as the family that lived there for many years not so long ago.

I didn't know what I was expecting to feel by being in such close proximity to my old stomping ground again.

Surprisingly, it didn't even encourage any reflection about Mum.

The need to visit must have been a spiritual thing.

For my own solace and nobody else's.

And then, as I remained standing unobtrusively across the road opposite the property, a young woman suddenly emerged through the front door. Whilst possibly only in her early twenties, she sported the battle-hardened, world-weary visage that I was oh so familiar with.

As she deposited a soiled nappy directly into the black dustbin, I presumed that she too was someone who had missed out on the pleasantries that life should and could offer.

She appeared devoid of hope.

Absent of aspiration. At a loss for inspiration.

She didn't spot me, her not-so-covert observer.

I had squatted to my haunches by this time, simply absorbing the surrounding scene and glancing idly at the occasional passing car and van.

The young woman shut the bin lid and sniffed her fingers.

I wondered if those same fingers were likely to get washed at any point in the near future. She duly scrunched up her nose before returning to the gloom of her hallway. The slam of the door presented a symbolic ignorance of the bigger world beyond the constrictive threshold of her own.

And there I remained, almost under the spell of the place, yet having no really discerning desire to be anywhere near it. It seemed inconceivable that my family's story started there within those four walls.

It seemed inconceivable that the Andrews family ever made it into existence in the first place.

Yet there I most definitely was.

In the flesh; alive and kicking.

A surviving token of proof that two dysfunctional, psychologically challenged parents might have just got something right between them amid their extensive catalogue of failure.

And my brother, of course. They got him right, too.

Couldn't forget Martin could we, dear reader?

And then at last, my flitting concentration centred itself on our late mother.

I would never know of the true extent of her disheartenment and desolation. She never fully opened herself up to me about her feelings.

But as her son, I sympathised with her plight regardless.

What a waste of a life.

Why couldn't she have talked to someone on that final, fateful day.

Did she truly feel so alone in the world?

The lump in my throat constricted my swallowing momentarily, as I faced off with the inanimate monument to my past.

And it continued to stare directly back at me, almost as if it didn't acknowledge my place in its history at all.

I recalled my last ever personal experience under its hallowed arches.

As I closed that front door behind me for the last time. With dear old Henry waiting for me on the pavement.

A movement in the shadows. A change of temperature in the air.

A noticeable shift in the mood.

A ghost in the darkness?

I'll never truly know.

But the memory served to reinforce why I was glad to be out of the place once and for all.

For me, there were no abiding memories lingering to be reawakened in Lodge Close.

Just a well-worn and long discarded script of misery and despair. And as I adjusted my bag onto the other shoulder, I was suddenly so grateful for that little bungalow.

That warm, welcoming house, that opened its arms to me in my most anguished hours.

Bequeathed to me by a dear friend.

And it was there that I now directed myself.

I spun on my heel and vacated Lodge Close.

At that moment my phone alerted arrival of a new message.

I was surprised to learn that Bobby was waiting for me at Glenfield Avenue.

A loving family environment beckoned me.

I hoped.

3
A POSITIVE REUNION

'SURPRISE! *Not*!'

Bobby's booming laugh provided the unmistakable wall of sound that greeted me as she pulled open the front door.

Despite my overspilling reservations about the situation, I felt genuine pleasure on seeing her again.

'You never answered my message, Jamie boy?'

'I was only around the corner. Thought I'd surprise *you* whilst *you* were trying to surprise *me*!'

She didn't answer me, preferring instead to pull my weary form into the hallway and embrace me extremely tightly.

'For Christ's sake, Bobby! Have you missed me *that* much?'

She drew away and exhibited her infectious smile once again.

'You bet I have! Christmas was a bloody long time ago! How was the journey? Sorry about the short notice and all that.'

I lowered my bag to the floor before kicking off my trainers.

'Could have been worse. The trip drags after Birmingham for some reason. I see you've bothered to hoover up this time?'

Bobby turned to look at the redundant vacuum cleaner and emitted a sparse chuckle.

'Less of that cheekiness! I'll hold my hand up and say that fetching it from the utility cupboard was as far as I got. I haven't yet managed to plug it in and use it yet, though.'

In fairness the house looked immaculate, but I wasn't going to let on, was I?

She was still giggling as we walked into the lounge.

'Right, then. First things first. Settee or camp bed?'

'Same as last time. Camp bed, please. But with an extra duvet this time if you don't mind.'

She exhibited a sheepish expression.

The sofa was not a comfortable option.

Why they hadn't yet put a proper bed in the guest bedroom was anyone's guess.

'It's still a bit junked up in there, Jamie. I haven't got around to sorting it yet. But you got a stiff back from the camp bed last time, though?'

It was suddenly calming to be back in the family fold again.

I was now quietly relieved that I'd been called to come back.

'No worries. I don't intend to be under your feet for any longer than necessary. On that note, would the hostess be an angel and put the kettle on? My throat is like sandpaper.'

Bobby curtseyed in a mocking gesture of compliance.

'Of course, sir. Which beverage is to sir's preference today?'

I watched her preen and prance around the room. Domesticity suited her and she kept a tidy nest. Since my stay last Christmas, she had moved ornaments and pictures around. There were new little items situated here and there.

She was a valuable influence around the place.

Just as well, really. I couldn't envisage my brother partaking in decisions concerning the décor.

She skipped into the kitchen and swung open the fridge door.

I couldn't help but laugh out loud.

'Orange juice, milk, tea, coffee or council pop?' she shouted.

'You're like a new-born lamb, Bobby. What are you jumping about the floor for? And how come you're not working? Can Johnny H cope without his best shift manager?'

Her inherently attractive features beamed at me from around the kitchen door.

'I'm excited to see you. That's okay, isn't it? And I'm starting work a little later today as I knew you were coming back. What is this, anyway? Twenty fucking questions, or what? Now, oblige me by answering one of mine. What drink did you want?'

I followed into the kitchen and in the end chose a glass of milk.

No idea why. Probably for speed of preparation.

'Don't worry about the stuff in the spare room, Bobby. I'll sort that someday. It's mostly Henry's gear, isn't it.'

Henry didn't have much to his name when he departed the mortal coil, but even all these months on I couldn't face the arduous task of deciding what to keep of his remaining possessions.

Just the sight of his box of tobacco pipes would likely send my waterworks into over-drive.

Bobby ventured to the second bedroom and after five minutes returned with a vigorous sense of accomplishment.

'Okay. Bed is set up.'

I placed my empty glass on the draining board.

'Thank you, hostess. I think I'll have a cup of tea now, please.'

'Right you are, sir. Kettle is going on.'

She hugged me once again before tending to the drinks.

As far as she was concerned, ten months was evidently far too long for me to have been absent.

And thankfully, her effervescence had swiftly served to disperse the negative anticipation that had accompanied me all the way from Wales.

*****

I sipped my drink as Bobby perched alongside me on the settee. It was like nectar from the gods. Stewed to a shade of deep orange just how I liked it. Brewed so strong you could stand the spoon upright in the mug. My first proper homemade cuppa for aeons.

And chocolate digestives as a bonus. I felt spoiled.

But we both knew deep down that all this flowery foreplay was masking the underlying issue.

Namely, the reason I was requested to be back there in the first place. I observed her quietly as she cradled her own mug in both palms.

She had changed her hair, but I couldn't convince myself as to what was specifically different about it.

Maybe a bit shorter. Perhaps a hint of a tint. Subtly coloured.

Who knew with her?

She had opted to dispense with the bob cut of old some months back. Short back and sides suited her profile much better. Her slightly pug features now looked sharper with a closely cropped style.

I had noticed back in the summer that she looked healthy and vibrant on the pictures she kept sending via text message.

There was a twinkle in her eyes which I couldn't help but admire.

It was still there now. That and the equally twinkling solitaire diamond in her engagement ring that had appeared just over a month ago.

'Let's have a look at that pip you're wearing on your third finger left hand then.'

She positively gushed as she thrust her splayed digits under my nose for inspection.

'Did I do well…or did I do *fucking* well?' she boasted.

I nodded and chortled with earnest delight.

'You did well, my girl. You did well. Congratulations!'

Nottingham and Glenfield Avenue were obviously suiting her down to the ground.

She jokingly referred to it as Life: Chapter Three.

Chapter One being a rocky childhood growing up in Northern Ireland.

Chapter Two commenced with her relocation to Blackpool.

Chapter Three was obviously proving infinitely better than both its forerunners.

But, at that moment on the sofa, she seemed more than a little reserved under the need for performance.

Still refined, composed and comfortable in her own dwelling.

Always acting the kooky hard nut.

But there was obviously something on her mind.

No prizes for guessing what that something might be, dear reader.

But I positively avoided verging toward *that* subject for the time being.

'You look the bees' knees, Bobby, if you don't mind the compliment. You look really good. Becoming a fiancée has certainly suited you. You're glowing.'

She fluttered her eyelashes as if pretending to react coyly.

'Thank you, Jamie. I take all compliments from handsome men. Me and your brother are so settled here. It's great. Come a long way, haven't we? By the way I have another question for you.'

'Sounds ominous. Hit me.'

'Did you *know* your brother was going to propose?'

'On my life I had no idea, I swear. But I'm so pleased for the both of you. So, I'm guessing Martin is back at school? When does he finish?'

'Three thirty. Why?' she replied pensively.

Her latent fears were not far below the surface.

'I thought we could go to the school gates and meet him out. Be a nice surprise? It's nearly two o clock, now.'

Bobby's features illuminated once again.

Her eyes brightened simply by the mention of her husband-to-be.

'Yes! Do it! He'd *love* that! It would be a great surprise. He knows you're travelling back today but to see you waiting outside school would be fantastic for him. I've got to be at work as soon as, though. So, you'll have to fly solo. How is Uni, anyway? It seems to be treating you well. You look so fit and tanned. Your hairs a little longer, too. Are you turning into a frigging surfer boy on us, or what?'

I sampled more of my tea and willingly obliged the mood of gentle humour.

'Oh, you know. If the new look works, then I stick with it. Chicks queuing up to greet me at every turn. It's been a hell of a great summer for them as you can imagine. Oh, and the beer. The never-ending *beer.*'

Bobby giggled at my sarcastic exaggeration.

She knew me too well and stared me out for a sensible reply.

'In all seriousness I'm really enjoying the journalism course. I don't think I've missed any lectures either yet, which is a miracle. But being here today breaks that record.'

‘I’m sorry, Jamie. That’s my fault, isn’t it. Hope you’re not kept here too long…I mean that in the nicest possible way. I’m so chuffed you’re back, though.’

Now it was my turn to chuckle.

‘I know you’ve missed me, silly. You’re only human, after all. And listen to me…don’t *worry*. All will be fine. This business with *you know who*. I’ll sort it.’

She gazed straight ahead, and an uncomfortable silence took root as Bobby eventually strived to steer the conversation back toward positivity

‘They let you back into living quarters on campus, then?’

I proceeded to dunk a biscuit. What a forgotten privilege.

‘By the skin of my teeth, yes. The student halls are only really meant for the first-year intake. So, I really should have slung my hook in June. I spent a fair bit of the summer working and sleeping on other people’s settees. My fault really but I was in the shit with no lodgings sorted. So, they’ve let me off for a while. Only thing is, I might have to end up sharing soon.’

Bobby smiled wryly.

‘Well, I’m sure you won’t mind that if they want you to bunk down with a female of the species.’

‘You know what? I honestly don’t know how I’ll cope if they throw a girl in with me. It will be sheer hell!’

Bobby read my open mirth as always.

‘Fucking God help *her* is all I can say.’

She squealed in delight, almost dropping her mug.

I laughed out loud again at her honesty

Bobby was always guaranteed to tickle my funny bone.

‘Are things okay this end with Martin’s return to school, then? Exam year this year! How exciting is *that*? Where has time gone? I’m sorry I didn’t get back for his birthday. A phone call doesn’t quite cut the mustard, does it?’

She threw me a feigned look of disapproval.

'He was disappointed not to see you, but he'll get over it. This makes up for it. Even though it's for different reasons.'

'I'll be sure to mark up the tenth of September on next year's calendar, so I'm guaranteed to be here. I can still get him a present now I'm back. Even if it *is* a month too late.'

'If you miss *two* of his birthdays in a row then you'll have *both* of us to answer to, Jamie Andrews, so think on!'

'Do you think he missed going to school in the summer?'

'Oh, he couldn't *wait* to get back. I think he truly yearned for the place. You know…the routine…the timetable and so? He's got some good friends there, too. Even if they are over ten years younger than he is!'

I was suddenly promoted to adopt the role of family preacher for some unknown reason.

'One thing I've learned about friendship. It doesn't matter about the age. It's the *loyalty* that is everything. *That's* the only thing that counts, Bobby.'

Finally, she relaxed and leaned back in her seat.

My presence was obviously soothing for her.

'I imagined you had fears about his return to education though, Jamie. I know I did. But you were right to encourage him. He's so clever. Leaves me standing. And in a way it's been good you not being here. He's had to fend for himself in terms of the social side of things. But he's getting there. He's a much more confident character, now.'

I nodded and set my empty mug down beside my feet.

Bobby's words confirmed what I had hoped to hear.

'It was no accident that I've stayed out of the way. You both need this space to yourselves. And you're both doing so well, Bobby. You're holding down a great job and he's holding down his academics. It's all good in the hood. By the way…please tell me you *are* going to work and didn't ring in sick just for me today?'

She threw her head back and smiled.

John Harrison warranted honesty.

'No kidding *you*, is there? No…I told John yesterday that I might need it off, but I'd go in later if you arrived early. He was fine about it. Especially because it's *you* I needed the time off for. He asks about you every single week, Jamie. He's very protective towards you.'

I needed to make a point of going to see John whilst I was back in Nottingham.

No excuses. I owed him a lot.

'Johnny H will always recognise the qualities in you, Bobby. And I'm glad you told me he's laying off the booze a bit. You'll be good for him just as much as he has been for you.'

Bobby went quiet as her visage visibly saddened.

She wiped her eyes with her sleeve as a discerning quiet descended on the room.

'You know, Jamie. We talked briefly on the phone about this in the summer. And I know you're more than happy living your own life now. But I feel I want to reiterate. Before I met you, I had no idea what living was all about. I had Martin, of course…but I kind of didn't *know* myself as a person. Does that make sense?'

It had become a bit of a habit for her to indulge in sudden pangs of personal sentimentality.

My absence of the past months had evidently left something of a big hole. I didn't realise the impact that my departure would have on her because I was too pre-occupied.

Expecting upset, I hesitantly encouraged her to divert away from the likelihood of negative reflection.

'We were all caught in the same trap, Bobby. But we got out. That's the way I see it, anyway. We are free souls now.'

Again, her eyes watered, and she breathed deeply to regain her composure.

'But *without* you, neither Martin nor I would have *been* freed. I dread to think what would have happened to us. It was like living in a spider's web. Each time we moved the spider would pounce.'

I raised a hand to stem the conversation.

It was too emotive for me and eternally depressing.

It was also a chat we had already had numerous times.

I didn't see any point in going over it again. And it brought far too much misery to the forefront of my thinking.

'You shouldn't keep dwelling on the way things *used* to be. It's not healthy. It's all in the *past*, Bobby. We live for the future now, don't we? That's my motto. Let history go. It's the only way.'

She dabbed her eyes again and nodded.

'Yes, of course. But I just want you to know I think you're a hero. And the way you've included me in the family. You know…drawing up the wills. Power of attorney and all before you went back to Uni in January…its very…overwhelming. I'm very lucky to have a loving safety net at long last. I want you to know that I don't take it for granted. Ever!'

I couldn't help but chuckle again, if only to break the fragile tension that was creeping into the air.

'Tying you in with the legal side of things was never an issue for me.'

Her hand reached over and gripped mine.

I felt the fear exuding through her fingers.

'I was and I still am indebted, Jamie. You and Martin are my true clan now.'

'Well…there's at least one person in the world that would disagree with you about the hero thing…but fuck him, eh? I don't need a pat on the back. Looking after what family I have left is my honour and duty. That's why I'm sat here now. I'm surprised your folks in Ireland haven't been in touch, though.'

Her glare was unwavering.

'I *have* no folks in Ireland. They're nothing to me. And haven't been for many years. What do you think I left the bastard place for?'

I didn't require any expansion.

Bobby was obviously another innocent victim of misplaced priorities within her own upbringing.

My attention again centred on her engagement ring as she spoke. More humour was required before we delved too deeply into any further unwarranted reminiscence.

'*You* are my guardian angel, Jamie. And no mistake.'

'Hey…*Roberta*…don't get all mushy on me. Today is a good day. Listen, you can get yourself to work now if you want. I'll go and get Martin from school and maybe drop into the Tiger with him for a pint. How's that sound?'

'That sounds perfect. Take my digital camera from the kitchen. Get some pictures for me. And *don't* call me Roberta or I'll take your teeth out with one swing!'

I loved teasing her.

Her aggressive reactions were always comedy gold.

Finally, the beautiful Irish smile returned to illuminate her temporarily downcast features. She then instigated a welcome change of subject that further lightened the mood.

'Hey, talking of which…guess what I got from work this week, Jamie?'

'No idea. And I really can't be bothered to guess so you'll just have to tell me.'

She clenched both fists toward me and her expression beamed with excitement.

'Only a fucking *attendance bonus*! Look! That cheque up there on the mantelpiece!'

Bobby jumped to her feet and retrieved the slip of paper from above the fire before parading it before me in close-up.

'Wow! A hundred and seventy-four quid? What's this in aid of then, Bobby? Is this how much you owe the swear box?'

She narrowed her eyes in feigned offence.

'Very funny! Apparently, I've managed so many consecutive hours without a break in service. I think that award covers the last two quarters of the year or something. Whatever that means. Twenty-six weeks straight, I think. It's linked to the T and A system. Christ knows how they figure it out. But it's better than a kick in the fanny, yeah? Stick that in your pipe and smoke it, Jamie boy!'

I couldn't prevent my amusement from spilling forth as she stood proudly swaying before me with hands on hips.

In that split second of natural jubilation, she seemed just like the Bobby Jones I first met at The Celtic Arms.

The quick-fire mouth was evidently still in fine working order when called upon. And so was mine.

'That will go some way to a nice romantic dinner for two, somewhere. But don't invite me, will you? I'm no good at playing gooseberry. Anyway, why do they give you a *cheque*? It's a bit outdated now, isn't it? I thought everything was done at source these days?'

Bobby folded her arms and rolled her eyes.

'Hark at you the frigging techno wizard! Still got your mobile phone, have you?'

'Okay yes, I know. I'm crap with modern stuff. So why the cheque, then?'

'Well, I asked the same question of John when he passed me the envelope and he said it was just the way the wages office wanted to do it. Cos its tax free or something? But it doesn't matter. When I get the chance, I'm going to put it in your savings account. The one you set up for the inheritance Henry left.'

I looked at her in astonishment.

She had predicted my earnest surprise at the gesture.

'There's no need to do that. *You've* earned it. *You* keep it.'

Bobby shook her head adamantly.

'Look Jamie. If it wasn't for Henry's generosity, we wouldn't even *be* here. It's my way of saying thank you to him in a small way. Will you pay it in for me? Perhaps tomorrow? I don't think I'll be going to town for a few days because of my shifts. You can put it in the savings, can't you?'

My sense of mirth was again exhibited from ear to ear.

She was still a determined bugger. I had to give her that much.

'Sounds really, unnecessarily, overly complicated, Bobby, but I'm sure that just like everything else we try and do it will fall together successfully in a big heap. It would be easier if you just kept the money to yourself though, wouldn't it?'

Bobby thrust her hands behind her back and squinted at me in mock frustration.

'Yes…yes it *would* be easier. But I want to do this *my* way and you *are* going to help me. Okay? I know I'm a constant pain in your ass, but this is very important to me.'

Bobby became lovingly agitated as she reinforced her position.

'I'm trying to give a little back instead of just taking. Get it?'

I couldn't help but rise to my feet and put my arms around her.

She had a soft heart behind the hard act.

'Okay, okay! Why don't I go to the bank for you this afternoon if I'm going out anyway?'

'No rush. Take my fiancé for a pint instead. You can go to the bank tomorrow when I'm at work. Besides I need to write you a slip when I've found my book. It'll give you something to get up for tomorrow.'

I sighed merrily under my breath.

'Ooh…*fiancé*. Sounds very *grand*! Of course. Leave it with me. For a forward-thinking woman you are wonderfully old fashioned. Payslips and cheques, indeed. I'll go to the bank in the morning. Anything to keep that amazing smile on your face, eh?'

She rested her chin on my shoulder and squeezed me tightly once again. I sensed the tension in her, though.

Even this little matter about the cheque had seemingly weighed heavily on her mind until now.

'Thank you, Jamie. You know my way is the right way. Now, you'd better go and meet your brother. And I need to get to work. I'll see you both tonight. Make sure you wait up for me, yeah? Don't forget photos!'

It was no small relief and possibly a minor miracle that we had managed half an hour in conversation without the direct reference to my father throwing a veil of despondency over proceedings.

But it was plainly obvious to me that his lurking presence was now beginning to assert itself in undermining the contentment that had successfully been nurtured at Glenfield Avenue.

And the unavoidable subject would not be kept out of bounds for very much longer.

I waved Bobby a temporary farewell as she trotted down the street in her uniform to catch the bus to work.

With time spare for another mug of tea I retreated to the kitchen.

Bobby had adorned the room with some lovely craft ware.

She had feathered the nest with a joyful eye for style.

And as the kettle hissed into life, I reluctantly acknowledged my distinct notion that the upbeat vibe within that little bungalow wasn't likely to last.

But for the time being, optimism reigned supreme.

Just about.

4
A WALK AMONG THE GRAVESTONES

It proved to be an altogether unprecedented and almost eerie experience venturing through town to meet Martin from school.

The upbeat exchanges with Bobby just an hour earlier were now relegated as a distant memory. My previously courageous streak had been gradually displaced by a nagging sheen of foreboding.

Despite having trodden that same path many times, every sight and sound along the route felt inexplicably novel.

The sudden sensation of unfamiliarity defied logical explanation.

Akin to voices in my head, age old landmarks audibly called out to be noticed, as if I was passing them for the first time.

Buildings in the locality that I had barely previously acknowledged in all my nineteen summers, now yearned for recognition.

I had only been living away from Nottinghamshire for the best part of a year, yet this place I knew so well now presented itself as alien to my ever-accepting eyes.

I passed underneath the arch of the railway bridge and onto the main traffic island in the village. I had lived in the vicinity all my life yet suddenly felt like a stranger.

Meandering along the main through road, I observed overly familiar houses jutted in and out from their plots and competing for my attention.

Up ahead, the recently constructed retirement residential complex towered above. Situated directly opposite across the road, the two-hundred-year-old building that was my ex nursery school now accommodated a dental surgery.

And I felt weirdly affronted by the fact?

The resonance of the persistent traffic pummelled my ear drums, as though I had never heard it in such proximity before.

The motorcycle showroom quirkily impressed me, even though I had never possessed any affinity for the machines whatsoever.

It was almost as though I was inducting myself on a voyage of renewed self-discovery.

A dimly painted post box begged me for a fresh coat of red. I briefly studied its dilapidated state and narrowly avoided stepping in dog muck that had been deposited and duly abandoned at its base.

As though somebody thought I had deserved such a penance for not fully concentrating on the surroundings beforehand.

I left the pavement and shifted up to the canal towpath.

The treeline that flanked the waterway leaned menacingly toward me, as if inspecting the appearance of the uninvited newcomer. Brown, dry leaves fluttered at my feet as seasonal change continued to weave its spell around my advance.

Many previously inert elements vied for spectacle.

I couldn't decipher the signals that my brain attempted to compute.

I continued the stride among the bleak canvas of my previous domain.

Did I truly belong here, anymore?

Was I suddenly classed as being so intrusive in my own territory?

The aura of the place was seemingly pushing against me.

Could it really be conceivable that my town perhaps held the perception that I had deserted it, and urgently wished for me to re-acquaint with its fixtures and fittings.

Or maybe something else was at work.

Perhaps these elements paraded themselves to inhibit me?

Maybe even to warn me off? To drive me away?

It was a most uncanny reception from a vista that I knew as well as the back of my own hand.

But I hadn't truly *seen* it before. I had only accepted it and ignored it. As I suppose we are all guilty of doing that at some time or other.

I was now finally being forced to appreciate what was on display in front of my eyes.

Albeit the items in view were of little consequence or importance to me at that moment. Or at any moment prior.

The school building of St George's issued the merest peek at its stone silhouette as it stretched upward in stature from behind the fire station.

I took the time to observe the family of swans that glided effortlessly alongside me on the surface of the water.

Mother leading out front.

Father guarding at the rear.

The grey-downy cygnets obligingly in single file between their parents. Receptive. Respectful. Cherished.

If only I could have been entrusted with such vital familial values.

Maybe I should have been born a swan.

Maybe I'll eventually be reincarnated as one?

I sure envied those little ones.

They lived contentedly under the protective shrouds of dutiful guidance and inherent endearment.

Then it occurred to me that I wouldn't be making the walk to meet my brother from school if we had been inducted in a better a way of existence in our childhoods.

My whole life had been an impromptu, reactive journey.

And I was privately resentful of the fact.

I was jealous of the swans.

But my lot was my lot.

I couldn't change a thing.

And so onward I marched with my distracting thoughts.

*****

I checked my phone as I waited beyond the school gates. Bobby had messaged to say she had clocked on at work and wasn't yet sure of her finish time.

It was getting a little chillier due to the dropping sun and I opted to keep walking into the school premises. Ten minutes until the kids were kicked out would enable me some time to explore.

From my vantage point among the parked cars, I observed the main structure of the building.

Its air of authority conjured many memories from my years there.

I found myself absorbed in the unique arrangement of the sash windows and burly formed lintels.

I embarked on a personal test to see if I could recall which windows belonged to which room number and the associated subject teacher.

It hadn't been all that long since I completed my formal education there. But my daily routine with the place had quickly faded into sad obscurity. It was like I had never attended St George's at all.

Yet how could it be that as a supposed gate crasher I still remembered so much?

I wasn't thinking in parallel lines that day.

Every image that registered in my mind grasped at me for some confirmation of why it carried such pertinence.

I can't explain the sensation, dear reader.

And I sympathise if you yourself are now a little giddy with all this alluring confusion.

But for me it was tangible, and its effect was almost nauseous.

Beyond typical rationale, certainly.

Weird didn't even cover it.

The graphic vividity of the place was unusually muddied. I almost felt prohibited to be within the property boundary, yet I similarly asserted the right to wander through the grounds of my own free will.

It was as though my earnest patronage of the place had been withdrawn. You work it out if you can?

I am still lacking a distinct conclusion to my apparent dismay.

Was I deemed the imposter?

The foolhardy and egotistical side of my personality fully expected that I might be greeted by an outpouring of warm hospitality.

Perhaps from ex-teachers that might have spotted me loitering with intent in the vicinity.

But of course, they were still teaching, weren't they?

How on Earth could they have had the opportunity to see me?

And anyway, who was I to distract them from their art and their craft and their duty?

I continued to advance my position until reaching the rear of the reception area and ultimately, I found myself in plain sight of the Sixth Form complex.

I was immediately transfixed by the dubious reappearance of telling mementoes from my past.

The external staircase. The double entrance doors of the ground floor foyer. The tarmac surface of the tennis court that doubled as a football pitch at break and lunch times for the lads to burn off their excess testosterone.

Showing off to each other.

Showing off to the passing females.

Fuck me - you already know where this is heading, don't you?

Yes - exactly where we don't want to go.

The path leading to one female in particular.

Who said she so enjoyed watching me fool about.

Who welcomed me to sit next to her on that bench on that day.

The one who stole my heart as I willingly took hers.

Aching recollections from a recent yet seemingly forgotten age.

Was that really *me* that fell in love so deeply, so willingly, and so unprotected?

That first romantic scene played itself out to the letter, as I stood leaning against the wire mesh surround of the tennis court.

The essence of a single moment in time returned as reliably and readily as a waterfall does cascade over rocks.

Clear, loud, and honest.

Consistent and unchanging.

And that clarity temporarily reigned.

I was no imposter.

I was *indeed* that boy.

I *was* Jamie Andrews.

And I *did* love.

Once upon a time.

But that boy, he didn't take her heart in its entirety as he presumed.

And that heart of his that she stole.

She never did return to him.

*****

I decided to bring my impromptu self-guided tour of the school site to an end. It was proving far too bewildering in a most unhelpful way.

In tandem with this, I detected the drone of the school's last bell of the day and swiftly re-positioned myself back to the front gates.

Across the road the Tiger Inn still enticed with an open door. It amused me to think of the times we had returned to our afternoon timetable ever-so-slightly under the influence.

I quietly wondered if current Sixth Formers still indulged in such a practice.

Or more to the point, whether the current landlord did.

Happy days. To a degree, anyway.

I heard the growing rumble as the school's interior corridors, walls and floors came alive with the vibrancy and animation of departing pupils.

The scraping of chairs and the echoing of voices.

Doorways flew open to release the uniformed multitudes unto their temporary liberation once again. I watched with growing enthusiasm as the gathering swarm of students began to emerge and rapidly envelope the car park and playground.

The hordes were headed in my direction as the gateway to supposed freedom beckoned them.

Their stride became ever more direct and determined. Their resonance ever more vigorous and indecipherable to my ears. A hundred conversations over-lapped and interwove as the onward charge closed ever nearer.

Not so long ago I would have been one of them.

But now I was invisible as the amassed teenagers ambushed me.

They pooled to my position and moved in all directions around and beyond me.

I was non-existent to them all.

And completely inconsequential to their missions.

And I suddenly found myself sensing pleasure.

Perhaps I was overdue a smile?

Perhaps I too remained burdened?

But I was overcome with youthful joy when standing amid that roving throng of teenagers.

It was certainly infectious.

The natural energy and easy fearlessness they emitted was an addictive combination. And as I grinned at them when they passed my position of invisibility, I felt simultaneously sorrowful that my adolescence was never as prosperous as theirs.

They had the divine right to greedily devour what life had already offered and would hopefully continue to offer.

My smile had now faded as rapidly as it had evolved.

But I fought back the dark thoughts and forcibly selected the God-given highlights to re-appear at the forefront of my mind.

A loving sibling.

Health and wealth.

Whatever we had been denied as youngsters we had eventually claimed back as our right to possess.

Fortune had eventually blessed our little clan.

Our turn had indeed arisen.

Albeit belatedly.

Delayed through circumstance.

But we were ultimately victorious warriors and had defeated life's villainous woes.

And as this thought dawned, I found that my expression of happiness had returned once again.

Mainly due to the vision that acquired clarity as it assimilated itself through the jostling melee playing out before me.

Evidently some years older than his classmates.

He *belonged* with them, though.

He was one of *them.*

He had immersed himself in his plunge pool of doubt and swiftly learned to swim with consummate grace.

Hearty laughter abounded from his group. I could see that the company he kept was vibrant and responsive to him.

That man of twenty-seven years had found his place in things.

And just observing him from afar made me so proud.

Martin kept glancing in my direction but hadn't recognised me yet.

He was far too engaged with entertaining his crew through his natural repertoire of witty observation. When it came to instantaneously humorous summary of what he saw before him, my brother was the very best.

Olympic standard as a comedian.

He was about ten metres away when I finally caught his eye.

We were separated by the heaving exodus, but the tide of bodies was also bringing him slowly closer.

Once we engaged acknowledging glances, his features altered accordingly. He was no more the showman just for his fellow pupils. He was now in a momentary state of mock disbelief as the joker returned take to the stage.

He stopped his stride and exhibited a visage of feigned panic.

He then clutched his right hand to his chest as if succumbing to a heart attack brought on by shock. With his left hand he reached out to me with extended digits and wide eyes.

His features grimaced and his voice slightly raised in volume.

A performance as much for himself, as it was for me.

'Oh no! He's found me! He's *found* me! He's come to take me away! Save me people…from his ruthless clutches! HELP!'

His school pals looked on in understandable bemusement.

I could do little else but chuckle at the exhibition.

My brother looked as handsome as ever.

A real A-list celebrity that stood out from the crowd.

And the self-assurance with which he now conducted himself was astounding.

His gaggle of friends remained none the wiser as he finally dropped the comedy act and moved toward me with arms open wide.

Helpless with admiration, I reciprocated the gesture.

Brothers back together as one.

We embraced tightly as though nobody else was around to see it.

It felt so soothing. It felt so accomplished.

The seconds passed before I whispered in his ear.

'So happy to see ya, big bro!'

His reply was typical.

'Well…I knew you were coming but I didn't bake a cake. How is my favourite younger relative?'

We pulled back slightly and gazed into one another's eyes.

'I'm great, Martin. And I'm all the better for being with you. Life is looking good for you too, so a little bird tells me?'

'Better than good, Jamie! Its brilliant. Did you know I'm the only pupil in the school who is engaged to be married? Pretty unique, hey? And what an extra special surprise to be greeted by *you* at the end of my school day. No one else can claim that honour, either! Fantastic! The icing on the cake…the cake that I forgot to bake!'

I was in stitches at being the recipient of his heartfelt silliness.

'Indeed. And by the way…congratulations! You've made Bobby a very happy woman.'

Martin looked at me blankly as though I'd committed a faux pas.

Not a trace of comedy could be detected in his forced switch of demeanour.

'You mean to tell me…. she wasn't happy *before I put the ring on*?'

I laughed again. Then Martin broke back into a giggle as I tried to be serious for one second.

‘It’s been too long, big bro. But I’m back for a little while I think.’

He glared at me and pursed his lips.

‘It *has* been too long, Jamie. Ten months is a punishment to leave me all alone with her. My ear drums were throbbing by March!’

‘Don’t let *her* hear you say that, Martin.’

‘Believe me. I tell her to her face. At least I would if I could get a word in.’

He was relentless with the patter as his attention shifted to his friends.

‘She has enough mouth for the three of us. And she knows it! Anyway…some introductions are in order.’

The puzzled onlookers had been very patient as they watched us become reacquainted. It was almost a relief that Martin eventually did the honours. With a glint in his eye, he patted each in turn on the shoulder as a gesture of reference.

‘This is Luke. This is Kieran. This is Daniel. My gang. My best buddies. My all-time favourite bosom chums. Apart from you. And my wife to be, of course.’

With a theatrical flourish of his arms, Martin finally announced my place in the grand scheme of things to the captive audience.

‘Gentlemen…this wonderful, nearly as handsome as me specimen standing before you is beyond any shadow of doubt, my all-time absolute saviour. The person I owe a life debt to. My knight in rusting armour. The lord of my prayers that I’ve not shut up about for over a year. I give you…my younger brother, JAMIE!’

The three fifteen-year-olds engaged me warmly with mutual smiles, and we avidly shook hands. It was a surreal experience seeing Martin with such appreciative companionship.

My heart was proud to bursting at that moment.

Then quite abruptly, he bid them a good night.

‘I won’t be walking with you this evening. But I’ll see you right here in the morning, lads. I need to spend some proper conference time with my brother. Okay?’

Without further word Martin's three friends duly nodded their heads, bid their farewells, and despatched themselves through the crowd.

'Okay little bro. Let's get home.'

Finally left alone together, Martin and I began to shuffle along the pavement. He was extremely excitable. I was struggling to get a word in edgeways, myself. And he claims his fiancée is the chatterbox!

'Did you see Bobby when you got to ours? Did she get to work okay? She works too hard. Bonus or not, the wage isn't comparative to the hours she puts in. Daylight robbery. But she is a born slave.'

He suddenly sounded grown up once his teenage audience had vanished.

I tried to respond accordingly.

'I *did* see her, yes. And she just messaged me to say she clocked in before three.'

'Okay, then she might be home about eight-fifteen if she's locking up the shop. That's cool. I ought to meet her if it's a late finish. Dark nights bring dark demons…you know?'

'I *do* know, all too well. You are obviously looking after each other. You don't need to worry about her, Martin. She loves earning a crust. So, anyway, how is school going? I'm sorry I've not been back this year. University is quite hectic. And I missed your birthday. Apologies.'

Martin eyed me with feigned suspicion before laughing out loud.

'You mean you've not given me a minute's thought since the non-stop partying and the endless girls, and the never-ending drinking kicked in? You're so thoughtless, Jamie. How can you even admit your shame? Who gave you permission to start enjoying yourself? Ha? Who?'

I had to stop and laugh again.

My brother was a natural born wit.

I tried to defend my corner.

'Where does everyone get the idea that being at Uni is like that? Honestly…its lectures and studying all the way. No fun whatsoever.'

Martin eyed me sheepishly.

'Yeah…and your nose is almost a metre long, now.'

'Never mind me, anyway. How is St George's treating you? Big exams year this year?'

Martin adopted an air of formality.

As ever, the comedian was not far away, though.

'Well, *I'm* being treated just fine. But Rufus got banned from site, again. Somehow every now and then he secretly hitches a ride in my school bag and jumps out in the middle of class to talk to everyone. He's very sociable but teachers say it can be a little disruptive. I think Bobby puts him in my bag when I'm brushing my teeth in a morning.'

I shook my head as we walked toward the canal path.

'Maybe she thinks Rufus will keep an eye on you at school?'

'Maybe so, little bro. But I'm a grown-up. I don't need Rufus supervising me anymore. I *used* to need him, granted. But not so much now.'

Martin was constantly tickling my funny bone without even realising it. I don't think he suspected that even the comments he made in earnest were likely to raise a smile.

I chipped in again to encourage his impromptu script.

'Really? I wonder why they might think he's a distraction. It's a sad sign of the times when mature pupils can't even bring their furry mascots into the classroom.'

Martin didn't acknowledge that I was teasing him.

'Well, Mrs Adams who teaches Maths says Maths isn't for bears. Which is kind of unfortunate as Maths is undoubtedly Rufus' favourite subject.'

I observed my brother's humourless expression as we stepped on to the canal towpath back towards home. By this time, I'd already totally forgotten about taking him for a pint at the Tiger.

'Do you ever take *anything* seriously, Martin?'

I could see him stop his stride and screw up his features in dismay.

'After the shitty life *we've* had so far? Erm…take a wild guess, Jamie. Same question to you…do *you* take anything seriously these days? Reality is a clusterfuck. Fantasy wins hands down every time.'

We continued our trek as dusk began to show signs of encroachment, dragging its grey shroud over the distant horizon.

It was so appeasing to observe Martin's calm demeanour.

After the initial opening period of joviality, my brother's next question was genuinely a little baffling and caught me off guard.

He stared straight ahead as he spoke in a stern tone.

'Can I ask, Jamie? How come you're back here? I mean, Bobby said you were travelling up today. But she didn't say *why*? Everything's fine, you know.'

I was suddenly in an awkward position.

I didn't know what answer I was expected to deliver.

Surely Bobby would have consulted my brother?

Especially if she was so concerned about the recent reappearance of our father?

But it didn't even seem to be on Martin's radar.

The only aspect baffling him was why I had suddenly appeared.

I thought on my feet and blagged a diplomatic reply, hoping it might be an acceptable one.

'I'm just checking in on you both. It's been too long, like you just said. That's okay with you, isn't it?'

Martin might enjoy playing the role of the jester, but he was certainly no fool. He shook his head as we both passed where the swans had been earlier. The feathered family were now grouped on the far bank of the canal and in ensconced in a process of collective preening.

My brother's mood altered noticeably as he suddenly manoeuvred across me and halted my stride.

He looked me in the eye to judge insurance of my honesty.

'You're a bad liar, Jamie. That's because lying doesn't come naturally to you. I'm paying you a compliment there, by the way. Now…once again…*why* have you come back? You haven't travelled two hundred miles just to *check in* on us. That's expensive, time consuming and impractical for your journalism studies.'

Well, he'd got me bang to rights, hadn't he?

And I was more than a little dismayed that Bobby hadn't fully enlightened him as to her concerns. But as I said, my brother was no idiot.

He would surely have had some inkling?

'Cutting to the chase then, I suspect you know very well why I'm here, Martin.'

Oh well, I'd managed to avoid the subject for a couple of hours.

No going back now. We were running with the baton, and someone had to take it.

'Okay yes, Jamie. I know. It's because of Dad, isn't it?'

An uneasy period of quiet descended between us.

I was certainly taken aback by Martin's choice of terminology. Once again, I was conjuring a response off the top of my head. But I hadn't realised just yet quite how astute my brother was. And I found it difficult to ascertain his standpoint on the issue.

He continued to stare into me.

As such, I had no other option but the truth, did I?

'Bobby phoned me last night. She sounded very worried. She said you'd seen him watching you across from the school.'

Martin seemed to shrug the revelation off.

'Yes. I did. That was last week, though. Why is she worried? What is there to worry *about*? He didn't attempt to communicate. He was just standing there. Hands in pockets. Watching me leave through the gates. That's all. Hardly worthy of a prison sentence, is it? There's no problem, here. There's nothing for her to get her head screwed up about.'

Now my brother was showing a chink in his armour. Our old friend, naivety. I had to try and shine light on the area he was evidently avoiding.

'Not yet, there isn't.'

Martin reacted to my veiled warning with apparent disapproval in his tone.

'And why *would* there be trouble ahead? *Why* would Dad want to bring any more misery to our door after two years apart? I just figured he was back in Nottingham to see some of his old mates. That's all. Its barely worth discussing, is it?'

For all his undeniable intelligence, I suspected an extremely worrying lack of awareness emanating from Martin. After everything we had been through, he didn't sense the danger that we might already be facing. And I quickly began to dispense my frustration.

'For crying out loud, bro. Our father's middle *name* is trouble. He's never given us anything *but* misery! You've got a short memory. He's not here to see his mates. Because he hasn't fucking *got* any mates! He's only here to cause upset to us. Because that's all he's good for.'

Martin was becoming distinctly aggrieved at my opinions, even taking a tentative step back to gather his own reaction.

'There's no need to shout and swear at me, Jamie. I don't like it.'

He didn't like it, no. And it was obvious why. He'd had a lifetime of being shouted and sworn at. But now it was my turn to unfurl some more of my fraying patience as we stood debating on the towpath.

The atmosphere had altered at the flick of a switch.

I hadn't anticipated an episode of sibling conflict so soon.

'Yeah? That's because all he ever did was bark at you. Isn't it? That's why raised voices scare you. It's because of that bastard? Well, *isn't it*?'

Martin let his gaze wander away into the distance. He evidently didn't want to talk about it. I'd touched a raw nerve. But I wasn't letting the subject lie without backing myself up with some proof.

'Show me your hands.'

Martin looked at me quizzically.

'What?'

'Roll up your sleeve. Show me your forearms.'

'I don't want to, Jamie.'

I grasped Martin's right wrist and tugged back his cuff.

The horrific evidence duly exhibited itself.

'That's what he did to you for *fun*! *That's* what good old *Dad* did! *You* told me that, *yourself*! Those burn marks are your inheritance from him. Permanent scars from the fucking scumbag that he was to you for all those years. And no doubt still would be if he's given the chance.

Don't tell me you've forgotten. How the hell can you ignore something like that?'

Things were becoming steadily heated between us.

We separated further to allow a group of pupils to pass between us. But the ceasefire was temporary, and we quickly drew arms once more.

'You don't have to patronise me, Jamie. I'm fully aware of Dad's previous. I live with what he did to me every single day. But I'm not inclined to go over and punch him in the face just for standing in the street. Last I heard that's pretty much illegal.'

I couldn't believe what was coming out of my brother's mouth.

And I struggled to rein in what was coming out of mine.

'Who's being patronising, *now*? And don't you fucking *dare* keep calling him *Dad* in front of me. He lost that privilege many years ago. Why the fuck do you refuse to see how this is going to go?'

I was now venting through frustration and despair, yet Martin retained his sense of perspective as he issued a snide repost.

'Okay, *Superman*? Now that you've obviously been called into battle. So, what does Bobby expect *you* to do about it?'

'What is *that* supposed to mean?' I snapped.

'I mean…what are you *actually* going to do, Jamie? Now that you've travelled up here. Are you going to lock me in the house and stake the school out until he shows again? Then what? Take to him with a bat? Employ a hit man to clip him? Look…if…as *you* claim…Dad is wanting trouble, then he's not getting it from me. I'm not going to allow him to invade my life again. It's simple as that.'

Martin was burying his head in the sand.

Perhaps through genuine disinterest.

But more likely through genuine fear.

'Please, Martin…please don't refer to him like that. I'm asking you nicely. He's never been a father to us. Never mind that other word. You're giving him stature. Why would you do that?'

Sarcasm was now being utilised by my brother as an escape route.

His mask of apathy was beyond ridiculous.

'Okay, Jamie. Sorry...Detective Andrews. You seem to have things under control. You tell me what he's doing back here, then? He's willingly blown his own cover. The secret is out. But he remains nothing to us. Why dramatize it?'

'Believe me, Martin, I'm not telling you this for effect.'

My brother held his hands out in a gesture of genuine curiosity.

'But why create a false scenario that isn't going to happen in real life? What happened is all in the past. And I'd really like it to stay that way. If that's okay with you and Bobby, of course?'

At last, I think I was finding my brother's wavelength.

He was wary of poking the hornet's nest.

Whereas I was already more than willing to kick it wide open.

Fine. I got that much. He was afraid and wanted to be cautious.

That was his justifiable right.

But if Martin truly believed that our father was just passing through then he needed educating as to the correct way of thinking.

No wonder Bobby contacted me in a blind panic.

We continued to walk together as a mode of serenity thankfully returned to the discussion. I attempted to convey the issue through a different approach.

'The point is big bro...I haven't got a clue *why* he's back in Nottingham. *None* of us have. Not *you*. Not *me*. Not *Bobby*. But the one thing we must do is stand together. We can't afford to start fighting between ourselves. If we do that...then he's already winning. And Bobby was worried because she loves you. That's it.'

Martin was now acting indignant. It really didn't suit him.

'Well, if Bobby was *that* worried then maybe she should have considered talking to her fiancé about it first before slamming the big red button.'

'Yes, you're possibly right on that score. But look how you've responded to *me*? You're very defensive about the whole subject. She obviously didn't want to upset you any more than was necessary.'

We continued our stuttering path toward home.

Thankfully the unwanted frostiness between us was thawing as rapidly as it had set in.

'Look, Jamie. I don't want to have any opinion on this. It's the previous negativity in my life that I really want to keep the door closed on. I've got you. I've got Bobby. I've got school. Nothing else comes into it for me. That's how I will deal with it. I'll keep it off my chart. Okay? Now…can we get to our house without any more falling out, please?'

Tranquillity reigned for a full five minutes as we approached the railway station and ambled under the shadowy arch of the bridge.

In the meantime, Martin had given himself plenty of opportunity to dig out some humorous remedy to the friction of earlier.

He suddenly stopped walking and shrieked.

'OH MY GOD, JAMIE!'

He made me jump in the semi darkness.

'What is it? What's the matter?'

'It's just occurred to me this very second.'

'*What* has?'

'The reason our father is back.'

I sensed I was being subjected to more imminent silliness.

'Go on, then. Enlighten me.'

'Do you think he wants to kidnap Rufus and demand a ransom?'

I willingly played along with the joke.

'Listen big bro…if he so much as goes in the same *postcode* as Rufus, I will knock his brains out. And then I'll get a hit man to finish the job off. Okay?'

'Good answer! That's the little brother I know and love!'

With the ceasefire fully restored we headed contentedly to Glenfield Avenue.

But both of us knew the subject was far from put to bed.

Our father would ensure that much.

5
A GLOOMY FORECAST

'Did you know that the guy that makes the batter puts beer in it to give extra taste?'

Martin's adamant declaration was followed with a supportive demonstration as he loaded his fork with fried cod and inserted it ravenously into his mouth.

Bobby and I gazed at one another, both unusually lost for words as Martin duly chewed his food, swallowed it, and slurped down some orange Fanta.

He was then ready to continue with the impromptu sermon about the evening's choice of supper.

'I mean…whoever thought it might be possible to get drunk whilst eating fish and chips?'

Again, I felt my attention drawn to Bobby's reaction.

Her natural instinctive smile was absent.

We studied Martin from across the dining table.

His relentless commentary threw a welcome veil of light-heartedness over the house. Indeed, Martin's God-given enthusiasm could adapt itself quickly to any given scenario. His candid and comprehensive observations were always entertaining and more often than not, would prove to be surprisingly informative.

I attempted to concur with his summary.

'I think most places do the beer batter thing now, bro. Not just The Dolphin chippy round the corner. It's very popular on menus almost everywhere these days.'

Martin nodded and attempted to convey another point through another mouthful.

'Well, I think it's about time we all went *out* to eat. At a real fancy place. Starters and desserts obligatory. Rufus too. The whole hog. What do you say, Jamie? What about tomorrow night?'

My brother's eyes widened in hopeful expectation of our reaction.

It was a good idea, but I wasn't sure the vibe was a particularly celebratory one at that moment.

'We'll see, big bro. Are you not hungry, Bobby? You haven't eaten much?'

She had seemed rather subdued ever since coming in from work. I did ask her earlier, and she claimed the shift at the store went fine. So, I could only presume that the problem was the perennial elephant in the room.

The subject that no one wanted to debate.

Yet we knew it would be impossible to evade it.

Bobby left work at seven to be home with the food by half past as arranged, specifically so the three of us could air our views in our own time and hopefully find some common ground.

It was very important for her to be present during the discussion, despite the trepidation she had conveyed to me about the situation.

I understood totally. Our father was as much of a negative blot on *her* landscape as he was on mine and Martin's. If anything, I had already picked up on the fact that my brother's stubborn disinterest in the issue would need some active encouragement.

Two on to one might just work.

But, as was his way, Martin's mind was anywhere but on the matter at hand.

'These chips *can't* be hand cut. They must be bought in frozen. The length is a big giveaway. Every chip is an average of seven centimetres. No off cuts. No small ones. All uniform. The staff wouldn't have time to cut them by hand like this. Plus, think of the wastage if they did. Impossible.'

I tried to engage Bobby's attention by staring directly at her across the table again. Involving her in such a numbing conversation might at least distract her from her other more potent concerns.

'Who would have thought a take-away would have provided such a stimulus for this insight, hey Bobby?' I quipped.

I was fairly certain she didn't even hear me speak.

Her eyes were fixed on an indeterminable point on the far wall.

Miles away. Glazed over.

Martin meanwhile expanded with his ramblings.

'And it's a sure bet that this curry sauce contains no authentic ingredients. Obscure powder and tap water. And it stains light coloured clothing forever. You could scrub for days on end, and it still won't shift. And it congeals like concrete on worksurfaces. But will come off laminate with a solid scraping instrument…imagine how it sits in your guts…'

Bobby set her fork down and rubbed her eyes.

It had been a trying twenty-four hours for her personally.

I could see that Martin's typically off the wall appraisals on all things irrelevant were something she could not be bothered with this evening.

She suddenly rose from the table. Her meal hardly touched.

I covertly observed as she entered the kitchen and switched on the kettle. This was perhaps my chance to talk privately with her while my brother continued happily in his own world for a while.

'Carry on with your dinner Martin. There's plenty more if you're still hungry.'

'Thank you. I think I will finish this first and then see. I don't want to be labelled a greedy guzzler, do I?'

I gave the thumbs-up to him and followed Bobby into the kitchen. She was leaning across the sink staring out into the darkness beyond the window. There was nothing visibly identifiable in the garden, but it diverted her attention, nevertheless.

I would soon find out just how sociable she was prepared to be.

To say the least, Bobby was giving off signals that indicated she was verging toward very unapproachable. I joined her by the sink and tried to analyse what it was in the bleak vista beyond the glass that she found so curious.

My first pre-emptive shot across the bow was woeful.

Pathetic, even.

‘Draws in quick now doesn’t it. I don’t like dark nights. Winter seems to go on forever once it’s here.’

I did pre-warn you about the mundanity of my effort, dear reader.

More seconds of silence followed.

Finally, she conjured the will to reply, which was delivered via a low hiss.

‘I can’t be doing with Martin, tonight. Does my head in sometimes.’

I wanted to laugh out loud as I could almost have read her mind.

But as things stood, I opted for a more diplomatic response perhaps lined with a twinge of comedy.

‘Bit late to decide that now. You’ve said you’ll *marry* him, remember? You’ve got *years* of this to come!’ I sniggered.

At last, the corners of her mouth suggested an upturn.

And the vivacious Bobby Jones of old made a fleeting entrance.

But it didn’t last for long.

Her demeanour was almost depressed.

This thing was weighing her down far more than I had presumed.

She addressed me with deep concern in her eyes.

‘The business with Jim. It’s giving me the willies. I’m not too proud to admit that I’m shitting myself here and now. I can’t help thinking that he’s going to turn up here and the merry go round starts all over again. I can’t go back to that life, Jamie. I can’t fucking let that happen. But I can’t talk to your brother about my worries. He’s on a different planet.’

I glanced over my shoulder to check that Martin was still eating.

I maintained the whispered tone.

I could feel her trembling.

This had really gotten to her.

‘Yes, I know. I talked to Martin about it earlier on the way home from school. He’s not willing to acknowledge the potential problem our father poses to the whole set-up here. My brother’s attitude is based on forgetting about the past and not letting it in again. It’s like he has completely closed the previous chapter of his life. If only it were that simple. But I’m with you on this, Bobby.’

She turned to face me and folded her arms.

I hadn't seen her carry such a fearful visage since first meeting her in Blackpool.

Our father's reappearance had already begun to drive a succinct wedge between the three of us. She was not holding back in her frustration at Martin's standpoint.

'There doesn't seem any mileage in even involving him in a discussion if he's blatantly oblivious to the situation. It is beyond belief to me that Jim seems intent on coming back to haunt us and all your brother is bothered about is the recipe for his fucking *supper*!'

I wanted to smile again.

But refrained, trying to stand on the side of common sense.

Yet Bobby's turns of phrase in referencing Martin were brutally accurate at times. I could fully sympathise with her apprehension because I felt it also.

Yet I was tempted to suggest that Martin's purposed aloofness was perhaps a policy we might need to invest in as having certain benefits.

If not least, in terms of keeping a level state of mind.

'Martin has an opinion. He's pretty clued up on how he feels to be honest. But he deals in blacks and whites. There's no grey area as far as he's concerned. The way he sees it our father has simply watched him from across the road. He doesn't read any more into it than that. He hasn't got alarm bells ringing like you and I have.'

Bobby nodded in vague agreement.

She seemed quite placated by the fact I had broached the subject with Martin already. I suspected she had grown weary of trying to convince him on her own.

'Yes, you're exactly right, Jamie. But what next? Where do we stand? What do we do?'

'Listen…we do nothing for now because nothing has actually happened, has it? Okay? We sit tight. That's the better option than going gung-ho with all guns blazing, I think.'

I could sense her now being caught between a rock and a hard place.

She was agitated because of her imagination working overtime.

But hopefully I had thrown a bit of sanity into the mix to help calm her down.

But don't get me wrong, dear reader.

My suspicions were on high alert, too.

I was backing Bobby's instinct all the way on this one.

But for now, the timing for any action was wrong.

'Look, Bobby. If it is any crumb of comfort, I understand entirely why you panicked and asked me to get on the train. In your shoes I'd have done the same. But we mustn't react in haste. The ball's in our father's court. It's his move still, isn't it?'

The rumble of the boiling kettle provided a minor diversion from the depressing subject matter.

She reached up to the cupboard for three mugs.

'Perhaps I was Little Miss Innocent in believing we'd seen the last of him when we came down here. More fool me, eh?'

'Not really. It's a case of self-preservation. Your response is a credit to your intelligence. He's still a dangerous and malicious bastard. And we shouldn't lose sight of that fact.'

At last, her striking smile stretched from ear to ear.

'Agreed, Jamie. And thank you for being here. You don't know how much better it's made me feel. Even in the last five minutes standing talking here. It's a bit less of weight, now. I'm too locked up in my own head with it.'

Our conversation was suddenly disrupted by a call from the dining table.

'Look! Clean plate! Did you say there was seconds if I had any room left?'

I retreated to the lounge and sat opposite my brother. The opportunity was there for the taking if I wanted to re-engage him on the priority issue.

'Glad you finished it up. The rest I will microwave for you in a moment. Listen carefully, Martin. Bobby and I want to be absolutely clear where we all stand with this business of our father turning up out of the blue, okay? No stressing like earlier. Everything's cool. But we are a family, and we need to discuss it like one. You on board with that?'

I hoped my prompt might resonate with him.

Still with cutlery in hand, my brother swiftly adopted a bemused expression.

'But we already spoke about it, Jamie. There's nothing else to say, is there?'

I glanced at Bobby who nodded her permission for me to continue.

The debate was open.

Whether Martin was interested in listening or not.

'But it's not quite that simple, bro. Me and Bobby are concerned about the fact that he's knocking around. He's playing it low-key like you say. But he has a motive. Surely you can see our point?'

Martin simply stared at his empty plate.

Bobby attempted to fortify my statement.

'A leopard doesn't change its spots, babe. Your father is rotten to the core. He's after something. He's not revealed it yet. But his true reasons for watching you will come out soon. Lord knows how long he's been sniffing around without our knowledge.'

Martin's next statement was hardly conducive to lifting her spirits.

'Yes, that's a valid point. If he's intent on confrontation, then he must know where we live by now.'

Not the declaration I particularly wanted to hear, either.

In fairness, she dealt with it reasonably well.

'Cheers for that, lover. That's made my frigging day. The icing on the bloody cake, so it is.'

After a few soundless seconds of deliberation, my brother decided to find his voice.

'By the way…on the leopards and spots thing. Did you know that the origin of that expression is in The Holy Bible. Jeramiah. Chapter Thirteen. Verse twenty-three…'

Bobby was understandably less tolerant this time.

'Martin! FOR FUCK'S SAKE! You see what I'm saying, Jamie? Waste of time.'

Her short fuse had predictably blown.

It was becoming obvious that my brother was unwilling to appreciate the gravity of the message we were trying to convey.

He fell silent once again as she attempted to hammer home the point.

'Never mind the bloody Bible. This is about the *real* and the *now*. We need to be prepared in case something *does* happen with your father. That's fair enough, isn't it? I'm not asking the Earth, am I?'

Martin lifted his gaze and focussed on Bobby as he returned serve.

'What happened is done with. I'm a happy man living for the present and planning for the future. That's fair enough too, isn't it?'

Bobby took a seat next to Martin and held his forearms firmly in her grasp.

'That's exactly my point. Your father will *know* that we are doing well. That's why he'll be pissed off that we have moved on. And being the kind of man he is, our success here will stir only one thing in him. Hatred. He was a monster to us *all*, Martin. How can you forget that? How can you be so casual about the fiend that abused you? That tortured you. That imprisoned you for all those years?'

I warily observed my brother.

The conflict was inwardly upsetting for him. I also noticed his brief inspection of the cigarette burn scars on his hands and arms. A permanent reminder of several savage experiences at the hands of the man who brought us into the world.

He seemed ready to speak again.

'Don't shout and swear at me, Bobby. I don't like it. And I don't deserve it.'

She reacted accordingly. Diplomacy resumed as she cradled his hands in her own. Her tone became softer and infinitely more accessible.

'I'm sorry, my darling. I promise I won't shout and swear again. I apologise. But you don't seem to see that I am really bothered by this.'

In an instant, my brother evolved from a logical, rational, sensible adult into a cowering child.

For all his independence, endeavour, and immense progress, he was still that little boy at heart. Among the impressive individuality he had acquired as an adult, the infant still lurked within him.

Bobby persevered, taking full advantage of Martin's sudden sheen of vulnerability.

'Okay, babe. Let's do a deal. Okay? If you *ever* see your father again, *anywhere*, you *mustn't* acknowledge him. You must not confront him or speak to him. Because that is exactly what he wants. But what you must do *instead*, is come straight home and tell me or Jamie about it. Because we need to keep a diary of events. Just in case we should have to tell the police. Okay?'

I remained the onlooker as Martin gazed into space and nodded.

Hopefully the sentiment was sinking in.

After teasing the pair of us for an endless period of quiet, he finally agreed with his fiancée's request.

'Yes. I understand. I'll tell you straight away if anything occurs. I now know this problem bothers you deeply so I will keep you informed if there is any more contact with him. I'm tired now. I think I'll go to bed if that's agreeable.'

Bobby smiled at me before kissing Martin on top of his head.

'You go and put something on telly. Relax. I'll be joining you soon. It's been a long two days.'

I watched them kiss goodnight and Martin then came and gave me a hug before retiring to the bedroom.

Fingers crossed the mission was accomplished.

Bobby turned to me and exhibited her broadest Irish accent.

'So, Jamie boy, how do you think that went as a final duel in the last chance saloon?'

I couldn't help but chuckle. When she occasionally addressed me in that direct manner it always recalled our first encounter in Blackpool.

An eternity ago.

At least it felt like it.

'You did very well, Bobby. Now full awareness is under this roof I think we need to chill and try and put the thing to the back of our minds if possible. We've rightly flagged it up. But we need to avoid nurturing our paranoia. We can do no more tonight. When you go to work tomorrow you might just feel a little better.'

Bobby Jones flashed that sarcastic expression that initially greeted me in The Celtic Arms.

'Okay, Jamie. You're the boss. Even if you *are* the youngest. What about you, though? Are you going back to Swansea tomorrow?'

I didn't show my true colours.

I might have played it down to bring closure for the evening, but my mind was secretly racing.

I had no intention of going anywhere.

'I'm gonna hang around to see if any dust gets kicked up. Plus, I'm going to the bank for you tomorrow aren't I. But no more needs to be said for now. Deal?'

Bobby rose to her feet and shook my hand.

'Deal! In fact, this calls for a little celebration. Fuck the tea. I'll get the whiskey out.'

'Good idea. Oh…by the way.'

'What now?' she gasped.

'Don't swear. Martin doesn't like it.'

Bobby mouthed further profanity as she retrieved two tumblers from the lounge cupboard.

A more congenial ambience resumed.

Whatever the future had in store, we decided to ignore it for the next few hours.

6
THE MORNING AFTER

'You were dreaming in the night, Jamie boy. I nearly came in to see if you were okay.'

Bobby's voice resonated rather too clearly as I scratched my head and yawned. She poured oats into a bowl and added some chopped banana before sitting at the table.

'Sorry I woke you. Must have been a night terror.'

She looked alarmed that I might be susceptible to such disturbances. In fairness it was probably the first one I had suffered for over a year. I needed a drink to perk me up.

'I'm making myself coffee, Bobby. You want one?'

'Yes, please. Was it a bad dream, you say? Like the ones you used to have before?'

I nearly dropped the sugar bowl whilst trying to recall some vivid detail.

'No. Milder. Less distinguishable. Not so intense. There was nobody involved in it that I knew, either.'

Bobby retorted through a mouthful of cereal.

'For saying it was mild you weren't half doing some calling out. Groaning for minutes on end, so you were.'

I sniggered to myself and joined her at the table with the drinks.

'Must have been the one where I turn into a werewolf. Nah…It was a bit nondescript to be honest. I was walking through darkness. I couldn't see a thing. Then a face appeared. A clown's face. Like the Stephen King clown, in fact. I thought it was friendly until I got near it. Then it frowned at me. Then it bared its teeth which were sharpened to a point. Not human at all. Bloody odd. Fuck knows where that one came from.'

Bobby's brown eyes widened in genuine revulsion.

Again, she spoke with her mouthful.

'Jesus of Nazareth! That is *fucking freaky*. I'm getting goose bumps thinking about it. Perhaps we'll lay off the night cap tonight, yes?'

I couldn't help but be amused by her blunt honesty.

'I don't think it was the whiskey that brought it on, Bobby. Besides, I didn't drink enough to feel rough today. I used to suffer these visions regularly. So did Mum. They were really bad just before I came to Blackpool that first time. But seemed to stop overnight for some reason. Believe me…I've seen some horrible things in my sleep. I've been to places you really wouldn't want to go to.'

Bobby observed me as she twirled her spoon among the bowl of oats.

I sensed another question coming.

'Yes, I bet. I don't need convincing any further. I remember you said you thought they were linked to your mother and Martin in some way.'

I blew onto my coffee to cool it a little.

'At the time I wasn't conscious of it. But I see now that they definitely were, yes. I've learned that there are forces in this world that we shouldn't mess with, Bobby. The next dimension definitely exists.'

She started laughing and reached for her drink.

'You sound like the intro to the fucking Twilight Zone! What was your *weirdest* experience, then?'

Where would I begin, dear reader?

Every single experience I've had in my life whether in slumber or wide awake could classify as very out of the ordinary.

I sipped from my mug and pondered.

Then it came to me. The clear winner by a country mile.

'When I was doing your job a couple of summers back, I heard and then saw an apparition that looked just like Martin at the supermarket late one evening. Inside the store and then outside in the car park.'

Bobby's features went white as her jaw hung open.

Even *she* was stuck for a response for once.

'Then there was the time I found Mum standing on her bed screaming. And the next day she swore blind that it was *me* who was screaming on *my* bed. I never did get to the bottom of that one.'

I could tell this business was interesting for Bobby.

And measurably intimidating.

'Did your mother have nightmares too then, Jamie?'

'Oh yeah! I don't think she had a decent night's sleep for the last two years of her life.'

Bobby shook her head as she attempted to balance the remainder of her breakfast onto her spoon.

'I can't imagine going through anything like that. Does Martin know about it?'

'There never seemed much point in dwelling on it with him. Besides which, you know his approach to stuff better than anyone. He doesn't think too deeply about such things, does he?'

She began to giggle.

'I'm not sure he'd buy into the talk of the *other side* and demonic horseplay. He'd probably advise you to take a Horlicks to bed.'

It was a pleasant change to see Bobby address life with a lighter heart. She appeared to be in a much better place than the previous evening. However, I took my mysterious night vision as a warning.

After all, I'd been here before.

Trouble was brewing.

And those on the *other side* were giving me the heads up.

Joy of joys.

And there was me hoping the spirits had given up the ghost long ago.

*****

As pledged, I would be setting my morning schedule around depositing Bobby's cheque into the bank.

I also wanted to have a look around town just to see if anything had altered since my last inspection of the place many months ago.

Martin had risen and left for school around eight. He was in a jovial mood as ever and couldn't wait to get out of the door.

His parting shot attempted to quash the unease I had evidently failed to disguise.

'And you don't need to meet me at the gate tonight. I'll walk with my friends. Everything will be fine, Jamie.'

I couldn't prevent the display of a knowing smile as I waved him off.

'Okay, big bro. Whatever you say. If you're ashamed of me, I can hack it. Heaven forbids that I should ever cramp your style.'

Bobby stood behind me in the hallway preparing for her shift at work.

'I didn't think you were in until ten, today?'

'I wasn't but John just messaged. One of the warehouse lads has rung in sick and he needs a forklift driver sharpish. That driver being yours truly. There's a big delivery waiting to be tipped. I don't mind. He let me be flexible yesterday so I can't really complain, can I?'

She began to apply lip gloss and eye liner as I debated whether to get dressed yet.

'You got time for a last drink, Bobby?'

'No, I've to be outta here as soon as possible. By the way…thank you, Jamie.'

I was puzzled by her gratitude.

'I was only offering you a cuppa.'

She lightly ran a brush through her shortened hair as she explained.

'Not *that*, silly. I mean thank you for coming back to us. It's a comfort. If you weren't here, I would never have let Martin leave the house alone today. But I suddenly feel safer. Safer than I did three days ago and that's a fact.'

She placed the hairbrush back in the drawer of the hall console table and let her eyes rest on me.

I could see the genuine relief in her demeanour.

'You don't need to thank me. I've told you. We are a family. Did you really think I'd tell you to naff off and stay put in Swansea?'

Her lips pouted in an awkward line.

‘Well, I thought maybe you’d see me as some wimpy woman that couldn’t cope. I had to flag it up. You’d have been annoyed if we *hadn’t* told you about your father, I’m sure.’

I moved toward her and placed both hands on her shoulders.

‘Hey…listen…I’m glad you let me know. Seriously. If it was up to Martin, he would have just carried on regardless and let things slide out of control. I’m just pleased that we all had our say yesterday and got a perspective on it. We can all think a little clearer, now.’

I finished making my drink whilst Bobby put the finishing touches to her appearance.

‘You’ve got a key haven’t you, Jamie?’

‘Yes. I’ll lock up. I need a shower before I go out, anyway. I’ll be here a while yet, I should think.’

Bobby re-directed the conversation back to the previous subject.

‘I’ll be straight with you, Jamie. Whilst this problem is hanging over us, I want you to stay with us. For as long as necessary. I know that sounds selfish, but that’s how I feel.’

‘Don’t fret. I’ve no plans to get back to Wales yet. Any lectures I miss I can catch up with. They’ll just have to learn how to party without me for a while, won’t they?’

Bobby kissed me on the cheek and pulled open the front door.

‘Big head!’ she chuckled.

‘You bet!’

‘Right Jamie, I’m finally out of here.’

‘Have a great day and play nicely. Give my regards to Johnny H. I’ll pop and see him soon. But not today, though.’

‘Will do! See you tonight!’

*****

As directed, I paid Bobby's work bonus into her current account. Whilst doing so I checked on the balance of the family savings.

A very satisfying figure was raised.

One hundred and thirty-five thousand pounds.

With some loose change added onto the back end of that.

Whilst my walk into town wasn't as unnerving as yesterday, I could not help but carry the niggling sensation that I might have been tailed.

I kept stern vigil and could not detect any signs of an unwelcome observer.

Nobody attempted to make themselves overtly known to me.

But my instincts on such things were rarely awry.

I picked up on the aura of another presence as soon as I had departed Glenfield Avenue.

It wasn't even anything that I might attach a physical familiarity to, but the sensation was with me for the entire journey on foot.

Even when I was in the bank, I felt something or someone over my shoulder.

My paranoia was perhaps taking hold.

But if my father *was* in the vicinity, then he was doing a sterling job of remaining secluded.

The transactions in the bank endured for less than five minutes in total.

I emerged gratified and thankful that our little trio was on a firm footing financially.

As for our collective emotional status, only time would tell.

7
SEEING THE SIGHTS

I stood outside the bank as the soothing wave of positive sentiment continued to wash over me. Henry had been so kind and the three of us were so fortunate that he had opted to provide for us in such a generous manner.

Having six figures in the savings account sure went some way to smoothing any potential bumps in the road ahead.

I didn't even class it as a rainy-day fund. The shock of being Henry's benefactor still hadn't dissipated if I was being honest. His gift was a foundation for us to lead the rest of our lives without money worries.

It was indicative of the love and respect Henry had for me but a totally unexpected gesture. I wasn't blood to him. He could have left his estate to anyone or anything he chose. But he chose me. I was humbled and will be eternally grateful.

In hindsight he treated me like his own son after Mum passed away. And when I returned from Blackpool with my brother and Bobby, he had no reservations about welcoming them into the fold. Even if it was more than a bit confined between the four of us in the bungalow.

The fact that I had sole control over the account has never been an issue for debate. Martin would not be interested in overseeing finances and Bobby understood that she would be benefitting from the windfall indirectly anyway.

Besides which, life had taught us all that money is only a means to an end. We had never previously had a penny in our pocket ever. Any possibility of the three of us being materialistic was completely out of the question.

Wealth was a foreign concept. And whereas the other two were perhaps wary of suddenly having so much cash in the coffers, they entrusted me to do the right things and make the correct decisions on their behalf.

I often thought of Mum when I thought of Henry.

She distanced herself from him as I grew up.

But she distanced herself from everyone, eventually. I think she was aware that Henry had bonded with me in my early teens. We became far more than neighbourly acquaintances.

Whilst she had no specific personal qualm with him, I suspect she was content to pigeon-hole him as just another nosey neighbour.

With the benefit of hindsight, I was more than appreciative he *was* another nosey neighbour!

I always presumed that Henry's initial interest in my daily life was due to the fact he was bored with his own routine and needed a distraction. He was also very lonely. He was a genuine and caring man with a heart of gold. Mum and I were a valued part of his everyday existence.

No one could have foreseen how his affection for us would extend after his death.

He was the nearest thing to a father I ever had, anyway.

My eyes glazed over as I wallowed in my pool of reminiscence in the middle of the High Street.

The sound of nearby shoppers brough me back to the here and now.

I observed my current surroundings.

In truth, the town centre looked to be in steep decline.

Traders had begun to feel the struggle over recent years.

Nothing left but charity shops, bargain stores and computer repair specialists.

I glared at my troubled reflection as I passed the endless line of long-vacated premises. A vain habit I know, but you'd expect me to inspect my appearance when the opportunity arose wouldn't you?

The cracked windowpanes that had survived or been replaced with chipboard were a monument to neglect.

I glanced briefly toward the betting shops and the place that promises instant cash for jewellery. Not much use to our family. Mum never wore a ring for obvious reasons.

I stopped and read the garish poster in one shop window.

One of those corrupt shitholes that will offer you a loan of ten quid if you agree to pay it back the following week with a thousand-pound interest piled on top. Where the hell was society heading?

My attention then centred on the smattering of stalls that were grouped together supposedly to resemble a bustling market. Another tradition dying on its arse by the looks of things.

A florist and potted plant seller. A guy flogging an assortment of Hi-Viz work wear. An open-sided butcher's van manned by someone in a headpiece and microphone that never stopped going on about his loin cuts and sausages.

To cut out the middleman there was a burger trailer situated twenty yards opposite and I was very nearly tempted to indulge due to the wonderful aroma of fried onions. But instantly resisted as I had no idea when I might make it back to the gym at Uni.

And that dear reader, was the basis of the town's market day.

Oh, I apologise. I forgot the pet food stall. How remiss of me.

I ambled onward noting the sparse footfall. It was twelve noon in a town populated by forty to fifty thousand. It should have been busier, surely?

Perhaps they'd heard I was back and were all in hiding.

I considered ringing Martin to see if he fancied a bite to eat on his lunch break, but in actual fact I was quite appreciative of the solitude for the time being. Revisiting the town of my childhood had been enlightening to say the least.

It was therapeutic in some ways.

Every building held a memory.

Every street corner I had stood on at some point in my younger life. And then as I prepared to alter my course and navigate a crossing point, another vision from the past emerged before my eyes.

A living, moving, breathing memento of a chapter that ended so sadly. I stopped dead in my tracks before pressing the button to engage with the green man.

No more than fifty meters away, through the threadbare gaggle of shoppers, I spotted Alex.

She was walking and laughing with a female companion.

I became unwittingly rooted to the spot as my conscience swayed in a sea of pained nostalgia. She was obviously still in the area. Possibly still living with her parents.

I couldn't recall exactly what academic plan she had embarked upon. After I left for Swansea over a year ago my energy had centred on *my* future as opposed to worrying about anyone else's ambitions. I quickly lost touch with everyone from the Sixth Form as my life took a new path.

I had never forgotten about Alexandra Lawley, though.

She looked serene as she strode confidently in dark coloured jeans that sufficiently outlined enough of her shapely legs to remind me of what her top half looked like.

It didn't appear as though she had cut her hair in a long while, either. Her brown curls bounced way lower than her shoulders as she threw her head back in a mirthful response to her friend's commentary on something or other.

I didn't recognise her friend.

Not from school, anyway.

It didn't look like anyone I could readily recall. Perhaps a fellow student from college? Or maybe Alex had ditched college and gone to work?

And then I remembered.

Economic Engineering. Nottingham University.

So, she must still be living with her mother and father.

Her unexpected appearance shook me rather.

I reacted the same way I always did when I saw her.

Jelly legs and a thumping heart.

She still flicked the same switch in me.

Electricity coursing through my veins.

But as I watched her walk, the bleak thought occurred.

What right did I have to feel like this about her anymore?

Okay, so we went out with one another for a year at school.

But the seal was put on that when she got into a little black sports car on the day I collected my A-level results.

The perfect storm - caught dead centre between Heaven and Hell.

I never did figure out *why* she decided to make that cameo appearance.

Revenge? Pity? Pleasure? Guilt? Who knows?

I always figured that I would probably never find out, either.

But I could not deny nature. My physical and psychological reaction to seeing her in the flesh once again was an overwhelmingly joyous experience.

But common sense would inevitably crash down onto the party that was beginning in my head.

Instinct told me to stay away.

To completely forget about any whim to exchange communication with her.

To pretend that I had not seen her that day.

To pretend that I had never seen her in my entire life.

Yet there she was walking with her mystery accomplice.

Directly opposite where I wanted to cross the street.

That's got to be fate, yeah?

I was tempted to discard all rationale and shout her name across the void. And then, as I frantically battled my own desires, the moment passed. She entered the coffee shop.

She had not seen me.

A certain blessing, indeed.

And I had to reaffirm my own standpoint there and then.

I was nothing to her anymore and had no future place in her life.

I had no justifiable motive to believe I would ever be anything to Alexandra Lawley ever again.

This was the mindset I adopted as I walked determinedly away in the opposite direction.

Away from the town centre.
Back toward Glenfield Avenue.
Back toward non-existence as far as Alex was concerned.
I can almost hear your thoughts, dear reader.
Because they are no doubt the same as mine.
Who was I trying to fool?

8
CONTACT

Emotions seemed to settle down a little over the course of the following few days. I spent my time helping around the house where possible, although there wasn't a great deal of housework to do as Bobby was proving more than proficient in the art.

Even so I still hoovered and dusted and polished and made sure it was pristine when they returned through the front door. I'm not sure where *my* apparent affinity for housekeeping derived from.

It certainly wasn't inherent.

Martin and Bobby resumed a routine resembling normal after the recent unsteadying episode. Contentment appeared to be seeping back through the cracks forged by our mutual trepidation.

I returned to the bank once Bobby's cheque had cleared and as per her strict instruction, I transferred her bonus into the family savings account.

When I eventually showed her the current savings account statement, her eyes welled up and her mouth dropped open. She was stuck for words and simply hugged me tightly.

The positives in life were establishing prominence once again and the anticipated dilemma surrounding our father's reappearance did not manifest itself further.

As such, it had crossed my mind to return to my studies in Swansea after ten days in Nottingham.

But dear reader...you will no doubt be waiting to hear me reveal the adage that all good things were bound to come to an end.

And your instincts are proving as sharp as ever.

Bobby was on a late shift on the afternoon in question.

Martin had arrived home from school at his usual time of around four-fifteen.

It was mid-October.

Slate grey skies had kept things convincingly cold outside.

As soon as I heard the front door open and close, I prepared the kettle and opened a packet of chocolate biscuits.

He didn't vocally announce his entry as he usually would, but that didn't strike me as particularly odd. He removed his coat and stood in the kitchen doorway, displaying an expression on his face which I could only initially decipher as unreadable.

My first question was by the book.

'Good day, big bro?'

His response, to say the least, hit the nail on the head.

'Dad spoke to me outside school just now.'

I was instantly weighed down by a mild state of nausea. I struggled to suppress any wanton panic as Martin's words registered heavily.

'You're joking with me, right? Where was he?' I stammered.

Martin seemed comparatively nonchalant.

'He was on the canal path as I walked past with my crew.'

The bastard must be following him.

He must know Martin's route home.

Despite forecasting such a possibility, it was a very real likelihood and a starkly unwelcoming premise.

'Sit down please, bro. I'll make tea. Your favourite biccies are there.'

I struggled to retain composure as I brewed the two mugs with my back to Martin. Perspiration moistened my back as my hands trembled.

This was not the news I wanted to hear.

And of the three of us, my brother was evidently most at risk.

Things could so easily have taken a nasty turn.

And yet Martin appeared completely unfazed by the encounter.

Considering he was the one who assailed our father on the back of his skull with five kilogrammes of concrete, his physical appearance at the dining table was thankfully unblemished.

So, what did our father want with Martin if not instant retribution?

I sat opposite and let my head settle down a little before my scrutiny commenced.

'Did he touch you? Did he threaten you in any way?'

Martin centred his focus on dunking a digestive into his drink.

It broke in half before he could raise it to his mouth.

'No. He just spoke. He came from behind me. Hands in his jacket pockets. It was getting dark, and I struggled to see who it was that called my name. But he kept a safe distance. He wasn't aggressive at all.'

I couldn't help but become angered by the depiction. I was frustrated by both Martin's apparent neutrality and our father's unswaying arrogance.

Jim Andrews standing from afar and spying on his elder son was one thing. But as for him having the brass neck to attempt communication at close quarters was something else entirely.

It was bravado on another level.

'So…he didn't shout at you? No swearing? Did he alarm your friends at all?'

'My friends have no idea about who he is or why he was there. Its business that I prefer to keep private from them. My history isn't something I ever want to discuss with anyone to be honest. It's tragic and its embarrassing.'

Wow. Such philosophy from a man who only deals in absolutes and black and white. I was a little taken aback by his mindset to be honest. It was the first time he had revealed such a standpoint about his family.

I sampled some tea and pondered the scenario.

The conversation needed kid gloves. I didn't want to become impatient and force Martin to clam up.

'Try and recall for me what was said between the pair of you. It's important, Martin. Any detail at all is vital.'

My brother looked me straight in the eye.

'I can recall all of it exactly. Word for word.'

'Please do so. For my sake.'

He took another biscuit from the packet.

'Okay. Well…I was with Luke and Kieran. Daniel had the dentist so walked the other way to town. We left the pavement and joined the towpath along the canal. Then I heard a voice that I recognised as Dad's. It called my name.'

It still incensed me that he continually referred to our father in such a manner. But I let it go for now.

'Okay…then what?'

'I turned around and he was seated on a bench. I had blatantly walked past him not knowing he was there. He then stood up but didn't move towards me. He remained at the bench. My friends were going to stay by my side, but I told them I'd catch them up.'

'Okay. So far so good. Then what?'

'He looked *old* close up. Much older than before. He asked me if I was okay and if school was going well for me.'

I fumed inside.

As if our father ever gave a single solitary *shit* about his son's welfare.

Since fucking *when* did he start getting interested?

But again, I strived to conceal my vexation.

I needed to hear everything that had been said between them.

I nodded an invitation for my brother to continue with his recap.

'I responded politely. I told him that things were going well for me. He just stood there staring at me. I wasn't going to divulge any more information than I had to.'

'Good thinking, bro. But I bet he wasn't content to play that game, was he?'

'He apologised for taking so long to come and see me. Something about struggling to find us. And something about getting straight his end. Then he asked about you.'

I knew it.

Our father was up to no good as predicted.

I was the opponent that he truly sought.

Martin was no threat to him. Martin wasn't the foe.

It was *me* that had proven my diligence and resistance to his hold.

It was *my* fearlessness that our father could not tolerate.

He wanted his youngest offspring.

I was sure of it.

'What did he say about me, Martin?'

'He asked about your university course in Swansea. He also wanted to know why you had come back to Nottingham.'

I became immensely concerned.

Our father already knew far too much detail about us.

'And so…what did you say to him as a reply, Martin?'

'Not much. That you were just visiting and were going back soon enough. Then he claimed he wanted to talk to you before you went back to Wales.'

The hairs on my neck stood on end.

'Did he say what he wanted to speak to me about?'

'No. And I didn't ask him, either. Because I said I needed to catch up with my schoolfriends. And so, I left him standing by the bench.'

'Are you sure? Are you certain he didn't follow you here?'

'I kept checking, Jamie. He didn't follow me.'

I continued to suppress my brimming fury.

Martin had given a resolute and concise account. In fact, I thought he had dealt with the situation admirably under the circumstances. He had shown infinitely more composure than I could have mustered.

'Okay, big bro. Well done. You did really good. Drink your tea. I won't ask you anymore questions I promise.'

As Martin switched on the TV and scrolled aimlessly through the channels, it dawned on me that I would have to tell Bobby when she came in from work later.

Even though the encounter had elapsed without incident, I could only draw the frustrating conclusion that hoping to keep our father at arm's length was unlikely to be a workable option.

He wasn't intent on going away in a hurry.

Perhaps it was only a matter of time before he would decide to confront me, too.

9
A PREMONITION?

I began to blink furiously as my breathing became laboured.

The punishment was vivid and unrelenting.

Not a vision like before though.

More a series of despicable, horrendous sensations.

Voices in my head.

Which became screams of desperation.

And then the silence resumed.

I passed through a zone where light became dark.

As if at the flick of a switch.

What was focussed evolved into blurred.

Pressure pummelled my body.

My skull. My chest. My eyes.

I could see nothing through hindered vision.

I could not resist the force that set upon me.

The oppression was tangible and mighty.

Suffocating. Smothering. Denying.

A gradual, perpetual loss of function encroached.

My lungs were aflame.

Every movement to defend myself rendered me evermore defenceless.

The battle was excruciating.

Yet gratifyingly short-lived.

Only seconds of sufferance.

And then.

Lifelessness reigned in place of life.

And I sensed the distant observation made by a stranger.

My very final thought before awakening, was of my family.

*****

The panic roused me from the distorted void of my imagination.

I had felt sure I was dying.

Yet I was obviously saved.

I sat up on the camp bed in the spare room, listening to the reliable creaking of the springs and hinges beneath me.

Beyond the curtains, night's presence was still in evidence.

Thankfully I did not disturb Martin or Bobby.

I wiped my sodden forehead with the palm of my hand.

Although I was alone in that room, another being had made itself known to me.

I had felt this spiritual acknowledgement before.

Doubt and then certainty.

Confusion and then clarity.

Storm and then calm.

The calling was beginning again...

10
THE TORCH STILL BURNING

Dear reader, I think I've been in your acquaintance long enough now to reveal my innermost secrets to you in confidence.

So, here's one.

But it will hardly class as scoop of the century and will likely be of little surprise to you, either.

You see the thing is, I never really came to terms with separation from Alex.

Did I hear a veiled sigh of disinterest from the back row?

Well, tough. I've got to get this off my chest.

We might only have been an official item for just under twelve months, but I now look back on that period as perhaps being the most accomplished of my life.

We connected so swiftly. Nothing needed prompting. There was no inhibition considering we were still so young. Our first real conversation still lingers in my memory. Word for word. On that bench. Near that sports court. You know the story as well as I do.

After all my covert and distant admiration of her that preceded our romantic union, it was ironic that she revealed that I was the only target on her radar too, and that had been the case for many weeks.

It was a credit to her wonderful sensitivities that she thought I was unattainable. That she thought she would always be at the back of the queue when it came to alerting my attentions.

We embarked on a relationship that was in essence, effortless.

We read one another's thoughts constantly.

We finished each other's sentences on a regular basis.

Cynics claim telepathy is a myth.

Well, the cynics know *nothing*.

It was understandable that her heart would break when I chose a different path to the one that we had planned to walk together.

I take full responsibility for that detestable deed.

And I still regret it every hour of every day.

I was the one that ruined our bond.

And in the most callous, obstinate manner.

I'm leaving. Come with me if you want. But I'm going, anyway.

What kind of a choice is that to present to the woman that loves you?

What kind of message was I intending to send to her?

That vision of her standing helpless as I walked away, amid the grip of her unrelenting distress, never fails to haunt my conscience.

And so, here I am, some two years or so later, faced with the eternal question: *what if*?

What if she had decided to come with me to Blackpool?

What if I had decided to turn my back on my brother in *his* hour of need in favour of choosing loyalty to Alex?

But neither scenario would have concluded happily.

That is the guarantee and the sole crumb of comfort from my perspective.

Eventually, resentment and remorse would have edged their way into the scenario.

In retrospect, Alex made the right choice for her.

And I made the right choice for me.

There's not much more to say, is there?

But being partially appeased by hindsight still doesn't prevent me from thinking about her.

Every waking second.

Whether she affords *me* another thought is another matter entirely.

And would be anyone's guess.

I would say that it is a sure-fire bet that her parents won't have the time of day for me. I can't say I would blame them, either.

They were protecting their young, as all competent guardians should endeavour to do. In fact, their response is exemplary when compared to the lack of responsibility my brother and I were shown by our own mother and father.

Of course, I fully accept that I caused Sarah and Kevin Lawley some pain and anguish by emotionally hurting their only child.

But it wasn't done willingly on my part.

Far from it.

Lord knows I had experienced enough heartache in my own existence to know that causing it for others was not a preferential option.

But regardless of the whys and wherefores and the who's and the when's, the image of Alex standing inconsolable that fateful Saturday morning at Nottingham station immediately left a mental scar that has never healed.

Perversely, estrangement from her has only given potency to my longing to make amends.

Surely, I'm dreaming?

Surely, it's got to be too late for any sorrows?

Well, *hasn't* it?

Taking the sensible standpoint, we have had our time and its gone.

Done and dusted.

The casual observer might feel entitled to say I blew it big style.

And occasionally, in those quiet reflective moments that I get a hell of a lot of, I might feel inclined to agree.

Until I saw her in town with her mystery friend the other day.

And all the misguided angst and contrition came flooding back.

The emotions didn't just stir.

They were whipped up into a storm of hurricane proportion.

A cyclone centred in my very core.

And I realised that I still hoped.

Like I said to you many moons ago when you first joined me on this epic journey, dear reader, hope is *everything*.

Hope is the only thing that drives us.

Maybe one day she might decide she feels the same.

She still looks and moves the same.

That aura of maturity.

The classic poise and practised physicality.

Minimal need for employing make-up.

She had a natural ability to make the best of herself.

She could look incredible in her *sleep* for crying out loud.

Radiance personified.

The flick of the hair.

The slight swagger in her determined gait.

She knew what qualities she possessed and always exhibited them with grace and efficiency.

Her B game was infinitely more impressive than most females' A game.

Jesus Christ. It's only just occurred to me.

I still loved her.

I wanted her back.

And it's all your fault for indulging me, dear reader.

Despite the passage of time, the desire remained unsated.

What am I saying? The prospect of reunification is ludicrous.

The likelihood of it reaching fruition so remote.

The consequences of ever broaching the subject with her don't bear thinking about.

Similarly, the opportunity to do so shouldn't even register in my psyche as even vaguely possible.

Should it?

Well, as you are now fully aware, dear reader, once Jamie Andrews sets his sights on tackling the supposedly improbable, he has a knack of accomplishing success.

The proverbial dog with a bone.

I had to try, didn't I?

Even with failure already casting its shadow across my landscape.

But it would not daunt me.

I had to pursue this most worthy of causes.

Wish me luck…

11
INTO THE UNKNOWN

Ashby Drive was definitively middle class. Compared to most other residential pods in the locale, anyway. It always conjured the sensation to me that I was a mere commoner when immersed within its fold.

Hardly surprising considering I was a born and bred council house boy.

The red brick semis of Lodge Close were in stark contrast to the modern detached housing plots of Ashby Drive. Inconceivably large footprints. Eloquently landscaped lawns back and front. Brand new Fords and Rovers typically perching in pairs on spacious block-paved plinths.

Well, these residents could afford a car each so why not display the fact?

A road predominantly inhabited by professional people who wilfully exhibited the evidence of their six-figure salaries.

Teachers; doctors; dentists; directors; accountants.

You get the drift, I'm sure.

And yet despite my humble background, I never truly felt out of place here though, as I always had sound motive for entering such hallowed territory.

Especially number eighteen.

The house owned by Sarah and Kevin Lawley.

And it was this house that I was currently headed for.

And at this juncture, dear reader, you have my permission to presume yours truly as having gone completely insane.

I honed my stride to resemble something akin to confident. Although my state of mind differed dramatically as I observed the frontage of the destination looming ever closer.

It was I believe nearly two p.m. on an indifferent Wednesday afternoon in late October. The very last person expected to be calling at number eighteen would be me.

But there was a strand of method in the madness.

There was a fair chance that if Sarah Lawley was at home, then she would be alone. I secretly wished this to be the case as I walked up to the front gate and checked the windows for tentative signs of life.

No car on the driveway was a clear indicator that Kevin would be at work. I kept my fingers crossed that Alex was also out doing her thing. Whatever that was these days.

The plan was in place. It was my aim to speak to Sarah only.

I could just about handle that much adventure at this early stage of the proceedings as I navigated through the gate and along the front path.

My right index finger hovered over the ornate brass doorbell before I suddenly changed my mind and loudly knocked three times.

I had an inbuilt distrust of doorbells. I've no idea why.

My heart raced in anticipation as I impatiently awaited movement on the other side of the frosted glass porthole.

The non-responsive seconds endured, and I mentally began to talk myself into a demoralising retreat when the distorted silhouette suddenly appeared in the hallway.

It grew in depth and stature as it centred on its journey to the front door to reveal the mysterious visitor.

When her expression materialised in the gap between composite and frame, the most apt description I could apply to it would be sincere astonishment.

I didn't think I had altered all that much in my absence, apart from the longer hair. But Sarah Lawley initially appeared to be struggling to fit my visage to a time and place.

Thankfully, I was much mistaken. And she readily recalled my name which was a promising start.

'Goodness me! *Jamie*? Jamie, it *is* you! Hello. How are things?'

Her expression was now evolving from cool disbelief to a warm acknowledgement. I was almost lost for words myself such was the surreal and unannounced nature of the encounter.

'Hi, Sarah. Great to see you again. I hope I've not called at an inconvenient time.'

More awkward seconds elapsed as we tentatively eyed one another.

If she felt any reservations about my uninvited visit then she was in good company because I was also nervous as a kitten, although I tried to conceal it with my Hollywood smile.

The magic touch evidently hadn't deserted me.

She pulled the door fully open.

'Not at all, Jamie. Please…do come in.'

I entered the familiar domain. The fragrance and décor hadn't altered one iota from what I recalled. The radio still echoed through from the kitchen just as it always did.

I kicked off my trainers, courteously awaiting her next instruction.

As I did so I glanced at Sarah and felt such a weight of sorrow.

It struck me that I hadn't exchanged a word with her since before jumping on the train to Blackpool over two years ago.

It had been an uneasy farewell to say the very least.

The best I could hope for was that she wasn't sitting in judgement on me after all this time. The fact that she took my coat and hung it on the stand showed positivity.

'You look well, Jamie. Please go through and sit down. Can I get you anything to drink at all?'

Okay. Ice broken.

No grudges on display, even though they might surface later.

'Please, Sarah. Coffee. Thank you.'

'Is it still milk and one sugar?' she smiled.

I nodded appreciatively. She remembered. That alone was gratifying. Perhaps I wasn't deemed the enemy of the state after all.

We sat together on the settee with our mugs, just as we did when I was lodging with them. And just as it did then, it felt right again.

Safe. Secure. Protective.

But of course, it was only fair that I started the ball rolling as to my motive for even being there after such a long time away.

'I felt I ought to come and make the peace, Sarah. I think you're due that much at least.'

Her face screwed into a pattern of confused lines.

'Peace? Why *peace*? When was war declared, then?' she chuckled.

The brief amusement did not mask the fact that the incentive for my unsolicited arrival was worthy and just.

'I just think that I owe you and Kevin. I don't know what you must have thought of me at the time, but the way I left Nottingham you would have been justified in slamming the door in my face just now.'

Sarah appeared somewhat puzzled by my attempts at self-persecution.

'What on earth would make you think that would ever happen?'

I observed the design on my mug.

A fluffy ginger cat gazed back at me.

It was a comforting image under the tense circumstances.

'Well, you know, because of the way I just upped and bailed out? The state Alex must have been in afterwards. Things were a right mess. You and Kevin were brilliant to me. I wasn't too brilliant to you both in return. I apologise for that.'

Sarah unexpectedly placed a hand on my shoulder and engaged my attention fully.

'Jamie…Alex explained everything to us. Your brother was the priority. Not us. When you went, I don't think you really had much of a choice, did you?'

The first person to verbally sympathise with my position.

She understood. I had no choice to make.

So very true.

'Even so, Sarah. The way it happened should have been more considerate. This is the first opportunity I've had to come and see you since the dust settled.'

'Kevin would appreciate your visit, Jamie. Believe me when I say this…we don't hold anything against you. We didn't then and we never will. In fact, if I remember, he even came up with the idea of taking you to Blackpool himself. It sounded a very complex and dangerous situation for a young lad like you to be involved with.'

I never really considered such a viewpoint before.

I was only sixteen. Willingly walking through Hell's gates.

Complex doesn't even scratch the surface.

'Yes…it *was* pretty unpleasant. I didn't realise *how* nasty things were until I got there, though. Alex was right to stay here in Nottingham.'

Sarah sipped her drink, and I sensed genuine interest from her now that the conversation had opened.

'How is your brother? Alex said he was back living here with you now?'

'He's good. He's enrolled at St George's as a mature student. He got engaged to his girlfriend a while back. He's turned things round superbly. She's been with him through thick and thin. They live just across town on Glenfield Avenue.'

'I'm really pleased for you all. And how about you, Jamie? How's *your* life taking shape?'

I wanted to laugh in abject sarcasm.

Would I really be honest and disclose recent events?

What a roll call. Where on the list would I begin?

That our demented and deluded father is back to haunt us?

That my nightmares have started again?

That I'm still in love with her daughter?

You'll be relieved to hear that I spared Sarah the depressing details.

'I got in at Swansea University after my A levels. Journalism. In my second year now. It's going well. I've just popped back to see Martin for a few days. So, I thought I'd make the most of it and fit you in too.'

'That's lovely, Jamie. So pleased you are all prospering. Alex is at Nottingham University. Economics. She loves it. I hardly ever see her nowadays. Even though she's still based here she's got a very active social life. There always seems to be another gig or party to go to. But I suppose you know all about that don't you? In fact, it's a shame she's missed you today.'

Not for me it wasn't.

I was privately relieved Alex was nowhere near us.

I was trying to tread around the subject very cautiously.

If Sarah suspected my true motives the atmosphere might not be so cordial. But how could I avoid the subject?

'In a way its perhaps best she's not here.'

Sarah's eyes widened in surprise.

'Why do you say that, Jamie? You're still friends. Aren't you?'

I took a deep breath. The discussion was sailing perilously close to my heart now. I didn't want to give too much away.

'I'm not entirely sure. It's been a while since we were in contact. I've got a new number now, too. I was hoping you might pass it on to her?'

Once again Alex's mother appeared bemused.

'Well…why don't I give you *hers*? Then you can ring her yourself.'

Wow, this mission was going *too* well.

Something was bound to trip me up at any moment, wasn't it?

'No honestly. I'd much prefer to leave the decision with her. If you get my thinking? If I make the initial contact, she might feel pressured. I don't want that.'

'Why would she feel pressured?'

Shit! Think on your feet, Jamie.

And make it quick.

'I just mean…she might be annoyed at knowing I've been here and took her number. She'll know we've been talking about her. If she doesn't want to communicate with me then I will soon find out, won't I.'

Sarah grinned broadly.

I think I got away with it.

'Well, that is extremely considerate of you, Jamie. Okay…I'll get you a pen and paper if that makes you happier.'

She watched intently as I scribbled down my mobile number on the yellow pad of post-it notes. My hand trembled as I wielded the pen. All I could think about was Alex's potential response.

Another coffee and another half hour of idle chatter feathered me back into Sarah Lawley's affections quite adeptly.

I had achieved far more than anticipated by the visit.

And like all wily gamblers, I seized the chance to get out while the going was good.

'Thank you for the drinks. It was great to come round again, Sarah.'

She followed me into the hall and retrieved my coat from the stand behind the front door.

'You're more than welcome, Jamie. And I'll make sure Alex gets that number into her phone. When are you going back to Swansea? You must come around for dinner before you go.'

My first and only thought regarding that generous proposal was to avoid it like the plague.

As terribly ungrateful as that might sound, dear reader.

Although I did conjure up a very diplomatic reply.

'Let's just wait and see if *Alex* wants me back around the dining table first, shall we?'

'She'll be fine! Trust me! She still talks about you, you know. There's no problem this end, Jamie. Honestly.'

'Okay. Well…I'll leave the ball in her court anyway. Let's see what happens, eh?'

Sarah leaned toward me and placed a kiss on my cheek.

'Bless you, Jamie. Take care now. Hope to see you soon.'

I departed number eighteen, Ashby Drive feeling rather satisfied.

The welcome from Sarah was earnest enough.

All things considered the plan had worked perfectly.

Considering my limited expectations of only an hour earlier, I could pat myself on the back for effort and determination.

Perhaps I wasn't such a bad boy, after all.

12
ANOTHER LEVEL

For all we had endured and survived together, I had never seen such trepidation in Martin before.

The moment in question ingrained itself on my mind indelibly.

The third occasion he returned from school with news of another development was the day which effectively began to change everything.

It had been over a week since the previous encounter between Martin and our father on the canal. I had informed Bobby that evening and despite her predictably emotive response, calm had gradually resumed within the walls of Glenfield Avenue.

But, of course, the fragile serenity wasn't going to last.

Because our father wasn't going to give in, was he? Now that I knew that I was a factor in his return to the area, it was obvious that there was a scheme afoot. And the first symptom of this wasn't long in being revealed to us.

My brother veritably knocked the front door off its hinges in his frantic desperation to get inside the house to me.

Jim Andrews had upped the ante.

As I fully expected he would do.

And now Martin was finally convinced of our father's deceitful intent, as his panting expression conveyed authentic concern over what had just transpired outside the school gates.

With her traditional sense of immaculate timing, Bobby was once again working a late shift. Just as well.

The sight of her fiancé in the throes of a sweat-laden panic would not have been good for her already pensive mindset regarding matters.

I had almost conceded defeat in attempting to convince my brother of the bleakest potential scenario.

He had thus far resisted my will to induct him in the ways that evil minds think and act. But it was this latest encounter which at long last had persuaded him to finally see the true light.

The perspiration glistened on Martin's nose and forehead as he displayed little hesitation in relaying the most recent chapter.

Once again, our father had veritably ambushed him.

Once again, he had embroiled his eldest son in conversation.

Yet whereas their prior meeting had been low-key and civil in nature, this follow-up had proved far different in design.

Again, it occurred on the canal.

Again, our father was perched in shadow on the bench.

But this time he did not hesitate to show his natural character.

Martin's personal space was immediately hijacked.

By my brother's account, the exchange was far more sinister.

'He demanded to know why I was shunning him, Jamie. I didn't know how to answer. But I've not been shunning him. He was aggressive. He used profanity. He had consumed alcohol. I could smell it on his breath he was so close to me.'

My initial response was one of intense frustration.

Frustration at the fact that despite my insistence, Martin had previously played down the stirring latent peril posed by our father's presence.

I also felt disgruntlement at the fact that I had been proved right.

That I *wasn't* making mountains from molehills.

Jim Andrews hadn't changed one bit.

I also felt relieved.

Relieved that Martin had looked into the eye of the beast for himself and now acknowledged the menace we could all be subjected to.

The supposedly buried memories of his life in Blackpool evidently were not buried deeply enough. The tension, the apprehension and the fear had re-surfaced swiftly. Martin was evidently very scared.

And rightly so. The monster had pursued us to our own doorstep.

It was on the verge of penetrating our vulnerable haven.

Safety was no longer a concept we could delude ourselves of.

I calmed Martin down and sat with him on the settee. Under a thin veil of composure, he expanded on what had happened.

I offered Rufus as a comforting presence, whom Martin promptly cuddled tightly under his chin.

'My friends got scared when Dad grabbed my coat. I think he's broken the zipper when he pulled me toward him. I really thought he was going to hit me, Jamie.'

This was not a progression I had expected.

I didn't anticipate such an overt physical confrontation.

Despite my undiluted negativity towards the man, I honestly did not believe that he would sink to the level of full-on assault.

Not in such an openly public domain, anyway.

Of course, he was capable. He was feral and a violent thug. But even I expected him to keep this side of himself in check for a while longer.

Laying a hand on his own offspring in front of witnesses showed me that he was not overly concerned with how he might be perceived by us. It was in principle a reckless thing to do.

But the leopard and the spots were still firmly in place.

Jim Andrews' penchant for talking with his fists had now aborted any hesitancy he may have harboured about coming to find us.

'Did he try and hit you, Martin?'

'No. Once he'd pulled me close enough, he let go. Then he began to whisper to me and kept looking around as if he didn't want anyone else to hear him.'

The method of approach was certainly in keeping with his mentality. But the motive remained far less transparent.

I moved position and squatted in front of my brother. He had been visibly shaken by the incident. Which was not like him at all.

I placed my hands on his knees and requested he lift his head to engage with me fully.

Surprisingly, I did not have to venture with further questions.

Even though Martin's voice was quaking.

'Jamie…he told me why he was back here. Why he had followed us down to Nottingham.'

My heart leapt with apprehension.

Surely our father must have been seeking retribution.

He wouldn't have taken that beating lying down.

But it was over two years ago now.

Yet the desire for recompense would still be in his blood.

Revenge was the only way he knew. It was highly unlikely that his willingness to make contact was borne out of savoury intentions.

But Martin sucker-punched me.

He now shifted position and relocated to the kitchen, still clutching Rufus under his arm.

I didn't see this one coming.

Despite my ingrained misgivings and inherent mistrust of the scenario, Jim Andrews' had perhaps been altered by circumstance after all.

Martin set Rufus down and placed both palms on the kitchen table.

He stared into the wooden surface as he deliberated.

'Martin…speak to me. What happened this time?'

'He said that he has some trouble with people up in the North. They are currently hunting him. He said bad people are after his blood. And he said that he knew we were able to help. Before it's too late.'

It wasn't a case of struggling to believe my ears. It was an outright, all-out refusal of acceptance. I tried to talk in response, but my throat was constricted by sheer incredulity.

'*Us*? He wants *help*? From *us*? After all these years of treating his sons like something on the sole of his shoe? Our father needs his *kids*?'

Martin rubbed his eyes which were on the verge of shedding tears but still he refused to look at me directly.

'He didn't fully explain. He was stressed out and drunk. He was slurring badly. But once I was close enough, he settled down a little bit. And he gave me this.'

Martin reached into his rear jeans pocket. He extracted a small piece of card and handed it to me. On the card was scrawled a mobile phone number, which was barely legible. I gazed back at my brother and widened my eyes to encourage him to reveal more, if indeed there was anymore.

Martin was being incredibly courageous under the circumstances and was willing to continue his disclosure.

'He wants *you* to contact him, Jamie. Not *me*. *You*. He knows that you will likely refuse, though. So, he said he's going to sit tight and wait for you to call. He promised he wouldn't follow you about.'

The anxiety I had harnessed was now releasing.

'We can't trust a word he says, Martin.'

'He just wanted to get this number to you. He said he didn't feel brave enough to confront you himself, but if you make the first move everything would be fine. He asks you to find room in your heart to ring him. If you can.'

I felt like laughing out loud.

Martin's last line was the killer blow.

Room in my heart?

A classic final touch from a practised fraudster.

The arrogance in the man obviously knew no bounds.

I shouldn't have been surprised, but even *I* didn't think our father had this much front.

Martin continued to glare at the tabletop. Our father's persistence had really rattled my brother's cage this time. That much was obvious.

My fury was brimming rapidly.

'You did really, really, good, Martin. You were very brave. And I'm sorry that he spooked you like this. He's got no right pouncing on you. But I won't be ringing him. I can guarantee on Rufus' life that I will not talk to our father ever again. And now you know I mean it, now I've said that. I wouldn't rely on him to tell me the correct time of day. The very thought of volunteering to be in his company again turns my stomach. I hope his enemies catch up with him soon. *Fuck him*.'

Martin became upset.

It could have been because of my language.

It could have been because of my standpoint.

It could have been because I mentioned Rufus.

And watching my brother cry instantly filled me with guilt.

I regretted my outburst immediately.

Perhaps I should have applied a little thought before opening my mouth.

And then the horrific possibility struck me.

That perhaps Martin might *want* to help our father.

Surely, such a prospect had to be beyond the realm of even *my* furtive and cynical imagination.

But one thing was already obvious.

Jim Andrews had exerted minimal direct interference so far, yet he had efficiently driven upset into the once peaceful domain of number thirty-two, Glenfield Avenue.

And it occurred to me that maybe this was his prime intention.

After all, the term is 'divide and conquer', isn't it?

Martin finally looked at me through a saltwater streaked grimace.

'Are you angry with me, Jamie?'

I slowly shook my head and embraced my brother.

I pulled him close and whispered words of reassurance.

As the inner hatred I had stored up for our father now pulsed through me.

'I could never be angry with you, big bro. Never think that I would be. But he is way out of order. I did warn you, didn't I.'

Martin nuzzled into my shoulder as his emotional release abated somewhat.

'But he'll get nasty with me, Jamie. If he thinks I haven't done what he wants. He might beat me again. And burn me again. Just like before. I don't want that to happen, Jamie. I'm really frightened, now.'

And there it was in full, unexpurgated glory.

This is exactly what the bastard wanted to achieve.

His own offspring, cowering in dread. *Because of him.*

Well, it wasn't going to fucking happen.

Not again.

I attempted to allay Martin's upset.

'I understand your worries, bro. But you are a grown up, now. You are stronger than him. Bigger than him. If he ever comes at you again, you've got my permission to lay him out. And I promise you won't get into trouble for it. Okay?'

Martin pulled back and wiped away evidence of his distress with his sleeve.

He wasn't emotionally capable of blanking this problem after all.

'I can't do that, Jamie. That's not me, is it? I only hit him before because he was hurting you so bad. I can't stand up to him without you beside me. I just can't do it.'

Was I really having this conversation with my own flesh and blood?

We'd come so far, together. Yet there was a tangible threat that the horrendous past we had strived to cast off was about to reclaim us.

'Listen, Martin. Our father just wants to use us. Then once he's got what he came for he will be gone again. Because that's what he does best. He chews people up and spits them out. Well, he's not getting near us. You agree?'

Martin focussed on my unflinching stare.

He might have been nearly a decade older, but he carried the demeanour of a petrified child at that moment.

'The thing is, Jamie...Dad *himself* looked worried. He might well need us. He seemed genuine to me. He had a very desperate manner about him.'

I wasn't prepared for this.

Realisation dawned.

Martin had been duped.

Our father's carefully honed performance had convinced his eldest son. My instincts were correct after all.

Martin actually wanted to fucking help the poisonous scumbag that had brought us into the world.

This train of thought needed nipping in the bud.

Against my better judgement I began to raise my voice one more.

I felt matters getting out of hand already.

'Bullshit, Martin! Get that crap out of your head NOW! HE'S *PLAYING* YOU! HE'S TRYING TO GET AT *ME* THROUGH *YOU*! BUT IT WON'T SUCCEED! YOU HEARING ME LOUD AND CLEAR? HE WILL *NOT* SUCCEED!'

Martin's prior convictions had seemingly been a source of solace.

His upset had ceased. He spoke with a worrying lucidity.

He had already drawn his own conclusions without my input.

My brother was totally adamant in his judgement.

'The way I see things, we have no choice, Jamie. You either communicate with him or he continues to pester us. I don't think he's in the mood to give up. And I also think that Bobby should give her opinion on things when she's home from work.'

I took several deep breaths to suppress my flailing despair.

Because Martin's words rang infallibly true.

Despite my ingrained abhorrence of everything the man stood for, Jim Andrews had played a trump card that we couldn't ignore.

This issue was not going to conveniently disappear of its own accord. How could it?

And Martin was quite right in pointing out that we had a third member of our little union that would be entitled to contribute her feelings to the arena.

We would consult with Bobby on her return home.

Though I could not even begin to predict how she might respond.

But the harsh truth now faced us squarely and we could not evade its far-reaching effects.

Our father was back in our lives, whether we liked it or not.

And he needed dealing with.

One way or another.

13
COME THE HOUR

The time was approaching ten p.m. The three of us had debated the situation for the last two hours. Bobby seemed remarkably collected in her thoughts which surprised me to say the least.

Perhaps she was automatically inclined to side with her husband to be. Who was I to try and interfere with or question such loyalty?

However apparently misguided I believed that loyalty to be in this instance.

But the verdict had been reached and I had been effectively outvoted.

I was tasked with carrying their wishes through.

The pair of them wanted me to convene with our father.

But I wasn't daunted by the prospect.

Despairing, yes. Daunted, no.

It was a challenge I was prepared to meet head-on.

The biggest obstacle for me was that I had to try and put my intensive resentment to one side, if that might be at all possible.

Despite her willingness to press forward with the ludicrous plan, I still saw the fear in Bobby's eyes that was perhaps in residence from the past.

She undoubtedly had her own vivid memories, and she was certainly not the forgiving type in most situations. But the next indeterminable chapter was not about forgiveness.

Nothing like.

It was simply a case of unlocking the mystery and solving it as soon as possible. And to think that I barely knew the man I was about to call.

Jim Andrews.

The ominous figure that had been a persistent black cloud over our lives since day one of our existence.

And here I was about to play the diplomat with that very same force.

My opinions were certainly not conducive to encouraging a family reunion, I can tell you that much. But my opinions were deemed irrelevant for the time being.

Dealing with the problem at hand was the foremost priority.

And it looked like I was faced with the shitty end of the stick on that score.

Martin had evolved in his thinking during the evening.

And he said he didn't mind that I had used Rufus as guarantor against what was about to happen.

He had transformed from weeping worrier into resuming the façade of indifference regarding what was about to ensue. The unenviable liaison with our father was an event that needed to transpire in his eyes.

Any of my doubts and pre-judgements were of little sway.

We were about to fly blind into the unknown and I was the unwilling pilot. And Martin was glad someone had relieved him of the burden he earlier perceived as solely his own.

Whilst I was nurturing a determination to resolve this unwanted episode in our lives, Martin was now apathetic to the cause.

And Bobby conveyed herself as edging on trepidation.

But it was not through fear of the unknown.

Something else was concerning her.

Something elusive that I couldn't quite decipher, but there were bigger fish to fry for the moment.

I figured that ringing from my personal phone would do little in the way of harm. I needed to contact our father and he would duly receive my number because of this.

If successful communication was to be a two-way street, then using a public telephone box would go some way to hindering the process. I took the piece of card and warily inserted the number into my contacts list.

The proceedings had suddenly adopted an air of cold formality.

Our father didn't deserve such standing in the family.

He didn't deserve my endeavour in obliging his request.

Bobby and my brother sat on the sofa holding hands as they observed me in silence.

I thought I could hear their hearts thumping in tandem, but both seemed fully addressed with the ins and outs of the current dilemma.

If I didn't make this phone call, the uncertainty of our father's intentions would only persevere in plaguing us. Despite my pig-headedness, I did understand that ignoring his wishes might well exacerbate the problem.

Jeopardy encroached, whichever way we turned.

This was not a choice.

This was simply following a pre-laid design.

As per usual.

The decision was not mine. Higher powers had already taken hold.

I positioned myself in front of the fireplace and offered my brother and Bobby a final, affirming glance.

They simply nodded back without word.

There was, after all, nothing left to say on the matter.

And let's face it. The real talking was now solely down to me.

With a tentative grasp of the handset, I selected the number and pressed call.

I waited for the connection to complete, and the ring tone eventually commenced.

The seconds passed as the three of us eyed one another with speculative expectation.

And then finally, the silence was broken by the gruff tone of a male voice, which resonated harshly from the other end of the spectrum.

It hissed a commencement to the dialogue.

'Hello? Who's this?'

I gulped in trepidation.

The moment to engage with the enemy was nigh.

And I was in no mood to embroider the exchange with pleasantries.

'It's Jamie. I got your message. I hear you want to talk.'

I didn't want to convey any hint of familiarity.

This wasn't a family issue. This wasn't even business.

This was duty.

The recipient's tone lifted slightly in mood.

'Yes, Jamie! Thank you so much for ringing me. Good old Martin. Knew I could rely on him.'

I shook my head at the inane facade of gratitude that echoed down the phone. In truth I wanted to vomit.

'I'm not making a social call. Martin's done his job for you. What the hell do you think you're doing? What the fuck do you want with us?'

Jim Andrews did not respond immediately.

Silence followed my question.

The onus was all on our father to convince me I was not going completely out of my mind in being willing to participate in this farce.

'I need to arrange a meet-up with you, son.'

The mere sound of his voice was intensely aggravating.

I heard the obscene reference to our blood connection but deliberately didn't bite back.

'Is that how you usually arrange meetings, is it? By grabbing a hold of people in public? By embarrassing your boy and scaring his school mates? By sending him home in tears?'

'I'm sorry I upset your brother. Tell him I'm sorry.'

'I've got a better idea…why don't *you* tell him you're sorry? I'll tell you why…because you're not sorry at all, are you? You couldn't give a toss about him. So, answer the question. What do you want with my family?'

Having purposely excluded him with my phrasing, I expected to detect a slight trace of anger in his reply. But our father remained strangely passive. My attempt to push his buttons was currently failing.

I wasn't convinced if he even picked up on my intended antagonism.

His next move was perhaps less of a surprise.

'Not on the phone. It's got to be face to face. Somewhere quiet. Where no one likely knows us.'

I glanced at Bobby. I whispered to her what had been proposed.

She shook her head as a silent gesture to dissuade me from agreeing to our father's request. I couldn't work her approach out. She had concurred with the decision to ring yet now expressed her reservations.

Yet physical proximity to our father was perhaps the better idea. I wasn't prepared to stand for much more of his sneaking around. And in truth I wasn't overly keen to expand the discussion over the phone, either.

Against my better notion, I opted to go with his suggestion.

'Have you got a location in mind around here? I'm not travelling miles and miles though. I've done enough of that lately.'

Our father was fully prepared with his plan.

'The Lunch Stop. Station Road. You know it?'

I just wanted to get this conversation done and dusted. It was late and I was tired.

'What day and what time?'

As I waited for details my legs tremored and the palms of my hands became clammy.

This was actually going to happen.

My heart screamed in rebellion at what my head was deciding.

Yet despite my personal protestations, I had very quickly evolved from refusal to compliance.

The expressions on the faces of Martin and Bobby suggested I might have taken total leave of my senses. I wished they would make their minds up which side of the line they wanted to stand.

Finally, as though delaying through checking his diary, our father set the schedule.

'How about this coming Wednesday? Ten a.m. Breakfast is on me. But just you though, Jamie. No one else must be there. You and only you. Deal?'

The fucking cheek of it.

Our father having the brass neck to dictate terms to me.

I offered a specification of my own in return.

I wilfully tried to offset his perceived glee.

'Listen up. I don't know what game you are playing and I'm doing this for the sake of my family. But if I get the slightest sniff that you are about to go pear-shaped on me then I'll have you. The police will be onto you like flies round shit.'

It was something of an empty threat, considering our father hadn't even committed a crime yet.

But he attempted to placate me, nevertheless.

'I promise. I'll be alone too. No funny business. You have my word.'

Now you know I would typically have reacted to that line with laughter, dear reader.

'Your *word*? Since when did that count for anything? I'll be there Wednesday morning. Whatever it is you have to say you make it quick and then you get out of our lives. You hear me loud and clear?'

Quiet prevailed once more.

Our father considered my albeit loose and whimsical stipulations.

He could take it or leave it.

'Look, Jamie. It's not really going to be as simple as that. But I will do my best. And thank you for ringing. I won't make you regret it. See you Wednesday.'

With that prophetic parting shot, our father ended the call.

My brother and Bobby studied me wide-eyed.

The imminent summit with Jim Andrews was an uncertain manoeuvre to say the very least. I crouched down before them and tried to offer some reassurance.

'Right then. It's done. No going back, now. And I'm doing this for us. Not him. He's nothing to this family, anymore. Hopefully this will be the first *and* last time I set eyes on him around here. Try not to worry, you two. Easier said than done, I know.'

Neither of them volunteered a positive or indeed a supportive reply.

And in truth, I couldn't fault them.

Because in truth, I was more fearful than they were.

14
OUT OF THE BLUE

Unsurprisingly, my recent sleep pattern had been sufficiently interrupted to the point where I couldn't recall what healthy slumber felt like anymore.

I'd been back in Nottingham less than a month and I was dog tired if I was honest. The need to maintain a mental balance was draining. I may have played down my nerves at the prospect of confronting our father, but Martin could see through the mist of my bravado.

And he knew I was having nightmares again.

I had to summon immense private courage to carry out that telephone conversation. For everyone's sake I needed to appear strong.

I dare not declare my underlying trepidation to Bobby or my brother. They hadn't dragged me back from Swansea to cower in submission.

To those two I was the brave heart of our trinity. I was expected to stand up and be counted and protect at all costs. And of course, that was my earnest intention. I suppose I should have seen their faith in me as flattery.

Our history together had proven me to be a capable and willing soldier in battle. I would never turn away from a challenge.

I would confront; not shirk. Sounds convincing, doesn't it?

Back to my nocturnal struggles and the portable camp bed was hardly a recipe for quality kip, was it? Although being in the spare room was infinitely preferable to being on the couch.

I had no clue what time it was when my bladder called on me for evacuation. As I shuffled past the closed lounge door toward the bathroom, I could hear Bobby talking to Martin, albeit in muffled tones.

I stopped my route march and listened, trying to decipher what was being said.

As it was, I couldn't understand the words being exchanged so blatantly I entered the lounge to disturb the flow of their discussion.

Bobby looked me up and down as I posed in my t-shirt, pyjama bottoms and evidently showing signs of long-term fatigue.

'You look worn out, Jamie boy. Sorry if we woke you.'

She smiled as she said it, whilst I shifted toward the dining table and rubbed my eyes. Martin was ready and waiting to pose a question as I slouched on a chair next to them.

'I'm sorry, Jamie. It's all my fault, isn't it. Have you had a bad dream again? It's all my fault.'

I yawned and stared at him before offering him fraternal assurance.

'Listen to me big brother. You will never have to apologise for anything. *Ever*. There are people in this world who *should* be weighed down by their own guilt…but you are not one of them. Okay? Besides…I haven't had a nightmare. I woke up to wee.'

Martin focussed on the tabletop as he spoke. A habit he had recently adopted. As though he might not want to observe the reactions to whatever he said.

'Yes…but if I wasn't here, you wouldn't have had to be phoning Dad. And I know you didn't want to, but you did it for us. It must have been so hard. I applaud your courage.'

That word.

I sighed heavily and shook my head.

'Martin…I've asked you this before and I'll ask you again. Please don't refer to our father like that. He's not *Dad*. He will never be *Dad*. Not in any way, shape, or form. *Ever*.'

'But he *is* our dad. Always has been. Always will be.'

Was I talking to a brick wall or what?

'NO! You must understand that he is our father. No more than that. He is our father genetically through biological default. But that's as far as the relationship goes for me and you. Understand the subtle difference, will you? Because believe me, there surely is one.'

He looked at me as if I had just issued my last statement in a foreign language.

His mouth began to form the beginning of an argument.

I raised my index finger as though to interrupt before he got chance.

'No, Martin. It's vitally important that you recognise the distinction here. Dads are *somebodies*. Our father is a *nobody!* Christ, Bobby! Help me out here, will you? Do I need ink and paper to explain?'

It was noticeable to me that Bobby did not intervene on the frustrating exchange. But I would not bow down. If I was back at Glenfield Avenue at their request, then I was more than prepared as the houseowner to pull rank when required to do so.

It was an unspoken rule that I was in charge. And dismissive as it sounds, dear reader, they should have been thankful that I was back to try and prevent them from ending up in any indeterminable mess that might come their way.

I dreaded to think where events may have taken them had I left them to their own devices concerning recent events.

Finally, after he studied the evident frustration etched across my face, Martin nodded his head.

'Okay. It's father. *Not* Dad. Rufus agrees with you, too.'

'Well thank the lord for Rufus. At least *somebody* has some grasp of the situation around here. Now then. Did someone say cup of tea?'

I moved from the table to make a brew.

My phone was fully charged on the kitchen worktop, and I disconnected it from the cable.

It was nearly two a.m.

There was a message notification on the screen.

It looked like Alex's old number.

I instantly smiled inside.

The fatigue and frustration experienced just minutes earlier was instantly eclipsed by a surge of excitement.

Premature reaction? Maybe.

I know. You're right as usual, dear reader.

Put the brakes on Jamie.

I hadn't even read the message yet.

Neither Bobby nor Martin wanted a drink, so I made mine.

I wished them both a goodnight and took both mug and phone back to my room to respond to the message in private.

The anticipation was slightly overpowering as I closed my bedroom door and perched on the edge of the camp bed. I felt slightly on a high. My physical chemistry had instigated a reaction that made me feel like I was flying.

And I still hadn't opened the message yet.

When I did, the wording clipped my wings to say the least.

I think the phrase that best applies would be *understated.*

Hi Jay. Mum said you had visited. She enjoyed it. Hope all is okay with u.

And that, dear reader, was *it*!

Not even a kiss to finish off with.

Distant. Disconnected. Unembroidered.

And somewhat deflating to say the very least.

Then I noticed what time it was sent.

Only nineteen minutes ago.

I slurped my tea and burned my tongue as the adrenaline flushed through me.

She might still be awake.

I needed to strike while the iron was hot.

And strike it with vigour.

But my reply required some consideration.

This process endured for about five seconds before I began typing.

Hi Ally. Gr8 2 hear from U. Wonder if U R free 4 a catch up anytime soon? Burger/drink/walk? Up 2 U what we do and when. Jay xx

Well like it or lump it she was getting two kisses from me.

One through habit; one for old time's sake.

I leaned back into my pillow.

And pressed 'send'.

And I sipped my tea some more.

And I scrutinised the phone screen, as the right palm it sat in slowly became clammy.

Even now I couldn't tell you what kind of a reaction I was hoping for or expecting, but the prevailing thought at that moment was just to see her as soon as possible.

My heart missed a beat.

I cannot put into words the elating sensation in my guts.

One minute passed.

Then two. Then three.

What was she writing in reply? A bloody essay?

And then, after four and a half minutes of personal, euphoric agony, her response came through.

You can only imagine my inner ecstasy.

Free tmrw. Where and when is your choice. Let me know asap and I'll meet you there. xx

The kisses, dear reader. You see them?

My charm still worked.

I thanked the lord above.

She actually *wanted* to meet in the flesh.

With this first massive hurdle overcome, my hands began to shake as I replied.

East Park. One pm. By the rain shelter. On the bench. Jay xx

More minutes passed by as if to exert further torture.

I studied the bedroom ceiling to try and reduce the demented focus on my phone screen.

But being woefully weak willed when it came to Alexandra Lawley, I could not take my eyes off it.

It practically demanded my full attention.

Then, after another period of oh so sweet agony, the confirmation arrived.

OK Jay. C U there xx

My mind drowned in contemplation of this wondrous reunion.

I was literally bursting at the seams to lay eyes on Alex again.

I placed my half full tea mug under the camp bed.

From Hell to Heaven in the space of half an hour.

I felt both thrilled and humbled at the premise of what the next day might bring. As I laid down my head, I could only wish that the pending twenty-four hours might just live up to the hype.

15
A RE-TEAMING

I picked the bench near the rain shelter for a specific reason. Alex would never have sat *inside* the shelter. Not even if it was raining. Or even if I offered her a million pounds.

Above all overriding temptation to be under cover, the outlying prospect of her seeing a spider would immediately negate any lure I might summon. But it was a nice, secluded spot. Away from the trail of cyclists and joggers. And it offered one of the most eye catching views of the parkland's greenery, although of course in mid-autumn it was more like *brownery*.

Such was my potentially misguided anticipation, I got there early. Half an hour early, to be exact. There was a chill in the air as you might expect, but I'd borrowed Martin's thicker coat for the job. He wouldn't mind.

I was nervous as a kitten. I had been pacing about at Glenfield Avenue like a tiger in a cage. Bobby was at work, so I was alone with far too much time to think. And boy was there a lot to think about.

Plus arriving early meant that if Alex herself arrived slightly ahead of schedule, she would instantly see me, and no doubt be relieved I hadn't stood her up.

Not that I would ever do that.

Knowing her she would have happily sat and waited. But you never know, do you. And I wasn't taking the risk. I wanted us to reacquaint on the right footing. Simple as that, really.

And I can possibly have a guess at what you are now thinking, dear reader.

Why would I feel at such pains to make a good impression on somebody that had been my girlfriend for a year? Surely it stands to reason that she would already know me inside out, right?

Well, I was still inwardly fraught about our history together and its emotional conclusion.

I had been - and still was - racked with guilt.

And regret.

So, sue me.

But two factors had lifted my spirits significantly.

Firstly. Sarah Lawley inviting me into her home again and taking my phone number.

And then secondly, but closing in rapidly on firstly, Alex even agreeing to be in the same postcode as me again.

Despite the fact I was physically there, the situation hadn't really sunk in if truth be told.

East Park seemed as good a location as any in the area. It was convenient, attractive on the eye even in the wetter, colder months, and offered peaceful privacy that a coffee shop or café would not.

I just hoped the vibe was still amiable between us. She would be entitled to arrive carrying certain unresolved issues from the past. She might be angry. Just as she might be pleased to see me. Even though last time we spoke she was on the arm of another man.

Maybe I was overthinking the whole situation as usual.

But I was balancing on the whims of human nature, wasn't I?

Whenever you care deeply about someone and then go and fuck it all up for whatever reason, you are always going to carry that burning inner desire to make amends.

Aren't you? Well, *aren't* you?

Help me out here!?

Of course, I didn't expect her to coming bounding around the corner with arms open wide, but if I detected there was ever the slightest chance of rekindling what we had, then I figured that life was far too short to ignorc that inkling.

I had to give it my best shot.

I *had* to try.

I lazed back into the bench and let my eyes wander across the relaxing scene before me. Every passing second drew my attention to a singular source of movement in the distance.

A dog after a ball. Every pushchair. Every infant. Every parent. The council rangers changing bin liners and marking football pitches.

Doddering pensioners just about being kept upright by walking sticks and Zimmer frames.

I scrutinized the soothing vista and the figures that flitted through its midst.

And I also kept one cautious yet excitable eye on the pathway to my right. Just to see if you-know-who was about to make her grand entrance at any given moment.

I imagined what she might be wearing. Crazy, yes?

Autumn had taken a firm hold so she would no doubt be sensibly attired in accordance with the temperature. I was glad to have Martin's fleece-lined parka on. My own lighter jacket would have already left me shivering.

Alex would certainly exhibit her inherent sense of style, whatever she was dressed in. Would she make a special effort for me, I wondered?

The imminent meet-up could never be classified as a date in the traditional sense, but if she was feeling even half as much in her heart for me as I was for her, then she might well be tempted to pull out all the stops.

But if truth be known, if she walked into view donned in donkey jacket and steel-toed boots, I would not think any less of her. The premise of simply being in the company of the woman was more than enough inspiration for me.

I sported blue denims and some older brown leather shoes from Glenfield Avenue. A dab of the aftershave that she used to love.

Just to offer the remotest nod back to times past.

Good move?

And maybe give a little impetus for times yet to come?

I wondered if she would recognise my cologne. She ought to, she bought it for me. I've not had call to wear it since we separated.

The wait on that bench felt eternal.

The yearning for our reunion made me ache with hope.

And then the inevitable doubts took to the stage.

Why was I still feeling like this about her?

What right did I have to invade her life all over again?

She seemed to be coping admirably without me.

Yet she was evidently open to a reconciliation of sorts.

Perhaps I slightly resented the fact my absence had not hindered her progress in life. That's just my ego talking though.

If truth be known, it was *me* that was struggling without *her*.

But there was no way I could openly admit that to her in so many words.

That would just sound pathetic, selfish, and perhaps even cruel.

Wouldn't it?

Who the hell did I think I was, anyway?

Her heartthrob for life?

This little escapade might well end up kicking me in the balls.

She just might hate my guts.

But I strived to console myself, and as I did so the black cloud of uncertainty was banished with a cleansing dose of realism.

She contacted *me*.

She agreed to see *me*.

Stop worrying will you, Jamie Andrews.

There are times when I wish I could switch my brain off.

Too many thoughts make it hum with overload.

I checked my phone.

No message or missed call.

I'd been sat for over half an hour, so technically, she was only four minutes late.

A brief glimpse of wanton sunshine bathed my face temporarily and I shut my eyes to its low, watery glare. Again, I envisioned her in my imagination. A futile mission really as I had only seen her the other day - albeit covertly.

I knew what she currently looked like. So why did I insist on teasing myself about her potential appearance?

The interesting thing was that she didn't know what *I* looked like. It had been well over twelve months since we last conflicted our interests outside the school gates.

I didn't think I had altered to any noticeable degree. My hair was longer, and I now kept whiskers more often than I shaved.

But aside this, I was the same old devilishly good-looking brute who could melt women's hearts just by entering the room.

Who's laughing at the back?

My eyes had been closed for just under a minute.

I opened them and again squinted into the tenacious rays of sunlight that battled with the ever-shifting slate clouds.

Instinctively, I looked to my right.

And there she was.

My Alex. In the flesh.

Striding confidently, indeed almost serenely, from the car park and onto the footpath. Then temporarily out of frame around the back of the rain shelter. Then back into view. Flanking the gardens and flower borders.

Her hair danced with every step she took, and that swagger was a permanent attraction. Jeans and jacket. Scarf looped loosely. Smart, seasonal, casual. Black suede boots with low heels.

Perfection to the beholder.

And then her eyes met mine and her determined features visibly illuminated.

She waved and smiled broadly.

So far - so damned good.

Judging by all current evidence on display, it was safe to evaluate that Alex seemed pleased to see me. When she got to less than ten metres away, I rose to my feet and involuntarily opened my arms.

Her expression beamed ever brighter as my legs now began to buckle ever so slightly. She gladly reciprocated my gesture with enthusiasm, and we embraced tightly in earnest, mutual contentment.

Our reunion rubber-stamped. No sense of hostility detected.

And I suddenly felt at peace with myself for the first time in so many months of self-persecution. I could breathe easy once again.

And her fragrance was divine.

As was the sound of her voice as she drew slightly back and engaged those crystalline pale blue eyes with my own.

I could do no more than watch her lips move as she commenced the conversation I had craved for so long.

'Well, you certainly surprised Mum by appearing as if by magic on the doorstep! She thought you were going to ask if you could move back in!'

United, we stood, and united, we chuckled.

'Maybe I was…'

The peck she placed on my right cheek was a wholly unexpected bonus to proceedings.

She was wearing the same perfume she always wore for me. The one I bought her for our one and only Christmas together.

Great minds thinking alike. Got to smell right, yes?

All the indications thus far were stupendously joyous.

We sat down together on the bench and after I'd settled into position, she slid sideways, so our hips now touched.

Dear reader…you must be reading the same signals that I was?

Or was I already running before I could walk?

And would you really blame me?

'So, what brings the stranger back to town, then? Local trouble?'

Did I really want to talk about myself? No. But her opening gambit forced me down that road to a degree.

'Don't ask. Same shit. Different year. How's Notts Uni, anyway?'

Her hypnotic gaze focused intently into mine once again, then her attention flitted to analyse my features, as though she were going through a swift process of refamiliarization.

I was secretly hoping that she would be impressed with what she saw. But I wasn't about to jump the gun on that score.

It was enough for me that she was there at all.

'Uni is good. I'm really enjoying it. Still at home with the oldies, but can't have it all my own way, can I? By the way, Dad was sorry he missed you the other day. He sends his best wishes.'

My response was cautious.

'Really? That surprises me!'

Alex leaned back and furrowed her brow slightly.

'Why does it? We don't hold grudges in our family, Jamie. He knows you made me happy. Mostly, anyway…'

I caught her grinning after that comment and contentedly let it go.

Not an area I wanted to revisit again in *any* depth.

'That's all good then. Are you happy nowadays, though?' I prodded, somewhat clumsily.

She hesitated in her answer.

I sensed her focus fall to the distant treeline of the parkland.

I might have touched on a delicate subject too quickly.

'I'm not as happy as I was, I don't think. But on the happy scale of life, I'm keeping a good middle ground. If that answer makes any sense whatsoever?'

She chuckled at her own muddled wording.

I was in a similar boat.

'I get you. Exactly. I saw you in town last week. With a friend. Going for coffee. I didn't want to ruin your day by announcing my presence across the street. That's really what inspired me to visit your Mum and leave my number. So that you could call the shots…so to speak.'

Alex turned to face me once more.

I detected a hint of sorrow in her eyes.

'You're not the devil incarnate, Jay. You haven't done anything to feel bad about. It was just life. Simple as that. If the boot was on the other foot, I would probably have done the same. You had no choice. Don't dwell on it.'

I didn't want to blurt out my reply, but lost control.

A glorious dive. Headfirst into honesty.

‘There’d have been one difference though, Ally. I would have gone with you. And I’m always going to be sorry for leaving you. But there’s not a lot I can do to put it right now, is there?’

Alex shook her head in condolence.

‘There isn’t anything that *needs* putting right, Jay. It’s history. It happened. No one owes anyone. No one showed disloyalty. We are still friends, aren’t we? By the way…I’m intrigued…’

She smiled the smile to enrapture all men.

I was becoming fanatical about her all over again.

‘*Intrigued*? About what?’

‘…about why you left your number with Mum. I’m glad you did. I’m just curious as to why? Why *now*? After all this time apart?’

I took a deep breath which bought me some time to ensure I said the right thing. More or less.

I wasn’t going to hold back now she had made the invitation.

‘Two reasons. First…I miss you. And I know you will believe me when I say that. Because it’s true. And I could never be anything but truthful to you.’

Her dark eyelashes fluttered, as though I had just conveyed something she really wanted to hear.

Her focus never deviated from mine.

‘Okay. And what’s the second reason?’ she muttered, coyly.

Again, I wasn’t going to beat about the bush.

‘Alex…I need your help.’

Her instincts were so finely attuned concerning yours truly that she had instantly assimilated the potential source of my current dilemma.

‘But you got your brother sorted, didn’t you? Mum said he was living in the house Henry left to you.’

‘Yes, that’s correct. Henry left me everything in his will.’

‘I heard he’d passed away. I wish you’d have mentioned it to me at the time. He loved you, didn’t he, Jay?’

‘So, it seems. But it never entered my head to tell you Henry had passed. We weren’t an item anymore. I didn’t think it mattered. Martin is in the bungalow now. With his partner Bobby, who he was with in Blackpool when I found him. She has just been promoted to his fiancée.'

Alex's features displayed a genuine exhibition of pleasure.

It was a refreshing change to impart some good news.

'Wow! That is *fantastic*! And all down to little old you, eh? So, it *was* worth your while abandoning me the way you did?'

I knew she was joking because she rapidly altered her expression to look at me through narrow eyes and a subtle hint of a smirk.

Again, I didn't acknowledge the gentle heartfelt dig. Besides, she casually moved the conversation on with her next question.

'So, do I take it all is well with the both of them?'

'Yes. They are doing fine.'

'And so, what about you? How is Swansea treating you?'

'It's okay to be honest. I'd get more assignments written if I did less socialising, but I've got no will power. Too many distractions.'

Alex laughed but I felt it might be forced and maybe even veiled a pang of jealousy.

Her next words pretty much prove it to be the case.

'Well, you always *were* going to attract you fair share of feminine interest, weren't you? Big girls now, though! Grown up girls! No silly shy teenagers queuing up quietly like they did at St George's, eh? I bet you're fighting them off from all angles!'

I could tell the matter caused her a little discomfort for some reason.

Again, she had wittingly implored me to speak from the heart.

It was now or never that I laid my cards on the table.

The conversation was heading exactly where I had hoped it might.

'Ally…since you…there's been no one. Not even to look at. I'm not interested in anyone else, either.'

A solemn silence descended between us.

I suspected I'd caught her off guard with my frank declaration.

She might have been pondering her doubt on just how *genuine* my declaration was.

Or perhaps she was privately overjoyed.

As regards the two of us, she declined to dig any deeper for the time being.

'So, you've gone from Romeo of the century to monk of the month in the space of three years. Is this what you're telling me, Jamie Andrews?'

The mood was swiftly becoming upbeat once more.

'I wouldn't say *Romeo*.'

She giggled and pointed an index finger in my direction.

'*I* would. And I just *did*! You certainly made my ticker go boom-boom anyway.'

I grinned nervously. The discussion was literally fantastic so far.

Just to hear her say things like that was like being in that first phase of love all over again.

'Is that right? Well, I never knew that! I bet I don't make it go boom-boom now though, do I?'

She reined in her reply and studied the distant trees once again.

Evidently, she had more to say on the subject.

And like me, she wanted to ensure that if it was disclosed, then it had to be the perfect sentiment.

Her smile returned as did her full attention on my face.

Her eyes flickered again as she scrutinised me.

And heaven did indeed open its doors.

I already sensed that my strategy had worked.

'Oh my god yes you *do*, Jay. More intensely than before, as well. When I came around the corner just now and saw you on the bench, my heart was racing, and I got butterflies. You still have the power, believe me. I'm still under your spell.'

As her announcement registered, I felt myself blush.

But not with embarrassment. With the adrenalin of success.

These were surely the most precious thoughts any woman could *ever* willingly convey to a man.

I wasn't accustomed to hearing such a poetic and powerful notion.

Indeed, how many men have ever experienced such a privilege?

For a guy like me who had heaped guilt onto his own shoulders for so many, many months, I suddenly felt elated and freed.

Redeemed and reborn.

The sudden awkwardness that evolved between us seemed wholly inappropriate and ridiculous, as though our mutual enthusiasm to pull all the barriers down had suddenly caused another one to be raised.

I struggled to summon the next line.

As ever, Alex came to my rescue.

She laid a hand on mine.

'So anyway, Prince Charming, going back to the second thing you mentioned. what exactly is it that you need help with?'

The answer to this question was supposed to be the easier of the two quandaries I had brought with me. Now suddenly this response demanded real articulation.

'It's not something I wanted to drop on you today, Ally. Especially now we've told each other how we feel.'

'But you all look pretty much sorted to me. I can't for the life of me think why you need *me* to be involved in anything.'

This was the supremely troubling part of the reunion that I was very hesitant to broach. Did I really want to drag her back into my mess after all she went through to stay away from it in the first place?

How could it possibly be fair to her? To ask her to walk with me again and guide me through yet another desperately unhinged chapter in the blighted saga of the Andrews family.

But she was so good at reading me. Before I could begin to formulate an explanation, she had the intuition to steer the discussion on the right course.

'So, is it something to do with Martin?'

No going back now.

I recounted the relevant recent developments for her, albeit in the scantest detail possible. I didn't want to overbear her with the dramatics. I could spare her that much at least. In all, with her responsive queries, she was fully updated within five minutes.

I awaited her impartial conclusion with bated breath.

I couldn't put my finger on it precisely, but as I watched her turn over the scenario in her mind, her eventual tone and manner suggested to me that I had woefully underestimated the powerful dynamic of our relationship.

In no uncertain terms, Alex declared that whilst I had been steeped in remorse about departing for Blackpool, her choice to stay in Nottingham had rendered her vulnerable to the same unshakable waves of sorrow.

Mutually drowning in our own personal despair had reinforced to us why we had both made the same mistake in turning our backs on one another when in fact we needed to be together more than ever.

Perhaps I was interpreting things incorrectly.

Perhaps not.

But the most pivotal phase of the conversation was still to come.

And it was only when I declared the reason for needing her support and assistance, that our reinvigoration truly blossomed.

The revelation regarding my father's unannounced return to Nottingham did not phase her one iota.

On the contrary, it served to cement her mindset.

Her words were sublime as she reached over and took both my hands in hers.

I got lost in those clear crystal pools that bore deep into my soul as she spoke.

'You needed my help before, Jay. And to this day I cannot believe I said no. I won't make that mistake again. You've offered me the chance to make amends. And I am going to take it. If you are truly worried about meeting your father alone, then I will be with you every step of the way.'

Both shocked and ecstatic beyond all measurable aspiration, I had to be entirely certain of what I had just heard her say.

That she was absolute in her convictions.

That she truly wanted to walk this path with me.

'Do you really mean that, Ally?' I stuttered.

‘Yes, I really mean it, Jay. I won’t ever let you down again. Let me make it up to you. It’s the very least I can do.’

Still holding hands, we pressed our backs into the bench and stared ahead into nothingness.

Both wondering what the blank canvas of our future might deliver.

Euphoria flooded my mind and body.

My best friend.

My confidante.

My soulmate.

My Ally

Alexandra Lawley was back by my side.

Literally and figuratively.

And I felt invincible all over again.

II
RESISTANCE

16
AWAITING THE ENEMY

The Wednesday in question came upon me far too soon.

D-day.

The first day of November.

Martin and Bobby obliged their usual weekday routine, knowing that my imminent personal agenda was far from typical.

They left the house with both hope and fear in their hearts I am sure, but it was an unspoken rule that the less said was infinitely the better until the meeting had transpired.

I mentioned nothing to them regarding Alex's involvement.

She was a secret saviour that I wanted to keep under wraps from everyone. My feelings for her had been rejuvenated on a galactic level.

The most precious gift had been offered to me a second time and I would endeavour to shield her as much as humanly possible from any collateral.

It was a grey and misty morning in town. Standard for the time of year. As you will recall with wary delight, dear reader, my father was responsible for choosing the venue.

I'm not sure where else I might have suggested that we convened but judging from the dilapidated exterior frontage of the café, it was in dire need of some TLC.

Much like me, I suppose. Cue the violins…

Suffice to say, my mind was already weighed down by intense anticipation and I was offered little further inspiration before even setting foot in the place.

I glanced at Alex who was loitering with intent further along Station Road. As per the plan, we had arrived separately. It was almost akin to a military operation.

Her visage presented nothing less than fortitude before she retreated to settle in her starting position.

It still hadn't sunk in that we were in this together again.

But that knowledge had thrown welcome shafts of golden light onto a previously extremely bleak premise.

The hinges of the door groaned in protest as I entered the place. And just like in every classic Western ever made, the occupants already inside the cafe simultaneously leered at me, with unjust suspicion being their first and only response to my appearance.

I would say I felt like Clint Eastwood for a few uncertain seconds. All focus falling onto the newcomer, as I observed my unwelcoming surroundings in the process of selecting somewhere to sit.

Eventually the half dozen onlookers sated their fleeting curiosity and reverted their attentions to their own business. I was grateful that their interest in me dissipated as soon as it had arisen.

Alex had appointed herself in a pedestrian cut-through which was across the street from the cafe, between an end terrace house and the railway line.

Out of sight yet keeping keen vigil on my location, we had decreed that no more than five minutes should elapse between my entry to the premises and hers.

Whilst a supposedly covert mission, it was hardly the stuff of James Bond, but potent enough in principle. At very least the plan should have ensured my father didn't harbour any suspicion he was under the scrutiny of a furtive third party.

It was a fair theory. After all, he had no idea who Alex was.

Her cover was impossible to blow. Bulletproof, for want of a far better phrase…

The idea being that I would freely engage in my father's request to meet and talk, and Alex would nonchalantly ear wig, whilst memorising any salient points in conversation that might arise.

Yes, dear reader. It was a crazily simplistic concept and almost childlike in its sincerity. I am in full agreement with you.

As I swiftly selected a table and removed my coat, certifiable insanity was probably exceedingly close behind me, but had not quite sunk its claws in fully just yet.

Although, as I settled into my chair by the front window, I did give myself cause to wonder how the hell I had ended up in this situation and why the hell I had agreed to partake in it.

Having adamantly proclaimed only days earlier that I wished to have no contact with our father whatsoever, I now found myself awaiting a rendezvous with the beast itself.

I could only conclude that it must have been my old friend destiny that looked to have intervened once again.

But I had only barely convinced myself of the belief that all this was the handiwork of higher powers and that I had no influence over my own decisions anymore.

If I could have stepped out of fate's grasp just for a moment, I would have adjudged the scenario to be ludicrous and would be siding fiercely with all inclination to abandon the mission altogether.

I peered through the greasy windowpane to the lifeless view beyond. It was just after nine-thirty. I had absolutely no idea if he would be early or if he was a habitual latecomer. But I was keen to obtain a clear view of *him* well before he set eyes on *me*.

Call it tactics if you will. But I sensed the need to attain the upper hand throughout the next hour or so. Being caught unawares on any level was not a tolerable situation.

And so there I sat, in expectation of the ogre's arrival, my mind now attuning itself to an oncoming yet indeterminable visitation.

By way of donning some psychological armoury, I began to mentally recount the many insidious aspects of the person I was about to encounter all over again.

This mentally distorted and inherently disingenuous man, who could never claim to be an authentic father figure. That role had been swamped long ago by his penchant for another way of life.

A distasteful, bitter, and poisonous character.

All the traits of a spineless brute, no less.

Every conceivable suspicion I had of him and more besides, had been embossed in Blackpool.

And I was sure his mantra was unlikely to have altered.

Violence and aggression were his prime artillery.

He held no understanding of his true place in things.

There was no compassion for his fellow man.

His instinct was purely to serve the self.

Callous and bullying in achieving his aims.

Negligent of his past and disarmingly reckless concerning his future.

At least he had been, up until now.

He must have finally reached breaking point if he needed *my* help.

Me? Of *all* people?

His youngest, unwanted offspring.

The *accident*.

And recently, his newly acquired nemesis.

The one soul he knew he could not conquer, was the one soul he now reached out to.

The boy that brought down an empire.

And the fallen emperor now pleaded for communication!

Jim Andrews wanting to talk in a civil manner at a table was the stuff of fairy tales. Especially when considering that his long-standing method of getting a message across was through employment of his fists or a handily placed weapon.

I should by this point have adopted an air of superiority.

By default, I had supposedly already attained the moral high ground.

But of course, this presumption would lead me to abject vulnerability once more. I had to keep up my guard and assume nothing about the impending summit.

I reserved nothing but doubt about his motives.

Our father was totally adept at enveloping himself in suspicion.

He had infiltrated my genetic instinct and poisoned it with mistrust.

Metaphorically, I needed my finger on the trigger.

This man had created a kinship with conflict.

For conflict was all he knew.

First and second nature.

But I was the hunter not so long ago. And he was the quarry.

And this dynamic was still the status quo of things.

I would not run and hide. I felt empowered to face this.

I sought closure - not confrontation.

Some might say I had effectively cast my father a favour by reclaiming Martin from his clutches.

Relieving him of the burden.

The inconvenience.

The embarrassment.

But I take a different view.

I take the view that bullies need a victim, or they cannot sustain their existence.

And the real tragedy running through all this, is that our father would never learn what a beautiful creature Martin truly is.

A young man blessed with physicality and intelligence that eclipses that of most mortals.

And it took his younger brother to retrieve him.

To give him back the existence he should have been privy to all his life, instead of leaving him lying at the bottom of the barrel, consistently watching the scum rising to the top.

Yet even now the question prevails.

Did I glean any pleasure from my apparent victory?

Did triumph in the face of adversity truly garner any personal satisfaction?

Not for me. No.

Possibly for Martin, it did.

But I did not go to war to win it.

It was simply my calling to go and fight the best fight I could.

The potential outcome was irrelevant.

The contest was the thing.

The utter, overriding priority.

Summoning the courage. Being brave enough to enter the ring.

There was no trophy to commemorate the outcome.

Only emotional cost could be attached to the apparently positive end game.

One scenario took precedence.

The disposal of another was unavoidable.

But life goes round in circles.

Circumstance usually dictates that certain situations will be re-visited over time.

And there I was.

And it suddenly hit me. Just to authenticate my theory.

I had been there before.

In that place. That very café.

Visited only once previously in my life.

As a younger version of myself. Sitting opposite Mum.

She had just passed the interview at Mason's Packaging.

And she treated me to a glass of orange and a sausage roll.

And I looked through the very same window that day as the rain lashed relentlessly against the windowpane.

Yes. The circle of life indeed.

But about to enter the fray was not Mum.

Instead, it was the source of her worst nightmares.

And I secretly prayed that she would forgive me for being there again for such a purpose.

I needed instant consolation.

So, I directed my train of thought elsewhere. To Alex. As I sat in that café at that table, I truly believed that I had got Alex back for good.

Yet today she was performing as a different kind of partner.

My undercover wingman.

Now crossing the road and approaching the front door.

Awaiting the moment to emerge and bear witness to what was to transpire.

The time was nine-forty-five.

I was nervous now.

Alex entered the fray and once again, all eyes inside rested on her sudden presence. Some inevitably beheld her with a lecherous slant. Understandably, most gazed in admiration of the striking female that had set foot in the establishment.

We did not acknowledge each other as she moved between tables and selected one adjacent to my own.

She removed her phone from her coat pocket in readiness to silently spectate and speculate.

And another sudden wave of trepidation washed over me.

What *madness* was this?

To win back the affections of the love of my life, only to throw her straight into the bear pit. To ask her to sit with me and wait for the demon to enter the fold? To render her helpless in the lair, vulnerable to the waking dragon?

Wasn't this exactly the situation I specifically wanted her to avoid becoming embroiled in all those months ago?

But perversely, we both now seemed addicted to the intrigue of it all. Especially regarding my father's physical demeanour.

How would he first manifest?

Not traditionally, surely?

Not with the shouting, the swearing, the anger, and the venom?

That couldn't work.

Not now.

Not here.

Besides, he knew I was not intimidated by his characteristic bluster.

But by his underlying intentions, yes.

This aspect worried me.

His motive intrinsically gave me cause to be anxious.

The time ticked on toward ten a.m.

Alex had ordered a coffee and pretended to scrutinise the tiny phone screen in her hands.

I allowed my attention to divert through the window once again.

The inaction was now beginning to agitate me.

But I had to employ patience.

The current mystery needed to be unearthed.

And then, as if out of thin air, he appeared in the street.

At the café door.

Through the sweating glass, he located my position and stared indeterminably. No visible reaction detectable in his features.

And in he strode.

Bold as brass.

Ugly. Repellent. Repulsive. As always.

He closed the whining door behind him and wilfully glared back at the pairs of eyes that duly inspected him.

But he was not deterred.

Because nothing troubled Jim Andrews.

Donned in black from shorn head to steel toed boots, he re-engaged with my table and slowly made his way toward me.

I sensed Alex looking my way, but obviously any instance of interaction with her was strictly forbidden.

He stopped his advance and looked down on me.

Not a hint of recognition in his eyes.

He glanced briefly toward the food counter and then focussed back to me.

I'm not too proud to confess that his low gravelly tone created shivers through my body.

'Alright? Fry-up?' he hissed.

The matter-of-fact manner of address could have been directed at anyone in the room.

The only indication that he was enquiring of me was the fact that his eyes bore into me with thinly veiled contempt.

In tribute to his blatantly dismissive attitude, I simply nodded without word.

I watched him turn and stride to the counter to order the food.

This was my one and only opportunity to briefly observe Alex.

She pouted and blew me a kiss across the void, before holding up both hands with fingers crossed.

As she readied herself to digest the meeting, I readied for battle.

No longer in the trench.

I was now over the top.

No retreat.

No surrender.

17
INTERROGATION

Jim Andrews ordered two full English breakfasts, both with extra black pudding and mushrooms. Four rounds of bread and butter. And two mugs of tea.

The lady at the till took the payment and presented the minimal change. She pledged to bring the teas to the table he pointed toward.

He returned to the seat opposite me, displaying the same sneer on his face that had been embedded in my conscience ever since leaving Blackpool. Yet as I studied his mask of disdain, I suspected it had become even more ravaged than I recalled from our previous contest.

The lines around his eyes and across his forehead were now deeper and darker. The nose appeared more prominent and the thin mouth more pursed. He had lost some weight too, which perhaps accounted for the apparent differences.

He checked around the room and then glanced through the window to the scene outside, as if to trying to confirm we were alone.

Or indeed, that his possible accomplices were in attendance.

Being as he didn't utter a syllable, the onus was on me to guess his next move.

As the quiet seconds evolved past the full minute, I had observed enough to see that he was certainly on edge. Pensive and uptight. A world away from the domineering tyrant that I had confronted first time round.

His whiskers looked over three or four days old and his balding scalp was also perhaps in need of a shave.

Strangely enough, by this point my nerves had all but vanished.

I think it was the waiting around that promoted my wariness. Now he was finally positioned across from me I sensed only a mild need to be cautious. He certainly didn't convey the air of menace that had been historically attributed to him.

To her credit, Alex was performing admirably.

This was her first ever sighting of my father.

She could have been forgiven for fleeing the scene in terror, but she held her nerve and her inconspicuous presence.

More seconds of inconclusive silence endured as he continued to exhibit the perceived act of cunning. This version of Jim Andrews was quite a contrast to the one I anticipated encountering.

The merciless fiend was perhaps attempting to convey himself to be as timid as a kitten.

And yet I still wouldn't trust him as far as I could throw him.

The parade of supposed meekness continued as he finally faced me and placed his elbows on the table and clasped his fingers together.

The distaste in his voice immediately belied the rehearsed facade of wholly unconvincing vulnerability.

Indeed, as if to unwittingly betray the act, he almost smirked as he grumbled under his breath.

'I bet you thought you'd seen me off for good?'

Delivering such an opening salvo seemed to generate a pang of pleasure within him. Yellowed teeth flashed a brief appearance, reinforcing my notion that this so-called father of mine was in principle a disgusting article both in mind and body.

But as I stated, I felt no personal concern for my own safety now. He had undertaken the onus to come and seek *us* out this time. He was the germ who had crawled out from under his rock to bathe in the light of day once again.

The fears of Martin and Bobby were hopefully in vain, but I understood they were well justified. For my part, I simply wished to establish the business at hand and get it signed and sealed.

Then this despicable specimen could disappear back from whence he came.

After a little deliberation, I decided to respond to him.

'In all honesty…I hadn't given it much thought. We've all picked up the threads back here. You aren't part of anyone's life anymore. So, I'll cut to the chase to save on oxygen. What are you up to?'

The uneasy hiatus was restored.

Alex listened intently from only six feet away, being astute enough not to attract attention to herself. She was very good at covert operations. She never moved a muscle out of place.

And I knew she wouldn't miss a thing that was said.

The waitress approached and placed two mugs of tea on the table.

She reached over to Alex's table for the sugar pot.

'Can I pinch this for these two, love?'

Alex looked up and was evidently a little startled by the intrusion on her concentration. I was grateful she recovered swiftly.

'Yes. I've done with it. Thank you.' she muttered nervously, before resuming tactical duty.

My father continued to stare at me as he chewed softly on his lower lip. He seemed almost offended by my bluntness. We might well have been parent and child in the eyes of nature, but I wasn't prepared to offer a shred of acknowledgement on that front.

If he anticipated any form of respect from his youngest offspring, I'm afraid that ship sailed many years ago.

The damage had been done. We were complete unknowns to one another so far as I was concerned. In fact, I would have probably afforded more time and attention to a *genuine* transient.

But his potential to become aggressive was always just simmering under the surface. I wasn't going to willingly antagonise the man, but if he took umbrage with my attitude then so be it.

'Jamie…you disappoint me…you really do…'

For a man who had made a life's work of causing hurt to those closest to him, his attempt to feign sensitivity cut no ice with me.

I felt no mercy and fired another arrow directly at the target.

'Listen…you aren't here for Martin and you're certainly not here for me. You hate the sight of us. And so, as I sit here, I can't think of any possible reason why you would travel down and consult with us. It's not to relive the good times, is it? There haven't been any!'

Jim Andrews shook his head and glanced across to Alex.

My heart stopped.

Surely, he hadn't caught on to our secret affiliation. How *could* he have? If he knew she was my accomplice, she would be immersed in this horrible scenario up to her neck and I obviously didn't want that.

Thankfully, my concerns were proved unfounded as he turned his attention back to me.

'I don't *hate* you, son. Why would you accuse me of that? Who put that silly idea into your head?'

That word made me squirm with revulsion.

Son.

When did he assume the privilege to refer to me as that?

He was actively mocking me to my face. Pure and simple.

I didn't show my contempt, however. I merely observed the contents of my mug and stirred.

And replied with honesty.

'*You* gave me the idea that we were hated. Who *else* would? And you are very convincing, too. But we are beating about the bush. So, I'll ask you again. What are you doing back in Nottingham? Why are you harassing Martin outside school? How would you even know he was back at school? How could you know where we were in the first place?'

His eyes burned into mine as he chuckled quietly.

He raised his mug to his lips and sampled some drink before checking furtively around the room once again.

'When you move in the circles that I do, information comes your way very easily. You find things out quickly through the network. I never left the planet, you know. I've been tracking you all for months.'

My jaw clenched with twinges of angst.

I shouldn't have been surprised, yet the revelation was still somewhat infuriating and unexpected.

'So why wait so long before showing yourself?'

Our private arena was disturbed momentarily as the waitress returned with the two fried breakfasts and the four rounds of bread and butter.

She placed the food before us.

I thanked the young girl, and she offered a grateful smile in response.

I was starving and more than ready to eat. Even if it was compliments of my father. It occurred to me that this was possibly the first thing he had bought me in his life.

Certainly, for the previous decade.

I could almost read his mind as he watched me pick up my cutlery.

Bacon and eggs. That's your lot, Jamie. Make it last you.

Pathetic bastard.

Jim Andrews doused his meal in salt before unwrapping his knife and fork from the napkin.

'I've not come here to cause problems for you, son. I'm proud of you all. You've made a better life for yourselves than the life I could have offered you. Martin is a revelation, isn't he? He deserves his second chance.'

I refrained from choosing my first morsel from the plate.

I spat a hateful response to the arrogant excuse for a human being sitting adjacent.

It was a struggle to keep my volume in check.

'*Second chance*? Since when did Martin get offered his *first* chance, then? Remind me. Because I don't recall it coming to light? And I would remember something like that, wouldn't I? After all, *my* first chance at life was also a bit like blink and you miss it, too. Wasn't it?'

My father studied the portion of sausage and tomato balancing on his fork. I kicked myself that my inner anger was surfacing, and this factor would be playing into his hands if I wasn't careful.

'Well…whatever you might think you know about me, son…I surely can't be as bad as you make out, can I?'

My grip tightened around my knife.

I was intrigued to know where this pointless conversation was leading us.

Possibly to a punch-up at that instance.

'Yeah? How do you figure that out?'

He continued to smile inanely as he swallowed some food and then slurped from his tea mug once more.

'Well, if I was the fiend that you think I am then you wouldn't be sitting in that seat, would you? You agreed to meet me here today. Speaks volumes that does. To me, anyway.'

I sat back in the chair and let my attention drift toward the miserably seasonal vista outside in the street.

My father had no bounds to his conceit and misguided view of life.

And as much as I knew so little about him, the same could said for his limited awareness of his two children.

He didn't know us, either. At all. He had precious little conception regarding what made me or Martin tick as individuals.

Again, I reinforced my mindset to him.

'I'm not meeting you here out of some long-held desire to socialise with you. I'm here as a measure of protection.' I sneered.

Baked beans steadied themselves on my father's fork as he considered my statement. He inserted the mouthful whilst pondering a suitable repost.

A crooked line of amusement broadened under his pock marked nose.

At that moment I was so thankful to have inherited Mum's looks.

Up close, Jim Andrews was one ugly son of a bitch.

On the inside and on the outside.

'*Protection*? Protection from who? Not me, surely? You don't have to feel threatened by me! None of you do. That's ridiculous.'

I assumed his plural reference included Bobby, although I was loathe to mention her at this point. Lord knows that she had seen more than enough of Jim Andrews' dark side over the years.

'Just leave my family out of this, will you? Just concentrate your energy on me and you. That's all that matters as far as you are concerned.'

I could see the ridicule welling behind his weather-beaten eyes.

He was enjoying testing my patience.

He carried not one shred of authenticity in his bones.

But at least he was consistent with this perennially offensive portrayal of himself.

'But I am pleased for you both. Honestly, I am. You've escaped the shit show and have turned it around. Cosy little house too, I see. Just a stone's throw from where you grew up. Very nice. Very…*domesticated*.'

The crafty bastard. He knew about the bungalow. He knew where it was. He must have followed Martin or me home at some point.

More details of our current homelife spilled forth.

'And darling Roberta is a manager now? Who would have thought it? Going up in the world! She's learned quick. She couldn't even take her bra off with one hand when I first met her.'

I ignored his casually disrespectful nod to Bobby.

Jesus Christ. How long had he been skulking around town watching us all?

Bobby would be beside herself with panic if she knew she had been under his scrutiny for such a protracted period.

'Okay. So, you know a few things. Like you said. But why didn't you want to speak to *them*? Why *me*? Why son number two?'

'Well, that's obvious. Isn't it? You haven't been around, have you. Swansea Uni, isn't it? I couldn't talk to the other two dopes. You're the only one that gets me. You're on my level. So, I had to be patient and wait for you to come back, didn't I.'

My father was underestimating me again.

'But I only came back because you started stalking Martin.'

'Well, yes. Granted. I eventually got bored of waiting. Things needed a little prod to get them moving. I could have spoiled the party last Christmas when you came back. But I took pity on the three of you. Even I'm not so hard natured as to fuck Christmas up for my kids.'

Now it was my turn to respond with a wry snigger.

'Unlike every *other* Christmas in our lifetimes, you mean. Why alter your habits now after all these years? And don't try to sell me the story that you suddenly give a shit about us.'

That line felt good to deliver.

My father promptly picked up a piece of bread and dipped it into his egg yolk.

I could feel my impatience beginning to simmer over.

'You really shouldn't think of me as being all bad, son. I've done many things that have caused me regret. But we can all improve with age, can't we?'

His false amiability was beginning to make my appetite vanish.

'You've never regretted *anything*. Besides getting married and having kids. Those are your only real mistakes. Your wife and your two sons. And God knows we have all been made to pay the price for your decisions.'

More tea was slurped before more bread was dipped in more yolk.

His face closed in across the table and the tone adopted a slant of malice.

'You sound like you're holding a grudge against me, Jamie my lad.'

My tolerance threshold was now fraying at the edges.

I was on the verge of getting up and walking out there and then.

But the under-pinning riddle had not yet been solved.

And so, I had to endure more of the tit for tat bullshit and undoubtedly forthcoming lies.

I fired back with the repeated ultimatum.

'If only you were that important. But you're not. You are to me and my brother exactly what we are to you. *Nothing*…and *nobody*. But I'm getting bored with you, now. So…for the final time of asking…what do you *really* want?'

18
A PLEA

We both temporarily resigned ourselves to eating breakfast as the futile exchanges were rapidly solving nothing.

Intrigue was my sole motive for staying put.

I had given up second guessing. It was leading to a headache.

The ironic aspect to it all was that even if he spilled the unequivocal truth about his reason for returning to Nottingham, I still wouldn't likely believe a single syllable of it.

We wolfed down our food amid an uneasy but possibly timely silence. Alex maintained her inconspicuous role and had now proceeded to tuck into a bacon bap.

Admittedly, I didn't think that my father's confession would take so long to materialise. Normally I would expect him to have the bullet loaded ready in the barrel and his finger firmly on the trigger.

This kind of delaying reticence was not his typical ploy when dealing with people who he needed to bend with him.

But I gradually began to sense that his character had perhaps softened over the passing months. He looked on his guard when he initially walked into the café. His eyes were everywhere.

Suddenly he put down his cutlery and cleared his throat.

The words he spoke I had already anticipated.

'The thing is this, Jamie…I need a hand-up, see?'

I stopped chewing and observed him studiously.

I was seeing okay. But was I hearing correctly?

This is the same line he sold to Martin, but I convinced myself that was just a ruse to get a figurative foot in the door.

My father, the most cavalier and callous individual I had ever known, wanted *my help*?

He now had my full attention.

'How do you mean? What kind of hand-up?'

He deliberated again and resumed with his knife and fork.

My shield was still up.

Whether or not honesty was about to emerge carried a fifty-fifty chance at very best for any bookmaker.

'Well, it's like this, son…'

That *word.*

He knows it grates my soul, yet he persists.

'…you recall the set-up I ran in Blackpool? The pub and so on?'

This was unpleasant ground to revisit, but I supposed it must have relevance somewhere along the line.

'How could I *not* remember? So? What about it?'

'You probably assumed I was the big man up there, yes?'

Deluded or what, dear reader?

'Get to the point, will you?'

'Well, everyone thought I owned the place as well as ran it. But I didn't. Me and the boys…we were only the front face of that little part of the operation.'

This was starting to sound like a repeat episode of The Bill or even Eastenders.

I was glazing over as tedium quickly descended.

'What *operation*? Drugs, you mean? Bobby mentioned it but I never took much interest. I had bigger things to concern myself with.'

For the umpteenth time my father looked over his shoulder and then again around at the other occupants of the cafe.

He lowered his voice to a whispered rasp.

'Well, it was true, yes. But it's not the sort of activity that generally gets discussed openly in the bar. Know what I mean?'

I still had little indication where this dialogue was taking us.

'Listen…you've got five seconds to put your cards on the table or I'm leaving. Up to you.'

'Okay. Okay. This is important, lad. Here me out.'

I suppose *lad* was slightly more palatable than *son*.

'I'm trying to hear you out. But you're not revealing very much Can you get to the point before one of us dies?'

I skewered the remaining half sausage on my plate.

'The major players of the crew are national. Not local. We were just the monkeys. The organ grinders are based in London.'

I finished my breakfast and set the cutlery down.

I briefly glanced at Alex in error but got away with it.

I swallowed my food and sat back in the chair.

'Right. I get you. So, what does this have to do with *me*? And what does it have to do with my family?'

'Things went tits up on us. Money and gear vanished almost overnight. The pub got robbed and then torched the following week. It was said they were hoping to catch me inside when it went up in flames. Things rapidly looked very dodgy for me. I got turfed out of Joseph Street and was warned to disappear before the real muscle caught up with me.'

A large pinch of salt might have helped my digestion of the sorry tale as it currently stood.

'So why did you have to leave your house?'

'It didn't belong to me, did it. It was just a safe haven. Where things got done. Call it the regional business office if you want. I was just the caretaker. The overseer. The house came with the job…if you get my drift.'

Feigning curiosity in my father's woes was becoming an increasing effort with each passing second.

I hoped he was getting to the crux of the matter very soon.

'You still haven't explained where I fit in to your shit mess.'

'The thing is, son…the finger of blame got pointed at me, didn't it. Loz and Ian both took a kicking because of me. Hospital jobs. The pair of 'em. And they can handle themselves. But I slipped the net and ran.'

He had no right involving me in this sinister palaver.

But my intelligence was of the sufficient level to comprehend that if he had become a moving target for his enemies, then it was only a matter of time before the punishment fell on somebody else's head.

Such as his children.

I remained very dubious about the entire affair.

'So, I take it you're now snooping around here looking for a hiding place?'

My father's gaze fell to the table and as he failed to respond I continued with my assumptions.

'And you figured that your youngest son was gullible enough to feel sorry for you? And by a sheer stroke of coincidence, he also had a place you could curl up in until the storm passes?'

He continued to study his now empty plate.

I'd nailed it for him.

Then his head rose slightly before he stuttered a follow-up line fishing for increased sympathy.

'I know what you'll now be thinking, Jamie. And in your shoes, I'd feel the same. I don't deserve any help. I deserve what's coming to me. But these people aren't your average neighbourhood ring. They must be seen to hurt you as an example to the rest of the operation. They'll kneecap you in broad daylight and leave you where they find you. And the cops won't go near them.'

I couldn't resist the opportunity for sarcasm.

'Sound like your kind of crew, I'd say.'

Even I wasn't sure just how much humour laced my retort.

If my father picked up on it, he didn't disclose the fact.

The way he now stared at me was not in any way parental.

It was a visage completely devoid of compassion, recognition, and affection.

Like everything else in his life, it was about self-preservation.

Pure and simple.

He rubbed his eyes before laying out the current scenario.

'Look…I'm on a mate's sofa in Mansfield. I've been at his now for three months. But I've got to shift my arse on. As I say, word travels fast in my circles.'

'So, what you're saying is…you want to know if you can come and sleep on *my* sofa instead?'

I thought I detected a hint of optimism in his face for the first time.

'Just for a short while. Just until it all blows over. If I wasn't desperate, I wouldn't ask. But I'm up the creek with no paddle.'

The fucking *nerve,* dear reader?

It no doubt seems incredulous to you that Jim Andrews even had the brass neck to show up in our lives again, let alone possess the steel balls to ask for favours.

This hateful and hated figure sitting just one metre away from me, was supposedly pleading a case for assistance, yet in his eyes I saw no strand of desperation or emotion whatsoever.

I backed away from encouraging any extension of his fictional yarn.

'You are dragging us into your problems. It's not fair. Your trouble is haunting you and you are prepared to sink low enough to involve your kids. After all this time. After all you've put us through. You now want a bed for the night and a shoulder to cry on? How fucking *dare* you?'

The employment of the f-word instantly attracted attention from the other tables. But I would keep my temper in check.

I would not lose control. I would not let my father see me buckle.

He needed absolute assurances as to which side his bread was buttered.

And I had no reservation in letting him know.

'You show no remorse or contrition for the way you treated the three of us. For the life you chose to lead and the lives you deserted us with. And now you want our help? You are well beyond the hope of that. You're never worth a second chance in my eyes.'

He raised a hand to interrupt, but I wouldn't let him as my restricted tirade continued.

'We might be blood, but that is as far as it goes. A chemical connection. I can't afford to let you back in. You would happily destroy everything again. Forget it. Forget we ever sat here and spoke. I am now going to leave the table and walk away. I want no part of this. I don't want to hear of you or see you ever again.'

He managed to interject, but only partially.

‘But Jamie…don’t you think…’

‘I don’t want to hear anymore. You’ve had your audience with me. I granted you that much. Now do us all a favour. Fuck off out of Nottingham. And I suggest in all seriousness that you leave tonight. Or *I’ll* be on your tail again as well as these so-called imaginary fucking drug lords you say you’re so scared of. Do you really think I’m fooled by this feeble tale? You’re not scared of *anybody*!’

I felt a sense of accomplishment as I rose to my feet.

It was a mean feat not to give Alex’s identity away, but somehow, I adeptly slipped on my coat and made immediately for the door.

Only to be halted in my tracks by my father’s outstretched hand as I passed him.

His grip was firm and unyielding around my forearm.

Almost painful.

But he held off from inflicting too much discomfort.

I bunched my fist in readiness for the inevitable.

He looked me in the eyes without blinking.

‘There’s no argument from me over what I have done to you two boys. Or what I did to your mother. I despise myself if truth be known. The things I’ve done I’ve got to live with. But please, just give me the opportunity to offer something in return. Instead of me taking from you again…let me give *back* to you both.’

My father’s eyes glistened with intensity as his grasp gradually increased its potency.

But I was not convinced at all.

Too much water had flowed under the bridge.

It was too late for a reprieve.

I stared down at his pathetic posturing.

His exasperating request for a chance at redemption.

His performance was far from authentic.

And yet still, he had more to say.

‘Jamie…hear me. If these people don’t get to *me*, they will make it their business to get to *you*. There’s no escaping it. You say you can’t get involved. But I'm afraid it's too late, son. You already *are* involved. Like it or not. You're *all* involved in this.'

I gritted my teeth.

I yanked my arm free from his shackle.

I then leaned toward him with my farewell message which was delivered in earnest.

'I've said my piece. We've nothing else to discuss. Thanks for breakfast. Goodbye.'

19
REVIEW

In hindsight I expected to feel far more fearful of the experience than it ultimately proved. Yet as things stood, an odd sensation of triumph flushed my veins as I closed the café door behind me and headed for the pre-arranged rendezvous point to wait for Alex.

I couldn't have cared less whether my father was telling me the plain gospel or not. He might have had genuine problems, but so far as I was concerned, they were all self-induced and not my business.

Money, booze, drugs, and gangs. It all leads to one place eventually and I had no sympathy for him.

He had made his bed for many years and if he was finally due a beating as opposed to dishing one out then so be it. It's an occupational hazard within the circles he indulges.

But I was adamant he would not be allowed to bring his toxic brand of drama to Glenfield Avenue. I'd fought too hard and lost too much to even consider the premise of taking him in.

His presence encouraged nothing less than assured destruction wherever he went. I couldn't do it to Martin and Bobby.

I would never forgive myself if matters took a nasty downturn.

He didn't care about us. We were his last resort. That's why he was sniffing around. Because he had absolutely nothing to his name and nowhere else to go. And after the thick end of sixty years riding roughshod over folk, he warranted nothing better than the predicament in which he now found himself immersed.

Whatever was coming his way, he would have to deal with it alone.

It might surprise you to learn that as I employed a determined stride through the town centre, I never once thought it might be necessary to look over my shoulder.

There was nothing to stop him coming after me, of course.

If he was as desperate as he claimed, he could have reacted badly to my rebuke of his character and principles.

But he would have been aware that his typical form of physical persuasion would not have fazed me one iota.

Perhaps he didn't favour the traditionally violent method anymore.

Perhaps the leopard *had* changed his spots to a degree.

Maybe age had mellowed him into a slightly more compassionate and considerate soul.

Like hell it had.

He was a trickster. He was performing.

His circumstances dictated that he should exhibit the humble approach. And if he thought I was the kind of mug that might fall for his display of false humility then he found out the quick way that I wasn't.

I had obliged his wish to meet up and speak. It was now done with.

I honestly never wanted to have any association with him again.

But even as these reactive thoughts marched rampantly across my conscience, I also knew deep down that I was fooling myself. This saga that had now entwined us all was destined to roll onward. And if you're as astute as I believe you to be, dear reader, you've already reached that conclusion for yourself.

As I motored along the High Street, my thoughts now turned to Alex.

I was very intrigued to hear what she made of my father's situation.

You will already be aware that her take on most things offered a far more balanced, considered, and usually philosophical viewpoint, than my typically testosterone fuelled knee-jerk responses.

She would present the scenario to me from an angle of logic and wisdom.

She would shine a light on dark areas that I hadn't even considered.

You might be slightly amused to hear that after conveying such bravado, I did eventually succumb to temptation as I strolled through the main precinct and reached the main traffic junction.

Yes, I looked over my shoulder.

No, I had not been followed.

Not a single suspicious character in sight.

I scanned the shoppers and the shop doorways.

Nobody appeared to be ducking for cover.

It looked like my father had arrived in town alone and had opted to stay in the café after my departure. Wallowing in his pathetic self-pity and contemplating his invitation that I had assuredly declined.

I turned and faced my next destination.

The ornate architecture of the library sat proudly nestled among its lovingly manicured gardens. This was the designated location where Alex was to find me. It was pre-arranged that she would leave the café thirty minutes after I did.

Solid plan, eh? Well, if it worked then I'd be content. It didn't need to be too technical. So long as it was fit for purpose.

The scheduled half hour hiatus would either provide my father with the opportunity to leave first or allow Alex the same luxury. Whoever happened to make the move it didn't really matter. The key factor was that no one in the vicinity would suspect a thing, would they?

I approached the main wrought-iron gates to the library grounds and ambled up the large stone steps to the double doors of the building.

Once more I glanced back into my wake before slipping inside.

I just hoped now that Alex would be able to execute her part of the mission unscathed.

*****

It was just after midday when I watched her majestic form appear at the library gates. My vantage point in the reference section allowed me to observe her feminine stride and I smiled inwardly as she trotted up the steps.

I swiftly moved to the double doors and pulled one side open to let her in. She shook her head and murmured half-jokingly as I closed the doors behind her.

'Jesus Christ, Jamie Andrews. Why did I ever get involved with this bloody family of yours?'

I giggled, albeit nervously.

'You *volunteered.*'

'I don't recall it happening that way.'

'Well, okay. I asked you if you wanted to be involved and you enthusiastically agreed. How's that sound?'

'Alright, smartarse!'

She was always beautiful, but even more so when annoyed. I really wanted to offer her a hug of gratitude but wasn't quite sure where the rules of touchy-feely started or ended at that precise moment.

We weren't officially a fully-fledged item again, so I supposed physical intimacy of any kind was out of bounds until she gave the order.

I'd happily settle for that.

For now.

And then, my old friend entered the fray.

Irony. My lifelong companion that had remained strangely conspicuous of late, suddenly decided to contribute to proceedings.

As I considered the potential folly of a wanton embrace with Alex, she jumped at me and wrapped both arms around my neck.

She squeezed tightly.

She meant it.

I was sampling a small slice of Heaven as the idyllic seconds in her protection endured.

Of course, I had experienced this sensation before, but never had her touch exuded such genuine affection.

Or - dare I say it - *love*?

We drew apart in the library foyer and I had the opportunity to fully lose myself in those crystalline eyes once again.

My god. Whatever possessed me to leave this girl behind once upon a time? What a fool I was. Yet there she was, back by my side.

On rare occasions, I guess, fate decides to work with us.

It made a well-deserved change to the norm.

'They do drinks here, Jay. You want a coffee? Cos I'm gagging.'

'Good idea. Where shall we perch?'

'It looks pretty secluded in the kids' section over there. I'll read you a fairy story to cheer you up!'

Out of sight from passing scrutiny, we sat quietly at a table and sampled our powdered caffeine.

I kept a loose eye on the movements of the two female clerks on duty, but thankfully they didn't seem overly interested in our reasons for being there.

'Well, what's your verdict on that little show?' I enquired.

'I have to say, Jay, I was very moved by your courage. He looks and sounds a real piece of work.'

I nodded in long-held agreement.

She carried an almost admiring expression, but I confess I didn't feel particularly brave about any of it. I played the hand that I was dealt. As is always the case.

'Do you think he's after more than he's letting on, Ally? I haven't made my mind up yet. But I can't have him anywhere near us. Bobby would throttle me on the spot.'

Alex cradled her plastic cup and leaned over to whisper.

'To be honest, Jay…I still can't quite believe what I witnessed.'

I was puzzled.

'How do you mean?'

'After all the things I've heard you say about him and all the strife he put your family through, it was totally surreal watching you both eating breakfast together at the same table.'

I sipped some coffee and pondered her initial feedback.

I never really considered how it might look to an observer who knew the background story. But we fully anticipated her to come up with something different, didn't we, dear reader?

'The bad stuff got much worse in Blackpool. I'm glad you weren't with us, Ally. Even though it broke your heart me walking into it. But it was a horrendous set-up. Unsafe. Really dangerous.'

She continued to stare into me. She seemed very touched by my honesty. I had no reason to hide my feelings.

‘We don’t have to keep reminding ourselves of that, Jay. Dwelling on that bit of misery eclipses the great stuff that happened before it.’

Her words were music to my ears.

So, she didn’t hold a grudge. Well, how could she?

I was officially still her knight in rusting armour, as Martin would affectionately put it.

‘You’ve never said it quite like that before, Ally. It means a lot. I thought you would have begun to hate me.’

Her features quickly formed into a mask of dismay.

‘Do you think I’d be sitting here if that were the case? Supervising myself in a stakeout over you and your lunatic father?’

I couldn’t resist dropping in a pinch of humour.

‘You’re a good judge of character considering you never laid eyes on him until today.’

We both laughed and the tension evaporated again.

‘The big question now Jay, is…what do you do *next*?’

I had literally no idea.

I hadn’t thought that far.

So, like all red-blooded males under pressure, I blagged it.

‘He’s been told to leave us alone. I’m hoping he’s got the message and that’s the last we see of him.’

I knew exactly what she was going to say.

And I know you’re saying it too, dear reader.

‘It won’t be that easy. Trust me.’

I trusted her.

‘Hit me with your feelings on this then, Ally. I’m relying on you for all the answers.’

She glanced around the room and moved her chair closer. I could smell her perfume. That same enticing aroma that always made me feel like I was floating on air. The memories flooded back to me, and I was lost in the elation of times past.

I loved this woman. And whatever happened now, I knew I always would. I regained concentration as she deluged me with her findings.

‘Point one. He’s in Nottingham. Point two…he’s scouted you out and knows exactly what you are all doing with your lives since you left Blackpool. And none of you even knew he was watching you until recently.’

I felt a chilliness descend.

‘That’s pretty scary when you put it together in that way.’

‘Point three. If he’s as much in the doghouse as he proclaims…why come back to his hometown? Especially when his family can’t stand the sight of him, and this is the first place his so-called enemies will look for him?’

I observed the frown lines that framed her stern expression.

She would make a very good detective.

‘So, do you think he really is in trouble? Or just on the scrounge?’

She pressed her back into the chair, folded her arms and crossed her legs.

‘Difficult to tell. It’s tricky, because if he has got bad company following him and he keeps hanging around here then he’s correct. Sooner or later, you could all get a taste of what’s coming to *him*.’

‘I know what you mean. I don’t want us to be put at risk. I don’t know how to play it, Ally. Like you say, he won’t be going anywhere.’

‘There’s no onus on you to do *anything*, for the moment. He’s your father. You can’t change that, and you certainly can’t stop him from creeping about the town watching you. So long as he keeps his distance. You can’t just cut the ties with him though, Jay. I know you *want* to. Of course, I do. But it’s not a realistic likelihood. Whatever his motives are.’

‘You think he will stick around, then?’

‘I can’t be certain, Jay. But if he’s anything like the evil colossus of legend I don’t think he’ll lose any sleep over kicking your door down and kicking your head in if the mood takes him. Get me?’

Oh yes! I got her, alright.

Loud and unnervingly clear.

Black and white with Alex.

I should have expected nothing else.

Her thinking was sound, and I wouldn't ever ignore her opinion.

I was suddenly overshadowed by trepidation again.

'Fucking hell, Ally! The mess we left up north could well end up being ten times worse down here, couldn't it?'

She smiled warmly.

'Now you're catching on, Sherlock! And I'll tell you something else. You need to tell Martin and his partner everything that was said today. You all need to be prepared if battle commences.'

We sat in contemplative silence for a minute or two.

Then she posed another corker.

'Do you want me to come with you? Back to the house, I mean. A bit of moral support for you when you tell your brother?'

There was an easy answer to this one.

'No. Absolutely *not*! I want to keep you at arm's length from all this. You've been so generous today by helping me out. I'll walk you home then I'll go and break the news to Romeo and Juliet. I'm sure they'll be utterly delighted that I haven't the foggiest what my father's next move is going to be. Come on. Let's get going.'

We departed the library grounds.

The afternoon air was now affirming its seasonal bitterness.

I wished I had the gumption to have held her hand, but I wasn't quite that confident yet.

We descended the stone steps and made out way to the exit gates.

Yes. You've guessed already, dear reader.

Irony abounded from the skies yet again.

Another thunderbolt struck from the blue yonder.

Alex grabbed hold of my hand and threw me an incredible smile.

The smile I knew so well, yet it carried a much more potent meaning this time.

My heart raced and I felt on cloud nine as we ambled along the two-mile route back to her parents' house.

If it weren't for the imminent storm brewing on the horizon, I firmly believe we would have officially rekindled our relationship that day.

Outside her front gate on Ashby Drive, we stood staring into one another's eyes.

Just like we used to.

No words necessary.

Until I felt compelled to convey the obvious ones.

'Thank you for today. I needed you.'

'I'm always here, Jay. Always.'

'I know. I won't ever take you for granted again.'

'Let's look to the future, eh? History's gone.'

'Yes. You're right. I'm sorry.'

'Look at it this way, Jay. If the past hadn't happened the way it did, we wouldn't be standing together now. None of this is your fault. You're just *cursed*. That's all.'

We both exploded into fits of laughter.

It was so inspiring to feel this way about her again.

To be so close. So mutually dependent. So reliant on one another.

And finally, she leaned forward, stood on her tiptoes, and pecked me gently on the lips.

'I'll see you soon, Jay. I'm at Uni tomorrow. Stay in touch though, yes?'

She retreated to her front door with a cheeky wave and a blown kiss. I watched her enter and disappear within.

For me, Glenfield Avenue now beckoned.

It was time to face my family.

And as I walked, my fragile mindset on the issue gradually began to degrade with every step.

I began to suspect I had made a huge mistake in refusing to assist our father so readily.

An overwhelming sense of regretful anxiety enveloped my previously clear conscience as I headed for the bungalow.

20
STRINGENT OBJECTION

'Are you out of your fucking mind, Jamie boy?'

Bobby creased her brow and offered me daggers across the dining table. On hearing my recounting of the meeting that morning, her mouth initially dropped open and silent.

But inevitably, this wasn't the case for long.

'Well, funny you should mention it. I have wondered lately if I am going nuts, Bobby. I told him to his face to get lost. But I'm having second thoughts. I think we should help him, if only to ensure he disappears as quickly as he arrived. I trust my gut instincts on this.'

She shook her head and slammed both palms down onto the table.

'Frig you and your gut instincts. My gut instinct tells me you've lost the plot and that your proposition is leading us to disaster. The man is a walking H-bomb. Or have you suddenly forgotten about that little detail?'

I was becoming steadily intolerant of the regular and instant negativity that she had offered in domestic debates since my return. It was testing enough to deal with a very uncertain situation, without the detracting foghorn rattling my ear drums every five minutes.

'Hold your horses, Bobby. Not so long ago I was the one who didn't even want to go and talk to him at all. But I went with your vote and bit my lip. I'm just telling you what he told me today. That's all. But my opinion is shifting already. I think I might have acted in haste by telling him to sling his hook.'

Bobby raised her voice and lost her temper a little further.

We were set on collision course.

'Well, bully for you with knobs on. Jesus Christ, can you lose your conscience for a moment. So, he wants a roof over his demented ugly head, does he? Next thing he'll be borrowing a tenner here and there. Have a word with yourself, Jamie. I can't get over the sheer cheek of the bastard. I really can't.'

Martin raised his right hand to venture an opinion.

I calmly addressed his request to intervene.

'Yes, big bro. Speak to me. Calmly, if possible, please.'

My brother took a deep breath and rested his hand on Bobby's arm.

'I sympathise with the both of you. But emotions are muddying the waters. If he says he needs help, then that must be for the first time in his life.'

Bobby brushed Martin's hand aside and snarled another offering to the debate.

'And you trust him too do you, darling? The man who beat us black and blue all those years. The guy who locked you up because he was ashamed of you. You are willing to ignore all that?'

'He's our *father*, Bobby. Facts are facts.'

She really was amid a resistant storm of turmoil.

Her expression and tone continued to adopt a furious edge.

'And so just because of that you're willing to give him the benefit of the doubt, are ya? Take a look again at those fucking scars on your hands and arms. Are you willing to forego those just because of a genetic connection? I can't believe what I'm listening to, here. This house is becoming a fucking looney bin, so it is!'

Martin suffered her predictable tirade before focussing his attention to me directly.

And what he was saying was pure wisdom.

'We agree that we are all aware of his true nature. It's because of this that we face such a dilemma now.'

I was keen to continue hearing my brother's viewpoint.

That was if Bobby could refrain from interrupting for long enough.

'Go on then, Martin. Keep talking while she gets her breath back.'

Bobby mouthed an obscenity at me as Martin expanded with his logic.

'It's quite simple, to me. Do we want him outside our tent pissing *in*? Or inside our tent pissing *out*? Unglamourous as the metaphor might be, that is the issue in a nutshell.'

As expected, Bobby now turned on her fiancé once more.

Though I admired his bravery in shoring up the argument.

'Well how glad am I that you've done your thesis on it. We can make his bed up now next to Jamie's in the spare room. Ring him up now. I'll make him some supper. Shepherd's pie alright for him? What planet did you two just visit? Because back here on Earth I'm about to commit to doing something silly that I definitely won't regret!'

But Martin was fully prepared to defend the standpoint in his typically casual manner.

'Don't shoot the messenger, Bobby. It's not Jamie's fault that our father has turned up here, is it? We've got to deal with it together. Not through squabbling. Falling out with one another is a path to oblivion, for sure.'

Sadly, Martin's imparted opinion only managed to stoke the fire further.

'Don't frigging patronise *me*, Martin Andrews. Can you recall the life you had with your father? Waiting every waking hour in fear of who was going to turn up at Joseph Street and give you a kicking just for the fun of it? Me locking myself in my flat for my own protection? Paying in kind for my fixes? Your tragically misplaced conscience is on the verge of betraying you. Has the sense of self-preservation deserted your corner of the universe in the past half hour?'

I didn't feel it appropriate to mention it at the time, but Bobby really was hilarious to observe when she was in the throes of anger.

It was becoming increasingly difficult to conceal my smirk as she vented her Irish spleen. Eventually I collapsed into complete failure, which resulted in her fury increasing by a thousand percent.

'I'll knock that fucking grin off your face so help me I will, Jamie.'

Her threat only served to evolve my mask of mirth into a full-on belly laugh. Hence, I thought it high time to try and bring the debate to a close as diplomatically and efficiently as possible.

It was understandable that Bobby felt somewhat outnumbered in declaring her reservations.

In all honesty, I sided with her caution.

She was justified and correct in every way.

But the overhanging problem remained unresolved.

And we needed to agree on a remedy.

My suggestion offered instant promise.

'Look. A night's sleep might make us all see differently in the morning. A fresh perspective, yes? It's been a tense day to say the least.'

Bobby was in the kitchen facing away from my brother and me.

But she was still listening, and she was still extremely annoyed.

'Fresh perspective, my *arse*! I don't know who your doctor is, Jamie boy, but I suggest you make an appointment and get a referral to have those rocks in your head extracted.'

Once again it was a battle not to giggle as I took one step into the hallway.

'Night, Martin. Night Bobby.'

The response was rude, full of gusto and above all, earnest.

'Go screw yourself, Jamie Andrews. And I hope you sleep tight, too.'

I was still laughing as I turned off the spare room light and climbed under the quilt.

21
MATTERS OF THE HEART

'Hardly the most romantic setting for a chinwag so you're lucky I'm hungry is all I can say.'

I chuckled as Alex pushed open the entrance door to McDonald's and we walked willingly into the predicted Saturday lunchtime scrum down.

'Well, I thought you might be. You never could think on an empty stomach, could you?'

'Cheeky sod!' Alex quipped, whilst playfully slapping my upper arm in the process. We joined what looked to be the queue to be served and began to scrutinise the overhead menu boards.

Despite the trouble brewing in the background at home, Alex was a tremendous distraction, and I now relished every single second in her company.

Not that I took her for granted before, but this time I was implicitly more appreciative of her companionship.

With the food eventually ordered and paid for, the assistant pledged to bring it over when it was ready. So, we took the opportunity to grab a recently vacated two-seater table by the front window of the restaurant.

Alex placed her coat on the back of the chair and with all the elegance and grace I'd come to associate with her, she set herself down.

'I could get used to waitress service in here, Jay.'

'Getting lazy in your old age, are you?'

Her disparaging glare was underlined by a captivating half-smile.

'That slap I gave you a moment ago is likely to be a rehearsal.'

'Rehearsal for what?' I queried.

'The fist that's gonna connect with your jaw if you keep it up!'

I perched myself opposite and gazed around the bustling dining room.

'Have we even been here together before today, Ally? I can't recall doing so. Not with you, anyway.'

Alex struck a thoughtful pose.

She had a better memory than I did.

'No, I don't think so. And thinking about it again, I suppose this is a *fairly* romantic place after all. Especially if you let me have the gherkin off your quarter pounder.'

Her enchanting grin never failed to capture my full attention in any scenario.

Not for the first time, I found myself completely absorbed in her majestic aura.

'Your wish is my command, your ladyship. Should you desire the gherkin, then you shall indeed *have* the gherkin. Luckily, I don't like gherkin, or you'd have to arm wrestle me for it.'

She narrowed her eyes and squinted toward the counter.

'Which milkshake did you order? It had better be chocolate.'

'*Shit*! No, I ordered Vanilla. Why?'

Alex laughed out loud.

'Brilliant! You are so clever! Vanilla's my favourite!'

Duped once again, Jamie Andrews.

'Why don't you take my fries too whilst you're at it? In fact, am I likely to be able to eat *anything* of my own order when it comes or are you having first dibs on it all?'

It was a sincere pleasure to be teased mercilessly by the beautiful creature opposite.

'I might do yet! Got to be quick with me around you know! Anyway, how's the vibe at Glenfield today?'

She seemed almost expectant of what I was about to say in response.

'Well, to cut a long story short…Martin is once again deciding to be totally emotionless to the whole thing. Whereas Bobby is still pretty much fuming with me.'

Alex briefly fixed her gaze to the ceiling and bobbed her head from side to side as if to weigh up the information I had just revealed.

'Right. Okay. So…how are *you* feeling about what to do next?'

I sat back in my chair and let my eyes drift to the scene of pedestrian activity through the window.

A view that offered absolutely no inspiration whatsoever. I clasped my hands behind my head and delivered a deep sigh of frustration.

'I'm totally in two minds now, Ally. It's a real headfuck. I don't know what to do for the best. I really don't. And I've had three days to think about it. But I've not contacted him again. Not yet, anyway.'

'It's good that you're taking your time. What's the rush, anyway? Make him wait. He can't just expect to turn up out of the blue and click his fingers for attention. Only *I* get *that* privilege!'

I sniggered. Fair point. I shouldn't be feeling pressured.

But at the same time, I quietly hoped for a solution to fall from the sky and into my lap as soon as possible. I certainly wasn't prepared to keep dealing with the same old issues for the rest of my life.

Alex made me forget my latent anger most of the time, but just bringing the subject of my father into a discussion instantly ground my gears.

'You would have thought he'd have learned that we don't want him around. We don't need him for anything. But he's here, nevertheless. So, yours truly has just got to deal with it, somehow.'

I wanted to change the conversation completely.

And I had a question that should have diverted our focus somewhat.

'So…anyway…what do your folks think about you hanging out with me again?'

Alex again glanced toward the service counter as she composed her reply.

'They haven't said anything, Jay. But I'm sure that behind the twitching curtains they probably think that I'm a reckless fool and that I'm stupid beyond belief for not learning from past mistakes and moving on with my life.'

That felt relatively harsh, dear reader.

Did you think so, too?

Give me a moment to deliberate before you get angry with her.

My return of serve across the table was justifiably abrupt, even though I now felt a pang of sadness regarding her comment.

'*Mistake*? Is that how I'm viewed by them, is it?'

Alex realised she had offended me with her choice of phrasing.

I did indeed feel slightly, quite rightly, hurt.

'I'm sorry, Jay. No. It isn't. Not at all. They haven't expressed any opinion. I don't know what they think. And it doesn't really matter, does it? We were both privy to the situation and parted company. And now we have realised that our relationship is worth preserving. The only mistake would be not to learn from the past. To avoid repeating it. Don't you agree?'

I contemplated her very considered statement as the server appeared and set down the tray with our orders on it. I thanked the young girl whilst trying to keep a grasp on the coat tails of the discussion.

'Well, we aren't likely to repeat it are we, Ally? Our days of wine and roses pretty much ended when I boarded the train for Blackpool, didn't they?'

Alex munched on her fries whilst avidly scanning the other items on the tray. I could tell that her cogs were turning because she wouldn't look at me. Always the giveaway sign.

She had something more to say but I sensed she wasn't convinced it was a good idea to disclose it. She poked two more fries between her pouting lips and continued to chew whilst scrutinising my burger.

Finally, she offered confession of her thoughts.

'Well, Jay…in my humble opinion…I don't think we gave ourselves much of a chance to blossom properly the first time around. You'd just lost your mum. It was an upsetting time all round. Life seemed to keep creating hurdles for us.'

I unwrapped my quarter pounder as her depiction of the past registered.

'Well, Ally, I think it's safe to say that not much had changed on that score, has it?'

She rolled her eyes and nodded down at the food in my possession.

Her rumbling stomach evidently overruling the need for any incessant small talk.

'Take your gherkin out before you start eating. You said I could have it.'

What was it with this woman? I took the top off my bun and extracted the three slices of green pickle and laid them on her box of fries.

And it was at that instance that I knew exactly what it was about this woman that I was addicted to.

I loved her with everything I could muster. I had never stopped loving her and I knew in my heart that I never would stop.

'Are you happy now you've got your bloody gherkin?'

She nodded as she pulled the paper sheath from a drinking straw and inserted it into the milkshake. Her cheeks indented with the effort of her initial intake.

'You are so generous to me, darling.' she teased.

Alex then exploded with giggles before sampling a slice of the pickle.

At that instance, when she briefly observed me as she sucked on the straw once more, it was reminiscent of our early courtship back in the days of the Sixth Form at St George's.

Carefree, dreaming and wallowing in one another's attention.

My pulse raced and the butterflies in my stomach suddenly roused themselves.

My head spun and I felt as though I were floating on air.

And just as in those early days, something was always liable to cause me to make a crash landing. The thought occurred that I needed to rein my emotions in. One silly declaration could well mess things up all over again.

But my reticence was unwarranted.

Irony intervened once again as she finally stopped cramming food into her mouth and weaved her spell with those incredulous crystal eyes.

And out of the shadows it sailed without warning.

As if spoken by an angel.

‘You know Jay, if we feel we are on the right track to address our, shall we say, unfinished business…I wouldn’t be completely *against* the idea. You know…us being an official item again. Just saying, like.’

I initially thought she was pulling my leg.

You quite never knew with Alex Lawley at times. She liked to keep me on my toes. But this time her face showed no signs of jest.

Her focus on me was unwavering.

I assumed that her declaration was honest.

But I requested confirmation, anyway.

‘You’re *serious*? You’d have another shot at us?’

She nodded without conveying any giveaway expression on her face. She looked slightly ill at ease with the time I was taking to respond to the idea. Alex expanded on her thinking.

‘When you analyse it, Jay, we barely had a reason to split up. Did we? We were in love. We were happy. We were faithful. It all seemed to get taken away from us. And I’ve scratched my head so many times thinking about what motive we possibly might have had for ending things. And I still can’t find one.’

I tackled a mouthful of burger, which was chewed and swallowed in haste. As ever, I seemed to be the one to put a dampener on our sunlit ambitions.

‘But things are even *more* restricted now, aren’t they? What about our Uni degrees? What about the issue with my bloody father? Yet again, life is already tripping us up before we’ve even re-started.’

Alex sampled more milkshake and frowned.

She spoke with the straw remaining clamped between her teeth.

Her addictive gaze drawing me further under her spell with every passing second.

As always, she hit the nail squarely on the head at the first time of asking.

‘How long do we wait then, Jay? Never mind what’s come and gone. And the future will take care of itself. But we are in the *here* and the *now*. Life isn’t a practice run. Snooze today and you lose tomorrow.’

I was in complete, euphoric bemusement.

I had to blink for a few seconds to establish this was all really happening. Right there in the middle of the restaurant.

And Alex detected my confounded mindset.

I had been desperately trying not to overstep the unspoken bounds of our replenished friendship and there she was, forthright and straight as the day is long.

'I'll say this Alex Lawley…you always retained that power to totally surprise me. I'll give you that much.'

She placed her hand over mine and pressed it down onto the tabletop. She leaned across until our noses were inches apart.

Her perfume was very persuasive to the senses.

'Promise me you'll think about it. No rush for an answer. Not today, anyway. But the least I can do for you is let you know that I still fancy you rotten.'

We grinned in mutual acknowledgement.

We finished our meal in comparative silence.

In the space of an hour, I had transformed from a being enshrouded by worry.

And into quite possibly the most contented man on the planet.

Be kind, fate.

Please, be kind.

22
OFF KILTER

'It's okay. I've become quite accustomed to them again. I had a year or two off. I suppose they were bound to come back eventually.'

The time on the oven clock was two-twenty-three a.m.

I had woken Bobby again with another nightmare of such horrific proportions that I couldn't even bring myself to discuss it with her.

The grimace on her face adequately summed up the intensity of what had visited me during my slumber.

'Well, it sounded bad enough. So, I dread to think what they actually *look* like in your head!'

I tried to employ sarcasm to lighten the mood.

'Feel free to borrow the next one if you want. They are queuing up in my brain it seems. I could even set up a library service. Rent-a-scare! Guaranteed to give you sleepless nights or your money back.'

She smiled at my hapless attempt to make light of matters.

I dove into the fridge and poured a glass of milk.

'I didn't hear you come in from work, earlier. How was your shift?'

Bobby rolled her eyes and yawned.

'I didn't get out until after ten. Fucking stocktaking. I hate it with a passion. But I was in bed by midnight and away with the fairies until you started to bawl the place down. So, thanks to you I've only had two hours kip and now I'm going to try and get two hours more. I'm glad you're okay, though.'

'Yeah…I'm fine. Having bad dreams goes with the territory, I'm afraid.'

She looked at me rather puzzled.

'What territory might that be then?'

'Having the surname, Andrews. What a burden!'

Bobby chuckled to herself in the lounge doorway.

I was relieved she had calmed down after our understandably emotive exchanges.

'Yeah. Poor *you*, eh?'

I didn't let her off the hook.

'It'll be poor *you* when Martin gets you up the aisle. You'll be an Andrews too, then!'

My comment was intended to be comical.

Yet it seemed that I had caused her some discomfort by letting it escape from my big mouth.

Despite being my brother's fiancée, her response was not indicative of a doting bride-to-be.

Far from typical, in fact.

'Oh yeah. I forgot about that bit. I think it be better if we just stay engaged. Less complications and all that. Just don't let on to the other half, eh?'

I wanted to find her statement amusing, but the tone of delivery and the look on her face suggested one description and one only.

Scornful.

Had I misinterpreted the signal?

It was only an innocuous parting shot from her, but it rocked me so much that even I felt stuck for a reply to volley back across the net.

Why should her comment have perturbed me as it did?

There was nothing in it, was there?

But it was the pronounced manner that bothered me.

Humourless. Matter of fact. Rather too sincere.

As if she truly meant it.

I let the moment pass. I was quietly hopeful I had misread her.

But then her next line was delivered through an even more negative and cynical demeanour.

'I suppose you've been filling your good lady in on all our family business then, have you?'

Why reference Alex at such a strange juncture in the conversation?

My intuition was proving correct.

Bobby was evidently aggrieved about something, and I was supposedly able to ascertain what it was that was bothering her.

I found myself suddenly sounding rather defensive.

'We've talked about things. Yes, of course. Why? Is that a problem for you?'

She continued to hover in the doorway.

Her features were unreadable.

'Not at the moment, no.'

So, dear reader, what the fuck was *that* comment supposed to mean do you think? Now I was really concerned about her odd tone.

'Explain, Bobby. You've lost me.'

She re-entered the kitchen and lowered her voice to a whisper. I presume this was so as not to disturb my brother, who was snoring like a drain anyway in the bedroom.

'Don't let her start pulling your strings about things. You need to be very clear on the road forward, Jamie. For all our sakes. Plus, I've given things some thought. I think you're right. You should help Jim.'

Yet again I found the reference to Alex to be unnecessary and even hurtful. Alex was my emotional anchor for everything.

My rock and my guiding light.

Who the fuck did Bobby Jones think she was pointing fingers at *my* girlfriend in *my* house?

And the first name reference to my father was distinctly weird.

Once again, I decided I wasn't going to get into a quarrel.

Everyone was tired.

The timing was all wrong.

But I was imagining nothing.

My faculties were responding perfectly.

The situation with my father was in hand.

'I'm going to contact him tomorrow. To meet with him again. I'm still not sure what he wants from us. But I'm not going to act on impulse. Don't worry. I won't decide anything without consulting you and Martin. Okay?'

Bobby was about to leave the room for a second time before she turned on me yet again.

She now carried a fixed, unyielding visage.

An almost dictatorial stance that I'd never seen her adopt before.

'You'd better be sure on the choices you make. That's all I'm saying. Sleep tight. If you can.'

I watched her depart the room and close the door behind her.

I was now rendered severely bewildered.

On top of everything else that was going on, I was the one that she now deemed fit to place under scrutiny. And her sudden U-turn on the issue with my father was baffling to say the least.

Here I was trying to watch everyone's back, yet there was obviously a fair degree of confusion and disgruntlement in camp.

I tried not to dwell on it too much.

I drank my milk and quietly retreated to the camp bed.

Hoping in my heart that the tangible unrest in the air would meet with a positive change tomorrow.

The story of my life.

23
TENSIONS ON THE RISE

'I'll tell you now, son…I don't like this one bit.'

I struggled to comprehend my father's statement as he placed a pint of lager in front of me on the table.

'You don't like *what*, exactly?'

'*This*. Meeting *here*. Too…*public*.'

I still wasn't clear on the actual problem as I observed him scrutinising the surroundings.

The apparent paranoia that draped around our first rendezvous at the café was evidently still shadowing him.

'That will be why they call them *public* houses. So that the public can come and go of their own free will.'

My sense of humour drew a disparaging glare from Jim Andrews as he removed his coat and positioned opposite me in the corner snug.

He sipped his Scotch as his eyes constantly darted to every corner of the room.

He still appeared to be afraid and uncertain - so unlike the legend.

'Don't be fucking sarcastic with me, son. If you knew who was after me. you'd understand why I'm so fucking edgy.'

The pub was surprisingly quiet for a Sunday afternoon.

And before you ask, dear reader, I did inform Alex that I would be having another meeting with my father in The Highwayman's Arms. A quaint little inn on the outskirts of town.

She of course offered to stake out again.

But we both agreed that a repeat of her covert presence could easily alert my father's attention. After all, what are the chances of the same girl being in the same café and the same pub as the pair of us within the space of five days?

Correct, dear reader - absolutely no chance at all.

So, I generously gave her the day off to slum it with her parents but pledged to report back with any progress.

I sampled some of my drink as a group of football fans across the room jeered at the action on the television. I too was struggling to settle. And being nigh-on tee total by this point, the alcohol tasted particularly sour on my tongue.

Much the same as the atmosphere that was prevailing between my father and me.

He was still trying to act the hard man in the face of his apparent adversity, and it was a source of increasing frustration for me. And I was still slightly fractious regarding Bobby's very odd attitude the previous evening.

All in all, my patience threshold would not take much breaching that day, and let my father know the score.

'The way I see it you're not in any position to dictate to anyone. Especially *me*. You're telling me you're up to your neck in it yet insist on giving orders out. I can get out of this chair and piss off if it suits me to do so. Then what are you going to do?'

'There's always another way, son. But I prefer to work *with* you as opposed to against you.'

An uneasy peace resumed between us.

We both took on more alcohol which went against my personal wisdom, but at least it helped us to relax.

My father edged closer to me across the table.

His eyes met mine as he whispered.

'So then…what have you got to tell me? You took long enough to make the call. I'd given up hoping to hear anything at all, to be honest.'

I watched him as he continued to scan the vicinity over my shoulder, just as he was doing when we ate breakfast the other day.

Every time someone entered through the main doors his head would spin to analyse the incomer. He was similarly curious when anybody went to leave the premises.

He was also preoccupied with the ever-changing patrons of the gents' toilet. Perhaps the suspected neurosis had indeed got him firmly in its grip after all.

About time he had a taste of it instead of everybody else looking over their shoulder because of *him.*

He was like a cat on hot bricks. Skittish and jittery.

Should I have felt out of order for finding a crumb of gratification in the fact?

Not likely.

It was strangely satisfying seeing him so unassured and jumpy.

'Don't get your hopes up. I can't offer you anything just yet. It's causing too much trouble at home.'

My father lowered his glass and raised his voice.

'Trouble with *who*? Are you trying to tell me your brother doesn't fancy having his old man around the place?'

I wasn't sure if he was deliberately acting ignorant, or whether time had indeed moulded him into the most insensitive specimen ever created.

I studied his deeply creased features that had been relentlessly ingrained with bitterness throughout his entire life.

'No. Not so much Martin that has the issue. To be fair he's taken a back seat on all this for the most part. He's very open-minded.'

My father nodded slowly and hissed his natural conclusion.

'Oh…so it's Roberta that's playing stick in the mud, is it? Gobby Irish cow. I can see her now wagging a finger at you and shouting the odds. Telling you how stupid you are and how disgusting I am. Well, it's not my fault. Not this time.'

Sarcasm strangled my reply.

'No. *Course* not. How could it *ever* be *your* fault? God forbid!'

I was prepared to bait him on purpose, such was my intolerant standpoint regarding the entire situation.

'For such a young kid you've got big bollocks showing me such disrespect.'

Christ! Here we go again. The plastic gangster acting all offended.

'And I wonder where I inherited that from? For an old has-been I think you've got big bollocks coming to *me* crying for *help*!'

He sat back in his seat and verged on a smile.

I could tell it was in there somewhere, but he held it back.

My father knew full well he wasn't dealing with an idiot, and I suspected a pang of appreciation might just have touched his conscience as we exchanged the pointless banter.

He drained his glass and placed the empty tumbler on the table.

'Fair point, I suppose. At least we are in the same room and talking. Considering everything, that is in itself a minor miracle.'

I wasn't convinced that my father truly understood the level of hurt that he had caused in the family.

His attitude to our history seemed far too casual and dismissive. As though nearly thirty years of his savage influence over the Andrews offspring didn't matter too much, anymore.

But I wasn't about to brush it under the carpet, was I?

The upset I felt was my defence mechanism.

'I'll tell you straight. I'm putting relationships at risk for this farce. I haven't even told Martin I'm here because I can't judge his reaction. How do you think that makes me feel inside? And as for Bobby…the jury's still out with her. She might go berserk at me again just for sitting here. I can't judge her at the moment, either.'

My father ran his hands over his smooth scalp and glanced to the bar again.

He was evidently ready for a refill.

'No, she wouldn't be mad. She'll be fine.'

'And what makes you say that?'

'I can say that because I know Roberta, don't forget. She's all front. There's a soft spot behind that loudmouth act of hers, I'm telling you.'

I was half-way down my pint. I didn't intend topping it up.

This was a strictly formal engagement. I couldn't afford to have my thinking muddied by drink.

'Well, until the three of us agree on what to do about you, you're stuck on your mate's sofa in Mansfield, I'm afraid.'

That was a declaration that pushed his buttons and persuaded him to drop the façade of being cool, calm, and collected.

The spittle formed at the corners of his mouth as he honed even closer to my face and delivered his disapproval.

'Listen here, Jamie lad. I haven't got fucking time to wait for your committee. Just get your brother on board. Don't worry about the Irishwoman. Besides, she'll be outvoted anyway if you brothers stick together, won't she?'

Were there no bounds to this man's crookedness?

He was completely sincere in his wish that the outcome of this business fell in his favour.

'She's part of the family. That word *family* still means something to some people in this world. Not that you can even spell it.'

His eyes burned into me with surfacing resentment. He probably wanted to knock my head off there and then. But that really would mess up his plea for charity.

It was satisfying to have the upper hand over him. He wasn't likely to upset the applecart. Especially if the yarn he was spinning turned out to be true.

'You're so fucking full of yourself aren't ya, young one. I can see you've inherited a hard and intolerant edge from someone. Probably your mother.'

I chuckled to his face.

Fifty percent genuine; fifty percent forced.

'I hope I haven't inherited *anything* from *you*. That's a fact.'

The ridges on his forehead drew ever closer for inspection as he placed his nose inches from my own.

'Okay then…if I'm such a repulsive scumbag, why are you even here? Why ring me to meet up again?'

This response came easy.

'Firstly, because I have morals. You're my father. I respect the dynamic if not the man. Secondly, I know you're not going to disappear in a hurry. So, I'm humouring you.'

Jim Andrews looked like he wanted to erupt with fury on the spot.

Yet I sensed him swiftly fighting for retention of his composure.

I briefly witnessed the noxious, untamed animal within him.

It still lurked beneath the surface, for sure. And that split second of recognition on my part cemented vindication of my caution.

I emptied my own glass and rose to my feet. He did not even look at me, fixing his vexed stare to the wall beyond my shoulder.

I offered a farewell sermon as I slipped on my coat.

'Well, this pointless thirty minutes proves that I need more time to think, whether you like it or not. You want me to make a leap of faith. I'm afraid I ran out of faith many years ago where you are concerned. Like you say, we perhaps need a family vote.'

I shuffled from the snug and my father's attention remained centred on the pub decor.

But he had a final offering for me too.

Couldn't help himself, could he?

'Don't be so cocksure of yourself and your cosy little family set-up, young lad. Unity is a very delicate commodity. But I have to say that you are absolutely correct in what you claimed just a moment ago.'

'Oh yeah? What's that then?'

My father finally turned to focus his raging eyes with mine.

Our minds dared one another into supplying the most potent parting shot.

'Rest assured on this, son. I'm going nowhere. I'm here to stay. And stay I shall.'

I gathered my thoughts before returning a considered sentiment.

'Fine. Stay put. Be the sitting duck for your mates to find. The best of luck. Sounds like you'll need it. I might be in touch again soon. Who knows?'

24
GROWING DIVISIONS

Despite my rather smug retort on departure from the pub, the declaration from my father was undeniably haunting. I couldn't erase it from my mind as I walked back through town heading for home.

On my return through the front door at Glenfield Avenue, Bobby's disposition had not lightened.

In fact, she was possibly more aggrieved than ever.

'I can't believe you went on your own again. I could have come with you, Jamie.'

'You were at work.'

'Only until two. You could have waited for me. Instead of playing this stupid game of secrets with him. When do Martin and I get a say in all this? Ha?'

It was fair to say that my supposedly hidden agenda did not meet with Bobby's wholehearted approval.

'Look. We are no further along the road with it. It was just a pint. That's all. I'm still weighing it up. But he's becoming impatient. He's not getting what he wants and he's beginning to show his old self again.'

Bobby was evidently incensed, and her voice raised an octave or two to rise over the volume of the television set.

'We are supposed to be in this together, are we not? I don't think you fully undertake the policy of democracy when you're sneaking off behind our backs. You said you'd keep us up to speed with stuff. I get the feeling I'm being left out on purpose here.'

This was getting ridiculous.

She really had a bit between her teeth about something when there was no reason for her to.

Unfortunately, she wasn't in a receptive enough frame of mind to accept where the actual truth might overcome her fictional version.

'Where's Martin?'

'In the bath playing with his fucking submarines.' she snapped.

Not an apt moment to laugh out loud, so I refrained.

'You need to calm down, Bobby. This thing with our father is getting to you. I'm doing my best to sort it.'

She suddenly rose from the settee and faced me.

Her nostrils flared slightly, and it was a shame that her naturally striking beauty was being temporarily contorted by exasperation.

'All that time we tolerated that bastard. Putting up with his barbaric attitude. All that danger we were in. And then you came and saved us from that fucking hell hole. And now you can't even make up your mind whether or not he's turned into Mister Nice Guy, all of a sudden. With his hard luck story under his arm. This stinks to high heaven, Jamie boy. And you want folk to calm down? I don't know who is going mental the quickest! You or *me?!*'

All fair points; expertly conveyed via her icy native dialect.

'Look, Bobby…I've told him we will make the final decision as a three. That's the last thing I said to him. No one in this house is being side-lined. Trust me.'

Sadly, my persistent attempts at orthodox reasoning fell on increasingly deaf ears.

'What fucking decision? Can't you see it, already? Are you so stupid *and* blind? *He's* already made the decision! He's *here*, isn't he? Get this into your thick head will you. We are stuck with him whether he gets his feet under our table or not. He will hound us forever and a day. There is no hiding place from this. End of story.'

Well, that was a whole plate of realism launched into my face.

And I couldn't disagree with any of it.

But I was also now tiring of being the target of her frustrations.

'Okay. If what you say is true, what now? Run away, again? Let him hole up with us? Pray he falls under a bus? Because you wanted me back here to deal with him and I will hold my hands up and say I haven't the first clue on how to handle things at this moment in time. Alright? There. Now you've heard it from the horse's mouth. Happy?'

My stark admission didn't seem to have any notable impact.

She simply left the room and checked on Martin.

I shouted through the lounge door to the hallway.

'Bobby, we need to keep talking. Don't you dare clam up on me.'

She returned to the living room. Hanging through the door frame, she carried a disgruntled, snarling expression.

I hoped that she might supply a grain of positivity to proceedings, but my hopes were in vain.

Her voice had steadied, but it was laced with a hint of dismissive resignation. She was becoming very resentful, too.

'Why don't you go and talk it through with your girlfriend. *She's* always got the answers you want to hear. But if you do go and see her, make sure you don't tell me or your brother about it first. Cos you obviously trust her more than your own flesh and blood. Honestly, Jamie boy. I thought you were a stronger man than this. You may as well have stayed in fucking Swansea.'

The slam of the lounge door resonated starkly in my ear drums as her words simultaneously cut deeply into me.

I could not compete with her current mindset.

She was so distant and disdainful.

Almost to the point of being untouchable.

I was bemused as to her sudden preference for all-out hostility.

But in fairness, Bobby was spot on with her final piece of throwaway advice.

Alex *was* always somebody that made everything seem very clear for me.

And if ever I needed her inciteful brand of intelligence, it was now.

25
A PORT IN THE STORM

I felt incredibly guilty. Alex had planned to spend the evening at a gig with a friend from university. But in fortunate balance to my selfishness, her enthusiasm when I phoned to suggest meeting up, was tangible.

In fact, I might go as far to say she sounded absolutely delighted.

At least somebody was happy to be in my company that day.

I met her at the end of Ashby Drive. Sounds rather unsociable but I didn't think my sorry looking visage would spread much joy by appearing at the Lawley's front door.

Besides which, it was too early to start getting overly familiar with her parents again. *Way* too early. And there was always the slightest possibility hanging in the air that Kevin Lawley may still wish to punch my head in.

Better safe than sorry, dear reader?

So, there I stood. One hundred metres away. Out of sight.

Waiting for the reliable presence of the woman I loved to sweep me up and away from all this strife and struggle if only for an hour or so.

I observed with undiluted excitement as her distinctive, swaggering silhouette came striding out of the shadows towards me.

And I know I've extolled the virtues of this before, but for a woman just twenty years of age, she really did exude elegance and class.

Just saying.

Again.

If only she was completely mine. Again.

Patience young Andrews. Everything comes to he who waits...

We embraced at the road junction and linked arms before commencing a slow ramble in the opposite direction from her home.

'Sorry for messing your plans up.'

'Its fine, Jay. It was only a student band in the city centre. No big deal. I'd much rather be walking around in the dark freezing my arse off with you, than being in a warm pub drinking, socialising, and dancing.'

I watched her try and stifle her giggles as the flitting amber hue of a streetlamp illuminated her face.

'Did you tell your folks you were seeing me tonight instead?'

'No. they think I'm still going with Plan A.'

I found her reply to be a little unnerving.

'Oh really? They don't know you had a much better offer at the eleventh hour, then?'

Alex chuckled and flicked her hair over her shoulder.

'To be fair I didn't really discuss it with them at all. Just got my shoes and coat on, shouted goodbye and left. They can always ring me if they are worried about where I am. Or who I'm with.'

My next question was understandable even though I felt rather awkward asking it.

'You would be honest if you were a bit reluctant to be with me again, wouldn't you? I wouldn't blame you. Not after everything that's happened.'

She stopped her stride and looked me directly in the eye.

'Are you asking me if I'm ashamed of you? Because if you are, then that is just *ridiculous*!'

'Well, you know…it's like you're giving me a second chance. People might sit in judgement. Waiting for you to get hurt all over again.'

She shook her head slowly and gently cradled my cheeks in her palms.

'I find it really upsetting that you can even have these thoughts, Jay. This past couple of years has really knocked your confidence, hasn't it? Please don't doubt your worth. Especially where *we* are concerned. Okay? Promise me that much?'

The relief washed over me, and we began to walk again.

'Yes. I promise. And yes, I've lost my touch a bit. Life can do that to you. People can do that to you, can't they?'

'Well…you know what I always say…'

'No? What do you always say, Ally?'

'I say *screw* other people! That's *what*!'

I was momentarily placated.

My spirit allowed itself to bathe in contentment once more.

But I couldn't quite leave the conversation there.

'So, you don't wish you were still with that guy who owned the black sports car, then?'

Alex laughed and squeezed my hand in reassurance.

'Now he *was* something to be ashamed of! I found out he was triple timing me! Could have been more than *three*! I mean, I know I wasn't in the running to be the love of his life, but he used girlfriends as if he was in a relay race! Drop one off and go round the corner and pick the next one up! No wonder the passenger seat was always warm. It took me a while to cotton on to his antics. But I got there in the end.'

It was mutually amusing for us to reflect on previous decisions and events. And errors.

I didn't dare tell her at that moment that I knew precisely who the love of *my* life was, and that I'd always been totally invested in the fact.

But this fleeting thought did prompt my next question as I sensed the evening chill factor begin to set into my bones.

'You know what you were saying before, Ally?'

She sniggered again as we crossed the road adjacent to the railway station.

'I think I need a clue on this one, Jay. I can never remember what I've said. Selective memory and all that. Great self-defence tactic, though!'

She was enjoying mocking me immensely.

And I suspected she knew exactly what area I wanted to cover.

'The subject was about you and me trying again. Maybe one day. When we feel the time is right.'

Even in the half-light of the street, I could see it was an effort for her to maintain a straight face.

'Oh God! *That* bit! Well, I must have been drunk at the time. I was hoping you weren't listening. Aren't I silly?'

Sometimes I wished she could act seriously for thirty seconds.

'Not in McDonald's you weren't drunk. Or being silly.'

'Oh yeah. That's where I said it, wasn't it. Okay. So, what about it, hotshot?'

Shit! Now it was *me* who was suddenly stuck for words.

I didn't really have a plan for the next stage of the discussion.

'Well, Ally…I just want you to know that when my family finally gets its priorities right, I think we should go for it. Properly, I mean.'

I walked straight into it, didn't I?

She wasn't being flippant, but I certainly deserved the reply she gleefully conveyed.

'Jay, the day your family sorts itself out we'll be grey and old and too knackered to be bothered with one another. If not that, then I'll wager that at least one of us will be six feet under!'

I knew what she meant.

The discord within and around the Andrews dynasty seemed never ending.

'On that very subject, I don't think I'm very popular with the other two inmates at Glenfield.'

Alex halted her stride again and pulled me closer. In fact, she pulled me so close I could have kissed her on the lips, and she wouldn't have been able to do a thing to stop me. Our noses were no more than six inches apart as she deliberated on what I just implied.

But the humour jumped in ahead of the issue.

'Well, I *am* surprised. You had your chance to snog me, then. Getting shy in your middle age or something?' she grinned.

'I'm far too much of a gentleman to take advantage in such a primitive manner. Sorry to disappoint.' I laughed in return.

'Yes. You are so very gallant, aren't you. And I'm not disappointed. I'm very impressed. I know I can trust you forever, Jay. *Always* and forever.'

We resumed our meander towards the town centre, which was typically quiet for a Sunday evening.

Her statement made me veritably float on air.

My concerns simply evaporated in her presence.

I didn't feel the autumn cold anymore. I was with my girl and on top of the world.

And then she had to go and burst the balloon with a distinctly unwelcome reference to harsh reality.

'So…family. Your father. You met him, today. What's happening? And why are the other two falling out with *you*? This is going to drag on and on unless something drastic happens. It's just a game for him but it's putting the brakes on life for everyone else concerned, isn't it?'

Oh, my incredible darling Alexandra.

You *always* understand.

Always.

'I don't know what to do about it, Ally. Helping his cause could be a terrible mistake. But so could ignoring him. I'm at a total loss with it all. It's really starting to affect things at home. Especially with Bobby. She's very temperamental towards me lately.'

Alex forced her arm to link with mine again.

'So…any thoughts on what I should do?' I begged.

'Yes. Do *nothing*! I told you in the library last week. *Patience*. Everyone is bound to be feeling the strain. I've never met Bobby, but she sounds like she's got her head screwed on properly. She'll come round. Just hang on until the ride stops. Did your father say anything of interest?'

'Yes. That he's not going to disappear and that he's running out of time. He's going to keep hassling me. I think I'm going a bit stir crazy with it all. Maybe a doctor might calm me down a bit, but I don't want sleeping pills or shit like that. The nightmares are back. It's like the cycle is starting all over again.'

Her mesmeric eyes bore into me through the blackness.

'You don't need the quack, Jay. I was thinking more along the therapeutic line. Your mum went to church for help. What about that avenue?'

It had never entered my head until she suggested it.

Alex continued making a very valid and earnest point.

‘I’m not religious at all, Jay. But that priest you went to see about your mum made all the difference to you. He changed your mindset for the better just by talking calmly to you. I can try and do that, but I’m not impartial to it all. He will be.’

Surprisingly, I found myself unopposed to the idea.

She continued as her warm breath spiralled into the cold air.

‘Perhaps he’s worth another visit? You’ve got nothing to lose. Things are too confusing for you to deal with all this effectively on your own.’

The light bulb went on.

Of course! That might well be the answer!

Alex had swiftly solved my inner dilemma.

I needed to source some form of psychological self-preservation if I was going to remain capable of handling the nagging domestic issues.

I decided there and then that I would go and see Father Carroll again.

‘Fantastic idea, Ally.’

‘Well, that’s what you pay me for, lover boy!’

We entered the High Street, and our randomly chosen route began to turn us back toward home.

I took a chance and grabbed her left hand with my right.

She didn’t resist.

I sensed her welcoming the gesture even if she didn’t vocalise her approval.

And yet again, she had eradicated yet another of my personal and persistent conundrums with a wonderful solution.

Alex always knew what to do.

She *always* knew.

26
A CONFIDANTE

Without the ever-invaluable insight of Alex, the bus journey I embarked upon the very next morning would likely never have transpired.

Sadly, it also served to encourage vividly painful memories of Mum.

It didn't seem so long ago that she had been laid to rest in East Park. Yet unbelievably, nearly three years had endured since her passing.

Not a day goes by that I don't wish she had chosen any other option but to end her sufferance in such a lonely, devastating manner.

Alex was aware of my plan for the day and was content to go to Uni instead of accompanying me. In fact, she insisted I go alone.

As for Martin and Bobby, relations were strained to the point whereby I wasn't particularly interested in consulting with them about anything for the time being.

Martin was still aloof to the emotive arguments of our past.

He hadn't mentioned Mum since his return to Nottingham. It wasn't a subject I wished to pressure him on. In fact, it had never seemed fit to raise the issue at all since our reunion in Blackpool.

But at least I knew where I stood with my brother.

Martin would actively avoid any scenario that he deemed potentially upsetting. He no doubt had opinions but would only convey them if, and when, he was ready. And I knew we could always converse in a civilised manner.

Yet Bobby's recent bouts of vocal inflammation were gradually making me wary of speaking to her at all. Even enquiring if she wanted a cup of tea was a question that increasingly carried the likelihood to annoy her. This gradual deterioration in communication was yet another problem I would need to address if it didn't find its own solution very soon.

Such was my hour-long preoccupation with life's rich tapestry that I almost missed my stop. I had made my connection in Nottingham okay, but once the daydreaming started on the second section of the journey, I lost all focus on where I was headed and why.

The first thing that grabbed my attention on alighting the bus was the looming spire that thrust a towering silhouette against the grey sky.

Without hesitation I entered the church grounds and decided to brave the biting breeze to perch on a bench for a moment of contemplation. The thought struck that Mum might not have approved of my visit to see Father Carroll.

On the other hand, it might well have made her proud.

Then again, it was only her state of desperation that forced her into this hallowed territory in the first place.

I don't wish to convey disrespect, but I always held the view that such an environment holds little appeal if all is supposedly well with one's life. Or perhaps that is a terribly sweeping statement?

I apologise in advance if you found offence in it, dear reader. But that's how I always felt about religion.

And my predicament then immediately slapped me full in the face. After all, consultation with a man of the cloth was indicative of being something of a last resort for a non-believer, wasn't it? And I sensed I was certainly reaching out for a last resort in some capacity.

But at least the priesthood managed to draw out Mum's innermost feelings, which is more than I could ever hope to achieve.

I think in retrospect this is why I was originally anti towards Mum's brief connection with the church and its mysterious representative.

In hindsight, my response initially was woefully immature.

But it was as though an imposter had swept into our lives, and then charmingly accomplished with ease what I could not.

Mum was a closed shop regarding her emotions, and I perhaps inherited that trait. Sometimes I wish I could dispense with them altogether, but then I suspect that whilst eradicating the negatives, I would prevent myself from experiencing the highs also.

What is it they say about pain being so close to pleasure?

They're dead right, too.

In my moment of remembrance on the churchyard bench under the whistling branches of a sycamore tree, I attempted to visualise Mum in happier times.

It was a contrived exercise as you might well imagine, dear reader. The source material concerning this little mission was minimal to say the very least.

The ever-present sorrow is that since her death I don't think I've missed Mum as much as I anticipated I would. And I know already that sounds like the most horrendous admission any son could ever make, but there have been too many other subsequent details to encounter which have served to distract my attention.

Almost as though life's events were purposely depriving me of the right to grieve. It's just my outlook. I can't help it, *can I*?

Maybe Martin sensed even less of a connection to Mum than I did? After all, his dealings with her ended when he was barely a teenager. Yet even before that they were hardly in what could be described as a close relationship.

Rightly or wrongly, even with Alex back by my side and offering her regularly inciteful input, the only aspect of life I felt I could rely on was in being true to myself.

To be honest about who I was and be trusting of my gut instincts.

Especially in those moments when I am alone. That's when I manage to briefly attain some strand of clarity.

It always seemed to be that my purity of thought swiftly becomes polluted when other people get involved.

I stared across the path at the neat arrangement of headstones in the tiny cemetery. Stark reminders that it would soon be time to visit Mum in East Park on the anniversary of her burial.

And it was as this very thought travelled solemnly through my conscience, a voice resonated from behind me.

'A pleasure to have your company again, young Jamie.'

The tone was soft, yet the words were conveyed with a certain familiar authority.

As well as being sleeved in that distinctive north-eastern accent.

Over my left shoulder some ten metres away, stood the stout, bearded figure of Father David Carroll.

Hauling myself from the seat, I waved my right hand in greeting, as he shuffled across the lawn towards me and beamed a welcoming smile.

The handshake was warm and affirming.

It instantly eased my nerves.

'Hello, Father. Did you see me come in through the gate?'

He seemed shorter than I remembered. But no older in appearance.

'Oh no. I sensed you were coming here today. Call it a feeling in my water if you like. You look fit and well. It's a joy to behold you.'

The phrase about his water amused me, momentarily. I could only guess that it was uncommon for a man of the cloth to express himself in such terms. Unless he was referring to holy water.

Not that I was overly blessed in experiencing the many chosen idioms of churchmen.

'It's a cold day. Would you be coming in for a drink of tea?'

I nodded gratefully and we made along the path leading to the main church building. His living quarters were in an annex to the south of the plot.

Despite feeling at ease by this point, I wasn't quite sure how to broach the motive for my attendance.

I wasn't even sure of the motive myself if I was honest. But such a trifling issue didn't concern Father Carroll. He was apparently sated by my allegedly anticipated appearance.

Besides, his incredible gift in foresight had already proved to have served him well.

He opened the door to his home and invited me to step inside.

'Take a seat if you will. Trouble at your door again is it, Jamie? It must be…you didn't travel twenty miles to be sociable over a cuppa, I'm quite sure.'

I sat down in the single armchair of his incredibly tiny abode.

In fact, it was the ideal setting for a man living on his own. As I had established just by entering the place, it wasn't designed for accommodating numerous bodies.

'There is always trouble at my door, Father. As you well know.'

His visage was soothing and sympathetic as always.

He turned away from the kitchenette and faced me with tea pot in hand.

'Please…no formalities. Not when you're my welcome guest, anyway. It's *David.* You know me well enough by now.'

I watched him fill the kettle and spoon tea leaves into the pot. As the water gradually came to heat, he joined me in the extremely snug lounge area.

'This is very cosy, David.'

'It's very *cramped*, you mean Jamie. Two's just about all the company it can cope with. *Three* inclines towards an eventual clash of heads!'

I chuckled at his gentle sense of humour.

It was a pleasant change to be in his company.

'Would you like to try a slice of ginger cake? My sister makes it. It is delectable, believe me. But don't take my word for it.'

'I didn't even know you had a sister.'

He winked and feigned an air of intrigue.

'Man of mystery, me.'

He was someone whom I could not fail to admire.

The lack of an authentic male role model in my life had left me short-changed to a large degree. But David Carroll oozed reliability and his authenticity effortlessly demanded my acclaim.

But despite being comfortable in his presence, I was still struggling to commence the conversation I truly wanted to.

Thankfully he observed my difficulty and took the reins.

'Your brother is okay, I take it?'

'Yes. He's fine. At school as a mature. Sailing it by all accounts.'

'And yourself? A-levels? University?'

How could he know these things?

'I did, indeed. Swansea. Journalism. Though I've not been there much this second year yet, unfortunately.'

'Excellent! So, your trek here today is due to concerns about a third party, I take it?'

By this point in the dialogue, I felt rather embarrassed. My intention wasn't clear in my own head and the whole experience already felt a little futile.

But one factor I was certain of was the sincerity of Father Carroll.

He would hear me out and take me seriously.

I just had to decide on what I wanted to say.

In the end, I got frustrated with trying to embroider what was basically a case of me being firmly wedged between the devil and the deep blue sea.

I related the pivotal aspects of the past month to him.

He didn't interrupt once. He encouraged me to keep talking and endured my stuttered silences with total understanding.

Finally, I felt I had managed to exhibit the necessary facts concisely. I sipped my tea as his mind registered events I had depicted.

A full minute or more passed before he raised his initial query.

'Do you think your father is a man of his word? To put a finer point on it...do you think he is telling you the truth about the reasons behind his arrival? Or do you believe there must be another incentive for him to suddenly want to reacquaint with his sons?'

I stared at the contents of my mug and leaned forward in the chair.

'Well, this is mainly why I came, David. I am very lost within it all. I can't see the truth *or* the lies. But matters need to come to a head sooner rather than later. I'm sure of that much.'

Father Carroll remained standing in the kitchenette as he sliced two portions of cake.

'The element of all this that I find rather contrived, Jamie, is the fact that he claims he requires urgent assistance from yourself. Yet he has spent his entire relationship with you wilfully spurning the opportunity for contact. Treating you as non-existent. It doesn't seem logical to me that he suddenly thinks you are in any position to actively protect him.'

I was already feeling sated by the conversation and the inquiring line of the questioning.

It helped dispel my confusion to a large degree.

'I'm not even certain about *who* or *what* I'm being asked to protect him from. He's very vague on the details. But I'm torn between the heart and head scenario. Bobby thinks I'm losing my mind even contemplating giving him the time of day.'

Father Carroll handed me a small plate containing ginger cake.

'Ahh, yes. Hearts and minds. It's the oldest battle in human existence, Jamie. Intelligence versus emotion. The logical and the illogical. There is no one who can truly advise on the correct course of action here.'

To hear such a vague proclamation from this man was disappointing.

In fact, it was the very last thing I wanted to hear at that moment.

'I'm staying back at the house with my brother and Bobby for the time being. Its causing tension as you can imagine. They kind of dragged me into this. I was happy at Swansea. But as yet, I don't feel I'm doing a very good job of sorting things out, though. Nothing has progressed.'

'Oh really? And who may I ask is the genius who designed the blueprint for dealing with such matters?'

I smirked at the sound of Father Carroll's quip and we both sampled some cake.

As he became more embroiled in the emerging scenario his northeastern tongue became broader and less restrained. I didn't expect him to conjure a magical solution on the spot. But just listening to him responding helped off-load some of my mental strain. It was a welcome relief.

Alex was superb at doing the exact same thing, of course. But I was reluctant to over burden her. She had made it clear that she would rather this fly in the ointment gets fished out by someone other than her.

Then we could then perhaps renew our relationship with no family issues in the background.

Father Carroll touched on a very salient aspect.

'Do you feel you might be letting your mother down by allowing your father to communicate with you both again?'

I sensed the ever-lurking upset within me begin to simmer at just the mere mention of my parents in the same sentence.

'It's crossed my mind every single day. I initially didn't want anything to do with him when he first showed up in Nottingham. But I figured quickly that ignoring the problem wouldn't make it disappear. He's already warned me about that very fact, as well. I can't win, can I? What Mum might have thought about it all is anyone's guess.'

Father Carroll narrowed his eyes to a squint as he sipped from his cup.

'The wondrous thing about having faith as I do…is that guesswork is rendered an irrelevance. Precision of thought is *everything* in *all* matters. She would be telling you to conduct this exactly as you are doing. With consideration of all outcomes and with due caution regarding his character.'

A comforting premise, indeed.

'Do you *really* know that is what she might be saying?'

Father Carroll engaged directly with me.

'You came here today as a matter of trust. Did you not? I would never lead your loyalty astray. But there is one thing that I must flag up to you and you must not be offended, Jamie.'

I was all ears, fascinated to absorb the man's inner thoughts.

'You couldn't offend me, David. Please tell me what's on your mind.'

Father Carroll set down his teacup and folded his arms.

His expression did not falter as he conveyed the judgement I had come to hear. And yet I would be jolted by his declaration.

'Employing the precision of thought that I just alluded to, I must convey this to you. I smell a big, dirty rat, Jamie. Do you smell it, too?'

The question was direct.

The terminology completely unexpected.

'I don't trust my father if that's what you mean. In what respect do you mean a rat?'

David Carroll re-positioned himself on the arm of my chair.

His expression was pensive. I was not accustomed to the aura of unwavering concern that he portrayed toward me.

'This goes far *beyond* the concept of mistrust, Jamie. It's his ulterior motive that needs to be unearthed into the open. I sense something severely amiss, here. To the point where you should not need to search too far for the answer you seek. Look closer to home and be guided by the responses of those around you.'

Now I felt a gnawing unease.

'You mean…my brother and Bobby?'

Father Carroll simply stared at me.

'Does anything seem out of place with their perspectives?'

I wasn't completely convinced of the non-specific portrayal he was trying to paint.

'Well, as I said there has been tension created within the home. There still is. But I think in general they are of the opinion that our father shouldn't be anywhere near any of us.'

Father Carroll did not even blink, such was his focus on my reactions.

He leaned ever closer toward me.

'Is that what they profess to you?'

'You don't think my brother would lie about his feelings, do you?'

'No. Your brother is blood. When push eventually comes to shove, he will be with *you* on this. But you said there is friction at home. With whom? Your brother's lady friend?'

I was gradually beginning to grasp Father Carroll's angle on things.

His implication of the potential trouble that lay ahead was almost as though he himself had endured a premonition.

My heart began beating a little faster.

‘Yes, I suppose. She just seems very quick to jump down my throat and dismiss my approach to most things since I got back from Swansea. I can’t weigh her up. She does seem to have changed her mind on matters, yes. She wants me there but by the same token I’m annoying her.’

Father Carroll’s evolving expression now presented a mask of foreboding that I had possibly not expected to witness that day.

‘Do you wish to hear my further feelings on the matter, young Jamie? Please say so if not.’

‘Yes. Definitely. Tell me. That’s why I’ve come.’

Father Carroll straightened his back yet kept me under his unswerving attention. A brittle, frigid silence inhabited the room as I awaited his next statement.

He stroked his grey whiskers as he assessed how best to proclaim his opinion.

‘The return of your father to the family he has abused for years is inconsistent with his thinking. Building bridges is not his policy. You are fully justified in your wariness. Foul play will prevail because he has unworthy desires. But I don’t know how you can begin to combat that which has not yet manifested itself before you. But the black clouds are beginning to form overhead. Believe me, young Jamie. I see them.’

I felt a shiver travel down my spine.

No longer was he the wise and embracing oracle conveying his impartial and measured overview. The demeanour of David Carroll was now seemingly conveying acute personal concern for my welfare.

‘When are you planning your return to Swansea, Jamie?’

‘I haven’t even had chance to consider that yet. The New Year now, probably. I didn’t think the issue here would become so in-depth. There seems to be no end in sight to it. So, I suppose I’ll have to stick around until there is some kind of conclusion to it all.’

Again, Father Carroll adopted the unsightly grimace.

He was now scaring me to a degree I never could have foreseen.

But I slowly realised he was putting me on my guard for good reason.

His eyes glazed as he focussed full attention to me.

The atmosphere around us suddenly embraced a sinister energy.

'I have a query you may find odd. Do you ever see the *good* in your father? Despite everything that has occurred in your life, could you honestly forgive him for his sins against you in the hope that he might possibly be redeemed?'

Another issue that had already deserved my genuine consideration.

My answer avoided direct commitment, to a degree.

'I can't help the nagging thought that to turn him away makes *me* a bad person. I've got to live with myself, after all. Maybe this is what frustrates Bobby. I'm too soft hearted.'

And then Father Carroll delivered what would prove to be his parting sermon.

And it made my blood turn to ice.

He clasped his hands and leaned forward once again.

His rigid glare claimed my undivided concentration.

'Being guided by your heart will put you in the severest of danger in this case, Jamie. You say you need to oversee the conclusion to this business before you return to your other, preferred life. But you can't see when or how peace will resume. Well, I can tell you, Jamie, as God is my protector, that the end is indeed in sight. And the loyalties and allegiances that you perceive among those concerned are convincingly veiled at this current time. But I don't wish to harbour deliberation anymore. It's not my place to do so. I've revealed my summation as you requested of me. That's enough from me, though. Go back to your family. I wish you God speed and all the power to you. But you must prepare for the ultimate conflict. It lies in wait for you. I am so sorry, my son.'

My mind was striving to assimilate the warning.

Father Carroll had always been a reliable and earnest spectator and I had willingly encouraged his assessments. But the prediction he delivered that day was overwhelmingly disconcerting.

We finished our tea and our cake. We said our reluctant goodbyes and I thanked him for his hospitality.

I exited the church grounds with the sorrowful belief that there would be no amicable ending to the quandary that had enshrouded us.

Despite the increasing weight of trepidation, I had at least made my own mind up as to what needed to transpire. I would reveal my decision to Martin and Bobby as soon as I got back to Glenfield Avenue.

It was with increasingly disturbing and deep-rooted reservations, that I deemed we had no alternative but to help our father. We would not turn him away in his purported hour of need.

And whatever God had in store for us, we would readily accept.

What I did not detect as Father Carroll covertly observed my departure from his home, was the grave misgivings *he* now stored in his own conscience.

And the overpowering dread that he now carried in both his head and his heart.

And the fear in his eyes that he had desperately succeeded in suppressing whilst in my company, that now finally allowed private tears to fall.

It was a given rarity that his own powers of provision could induce such a reaction of consuming anxiety within himself.

Of course, I had no knowledge of the fact that David Carroll secretly wished that I, Jamie Andrews, had not visited that day.

For he knew that the misfortune awaiting that boy, was nigh.

Sadly, pre-determined.

Inevitable.

And unavoidable.

27
CONCESSION

The reactions were predictable when I announced my decision the following day. Martin's indifference to consequence only seemed to add fire to Bobby's furious bluster.

But they wanted an answer to the issue.

So, I bluntly presented mine to them with little due care for their responses. Full agreement as a trio was a pipedream.

I left the house to meet our father who was already on his way from his digs at Mansfield at my request.

Understandably, I gave no mention of my unnerving visit to Father Carroll to Bobby or Martin. And as before, Alex agreed that her absence would be wholly beneficial to a smooth negotiation.

If Jim Andrews should ever have suspected that he was being spied on then I was quite convinced his current if frail façade of diplomacy would be abruptly dispensed with.

The Lunch Stop café was again designated as the preferred meeting place. Midday was the appointed time. As before, I was there early and at the table by the front window.

My heart thumped a symphony of apprehension as I awaited the arrival of the unknown.

He had no grasp of my proposition yet.

I kept a keen vigil on the scene outside and the door of the premises.

Much as it pained me to admit it, and much as it went completely against all my gut instincts, an olive branch seemed to be the only possible method of encouraging our father to disappear again.

Whether such an apparent contrast of intention would offer this result, only time would tell. But the need for deliberation was surely over.

It was time for deed, not word.

I had been in my seat for ten minutes when the young waitress approached and asked me if I wished to order.

The last thing on my mind was food.

I politely declined her offer, claiming I was waiting for someone.

I was about to take a massive gamble that could, and likely would, affect lives indelibly.

Not just my own, but also the seemingly contented existence that Martin and Bobby were previously enjoying.

Martin knew I was here and that our father was about to be invited back into the fray.

It felt like a ludicrous, lose-lose scenario for all of us.

I felt rotten inside.

Physically upset; mentally drained; spiritually on the wane.

But despite all the signals now repeatedly pulsing their warnings, I had ultimately convinced myself that the course of action I had selected was the correct one.

I had been in my chair for nearly twenty-five minutes when he eventually appeared outside.

He glared at me through the large front window of the café and nodded in acknowledgement before approaching the door.

I just stared back. I felt nothing for him.

My father's imposing form strode through the doorway carrying a small holdall which I presumed were possibly his remaining life's possessions. Or somebody else's, which was not beyond possibility.

As on the first occasion in this chosen arena, he momentarily studied the curious faces at the occupied tables as though confirming he was not under scrutiny.

Finally, he centred his attention to me as he unzipped his coat.

'Breakfast, son?'

'Nothing for me.'

'Suit yourself.'

A minute elapsed whilst he attended the serving counter and then came to my table with a mug of coffee in hand. He draped his coat over the back of the moulded seat opposite and slammed his backside into it. He saw little scope for small talk and subsequently wasted no time in getting to the point.

'I hope I've not come here for nothing again, lad. I'm becoming bored and I'm running out of tolerance.'

You wouldn't have thought I was his lifeline, would you?

The inherent ingratitude and insensitivity of the man was consistently astounding.

I tried to dissect the truth behind those devious yet apparently desperate eyes of his.

They yielded no clue as to the authenticity of his soul.

Again, I used the opportunity to study the scarred mask of self-interest that he exhibited so proudly. Etched with ridges and peppered with damaged tissue, he effortlessly portrayed an aura of menace and controversy to the uninitiated observer.

But he was no figure of fear to me anymore.

I had exposed him once.

I was fully prepared in case I was called to repeat the feat.

His features betrayed a life of danger. He had courted dissension for nearly six decades.

Supposedly untouchable.

Certainly penetrable.

Disregard for priority had led him along a chosen path of violence, where infliction of pain was the customary currency and death the ultimate if only occasional calling card.

Never once had he been given cause to assess the sufferance he left in his wake. The countless lives he must have invaded and destroyed.

Now irretrievable. Forgotten by him for sure.

No guilt. No penance. No conscience.

But now the tables were purported to have turned.

Now this self-appointed fiend of repute was allegedly tasting his own brand of insidious medicine.

And there he was. Somehow still living and breathing.

Across the table from his youngest boy.

Crawling back to his offspring.

Begging for help.

My brief study of his image, whilst being bombarded with arrows of foreboding, had not dissuaded me from answering his question.

And strangely enough, when I spoke, the words came easily and with conviction.

'Okay. What do you need me to do?'

His eyes widened. But not with pleasure or surprise. More likely that he recognised the scent of opportunity, and it excited him.

But the frontage of my father soon resumed its customary, battle-ravaged veneer.

He leaned across the table to inform me in a villainous whisper.

'Primarily…I need cash.'

I scanned the interior of the café to ensure we were not overheard.

'How much? And when?'

There was little hesitation in his request.

It was uncanny. As though he already knew I would comply with his needs. His tone was incredibly serene considering I could just as easily have told him to sling his hook.

'Twenty-five thousand. As soon as.'

I sat there staring at, of all things, his flaring nostrils. As though they were reacting to a long-denied source of oxygen. He could already sense the pathway being cleared for him and his features slightly contorted in greedy anticipation of my award.

He was an unpleasant specimen for sure. Both inside and out.

And as I now re-discovered, self-serving beyond all thresholds.

And then a very unsettling thought began to descend.

How could he know I had such a quantity of money to gift him?

If I were penniless, would he have pursued me so avidly?

Would he have even bothered coming to Nottingham if the family coffers were empty?

Father Carroll's dour assessment now carried real gravitas.

Motives. What was the *incentive* for his return?

'You never said you wanted money.'

My father tried his hardest not to laugh in my face.

His broad smirk displayed an uneven arrangement of stained and crooked teeth in their full technicolour glory.

'Now come on, son. What do you think this is? Bad people only deal in money. And they won't accept luncheon vouchers. Now, are you getting the dollar for me or are we wasting our time even sitting here?'

His cold dismissal of consideration for any other living beings was profoundly despairing.

There really was only one person in his life that truly mattered.

Survival of the fittest was the be all and end all for my father.

'That's a lot to ask for.'

'Not in my world, son. Now when do I see it?'

'I'll need time. Today is Tuesday. I need to go to the bank to arrange the withdrawal. They might only authorise me a cheque, though.'

Again, the toxic grin emerged under his nose.

'Grow up, lad. It's cash only, I'm afraid.'

He was wittingly stirring my impatience with his attitude.

'But what if the bank won't play ball?'

He shook his head in misguided expectation.

'I've every confidence in your charm paying off, my boy. I need the money in note form. The people I deal with don't want a trail of receipts. If you get my drift? If I went to them with a cheque, I'd likely lose a finger or two for the insult.'

I continued to mentally absorb the creature sitting opposite.

A despicable, callous, egotistical freak.

Was he truly the person responsible for my arrival into this world?

I couldn't resist taking the conversation along a little detour.

His presumptions had angered me.

'What if I don't have the funds? Then where do we stand?'

His reply now intrigued me.

And as it registered, I became perturbed by his assuredness.

'Look, son. Don't fuck me about. You've got more than enough. And I know you can get it for me.'

I wasn't going to bend over that easily.

'You're not showing me much appreciation as your last hope considering you're supposed to be up to your neck in it.'

He moved his face closer to mine. I was now beginning to test his restraint and he started to let his act of cool slip a little. I was tormenting him. I was dangling the carrot he coveted with a very long stick.

He clenched a fist and lightly banged the tabletop between us.

'Listen, lad. Along the paths I walk, appreciation is what you feel when the bullet just misses the back of your head and hits the brickwork. *That's* the point you find yourself appreciative. *That's* the point when you know someone is looking out for your interests. Not before. Not after. Just that moment. *That's* what counts. Nothing else.'

Well, he invited the obvious return of serve, dear reader.

'Not even your own family?'

My wilful prod didn't even cause the mildest reaction in him.

'Don't worry. I know the score. You all resent my very existence. So, we'll keep the history lesson out of things, yes? We'll stick to talking business. The deal is simply this. That once I'm off my creditor's radar, I'll be off *yours*. Fair enough?'

I felt like telling him he was getting nothing from me.

I truly wanted to antagonise the bastard.

Just for the sake of seeing the fireworks erupt.

'You miss the point. You could at least *pretend* to be interested in your sons. Even if it's just a passing acknowledgement toward the fact that your children even exist. That would be *something*.'

He begrudgingly shook his head again and perhaps muttered the first and only conveyance of honesty in his entire life.

'It's not in my nature, son. Sorry. I don't do affection very well. But you don't need me to tell you that, do you?'

Can you believe he openly chuckled at admitting to his own parental incompetence and abstention from responsibility?

My own father, literally wallowing in his reputation as a failure.

Not a shred of contrition. But why on earth should I have felt such emptiness in acceptance of such a fact?

After all, Bobby had been hammering the same message into my head for several days, now.

Yet for better or for worse, there I was.

Succumbing to my foolish sense of moral obligation.

And with absolutely no idea who I must have inherited such an affliction from.

My next question sounded defeatist, but I wanted to discover just how much of this scheme my father had planned before our meeting.

'I suppose I have no choice in all this.'

He merely lifted his mug of coffee and his eyes narrowed as he drank.

So naturally, I probed him again.

'What about your mate in Mansfield?'

'What of him?'

'Are you still going to be lodging there?'

He paused before answering.

Another loyal associate about to be abandoned.

'I bailed out this morning before boarding the train. Told him my sons are putting me up from now on. Well, for a while anyway.'

The despicable stench of ingratitude oozed from his every pore.

He had no scruples or standards.

Was everyone just a stepping-stone to his personal gain?

I rose to my feet.

Not realising that during this development, I had completely dispensed with the concerns conveyed by Father Carroll only the day before.

I just wanted to roll with momentum now.

'Finish your drink, then. Let's get out of here and let's get this over with.'

*****

When I opened the front door at Glenfield Avenue, Bobby was in the hallway drying her hair after a shower. Her afternoon shift beckoned. On noting my entrance, she switched off the drier and threw me an expression that conveyed both expectancy and worry.

She instinctively knew who was waiting outside beyond the front gate.

She was still attired in her bath robe.

This needed remedying before anything else.

'You might want to get dressed.' I muttered, unsure of her current mood.

She looked past my shoulder as if to see through the door.

'Is he out there? Now?'

I nodded reservedly.

'Fuck my life, Jamie boy. No going back now then is there. Gimme a second.'

She re-appeared a minute later, now donning t-shirt and jeans.

I pulled open the front door and gestured for my father to come in. He stepped over the threshold not unlike a strutting celebrity meeting a queue of fans wanting autographs.

I enclosed him by shutting the door.

The wolf was now firmly entrenched in the fold.

He placed his holdall on the hallway floor and immediately let his attention centre on Bobby. who was in the lounge doorway carrying the response of a rabbit caught in the headlights.

He immediately grew a smile across his face. The pleasure of seeing her again seemed genuine for once.

I could barely look as he conveyed his insipid greeting.

'Hello, Roberta. Long time, no see! You missed me, then?'

I reluctantly engaged with her disparaging stare.

I knew she was beyond furious, but I was also thankful that her tone remained moderately affable.

'You can dispense with the mock pleasantries, Jim. Let's just get this sorted, okay?'

He turned to me and performed a perverted wink.

'Now I do like a girl that just wants to get down to business. Saves a lot of wasted time. First things first, though. You got any beer in?'

It wasn't even one p.m. Bobby shook her head in perceived disgust. I was trying to maintain a diplomatic atmosphere but sensed I was losing that battle already.

'I can get some. There's an offy around the corner.' I pledged.

'Second thoughts. Cancel the beer. Whiskey is the tipple for the occasion, I think. To celebrate our little reunion. Talking of which, where's my elder son?'

'Martin is at school. He finishes at three-thirty.'

'Oh, yes. I *know* he does!'

'Yes. Of course, you do. He'll be home about four. Give or take.'

'Won't he be overjoyed to set eyes on *me*!'

Bobby folded her arms and tried not to vocally disparage my father's presence.

Meanwhile he opted to take himself on a quick inspection of the house before setting himself down on the sofa.

'Nice little place you've netted here, boys and girls. I think this settee will suit me fine for the foreseeable. If that's alright with everyone?'

He was enjoying playing the unwelcome tormentor.

Just as well, as the role suited him down to the ground.

Bobby broke her barely tolerant resolve.

'Don't get too fucking comfortable. This is a short-term fix.'

Predictably, she encouraged a cackle from my father.

'Don't panic, Roberta. I'll be out of your hair as soon as possible. Unless you decide you like having me around again, that is. I've not got to rush off anywhere. We could even re-enact the good old days. I'm up for it if you are. You're still a fine-looking woman.'

Bobby duly took the bait and lost her temper.

My endeavours to keep matters on a civil footing had failed within two minutes of him being in the blessed house.

'Don't be disgusting…you sicko! I'm engaged to your son, you fucking inbred. So far as I'm concerned, the sooner you're gone the better. I'm off to work. Please don't wait up.'

Bobby brushed past me to the bedroom to don her work tunic. My father's inane sense of fun remained plastered across his weathered features until we both heard her tramp along the hallway and slam the front door in her wake.

He seemed wholly amused by the entire charade.

'Moody cow, that one. Always was. Good in the sack, though. Knows her stuff.'

My stomach turned in disbelief at what I was hearing.

For a moment I had completely forgotten that the thug sprawled across my settee was a relative. If he wasn't blood, I would perhaps have punched his lights out there and then.

Once again, I attempted to pour oil over troubled waters but sensed imminent failure.

'You need to toe the line if we are going to get through this cleanly. We don't want trouble in this house. Understand?'

He craned his neck to focus on me directly.

'I promise you won't even know I'm here, son. Now then…are you going out for that Scotch, or what?'

'I'll lock you in. I'll be ten minutes.'

My father issued a demonic snigger. He kicked off his shoes and stretched his arms behind his head.

'Thank you…I'm so…*appreciative*. I know you like that word, don't you. I think you like having me here already.'

The echo of his snide commentary followed me out of the house.

If I previously suspected that accommodating him might be a bad idea, then I was now absolutely convinced it was.

But I had crossed the line now.

I had no scope to reconsider circumstances anymore.

Jim Andrews was in charge.

And it was far too late for regrets.

28
REALISATION

‘You see, son, the thing no one understands about me, is how difficult and distressing my life has been.’

Martin and I watched my father stumble around the dining table in search of the whiskey bottle. It was a sorry and pathetic experience.

The Scotch might have softened his edge initially but was now having the opposite effect. His mouth was now a conduit for a never-ending procession of self-pity, profanity, and projected bitterness.

I knew from first-hand experience that the policy of drowning sorrows was a downward spiral to feeling a whole lot worse than was necessary. It was also repellent to friends.

But the self-deceit arrives via the perception, that if you bemoan your place in things often enough, then that negative perception gradually hones itself as the actual truth.

Yet I swiftly figured that instead of switching off to his mumbling chronicle of despair, I might find it useful to listen to him.

Although the current subject under debate would never have been my first choice.

‘I know you both blame me for what happened to your mother. But believe me, she was in a much worse state *before* I met her. And I tried to do my best for her before you two came along. But in the beginning, she was firmly under the spell of her parents and that fucking sister of hers. Control freaks they were. The lot of ‘em. It was a battle to see them off, I can tell you. In effect…I *saved* your mother from them. But nobody acknowledges that, do they?’

I glanced at Martin, who as usual was content to offer no opinion whatsoever.

Neither of us had any recollection of our grandparents. And certainly not of our Aunt Shirley. She had surrendered to the ogre that was her brother-in-law before we were even conceived. Mum had rarely mentioned her, either.

My brother had observed our father remove the seal from the whiskey bottle at just after four p.m. on his return home.

He simply dropped his school bag and made himself a sandwich.

He wasn't about to let his routine be interrupted by the turgid human being that was occupying his space on the settee.

Three hours later, that same bottle was now three quarters empty.

Like me, he had tolerated our father's inebriated rambling.

Martin was a pivotal part of events but had nurtured the trick of seemingly being detached from making any contribution.

Until of course there was a point of issue that would likely inflame tempers.

This occasional problem had been swiftly escalated by our father who had committed the one disclosure that I wished he had kept secret.

Namely, the amount of money he had requested from us.

Martin inevitably had a vested opinion on this. Oh yes, indeed.

'I don't think the bank will issue that much currency over the counter, Jamie. A printed bank cheque yes because it carries guarantee of funds by default. But not used notes. It's a security risk to all concerned. And nobody needs to deal with that much physical currency these days, anyway.'

Jim Andrews threw a scornful grimace toward his elder son as he precariously directed the lip of the whiskey bottle over his empty tumbler.

'Well, well. Who rattled *your* fucking cage, smart arse? Suddenly found your tongue, have you? What the fuck do *you* know about it, anyway? Suddenly a finance expert, are you? That's what banks do, you know. Issue money. Stick to what you do best, son. Teddy bears and kids' cartoons.'

Martin's desire to barter the point only served to add further distress to our father's obviously reactive temperament.

'Well, I know for a fact that in The States any withdrawal over ten thousand dollars is subject to a client report and finance company procedural assessment so it can be lawfully deposited and then traced.'

Thankfully, under considerable if unwitting encouragement *not* to do so, our father opted to retain control of his ever-simmering anger and switched position in his chair to turn his back on Martin.

He then proceeded to pour his umpteenth shot down his throat.

'Jamie, son. Tell your brother to shut his stupid mouth. And also tell him that you will be able to arrange things at the bank for me tomorrow. Go on…*tell him.*'

I honestly could have well done without this futile sideshow, dear reader.

Seriously pointless bickering was going to get us nowhere.

As I studied Martin shaking his head in what was quickly revealed as unbridled amusement, my priority was to douse the growing antagonism that was being promoted between them.

Martin's comments were purposely causing a potentially toxic atmosphere to become a distinct reality.

But it wasn't *his* fault that he only dealt in logic and fact, was it?

Our father would never be able to understand such concepts.

The casual observer could rightfully proclaim that Jim Andrews' currently delicate status should by default dissuade him from reacting negatively to anything.

He had a lazy and vindictive mouth which unfortunately we just had to accept. But if he made any move corresponding to the violence of before, he knew he could kiss his money goodbye.

Yet, Martin was correct. And I was willing to back him up.

'So long as I can prove who I am then I don't see an issue. The funds are there. But they won't have it ready for at least a day or two. No bank would do that any quicker.'

Our father didn't deal in maybes.

The Jim Andrews of old was trying to seep through the cracks of the comparatively civilised version that pointed toward me with malt glass in hand.

Anything that didn't align positively with his plan he was ever ready to shoot down.

He stammered a slurred, bleak warning.

'Tomorrow, my lad, I will be coming to the bank *with* you. And believe me…there won't be any problem at all.'

Despite my best hopes and covert contingency, most of my father's objectionable characteristics were now being ably exhibited.

The greed and the malice were on show.

The bully was back in the room.

The harsh, heartless individual that I had pledged to help was intent on giving me every reason to make me wonder why.

'You might be our father and I might have agreed to shield you, but rein yourself in. You're not in authority here. I am. I hold the cards. Not you.'

His screwed and spiteful visage centred its attention on me as he rose to his feet and staggered across the carpet.

'I've said it before, and I say it again. You've got balls Jamie, my lad. I must take my hat off to you on that. You must get that from me. But I'm *back* and you'd better get used to it. We all secretly know who truly wears the big hat around here, now. Even if you don't have the good sense or the honesty to admit to it.'

I was now losing my own composure and willingly went nose to nose with him.

'Sit…the fuck…*down.* And calm the fuck down. Bobby will be home from work in a minute. Try and sober yourself up for her. You think she will be impressed with you acting up? This is her house as much as anyone's. If she sees you pissed up, she'll have you out. Pull yourself together for Christ's sake.'

He wouldn't back away, but at least I had now given him cause for amusement instead of confrontation.

'Don't you worry about the wonderful Roberta. She will *never* be upset with me. She knows which side her bread's buttered.'

It was becoming a humungous effort not to lay a hand on him.

'You're talking crap, now. And if she knew how much money you were getting from me, she'd probably kick *me* out along with you.'

My father's expression leaned toward the notion of sobriety for a split second. I appeared to have struck a chord in his head which seemed to cause him genuine deliberation before he bit back.

'Oh? Suddenly, it's *your* money, is it? Well, well. That's a turn up for the books. Then again, you always were a naïve little sod.'

Martin decided to make his excuses and retire to bed.

And I couldn't say I blamed him.

The company was to say the least, testing.

He signalled for me to follow him into the hallway as our father successfully navigated his backside onto a chair at the kitchen table.

'Tell, Bobby I'm tired. Its near enough to the truth. I'm sick of the sight of him already. Jamie…I hope you know what you are doing. Our father is a wild animal. And he's out of the cage now. I would say goodnight, but it looks like being anything but a good one on current form.'

I nodded dejectedly. Remorse pummelled my conscience.

What the hell had I done?

I hugged Martin and watched him enter his bedroom and close the door. There was little option for me but to return to the lounge and continue to try and abate my father's whimsical outbursts.

Why did I agree to get him the Scotch? I must have been out of my mind on that score as well as everything else.

Well, of course I was. I had been out of my mind for years.

Slumped at the dining table, Jim Andrews recommenced his deranged lecture.

'Fuckin' know-all, your big brother. Isn't he?'

'He's smarter than anyone I know. Yes. So? What about it?'

Our father didn't venture to continue his point.

Instead, his mind focussed back to the earlier digression about the money.

'I've been thinking while I've been drinking, son. I'm going to have to increase my demand.'

I felt my feet being pulled from underneath me.

The worst-case scenario was rapidly becoming a disastrous truth.

Why didn't I listen to Father Carroll?

My head should have overruled *everything* else.

My father knew he could back me into a corner now I had exposed a chink of sentimentality.

'There is no more money. What the hell have you been doing to owe so much?'

He didn't even have the manners to look at me as he spoke.

'It's got to be thirty grand, now. And the longer you dawdle about getting it, the more the interest piles up. Not my fault. That's the rules of business, I'm afraid. I hope things come together tomorrow, son.'

Already being submerged by personal guilt, I now fully realised I should never have succumbed to his hard luck story.

I should have let the vultures have him.

A mistake I could not rectify.

The onerous figure that was my father looked to be gradually surrendering to slumber as he nodded at the table.

I could only hope that fate still held some influence over events and that the three of us would come through the other side of this unscathed.

Aside being a little lighter in the coffers.

The financial loss would surely be worth it.

I envisaged a nightmare situation on the horizon if I did not bring closure on matters and ensure his exit.

The sooner the better.

29
GREEN SHOOTS OF DIVISION

Saturday evening. Ten-fifty p.m.

'Where is he?'

Bobby stood in my bedroom doorway having again just walked in from work. She had hands on hips and displayed a disgruntled scowl. I surmised that, having been kept back on overtime, she wasn't in the frame of mind for guessing games.

I sat up on the camp bed and yawned.

I rubbed my eyes to gain some clarity on the impatient figure hovering before me.

'Where's who?' I muttered.

It was a bad move to answer a question with a question.

Schoolboy error, I think they call it.

But at that particular juncture, answering a question with a question was nothing less than calamitous.

'Santa Claus. Who you *think*? YOUR FUCKING *FATHER*! THAT'S FUCKING *WHO*!'

Oh dear.

Her frosty disposition of recent weeks hadn't thawed to any noticeable degree.

'No need to shout I'm only three yards away. What's the problem? Is the house on fire?'

Humour was wholly inappropriate.

Yes, dear reader I know.

You don't need to enlighten me on that score.

Another bad move. I should have been aware of that much, at least.

'I'll tell you what the fucking problem is, Jamie boy. You jumped through a lot of hoops to yank thirty big ones from our savings and gave it to that piece of scum, yesterday. Who then proceeds to stuff it in his bag. He wasn't here when I left for work at dinner time, and I come home from work and he's still not fucking here. So, I repeat the question hoping it penetrates through your cloth ears and into your sponge of a brain. Where has he gone with our money? I think I'm entitled to ask, don't you?'

I was developing a headache already.

'Bobby…please put the kettle on. Don't wake Martin.'

'I think I'd *like* Martin awake. He's the only one around here that talks any frigging sense anymore. Yes! That's how screwed up all this has become!'

I couldn't argue with that.

I staggered upward to my feet and navigated a path to the toilet. As I evacuated my bladder, I could hear Bobby banging and crashing in the hallway.

The very last thing I needed was further conflict with her.

Our relationship had taken a fractious turn of late. She was constantly on edge, but not so much due to *fear* of my father.

Moreover, she seemed unduly curious as to his movements and whereabouts. Almost concerned at times.

She had a persistent whim to know where he was and what he was up to during the day. But he was apparently no longer the figure of dread that not so long ago had her cowering for cover in her own shadow.

I told her I still had my hands firmly at the helm regarding the situation, but things were fragmenting a little.

I entered the lounge to be greeted by further disapproval.

'Look, Jamie! He doesn't seem to be planning on a comeback any time soon. Everything he brought with him has gone.'

She was becoming consumed by rage, and I couldn't fully understand what it was that had caused such an inflamed reaction.

And she was now aggravating my own temper in the process.

'What are you so pissed off about? That's the whole idea, isn't it? Pay him and get rid of him? I thought you'd be pleased.'

Yet another ill-advised comment. I was on a roll.

'*PLEASED*? HE'S WALKED OUT OF HERE WITH ALL THAT MONEY AND WE HAVEN'T A SCOOBY DOO WHERE HE IS.

WHAT IS THERE TO BE FUCKING *PLEASED* ABOUT? TELL ME THAT, IF YOU CAN.'

This wasn't making any sense whatsoever, anymore.

Only two weeks ago she was adamant she didn't want him around us at any cost. Now she's complaining that he's not visible!

I literally scratched my head in trying to work my way through the ever-thickening fog that was building within the walls of number thirty-two, Glenfield Avenue.

'Perhaps he's gone back up north? He said he wasn't going to hang around.' I tentatively offered as a reason.

She turned on me carrying a glare of sheer venom.

I felt physically vulnerable myself, by this point.

There was an air of combusting desperation about her.

'Did he not say a word about leaving for Blackpool, then? Surely to Christ he didn't just piss off with the cash?' she barked.

Her uncivil attitude was pushing my buttons now.

'He said nothing. But I'm not surprised. He's not big on communicating the finer details, is he? Blackpool is just my assumption.'

She shook her head and rubbed her eyes.

'By now he could be fucking *ANYWHERE*! Conniving, conning bastard, that he is.'

Bobby seemed intent on unleashing her wrath on me.

Then a thought struck.

I insisted my father kept quiet about the increased amount.

And he swore to me that no one else would be told.

'How did you know it was thirty grand?'

She suddenly altered her demeanour as my query registered.

'What?'

'The thirty grand. Did Martin or our father mention it to you?'

Bobby seemed to be caught off guard by my genuine query.

'Who do you think told me? You can't trust him and his mouth. Here's me earning a pittance on regular afternoon shifts and you're giving our savings away to that arsehole!'

Despite our legal arrangement with the solicitor, it was rather presumptuous of her to refer to the money as hers.

And it wasn't the first time, either.

Bobby shadowed me into the kitchen as I switched the kettle on.

Another idea lit up in my head as she hovered behind me.

'Perhaps he's gone back to Mansfield to his mate?'

Again, my suggestion only served to vex her further.

'The manipulative waste of oxygen. How can you be so fucking chilled about this, Jamie? You may as well give him *everything*. The house. The lot. Cos he will only blow it. You'll likely not even see him again. He's a parasite and a born cheat.'

The sound of her irate voice was now beginning to cause me severe annoyance.

How did I ever become the target for blame?

I was anti this plan from the off, wasn't I?

'Yes, Bobby. And he's *gone*! Just as we wanted. Just as *you* wanted. Now fucking give me a break, will you? This is no picnic for me either you know. I want it done with just as much as anyone. I've missed two months of Uni dealing with this mess.'

Her eyes were untypically tinged with animosity and her tongue became even more hostile.

This wasn't the Bobby Jones I thought I knew.

'Give *you* a break? I asked you back here to *help* us, Jamie. Not clear us out!'

She had overstepped the mark, now.

If she wanted to fall out with me then reluctantly that was the path I would also choose to follow.

'You *what*? Short memory, haven't you? Who was it that came and got you away from that hellish existence up on the coast? Who was it that gave you the chance of a new life? Who helped you get back your self-respect and start afresh? Who encouraged you to take the job and build your confidence up? Don't you fucking *dare* lecture me about anything ever again, Bobby. You'd be destitute and in the gutter without me. It's not an exaggeration to say you might not even still be alive the way things were going in Blackpool. And by the way, the money you are so keen to worry about was a gift to me from my friend. It will never be OURS. We are just custodians of Henry's memory. The money he left behind is not the be all and end all for me. It doesn't matter. It's not life and death.'

She was unrepentant and pressed for the joust to continue.

'And you think that Henry would approve of you giving a fair chunk of it to that low life of a father of yours?'

I gritted my teeth before things really went beyond retraction.

She wasn't getting the drift at all.

She had breached her bounds by a country mile this time.

'What Henry would have wanted is not *your* concern! But he would have trusted *me* to try and do the right thing. And that is all I have done. As for you, I don't know what message you are trying to send me these days. You must have a fucking groove in your arse cheeks from sitting on the fence so much. At least I've made a *decision*. Rightly or wrongly, who knows? Time will tell. But now I've got to live with it. If you can't handle the way I do things, it's just tough. I've fucking had enough of it all. If we ever set eyes on him again, then I'll be as amazed as you. And if we don't ever see him again, then its mission accomplished. Now get off your high horse and get off my back.'

I exhaled a long relieving, exhausting breath.

I had said my piece.

For once in her life, Bobby Jones had finally been stunned into silence.

A fragile ceasefire was temporarily resumed.

But her remonstrations had unnerved me considerably.

Glenfield Avenue was steadily evolving from a haven and into a focal point of persistent conflict.

She didn't summon the desire to respond further and brushed past me to go to bed.

Whatever the opinion was about my father's scheming, the lost money, or my command of the situation, I knew I could hold my head high in claiming to have acted with the three of us as my absolute and only priority.

Yet worryingly, I now sensed even darker clouds forming above.

Possibly the very same clouds Father Carroll had forecast.

But I could not source a possible reason why this should be the case.

For the first time in the close-knit relationship that the three of us shared and supposedly cherished, I detected serious unrest on the cards.

How that might present itself remained to be seen.

But it was coming.

30
THE SHADOW OF DECEIT

Six days had crawled by and led us to the end of November.

We had heard nothing from our father.

This ongoing dynamic had drastically altered my perceptions of the entire situation.

Don't get me wrong. His absence was somewhat relieving and the recently arising friction in the house had reduced considerably.

But Bobby knew.

And Martin knew.

And I knew.

He *would* be back.

After all, it could never have been as easy as all that.

Just to give him what he wanted and watch him walk into the sunset a happy man?

Not a chance.

Jim Andrews was consistently unpredictable.

Always liable to turn up at any given time.

And unlike the privilege denied to his sons, it would be Jim Andrews who would be making the next decisive move.

Fate's role was currently academic.

The sense of smothering disconcertion now enveloped every aspect of our lives.

*****

I was with Alex on the following Friday in Nottingham City centre. Christmas was already in our thoughts. We'd browsed several shops and bought tickets for an early afternoon screening of Casino Royale. I was eager to see James Bond in his all-new blond-haired guise.

We had immersed ourselves in one of those infrequent pockets of contentment that never seem to last.

And as half expected, our plans were quickly rendered null and void.

We would never get to see the film that day.

Nor would we make our table booking at the Italian restaurant afterwards.

All in all, it was supposed to be a wonderful afternoon.

Quality time that would supposedly present an unfailing mixture of excitement, romance, and laughs.

But our hopes were swiftly left flailing in the brewing hurricane.

As we held hands and decided to exit the Victoria Arcade and head for the cinema, the phone call duly came through.

The inevitable S.O.S.

Bobby sounded distraught on the other end of the line as Alex instinctively rolled her eyes in justifiably cynical fashion.

Our private schedule had been well and truly hijacked.

I had been summoned back to Glenfield Avenue.

*****

Jim Andrews was in no mood for delay. He scowled at Bobby and spat his impatience across the lounge.

'Where the fuck is he, then?'

'Jesus Christ, Jim. You've just this minute watched me talk to him on the phone. He's coming back from Notts. He'll be an hour yet. You didn't exactly give us much notice you were dropping by to say hello.'

Jim Andrews was flustered and looked like a man at breaking point.

Luckily Bobby Jones knew just how to keep him relaxed.

'Did you sort the issue with this McCafferty fella?'

'Never mind that for now. Where's the retard?'

Bobby looked at Jim with a degree of contempt.

'Don't call him that. His name is Martin, he is your son. And he is at school.'

The sentiment didn't register with him one iota.

‘What…*again*?’

‘Well, yes. It’s a kind of legal obligation to attend every day, you know. They give you weekends off though! So anyway, back to business. What’s the story from Blackpool? And how the fuck did you get here in that old banger out the front?’

Jim Andrews glared at the twelve-year-old Ford Mondeo through the front window. His gaze never diverted from the inert wintry vista beyond the glass.

‘The car belongs to a mate. And the story from Blackpool, Roberta dear, is that I need more dollar. That is why I am making this flying visit.’

She watched him sink into the armchair and kick off his boots.

‘What? The cheeky bastards!’

Jim Andrews cackled at the sound of Bobby’s indignant reply.

‘Come on, Roberta. You know the game better than anyone. There’s always another stiff to pay. The fucking queue never ends once word gets about you can pay up.’

‘But surely thirty covered it?’

‘Not quite. Don’t worry. Our rainy-day fund is already looking healthy. I just want a top up. Bit of security, you know? A few more crumbs from the table, so to speak.’

Bobby perched on the arm of Jim’s chair and proceeded to play with his shirt collar.

He looked up to her and smirked slyly.

‘You can arrange the withdrawal, can’t you? Save the waiting around? You’ve done a fine job of fooling the masses so far.’

‘No, sorry. My name’s not on it.’

He shunted forward from her touch and looked her squarely in the eye.

‘Are you winding me up, Roberta? You mean to tell me we are sitting on a fortune and he’s the only one that can unlock the chest? Some fucking level of trust that is from you!’

‘I don’t know what you’re complaining about, Jim. Your first bite at the cherry was pretty hefty. I didn’t think you’d want more than ten. If

I suspected that you were going for the job lot, I wouldn't have told you about the inheritance in the first place. We can't leave your sons bone dry, so we can't.'

Jim softened his attitude.

He reached up and held her hand in a very rare gesture of affection.

His tone altered to convey the same.

'Don't panic. They won't be left destitute. Perhaps another ten…or maybe twenty should alleviate things properly for you and me. And we can sell that diamond on your finger. I don't know how you're going to make your big reveal to them though. You've gotten pretty tight with the boys this past two years, haven't you?'

Her attention fell briefly to her engagement ring.

'That was the whole idea, wasn't it?'

'Yes, Roberta. Yes, indeed. I'm not criticising you. I'm *praising* you. You've been a good ally to the pair of them. But when they realise the truth of things it could kick off badly. Just saying…I hope you're prepared.'

Bobby gazed straight ahead into space as if lost in thought.

'Well, I don't feel worthy of praise, Jim. I'm doing an unforgivable thing. They are like *my* own brothers, now. The betrayal will be horrendous for us all.'

Jim Andrews sat forward and attempted to obtain her full attention as he placed his hands on her shoulders.

His demeanour was untypically calm and persuasive.

His ambition was now so close to bearing fruit.

'Hey…don't start getting a conscience on me, girl. You're far from squeaky clean in all this What we are doing here will mop up a lot of mess for the pair of us. Once it's over then we are off everybody's wanted list and free as birds to fly wherever we wish.'

Bobby shook her head as upset swiftly took a firm grip.

She covered her face with both hands as the reality of the impending scenario hit home.

Jim adjusted position and cradled Bobby's moistened features.

‘Hey, come on, this is the order of things. No tears now. This is the way it must be. You can’t hide from your destiny, Roberta. We all make mistakes. And we all do bad things. It’s our way. We do stuff and we run. What’s important is the running. If you stop and look back for just one second, then you’re fucked. *We’re* fucked! Cut out the emotional stuff. Don’t go all soggy on me now. There’s no space for that. We are too near the finish line, now. You’ve already done the hard work.’

She wiped her eyes and nose with the sleeve of her cardigan.

‘Jesus, Jim…you make it sound like a doddle. I’m such a bad person for this.’

He smirked as if impressed by her admission.

‘So…you’re a bad person. Fine. So am I. But the key thing is not to dwell on it. Keep moving forward, my girl. It’s the only way. Living with the knowledge and ignoring the guilt is a skill and takes practice.’

‘I don’t think I can live with it, Jim.’

‘Rubbish. It’s when the regret doesn’t affect you anymore. That’s the *real* deal. That’s when you know you’ve mastered it. This is just business. Pure and simple.’

Her eyes engaged directly with his.

‘It’s not business, Jim. It’s treachery.’

Jim Andrews’ voice took on a much sterner edge as he took her face in his palms again and forced her to listen.

‘Don’t you dare hide behind your false morals now, Roberta. We are so nearly there. Within touching distance. The job is almost done.’

‘Well bully for the job. It must be lovely to live with no feelings.’

The crooked, yellow-toothed grin emerged on his face again.

‘It *is*! It’s *brilliant* to exist without caring! Don’t think you can jump on board with me and then decide to be all sensitive about it. Just carry on what *you’re* doing, and I’ll take care of the rest. Okay? We will be fine.’

‘It’s not fine for *me*, though. I’m the worst person in the world right now. To disregard and then discard the faith that your sons have shown in me. Its unthinkable.’

Jim Andrews annoyance was beginning to flare.

He didn't partake in morals and had no patience for those that did.

'Then don't fucking think about it! Otherwise, I'm going to have to reconsider our secret little arrangement. I need you fully on side with me, Roberta. If you want to bail out, now is the time and we'll never see one another again. I'll be gone tonight. Forever.'

Bobby looked at Jim and conjured a pledge of her commitment.

'Don't say that.'

'Right then, stop your whining. Just hold on tight and ride the bumps with me. No one said it was gonna be easy. But this is for the both of us, you know. The debts you have back up there won't just vanish. It needs sorting. Don't you think I've had enough too? I'm sick to death of being on my toes with it all. McCafferty's lords keep close vigil on who is next due for a kick up the arse. It's my turn at the moment but they can't keep up with me. But *you* could be next in line. I'm trying to avoid that for our sakes. Just hold yourself together for a few more days. That's all it will be.'

Bobby whispered in sorrowful if reluctant agreement. But she seemed barely convinced of Jim's confident standpoint. Frustration got the better of him again as he scanned the empty street once more.

'Fuck waiting around for Jamie. I might try and get what I can from the bank myself. Is his card and ID knocking close to hand?'

'I can't let you do that, Jim. It's bad enough playing this charade. I can't let you just steal it. It's getting crazier by the hour. Jamie won't let you have any more money anyway.'

Jim rose to his feet and began to check the cabinets in the lounge.

Having no success, he turned his intention to the kitchen and commenced emptying the drawers.

Paperwork and expletives flew in every direction.

Bobby was becoming overwrought at the display of desperation.

'Jim will you just stop it! You lecture *me* about patience. Show some yourself. You're better off leaving without me if you can't control your temper.'

He turned to face her, now almost slavering with fury.

'If you're on my team, Roberta then you'll help me find the bank card.'

Bobby screamed as Jim's manic hunt continued beyond reason.

'It isn't likely to be *here* is it, you fucking *idiot*. Jamie will have it on him. Just get out of here for a bit. I'll tidy up. He won't be long.'

But her words were to no avail.

And our father persisted with his misguided, futile hunt.

Bobby retreated to the bedroom in helpless defeat.

Several minutes passed before the clattering and shouting subsided, to be replaced by a soothing silence that settled through the house.

The soundless seconds ticked by as Bobby Jones listened intently from her pillow.

Then the slam of the front door shattered her peace of mind.

As Jim Andrews departed Glenfield Avenue once more.

And the stirring of unseen influencers continued at a pace.

31
A CONCERNING NEW PERSPECTIVE

As you would rightly imagine, dear reader, Alex wasn't exactly overjoyed on learning the news that our mutual intentions for the day were to be unavoidably postponed.

But being the loyal comrade that she is, it was her suggestion to go with me to Glenfield Avenue once we had journeyed back on the train.

Few words were exchanged between us as we departed from Nottingham station. She might have volunteered herself as a willing companion, but she was far from enthusiastic about the situation that likely awaited us.

We still held hands on alighting at the platform at Little Henton and walking through the estate. But the apprehension was increasingly palpable as we approached the unknown.

I had little idea of what lay in store as I placed the key in the door at number thirty-two.

The first surprise was that it was unlocked.

Once inside, I nigh on gasped in despair.

The place looked as though it had been hit by a bomb. The contents of every drawer and cupboard lay on the floor.

Alex opted to uphold her resolute silence as she stepped carefully amid the debris. I ventured through the lounge and kitchen almost feeling like crying at the mess that had greeted us.

Back out in the hallway, I called for Bobby.

A few seconds elapsed before her tear strewn face emerged through the gap in the bedroom door.

There was no sign of my father.

'What the hell happened here? Why are you upset? I thought you said on the phone that he had come back?'

She shuffled into the hallway as Alex smartly positioned herself in the lounge doorway to gain good vantage of us both.

I wasn't quite sure what kind of explanation I anticipated.

Through her streaked visage, Bobby attempted to convey the events that had occurred in my absence.

'I didn't know he was coming back, today. Did you, Jamie? He just turned up in a temper and demanded more money. I think he'd had a drink. That's why I rang you in a panic.'

Knowing my father's usual routine, I presumed he would be under the influence of something. That was the only way he could deal with life these days.

'It's okay. You did the right thing, Bobby. What did he say before erupting?'

She blew her nose on a tissue and wiped the mascara that had run around her eyes.

'Well, he wanted to see you so you could take him to the bank. Then he asked *me* to go with him, but I said I didn't have the account card. He didn't believe me when I told him that you were the sole named holder.'

I gazed round at the scene of carnage.

'Okay. So, what happened to the house? As if I need to ask.'

Again, Bobby mumbled through a veil of verging emotion.

'He got nasty. Started ranting like he does. Then said he was going to the bank himself as he couldn't wait for you.'

I briefly glanced to Alex, who was inwardly just as furious as I was, if not more so.

To the point of refusing to speak to or even acknowledge Bobby, which was ridiculous and somewhat tragic considering it was their first ever face-to-face encounter.

To say the very least, I was extremely disappointed with my father's actions. I thought I had read him more astutely than that.

More fool me, dear reader.

'The greedy bastard. Did he say what he wanted the extra money for?'

Alex moved closer to the pair of us and folded her arms defiantly. She seemed very intent on absorbing Bobby's personal account of things.

And I noticed that her expression conveyed nothing less than abject distrust and suspicion regarding matters.

'I haven't a clue. But as you can see for yourself, he was angry and desperate. The old Jim Andrews was back in place, today.'

I asked Alex and Bobby to take a seat and I prepared us a drink before attempting to attack the process of cleaning up. In truth the tangle of paperwork was not as bad as it looked. It seemed my father had lost his temper and lashed out at anything close to hand. Surprise, surprise.

It was fortunate that Bobby hadn't been on the receiving end of one his habitual right hooks. She had suffered with such before. Yet thankfully today she had escaped unscathed.

In some respects, I was glad I wasn't there when he appeared.

It would have gotten out of control without any shadow of doubt.

'He won't get much joy from the bank. That's a certainty. Did he say anything else before leaving?'

'No. I went into the bedroom to get out of his way. Then I heard the door slam. That's as much as I know.'

Again, I observed Alex's body language as she sat next to Bobby.

She was very cold and defensive. No concern offered whatsoever.

I could tell that her personal conclusions were already formulating.

'Okay. At least he didn't lay a finger on you, which is more than can be said for this cupboard door.'

'But what if he gets more money and then splits again?' Bobby queried.

'He won't. He can't. The money's secure, don't worry.'

Bobby rose to her feet and wiped her eyes.

'Listen...I'm needing to get ready for work. Thanks for coming back.'

I was rather shocked to say the least.

'Are you sure you're in any fit state to go to work after this?'

'I'm fine. Work will take my mind off things. I'm going to get my tunic on and get going.'

There was no changing her mind. There never was any point trying.

With Bobby out of the room and out of earshot, Alex joined me in the kitchen and assessed the damage.

In hindsight I was relieved she was there to try and deflect some of my mental bombardment.

'Well, Jay, this wasn't quite the afternoon we had mapped out, was it? Nevertheless, all good fun though!'

'I'm sorry, Ally. I'll make it up to you.'

'Dead right you will.'

The fact that she smiled at me regarding our cancelled plans made everything instantly seem so much better. I had an idea.

'We could sort this quickly and go back into town if you wanted? Martin can let himself in after school. He doesn't need babysitting.'

Alex's expression conveyed a strange combination of dismay and deliberation regarding what she had just witnessed.

She came closer and pursed her lips as if to speak in a whisper.

A hiatus endured as she thoughtfully composed what she wanted to say.

'Are you okay, Ally? You weren't very sociable toward Bobby. Not ideal circumstances for a first introduction, I grant you.'

She nodded toward the hallway where Bobby was nearly in readiness to leave. The hushed volume was maintained.

'Jay…are you actually buying all this?'

I was perplexed by the question.

'I don't understand what you mean, Ally.'

'Look…tell me if I'm speaking out of turn here, but this whole set up is ringing serious alarm bells for me.'

Normally I would be genuinely interested to embrace Alex's opinion.

But at that juncture, I felt I had bigger fish to fry.

'Is this one of your conspiracy theories, again? You haven't thrown me one for a while.'

Alex glared at me and furrowed her brow.

I don't think she was very receptive to my attempt at sarcasm.

Again, she checked to see if Bobby was still out of the room and whispered.

'I'm not messing about, Jay. I'm serious. I can't put my finger on it, but in my eyes, something is very wrong here.'

I raised my hand to warn that Bobby had entered the room.

'I'm off. I'll be seeing you both again soon. Short but sweet, Alex. We'll try a bit harder next time, eh?'

Alex did not even turn around to observe or acknowledge Bobby's departure.

'Indeed.' was Alex's only reply.

The abruptness in her mannerisms was most unlike her.

I swiftly attempted to bridge the gaping chasm in the room.

'Take it easy at the shop, Bobby. Tell Johnny H you need to come home if you're not right. Okay?'

'Will do. Bye!'

Alex and I heard the front door get pulled shut.

At last, we could talk freely about her concerns.

She faced me with those wide, pale, beautiful eyes and forced another smile as she spoke.

'Okay, Batman. Now what do we do? Wait around here for the return of the Incredible Hulk?'

I couldn't help but chuckle at Alex's inventive and timely quip in the face of our continuing adversity.

'Yes. I'll wait. I've changed my mind about not babysitting Martin. Who knows what state our father might come back through the front door in? I'm not sure it's a good idea you stick around, though, Ally. Crossing paths with him is something I'd like you to avoid, if you know what I mean. You're the only free spirit left among us.'

She seemed strangely disappointed on hearing my suggestion.

'You're sure? I don't mind staying with you. It should prove interesting to say the least.'

My father was no fool. He would have recognised Alex from the first meeting in the café. The cat would be out of the bag immediately.

'Terrible idea, Ally. Seriously. I need you to stay clear of all this until I'm over the finish line with it. I can tell you something that I *would* like you to do, though.'

She exhibited a knowing expression of affection.

'What's that then, Jamie Andrews?'

'Kiss me.'

'Why?'

'Cos I really need it.'

Our embrace was close, warm, and meaningful.

Confirmation at last, that our endearing compassion for one another had been fully relit.

We said our temporary goodbyes in the doorway of number thirty-two, Glenfield Avenue.

The brief loving exchanges were idyllic moments to wallow within.

She began to walk down the path to the gate.

I called her name and she stopped and turned to me.

'What is it, my handsome prince? I'm supposed to be doing a disappearing act before the Jolly Green Giant returns.'

I laughed out loud.

'I forgot to say something, Ally.'

'Well, hurry up and say it its cold.'

My heart sprinted with elation at the wondrous vision standing on the pavement.

I had so wanted to tell her again over recent days and only now, of all times, could I summon the courage.

'I love you, Alex Lawley.'

Thank goodness the sentiment was received positively.

She trotted quickly back to the front door.

Those crystal eyes shone. Her incredible presence sated my soul.

Cradling my face with her palms, she let her lips connect with mine for a few more seconds of undiluted paradise.

She drew away once more, never allowing her hypnotic gaze to divert from mine.

Finally, she uttered the words I had so longed to hear her say back to me.

'I love you too, Jamie Andrews. You'll never know how much. We'll get through this you know. Then me and you will be going places. I promise. Ring me as soon as you can.'

I nodded as the myriad of sensation relentlessly intertwined.

Adoration. Admiration. Exaltation.

I was now completely swept away by her.

What higher praise could I offer this woman, dear reader?

My emotions created a tumultuous inner concerto as I watched her finally depart Glenfield Avenue.

Away from the danger that now constantly resided.

And would no doubt soon be returning to the very same doorstep she had just departed.

But alas, fate was still the master puppeteer.

And had already rubber stamped its schedule on matters.

Neither Alex nor I were to know it at the time, but our passionate farewell and ultimate declaration to one another on that day would never be repeated.

We had no knowledge of the fact that our paths were already ordained toward totally different destinations.

Indeed, it would prove to be the very final occasion in our lives that we would ever set eyes on each other.

III

JUDGEMENT

32
FINALITY CREEPS

Martin continued with school.

Bobby continued with work.

I continued to wait.

Permanence of absence was never my father's true ambition.

I knew he would return.

Bobby disagreed to my face.

Martin, as ever, was adamantly non committal regarding his placement within our entire, strife strewn saga.

But I had an instinctive feeling.

I knew absolutely.

Because the calling had been guiding me for weeks.

And our stories were still being played out by the unsuspecting participants of the very suspecting world.

I had become very unsettled during the days since our father's latest disappearance. I had even rung his number to no answer and to no avail.

I was fully accepting of the inevitability that there would be another chapter of distress to embark on.

This business was not yet finished.

Not by a long chalk.

I had begun counting the hours.

Which then evolved into counting the days.

The year had evolved into the second week of December.

A month that holds only sad tidings for the Andrews brothers.

I had pledged to take Martin to East Park to visit Mum's grave on the twenty-second day. We could pay our respects to Henry, too.

But Mum's final resting place needed honouring with the presence of her sons.

He had agreed to attend with me.

But before then, there was another episode to confront.

The ultimate meeting of minds was imminent.

And I was at my post, awaiting the arrival.

Akin to being in the trenches, awaiting the Big Push.

I had telephoned Alex over a week ago to stay away from Glenfield Avenue until the coast was clear.

We had exchanged many loving text messages since.

But she too had seen the horizon becoming grimmer.

The looming silhouette that relentlessly advanced our way.

Indeed, to her credit, she foresaw far more of fate's intention than I could ever have detected.

We promised to meet up soon enough and discuss our relief and our gratitude.

Our hopes and our fears.

But only once the storm had passed.

This was now the calm.

And the true event was almost upon us.

*****

It was nearly six p.m.

A Tuesday evening in mid-December. I cannot recall the date.

Could have been the twelfth. Or the thirteenth.

Not that it matters anymore.

Bobby had taken a much-needed day off from the supermarket.

Apparently, Johnny H wanted to take me for a festive drink before Christmas arrived.

Time had flown since my return to Nottingham in early October.

I had asked Bobby to pass the message back to Johnny H.

We would definitely meet for that long-awaited pint.

There was still time to fulfil that pledge.

I had decided to treat Martin and Bobby to dinner at the local carvery restaurant about a mile from home. The three of us agreed it would present a welcome if brief diversion from recent troubles.

As you can rightly imagine, any subterfuge was welcome.

As things transpired, the diversion that did arise was not the one we anticipated. Far from it, dear reader.

Despite our best collective intentions, the days at Glenfield Avenue were now tinged with persistent negatives.

The slope becoming ever more precarious and steeper.

As we gradually started to lose our footing and began to slide.

The perennial sense of dread was something we had all learned to live with by now.

I had spent an hour on the phone talking to the registration secretary at Swansea University. They had apparently been attempting to contact me prior to that day but to no avail.

My record of absence had now officially run into its tenth week.

I think I successfully convinced them of my intention to return to my studies in the New Year at the latest. All sounding very familiar, isn't it?

The cycle of my life spans ever forward but only to the next repeat showing.

Then it's back to square one.

I explained to the secretary that I never intended being back in Nottingham for this length of time, but as per usual things were a little beyond my personal control. I had priorities here and they needed my attention. It was as simple as that.

I just had to keep my fingers crossed that the situation with Uni would be recoverable. Well, I'd done it at St George's, hadn't I? I was now something of an expert in catching up with my peers. No sweat.

It was understandable that the festive season had kind of lost its albeit flimsy appeal this year.

I hoped that a trip to the pub might give the three of us the inspiration to embrace Christmas with at least some mild enthusiasm.

Tough call, I know.

I pined for Alex, but I knew she would be willing to wait should I not get the opportunity to see her until after the big day. I was looking forward to making up for lost time with her, as you can well understand.

If only looking forward could have enabled me to depict the harsh reality that awaited us, as opposed to indulging us in such fleeting, futile fantasy.

But the dish of frivolity was seemingly never going to be ours to sample.

As the grip of destiny grew ever firmer.

*****

Surprisingly, Martin and Bobby were very excited about the evening's dinner arrangements. I had asked Alex out of courtesy to join us but as usual she aired on the side of logic and wisdom and politely declined the invitation, offering the view that we as a three needed some quality family time together.

Our taxi was booked for six-thirty.

Unbelievably, all three of us were ready in plenty of time and were about to indulge in a pre-departure beverage or two.

I must say we had rarely looked better as a trio.

Washed up and brushed up, we cut a dashing ensemble, even if I do say so myself.

Martin's naturally handsome looks were set off to a tee by a crisp white shirt and blue jeans. He had cheered up after an hour's sulk regarding the fact that I gave him the eternally disappointing news that Rufus wasn't allowed to attend the carvery.

After some routine exchanges about his loyal teddy bear, my brother conceded that it ultimately might be best if Rufus stayed on guard at home.

'He'll start to complain I never take him anywhere, Jamie.'

'You've been best friends your whole life, for crying out loud. Missing out on tonight won't dent his allegiance to you, believe me.'

I could see my brother's brain working on a solution.

'I've got it! I just won't tell him we are going out. That should do the trick. He can't get upset about what he doesn't know about, can he?'

I loved Martin's untainted innocence in such things.

'Good plan, big bro. Good plan.'

As our well-worn conversation reached its latest conclusion, Bobby entered the room and it's no exaggeration to say that she took our breaths away. She always had the style and figure to carry off a dress, and I had forgotten how glamorous she could look when she wanted to impress.

Her dress was black, short, and close fitting, with three-inch heels to finish the look. She was going to make us proud to be seen with her.

As for my brother, he termed it rather more acutely.

'You'll have tongues hanging out at every table looking like that. And to think how jealous they'll be because you're all *mine*.'

Bobby laughed at the long-routed compliment.

'Well, if I'm going to escort the Andrews brothers to dinner, then I don't want to be showing them up now, do I?'

I simply stared, evidently displaying my inner reactions all over my awestruck features.

'What's the matter, Jamie boy. Never seen a beautiful Irishwoman before?' she chuckled.

My response was honest, if short.

'Wow! That's about all I can say, Bobby. *Wow*!'

She looked me up and down.

'Not scrubbed up bad yourself for a young 'un. Five out of ten each for the pair of you.'

I had opted for a pair of brand-new tailored trousers and jacket.

I wasn't going to make a grand effort but thought that spoiling myself might alleviate the misery of recent times.

It was perhaps the first occasion I had donned such an outfit since Henry's funeral.

'Are we cracking this plonk open or what? I'm more than ready for a booze.' gestured Bobby toward the kitchen table.

We each took our glasses and wished one another a Happy a Christmas as might be feasible. There was an element of joy in the house at long last.

And as the wine flutes clinked together, we actively praised one another once again for looking so damned fine.

The mood was vibrant, and we each drank quickly in readiness for a refill.

It was the first occasion for many weeks that the atmosphere within the walls of thirty-two, Glenfield Avenue, could be termed as positively contented.

For the moment our troubles were put to one side.

But dear reader, you might well have already guessed that my talent for speaking too soon swiftly reared up and bit me on the behind again.

It was when we prepared ourselves for a second toast to our stoical togetherness, that we simultaneously heard the raucous screech of a car braking outside in the road.

The mutual appreciation of our union was about to be interrupted.

We gazed at one another in wonder before Martin supplied a morsel of mirth.

'If that's the taxi just pulled up…then I'm *walking* to the pub.'

Bobby and I smiled with mild curiosity as we simultaneously shuffled to the front window to ascertain the cause of the disturbance.

The scene was difficult to visualise through the darkness.

Glimpsed under the partial illumination of a streetlamp, I struggled to identify the vehicle beyond the front gate.

Then I observed Martin, who had already ventured out through the front door and down the path to inspect the car in question.

He stood for a few moments in the evening chill, apparently scrutinising the motor that had abruptly come to a stop outside.

The driver was proving quite adept at sounding his horn and did so every ten seconds.

I glanced at Bobby and conveyed my initial response.

'What a clown. Teenager just passed his test, no doubt.'

She did not respond, continuing to squint through the windowpane.

Martin re-entered the hallway, his cheeks flush with a combination of the cold air and bubbling enthusiasm.

‘It’s *beautiful*, Jamie! Audi A4! Brand new! I’ve changed my mind. If that’s the taxi I’m calling shotgun!’

I was now keen to establish what was going on outside, as were several neighbours due to the repeated use of the horn, which was now accompanied by deployment of the pounding stereo speaker system.

The three of us emerged from the house and positioned ourselves at the pavement edge.

I noticed curtains were twitching and one or two residents had also appeared at their own front doorsteps to ascertain the source of commotion.

The driver was evidently attempting to attract the attentions of somebody. I turned to Bobby.

Was I still so naïve? So *innocent*? So unaware?

‘I’ll see what the noisy twat wants. You two…wait here.’

I marched around the rear of the car to enquire what the occupants thought they were doing.

I didn’t get to the driver.

Because the driver got to me first.

His door opened without warning, courtesy of the sole of his boot.

It soon became very obvious that the exhibition of noise was for the benefit of the occupants of number thirty-two.

My heart beat a little faster as my father slid out from behind the wheel and stood before me.

I glanced back to Martin and Bobby who could now also readily identify the visitor.

Bobby turned to my brother.

‘What the fuck is *he* doing with a chariot like *that*?’ she quipped.

‘If the car’s not stolen and uninsured then I’ll be a monkey’s uncle.’ Martin replied, whilst still gazing in sincere admiration at the transport our father had arrived in.

Whatever he had come to say I didn’t want to hear it and I promptly ushered Martin and Bobby back up the path.

The three of us shut ourselves inside the house.

Strangely, Jim Andrews didn't appear to be in any hurry to take up pursuit.

We watched from the lounge window again as he calmly turned off the engine and locked the car, before approaching the front gate.

His demeanour appeared affable. We were soon to find out whether this was a falsehood. The eventual knock on the door carried a vibrancy that resonated heavily through the lounge.

He observed us watching him through the bay window.

He grimaced as his frosted breath billowed skyward.

'OPEN UP OR I KICK MY WAY IN. YOUR CHOICE!'

I glanced at Bobby who had remained unusually quiet.

I promptly issued an order.

I hoped it would garner support.

'I don't know what he wants but he doesn't come in the house. I'm not having him turn the place upside down again.'

Bobby observed me wide-eyed.

'So, what do we do? He'll barge his own way in anyway if we don't go and talk to him.'

Unsurprisingly, it looked like I had been unofficially nominated to be spokesman as usual.

I decided to engage with my father where he couldn't repeat his party piece and ransack us.

'Wait here, then. Lock the door when I'm outside.'

*****

My opening salvo didn't invite any scope for misinterpretation.

'Don't do this. Not tonight. Fuck off and pester somebody else. We aren't in the mood. We've had enough.'

Jim Andrews gaze fell to the lounge window.

'Can't I come in, then? What they shut us out for?'

It was instantly apparent that our father was again inebriated.

He swayed as he stood. He slurred as he spoke.

‘We don’t want you here. You trashed the place last time. You can’t just turn up out of the blue. We’re on our way out to dinner, anyway.’

I could smell his breath even though I was three or four meters away. Christ could only guess at how much he had put down his throat before deciding to drive.

‘Bit rude, son? I always thought guests should be invited inside. Not be made to stand outside freezing their bollocks off. Especially at Christmas.’

This conversation was already bordering on pathetic and way beyond pointless. Especially as we had now attracted the distinctly unwanted attention of several fellow residents.

‘You’re no guest of ours. If you want to talk then ring me tomorrow and I’ll meet you somewhere. Just not tonight. Please leave my property.’

Jim Andrews smiled broadly in the bleak half-light.

But it was not in humour.

He ran his fingers across his bald scalp and furrowed his scarred brow as his frail capacity for balance successfully steadied him once more.

Yes. He was back for conflict.

Just as the script predicted.

He advanced a few paces toward my position.

‘Ooh…you’ve changed your tune, son. *Your* house again now, is it? I always thought it was your brother’s. Since when did this little arrangement get sorted, then?’

His persistence was an intrusion on my intelligence.

‘None of your fucking business! Never has been and it never will be.’

My father shook his head before he sneered an odd response.

‘I wouldn’t be so sure of that. Look, son. I’m not here to fall out. I just need a little more of that stash that you keep under the floorboards and then I’m gone again. Easy as that.’

My composure was being pushed to the limit.

My patience was already long gone.

In turn, I was aware that his temper was also likely to fray imminently as the discussion ensued.

'Not a chance. You've had all the money you're getting. So, you can just climb back into your shiny new car and disappear. Okay? But try not to kill anyone on the way there.'

Our father glanced over his shoulder toward the Audi.

He then turned to me once more, his voice emitted through a snarl.

I would not be goaded, however.

'That's just a little something for the old man. I don't get much out of life, do I? Thought I'd treat myself.'

I couldn't help but laugh at the sorry specimen standing before me.

'You mean to tell me that you didn't nick it?'

'How could you suspect me of such a thing? No. It's all above board, son.'

'There's no way *you* paid for that!'

He grimaced knowingly.

His answer already cocked in the barrel.

'Nah! Of course, I didn't pay for it. *You* did!'

My brewing fury was beginning to get the better of me.

I had tried so hard to humour this man who had no apparent purpose on the planet other than to inflict unbridled hardship on others.

I had tried so hard to cajole him into leaving, albeit with a persuasive bundle of money tucked under his arm.

I had tried so hard to forego the past, in order to give the three of us the chance of some grounding for the future.

But it was obviously a lost cause.

He remained firmly in his place hanging over our heads.

Still exerting his poisonous influence.

Gloating.

Inciting.

Glorifying malevolence with every single syllable he uttered.

And it was becoming increasingly impossible to resist giving him the fight he so obviously and so dearly craved.

My better instincts kicked in as I spotted Martin still hovering at the front window.

The next I knew my father had grasped my right arm at the elbow and was pulling me through the gate onto the pavement.

'I know you can't really see too much in the dark, but she is a beauty isn't she. I suppose I should thank you.'

I didn't want things to become publicly physical. I truly didn't.

'I couldn't give two shits about the car. It won't stay in that state for long, anyway.'

He continued to cajole me toward making a closer examination.

'Cheeky little fucker! I'm a *great* driver! Don't worry. I'll look after her. She won't get a scratch.'

'You shouldn't even be on the road. You're either pissed or high. One or the other. Or both?'

He pressed his nose close to mine and hissed a feebly conveyed warning.

'Show some respect to your old fella Or I'll teach you the cost of bad manners.'

That was the last straw. I'd heard enough.

I squared up to him and glared into his wild and dilated pupils.

I clenched my fists in readiness to launch.

'You are an alcoholic and a bully. You've done what you came to do. You've rubbed my nose in it. Now leave. Just go.'

Unbeknown to me as I engaged in exchanging unpleasantries with our father, Martin had re-emerged from the house and ambled down the path towards us.

He made straight for the car and began to drool.

'Amazing! Can we go to dinner in this, Jamie? Please? Dad will take us. This is the ultimate! Can we, Dad? You could have carvery, too!'

I couldn't believe what I was hearing.

That word again. On top of everything else. *That word.*

The last thing I felt like doing now was going out.

Our evening together destroyed before it had even begun.

But Martin's fascination with the Audi had diverted our father's attention toward an unanticipated proposal.

A proposal of the very worst kind.

'Fancy a ride do you, son?' he jeered, whilst eyeing my reaction.

My instincts were screaming at me.

This was wholly unexpected and rendered me completely off guard.

'No, Martin!' I interjected. 'Forget it! You're not going anywhere with him. *Especially* if he's driving.'

My order to my brother was in fact a lightly veiled plea.

The situation was already sliding beyond recovery. Yet before I knew it Martin had approached the passenger side, pulled open the door and was getting in.

'MARTIN! I SAID *NO*! BACK IN THE HOUSE! NOW!'

Our father seemed to find the unfolding events more than a little amusing. He was enjoying himself immensely by interfering.

As always.

He was evidently determined to indulge in making the problem even worse and re-positioned himself beside Martin's open door.

'Put your belt on, lad. That's it. We'll go for a little spin. Yeah?'

I moved between them to try and reclaim Martin from the car, but my father ably obstructed me.

'MARTIN! PLEASE! DON'T DO THIS!' I barked in desperation.

My brother's reply seemed so young and unseeing.

'Just one ride round the block, Jamie. Let me do this one thing with Dad. I never had the chance before. Not like you did. Please, Jamie.'

I grappled with my father who was now cackling loudly at the sight of my encompassing distress.

'MARTIN! PLEASE DON'T GO WITH HIM! I'M FUCKING BEGGING YOU! DON'T DO THIS!'

'You're swearing and shouting at me, Jamie. I don't like it.'

I was temporarily distracted by the sight of our pre-booked taxicab pulling up a few metres along the kerbside.

But our plan to dine out had already been forcibly abandoned.

My distraction allowed our father to shift position back around to the driver's side and he pulled his door open.

'We won't be long, son. Just a little tootle for my eldest boy!'

I helplessly observed Martin's excited form as Bobby joined my side. She appeared ridiculously unmoved about developments.

It didn't make any sense whatsoever.

I turned to her as my emotions quickly got the better of me.

'BOBBY! FUCKING STOP THEM, WILL YOU?! HE'S PISSED!'

She moved to the driver's side to speak with my father. I couldn't decipher the details of their muttering. It was almost as though I was being purposely excluded for some reason.

The episode was becoming more bizarre and terrifying with every passing second. I was becoming frantic.

'BOBBY! WHAT IS GOING ON? WILL YOU GET MY BROTHER OUT OF THE BLOODY CAR?'

Her response was absolutely surreal, and for me at that moment, completely debilitating. She re-joined me on the pavement.

'Martin will be fine. Jim's just going into town and back. Five minutes. Let your brother enjoy himself for once, will ya? Chill yourself down, Jamie boy.'

My brother's yelps of undiluted delight resonated along the street.

Under normal circumstances I would have been elated for him.

Under normal circumstances the sound of my brother's happiness would be music to my ears.

Yet at that juncture I sensed something sinister was at hand.

A nightmare scenario was transpiring before my very eyes, and I was powerless to prevent it.

'Bobby! I can't believe you. Are you smoking the same shit that he is? He's off his head for fuck's sake! Can't you see it?'

Bobby raised the palm of her hand.

'Be still, Jamie. You worry yourself for nothing.'

I glanced again to the waiting taxicab. I felt lost in a mental fog.

Either I had lost my perspective completely or I was indeed on the verge of insanity.

The Audi's engine roared into life and the speakers began to thud once again. Our father began to rev the throttle.

Even with the car windows shut I could hear Martin's squeals of sheer exhilaration.

I glared at his fiancée once again.

What the hell was happening to us?

'Where is he going with my brother? Are you out of your mind letting this happen, Bobby?'

She continued to blatantly ignore my pleas.

Instead, she maintained her attention on the front seats of my father's car.

And then, above all else, after all that - she smiled.

A loving heartfelt expression that left me reeling with further bewilderment.

And then I thought of Alex.

And the concerns that she implied to me a few days earlier.

And the suspicions that she intimated were now materialising before my very eyes.

I only had one remaining option.

'Fuck this! I'm calling the police.'

It was only on hearing that proclamation that Bobby decided to finally engage with me.

'Don't do that, Jamie. There's no need. They won't come, anyway. There's no crime being committed, is there? Let the father and son have some quality time together.'

Was I in the midst of another nightmare?

Was it at all possible that my imagination that could have invented such a precarious scene? Or was this actually happening?

My blood ran cold as I studied the vision of my brother in the passenger seat, laughing heartily at the actions of our demented and intoxicated father.

And Bobby, who had seemingly shed her years of harboured, inbuilt fear in an instant, and was willingly placing her trust in what was sequencing before our very eyes.

Could she really be forgoing the demons that Jim Andrews had instilled within her soul?

Had I misjudged her so erroneously?

It appeared so.

She went to snatch the phone from my grasp as I battled successfully to dial nine three nines.

The audience in the street was growing.

The situation was becoming more irretrievable by the second.

And then the confirmation I needed was in plain sight as she suddenly became violent toward me.

Screaming. Kicking.

Punching. Scratching.

The personality switch was ominous beyond belief.

I backed off under the intensive physical duress and managed to speak into my handset to the emergency services operator.

It was a physical feat to convey the predicament as Bobby's relentless objections rained down blow after blow.

I supplied the registration plate of the Audi and our location.

I insisted that a kidnap was in progress.

Confirmation came swiftly that assistance had been alerted and would arrive very shortly. I hung up and exchanged scornful glares with Bobby as she backed off and stooped for breath.

I could not believe the hatred that swelled in her eyes.

Who *was* this woman?

Had I really been fooled so easily?

And what was my brother's part to be in this terrible scheme?

'You shouldn't have done that!' she screeched. 'You stupid fucker. You'll lose *everything*, now! EVERYTHING!'

She ran to the driver's side of the car to talk with my father once again.

This time I heard her loud and clear.

'Jim…the filth are on their way. Your stupid cunt of a son has called them on you. You need to go. NOW!'

He alighted the car and turned to me with index finger outstretched.

His face etched with indescribable menace.

'I'll be back to sort you, laddie. Once and for all. Always the fucking hero, aren't you. Well, you've done it once too often, this time!'

With that warning he jumped back behind the wheel.

I knew then in that instance that I had no choice.

I had to go with them.

In the five seconds it took me to reach the rear of the car, pull open the rear nearside door and jump into the back seat, the throttle was at the floor and the clutch was being lifted.

The sudden acceleration threw me backwards and caused my door to slam closed. Adrenaline coursed my veins as I made sure I was secured in with the seat belt.

I quickly checked over Martin's shoulder to make sure he was too.

I then glanced across to our father.

Akin to current form, he had not buckled up.

We approached the first T-junction at ridiculous velocity.

There was no time or room to stop at the give way line.

Just as well, as our driver had no intention of obliging the highway code. Martin squealed with delight as our father navigated along the amber lit road at breakneck pace.

I could observe on the speedometer that he was pressing sixty miles an hour around the residential estate.

We collided with and careered upward at every speed bump in our path, causing not a little amusement for my hapless brother.

It was too dark outside for this kind of recklessness.

But Martin was delirious with the unplanned adventure and turned to me as I glared in horror through my window.

'Jamie, you'll love this! This will be a real thrill! The best ride ever! It's going to be superb!'

Our father gripped the wheel in his fists and barked a warning to me as he scrutinised the uncertain view ahead.

'You're going to regret what you just did, young one. Big mistake involving the coppers. You've messed things up for me for the last time.'

I didn't respond to his idle ranting.

My focus was centred on the view of the semi-lit town centre that flashed past us.

And only one singular thought hammered away at me as we travelled.

That for so long I had dictated matters.

That my influence was unhindered.

That I had attained and retained control of my family's affairs.

And as the Audi screamed along the bypass heading out of town, the realisation had already dawned in my mind that I had now entirely surrendered my authority.

The Gods were now spectating.

My brother and I were trapped in the one position that I had strived for so long for us to avoid.

We were both confined by and now at the mercy of, our one and only true enemy.

Jim Andrews held total power of government.

And just as I had once prayed for Martin.

I now had little choice but to silently pray for the both of us.

33
FOR WHOM THE BELL TOLLS

Jim Andrews was no novice behind the wheel.

The gear changes and dextrous manoeuvrability were akin to the skill of a rally driver as we motored with incredulous ferocity along the dual carriageway toward Nottingham.

Roundabouts and traffic lights bore no effect on our journey.

Our father might have been very capable at handing the vehicle, but the risks he was willing to take sailed increasingly close to the wind.

Martin of course identified none of the danger.

Only the thrill.

From my position in the back seat, I felt helpless in this ensuing void of peril. The ultimate unwilling observer.

And then, at perhaps the most inappropriate moment, our father turned to me as though to commence a conversation, before his attention was demanded again by the view through the windscreen.

Streetlamps, houses, and cars flashed by in a blur of amber and black then by turn white and red.

We were way over the speed limit with the only crumb of comfort being that the traffic around us in both directions was comparatively light.

We careered through another large island spanned by a footbridge and with his foot to the floor to enter the straight beyond, our father turned to taunt me yet again.

'Well, well, well…this is a rarity, isn't it boys? Dad spending some special time with his sons. What a treat for us all, eh?'

I felt like knocking his head off there and then.

But I could do very little to inhibit the madman at the helm.

My brother and I were in a no-win situation.

Despite the insufferable scenario, I was powerless to intervene physically without putting us all in severe jeopardy.

Martin's gullibility only served to fuel my overspilling rage.

‘This is *brilliant*, Dad. You’re a superb driver. I wish Rufus could have shared it. I should have brought him along. We could go back for him, couldn’t we?’

I cringed inside and steadied the involuntary instinct to vomit due to the overwhelming quandary we found ourselves in.

All those months of starting over. Of knitting our lives back together. And yet he we now were.

Hanging on the whims of a truly deranged monster.

On top of everything else that he had done that was not merited, the very last thing Jim Andrews now deserved was acclaim from his elder boy.

And yet Martin’s persistent referral to him as *Dad* undermined the principles and morality of every abiding and loving role model on the planet. And our father revelled in every second of it.

‘Glad you’re enjoying yourself, lad. It’s about time. And the ride’s not over yet! Oh no! What about my young un in the back? Having a good time too, are ya? Are ya pumping yet, son? Can you feel the G’s?’

His manic laughter formed a sinister accompaniment to this acutely hazardous latest chapter of our lives.

I again calmly requested that he stopped the car and let us out.

‘Don’t be a spoilsport, young ‘un. Are you not enjoying yourself, then?’ he yelped above the thrum of the engine.

My tolerance threshold had been shattered many moons ago.

‘What do *you* fucking think? Where the hell are we going? You told Bobby we were staying on the estate. And slow down for crying out loud!’

I was wasting my breath imparting any plea for reason.

‘It’s just a little mystery tour, that’s all. I haven’t quite decided myself where we might end up yet. It’s just nice to give this little beauty of a car a proper workout. Get some air in her pipes if you know what I mean. Burn some rubber!’

‘YAY! BURN SOME RUBBER, JAMIE! I LOVE IT! DO YO LOVE IT, TOO?’

Martin's injection of childlike enthusiasm was woefully misplaced.

As was his follow-up query.

'Are we going to the zoo, Dad? Or the airport? Can we go to the airport?'

I felt the harsh pull of the engine as the car hurtled past the Queen's Hospital at nearly eighty miles an hour. We seemed to change lanes every five seconds, with the mirrors undoubtedly being rendered redundant during the process.

Our father's true satanic colours were ably surfacing as he replied to Martin's innocent bout of hysterical wonder.

'Fucking idiot. Of course we aren't going to the *zoo*. Its *shut*. And why would we be going to the airport? Its pitch black. You won't be able to see any planes. You clown.'

Martin was stunned into quiet by our father's nastiness.

But his reticence to reply didn't last for long.

'To see the animals! Why *else* would we go to the zoo? Anyway, I'm not the idiot! *YOU* ARE!'

A concerning silence descended within the car.

It was the first time I had ever heard Martin respond in kind to our father's vindictive tongue.

Part of me wanted to cheer and pump the air.

But the more intelligent side of me rose to the fore and dictated extreme caution.

Unfortunately, Martin wasn't so considerate in his choices.

And inevitably he paid the price.

He never anticipated the back of my father's left fist coming into a clean and heavy connection with his right jawbone.

I heard Martin wince with shocked agony and then watched as he closed both hands over the area of contact.

Our father directed a warning as random headlamps glinted towards us, temporarily illuminating the interior.

The strobe-like scene beyond the windows flashed past at lightening pace as our father issued his verbally dishevelled sermon.

The atmosphere between the three of us had taken a sudden and concerning downturn.

'There's more where that came from, you cheeky little bastard. Why can't you keep your mouth shut like your little brother? He's learned it's the best way. But you must keep on with that stupid gob of yours, don't you? Gets on my tits, it does. Stay quiet for a while. It will prove to be a lot better for your health. Isn't that right, our Jamie?'

The euphoria that Martin was enjoying had now been eclipsed by the rapid onset of thumping pain.

He fell into soundlessness as I attempted to jump to his defence.

I leaned forward from my seat.

'He's only copying what *you* say to *him*. He does it all the time. But you wouldn't have a clue about that, would you? If you don't use certain words, then *he* won't use them. You've really hurt him, now.'

Our father showed little interest in my request for lenience.

Instead, he conveyed another malicious and misguided theory.

'That's where I went wrong all these years! I didn't dish out *enough* slaps to keep you both in line. Paying the bloody price for my kind heartedness now though, aren't I? What a pair of fucking brats!'

Not for the first time, I couldn't believe what I was hearing from him. I could not restrain my urge to commence combat.

'You what? *Kind-hearted*? The only talking you *ever* did to us was with your knuckles! You're a fucking disgrace! A bully! A horrible piece of work. You always have been!'

Jim Andrews began to chuckle as he wrenched full left lock on the wheel to take the first exit from the imminent traffic island.

As our tyres screeched against the revving pistons a car horn sounded in protest from behind us and then disappeared away into the evening gloom.

'Who's told you that I'm a bully? Was it Roberta? Well, if you haven't yet wised up to the fact that *she* is a born liar, then I've badly underestimated you, my boy. I had you down as someone with at least half a brain, too!'

The car lurched from one side of the carriageway to the other.

More horns in front and behind bleated in desperate protestation at the Audi's wild tracking.

I tried to ascertain our position as I squinted through my door pane into the dimness beyond. We weren't heading to the city centre anymore.

We had remained on the dual carriageway on route to Grantham.

I continued with my bold effort to prevent Martin interjecting with another potentially careless contribution. My father was not in an obliging mood where his elder son was concerned.

I studied the dazzling brilliant streaks of the car headlamps out front of us, and the retreating crimson lights we subsequently left in our wake. Adrenaline now fuelled my rampant desire to bring this frenzied and extremely frightening charade to a close.

'I don't understand why you've brought us out here. What's the point? Can you slow down, too? We are touching ninety, for Christ's sake!'

Our father blatantly ignored my requests.

He had seemingly become distracted by ensuing activity behind us.

Possibly for the very first time since starting the engine back in Glenfield Avenue, Jim Andrews studiously addressed the rear-view mirror.

His tone remained passive, which was surprising considering the scene he was witnessing. He then uttered a despairing declaration.

'Well, looks like you got your wish, young 'un. Coppers are on to us. You stupid little fucker.'

I spun around in my seat to analyse the source of his interest through the rear windshield.

About a mile back in the open flow of evening traffic, two sets of blue flashing lights made keen pursuit with the sirens vaguely audible.

Relief instantly washed over me.

The instantly soothing thought that our fretful journey was nearly at its end sated my conscience. I felt inwardly grateful that this temporary madness was about to be halted.

But appearances were deceiving.
How could my presumption have been so false?
If only I could have employed some powers of prediction.
Because in truth, the real nightmare was yet to flourish.

34
THINE IS THE KINGDOM

We had been travelling as prisoners at our father's behest for nearly half an hour. The A-road had slimmed down again to a single-track carriageway. But it had not altered the insidious nature of the journey.

Our pace had been relentless. I checked again through the rear windscreen. The police were still on our tail but unsurprisingly were failing to gain much ground.

I attempted once again to process some common sense to the psychopath at the wheel.

'Just give it up, will you? You can't achieve whatever it is you want to, now. It's over. At least let me and Martin out of the car. Then you can do what you like for all I care.'

Once again Jim Andrews delivered a raucous peel of laughter as my words registered with his twisted mindset. He simply gripped the steering wheel ever tighter and pressed down on the accelerator even harder.

'Sorry, boys, but if you hadn't guessed already, I won't be letting any passengers off. You're in for the full experience now, I'm afraid. And anyway, thanks to you young one, and your interfering, I couldn't stop even if I wanted to. Because the pigs will be right on top of me. That's *your* fault. Sorry, but we are all stuck with it!'

I checked behind us again.

There was no sign of the flashing blues at all now.

My automatic puzzlement at their sudden disappearance combined with intensive deflation.

I privately hoped to God they hadn't given up the chase.

And then just as my devastation blossomed, my eye was swiftly attracted to something in the sky.

Red flashing lights and a search beam.

Another method had been deployed by our pursuers.

Surely now, the end of this treacherous trek was upon us.

The rig of safety lights illuminated the undercarriage of the police helicopter as it travelled a hundred metres above us. I thought it only right that my father should heed the new development.

'Funny you should say that. Because the cops are *already* right on top of you. That's it. Game over. Stop the car!'

Our father snorted in rebellion as he veered the Audi lazily across the white centre line and recovered control.

'Not a chance. This is *your* doing, young 'un. I only wanted to take your brother for a little ride. But you had to stick your beak in, didn't you? Couldn't resist stirring the pot. Just like you always did. Even as a nipper you were always getting in the bloody way. Always the accident fucking things up for everyone else.'

Even now, after all these years, it cut me so deeply to hear my father refer to me in such a way. It was always obvious that he hated his sons. We were nothing short of a total inconvenience to his pathetic, insular existence.

But at that moment, emancipation happened.

Despite ruing the dying embers of any compassion that had put us in this horrendous predicament in the first place, I now finally accepted my own truth.

I detested the man.

I resented every single fibre of his being.

I observed in distaste as he fitfully tried to ascertain the position of the helicopter through the front windscreen and his own side window.

His ineffectual quest to remain evasive in the chase was still at the forefront of his thoughts.

But I knew it was now too late for him.

Our apprehension by the police was pending and unavoidable.

A sure-fire case of not *if*, but *when*.

Yet still he persevered, dear reader.

Even past the point of surrender, with the slim odds that might have once been in his favour all but evaporated, he would not and could not accept that he was staring defeat in the face.

The situation was fraught beyond imagination.

Yet still we rampaged along the black, featureless road.

Still our father acted on his blind compulsion.

And then, at the most inopportune of moments, Martin once again opted to supply his own brand of commentary as our carrier continued its uncertain path into the night.

'Is it the seaside, Dad? Is that what the mystery tour is? We'll get there very soon, won't we? Before everybody else at this rate.'

True to form, our father was instantly dismissive of his elder son's enquiry.

'Shut your mouth, retard. *Fucking seaside*. I'll give you fucking *seaside*.'

Martin could not heed the warning signs because he never even saw them. Unbeknown to my brother, his gentle and almost infantile curiosity was now his own worst enemy.

'Is that a *yes*, then? Or is that a *no* then, Dad? Don't you build my hopes up and knock them down, again. You *always* do that!'

I sensed our father's albeit limited reservoir of patience had nigh on run dry regarding his elder offspring.

And once again I was too slow to prevent the punch.

The impact of the second assault hurt Martin all over again.

This time delivered by our father's right fist. The knuckles connected keenly with Martin's right eye socket. The car lurched again due to the temporary absence of control.

Once again, my brother recoiled in agony.

Not knowing how to respond to the violent treatment that he had done nothing to deserve.

But being deserving of such punishment was irrelevant.

It was the story of Martin's blighted and tragic life.

I sat in the back seat, now shellshocked at our father's blatantly jagged and abusive nature.

Again, I was rendered impotent in the current situation.

I could not intervene in any way.

We were already at significant risk as it was. I was emotionally lost amid the stirring pity for my brother, as he whimpered like a juvenile in front of my eyes.

I furtively scanned the scene beyond the rear windscreen once more, hoping that the police were still close by.

I couldn't visually detect their proximity.

But on winding down the rear window, I could hear the deafening grind of their rotor blades now no more than fifty metres overhead.

Not long now.

The relentless blast of freezing night air smashed into my face as I extended my neck further through the gap.

But our father was not appreciative of my curiosity.

'CLOSE THAT FUCKING WINDOW! NOW!'

I felt as though I might be able to touch the helicopter it seemed so low. I drew my head back into the car and sealed the window as ordered.

Separating us from our saviours as my renewed hope for respite gradually encroached.

Surely this hazardous mission was about to be aborted.

Surely our father was about to see sense and surrender.

Then suddenly, as if in an act of panic, the car veered left and departed the main carriageway to engage with an unlit narrow country lane.

And it soon became clear why our father had opted for the improvised detour.

I glimpsed back at the road we had just exited.

A wall of blue lights lay in wait at the roadblock some way ahead.

Promoting our father's unannounced measure to swiftly divert the car along its now totally unfamiliar route.

Whether this would ultimately entail our escape, we did not yet know.

And then a police car appeared behind once again in hot pursuit, along the darkened winding track that our father had hastily decided to utilise.

He had no choice but to apply the brakes, now.

Blind bend followed blind bend in the pitch murk.

Despite the enforced reduction in speed, Jim Andrews would still not concede his position.

I gripped the back of Martin's seat. We were being shaken like rag dolls. The car felt as though it lost traction at least two or three times.

And then I witnessed Martin suddenly switch position as he now faced our father squarely from the side.

And the retribution commenced.

Blow after blow. Punch after punch. The combinations landing on his target's face and head were clean, powerful, and potent.

Martin had finally and literally lost control of his mind.

His fury was now incessant as it was ruthless and efficient.

And our father was suddenly completely defenceless as he battled gamely to retain the wheel, whilst trying to fend off his elder son's pent-up physical outrage.

The assailant made no sound. No words were deemed necessary.

Every strike he unleashed would serve to fuel the next.

Energy rained down on Jim Andrews like bolts of lightning.

Hit after hit. Martin pummelled his target with repeatedly precise assurance.

Until eventually, my brother's energy levels began to subside.

I leaned between the front seats and attempted to obstruct my brother's access to his victim.

'MARTIN! ENOUGH NOW! WE NEED TO GET THE CAR STOPPED! PLEASE, BRO! THAT'S IT! LEAVE IT, NOW!'

Despite the potentially lethal altercation that played out before me, the car continued to rocket along the uncertain trail laid out ahead of us.

More blind corners. More sharp bends.

Only the headlamps reliably guided us away from potential collisions with the grass verges and stone walls.

Heavy application of the anchors was followed instantly by restored acceleration. I scanned the surroundings beyond the glass.

I could not detect the current whereabouts of the police, either on the ground or in the air.

Surely, they hadn't lost sight of us, again?

My attention centred once more out front, where Martin had thankfully decided to cease his maniacal onslaught.

But my appeasement was to be short lived.

What occurred next instantly placed us in irretrievable danger.

Martin simply glanced back at me, then engaged with our father.

'Don't worry, Jamie. I'll save us. I'll stop this right now!'

My brother made no other prior announcement as he reached over with both hands and wrenched the steering wheel from our father's grasp.

Now, nobody was controlling the car.

It sped along its own path, under its own momentum.

Just as fate would have ordained.

At nearly seventy miles per hour, the untethered Audi A4 containing a father and his two grown-up sons, left the unmarked road with unstoppable impetus.

Through a privet hedge; across a cattle paddock.

The new direction ricocheted the passengers around the interior of the vehicle with even more frenetic power.

I hoped we would soon lose our speed.

But the opposite was in fact in process, as our father's right foot remained firmly depressed upon the accelerator.

And horrendous calamity was about to befall those passengers.

That father and his two grown-up sons.

Down a gradient the car sailed freely.

Gathering a renewed propulsion as gravity joined the party to ably compound the peril that already enswathed us.

And through a moment of terrifying illumination, our headlamps offered only a fleeting glimpse of what awaited.

An inescapable, unrelenting snare.

The picket fence that bordered the gravel pit was effectively demolished on impact.

And then for two seconds, life stood still.

Absolute silence preceded the car entering the water, as the three souls aboard pre-empted their doom.

The nose of the car plunged through the surface first at a steep angle. But any light offered by the headlamps was short-lived as the freezing lotion instantly invaded the fuse box.

My severely limited vision could barely identify what was happening in front of me.

It was evident from the hysterical reactions of Martin and our father, that the footwells in the front of the car had begun to fill.

In turn, lending a distinctly uneven distribution of the vehicle's weight.

My mind went blank as I blindly listened to events beginning to play out in slow-motion before me.

With the three of us inhibited by the shrill shock that rapidly enveloped and the reality that was rapidly overpowering our bodies, I felt paralysed by fear as the car began to sink.

And the dominating thought lodged itself.

That fate had decreed this final event.

To the order that this day…

…was looking likely to be our very last…

35
THE POWER AND THE GLORY

The irony was merciless.

As was the unstoppable influx of icy liquid.

For the first time I could recall in my entire existence, I needed my father's help.

I wanted my dad.

I needed him so badly.

As did my brother.

But I already knew the ensuing scenario was beyond retrieval.

I heard the primeval screaming of my brother and our father.

But I could not see them due the darkness of both the sky and the turgid clinging cloak that consumed us.

Yet as my body began its own process of panic, my mind found increased sustenance in the face of such incurable desolation.

It was akin to suddenly transposing to another dimension.

In another life.

In other people's existences.

Not in ours.

Surely it could not have been deemed to end this way.

Of all the traumas God had set aside for us and forced us to abide, it appeared he had saved the most harrowing penance until last of all.

I wanted to divert my imagination from this brutally measured torture and try to clearly assimilate what action I needed to take.

Yet our plight was becoming more unforgiving and inescapable with every passing second. I unclipped my seat belt.

I was only immersed up to my knees due to the angle of the car's entry. I could reach forward and feel that my father and brother were now submerged to at least chest height. I leaned across Martin whose wild flailing and piercing shrieks made it nigh on impossible to reach his door catch.

I then grappled under the water for his seatbelt socket.

Freeing him from his harness had to be the first step to escape.

I could not see that our father had successfully unlatched the door on his side and was now attempting to force it open with his feet against the powerful pressure beyond.

The reservoir was claiming the vehicle at a furious rate.

I glanced forward as the view through the windscreen exhibited a stark nothingness.

Due to the car's swift intake, I could not ably reach Martin's door to release it.

I persisted once more with my efforts unbuckle him.

I fumbled around as the water's occupation was now teeming at Martin's neck. My brother was beyond frenzied.

Clawing at me in absolute terror, he was rendered defenceless as the levels finally rose high enough to take him under and into its maw.

He tried to speak to me as water smothered his mouth and nasal cavity. I couldn't decipher a word. I couldn't observe the fearfully fraught expression he must have been carrying.

Completely without vision, I now had to fight Martin off to try and continue my futile mission to save him. I re-inflated my lungs whilst the remaining pocket of air under the rear windshield was still available.

I unleashed one last anxious effort to try and work around my brother to release his door.

I got nowhere near the designated target.

I resorted to trying his seatbelt again.

The endeavour now felt mountainous.

But I could not give up on him.

I was required to be his salvation once more.

Fighting the formidable ultra-chilling swell and it's all consuming, malevolent blackness, I too was on the verge of conceding to fate's order.

With all my remaining mettle I combatted the suffocating temperature and the disabling rumble of pending acknowledgement.

I reached down with a final breathless lunge and finally succeeded in freeing the buckle from its housing.

But my success came too late.

Martin's seatbelt floated freely away from his lifeless, infested body.

It was now harshly evident that I too was not destined to triumph.

My head and hands were still above the incoming rush.

But it was futile. I didn't have long left to impart an escape attempt of my own.

Martin had now succumbed.

The car was almost completely immersed.

He was still effectively restrained by the closed door beside him.

His potential liberation and survival now a lost cause.

My energy levels were depleting swiftly due to the merciless decree of nature's ravaging elements.

With the moment of resignation almost upon me, I calmly sat back as the water level rose further to my chin.

One last intake of oxygen was all that I would be afforded.

One final breath on this callous, unforgiving, hateful Earth.

One final breath.

For one final act.

However, the remnant of my strength would not be utilised to make any further attempt at personal salvage.

But to bid goodbye.

I filled my lungs with air for the final time in my life.

I closed my eyes and leaned through to the front seats.

I found my brother's right hand in the inky, unforgiving soup.

His limp form now fully overcome and deceased.

I then reached to the driver's side to take our father's left hand.

It was inevitable that he too would no longer be the living, breathing monster that had successfully conspired against us.

But I could not attain any physical hold on him.

I held Martin's hand ever tighter as I grappled and grasped in the space where Jim Andrews had been positioned only twenty seconds earlier.

And the stark realisation hit me that he was no longer in the car with his two dying sons.

My last calling now laid itself out before me.

Alone, as the remaining sufferer in that fatal watery tomb, I continued to clasp Martin's hand as destiny claimed its prize.

And then it claimed us absolutely.

The deluge served to fully engulf.

A soothing acceptance presided as the noxious drink completely occupied my body and soul. With my chest veritably exploding for a release, I finally and willingly allowed destiny to be the victor.

The lake vented its path into my body's every sinus.

I fought the reflexive urge to be fretful.

I would not be taken under protest.

I would obligingly join my brother.

We would cross the barrier together.

The fluid trap had now fully inhabited my being.

I would submit with dignity.

If this was truly how it was meant to be.

As our imprisoning cell descended the fathoms and hit the bed of the reservoir, the pressure on my lungs, eyes and ears was unbearable.

But I still wanted that instance to come.

When my suffering would end, and my passing was complete.

The visual flashbacks commenced in earnest.

Indicators I was getting close now.

Mental pictures of a life undersold.

Undervalued.

Images from my history paraded in rapid succession.

Until one remaining thought became lodged.

One ultimate acknowledgement before I departed.

I thanked God.

For everything that had preceded in my existence.

And for the fact that my existence was now, at long last, concluded.

*****

It was some twenty hours later when the police rescue team finally completed their unenviable mission on the frosted banks of Collinson's Reservoir.

The need for daylight and the sheer depth of the gravel pit had ensured that any retrieval operation had to be delayed for the safety of the members of the unit assigned to the task.

The time neared two p.m.

Winter's rigid grasp harnessed the scene in a white sheen.

From a distance of two hundred meters and positioned behind the police cordon, Bobby Jones observed in the company of her designated family liaison officer.

She shivered with arms folded in the face of the stiff December breeze and watched without obvious reaction, as audible communication between the teams at the site confirmed that the car had been located and the recovery process had started.

The hideous spectacle endured for nearly sixty minutes.

Once liberated from the bottom of the lake, the vehicle was drawn up to the bank in a motion absent of unforeseen obstruction or uninvited hindrance.

The female liaison officer dared glance at the unreadable features of Bobby Jones, as the mystery encasing the harrowing events of the previous evening were granted an awful clarity by the eventual emergence of the car from the clawing fathoms.

There were no evident signs of emotion from Bobby.

She stood seemingly transfixed by the unfolding episode yet shed not a single tear in response to it.

Almost as though she had no connection to the incident whatsoever.

And as if the people that had subsequently perished in such unspeakable circumstances had never touched her life in any way.

Nor she theirs.

She retained a coldness akin to the body of the lake itself.

Portraying an unmoving, almost sinister curiosity.

The epitome of detachment.

The liaison officer gently touched the arm of Bobby Jones as if to try and encourage some form of response.

And then the delayed reaction duly arrived.

Delivered through a matter-of-fact expression and a tone of puzzling, untypical forthrightness.

'I'll identify them all. Now. If you want me to. If it's okay, that is.'

The female constable cast an element of doubt over the request.

'I'm not so sure that's such a good idea at this moment, Miss Jones. Let me contact…'

But Bobby Jones did not possess the necessary allegiance to protocol. She would not wait for permission to be granted.

She stooped under the blue and white barrier tape and swiftly embarked on her privately selected path.

Still with arms firmly crossed over her front, she made careful yet assured steps toward the eight-man diving squad that had performed their unholy occupation.

Bobby ignored the calls from over her shoulder.

It was inevitable that somebody would attempt to obstruct her advance.

A forensic sergeant donned in white overalls marched up the bank to meet with Bobby and cut her off.

He held up both hands, one containing his radio.

'I'm sorry, Miss. No further. This is potentially a crime scene.'

But Bobby Jones was in no mood to tolerate procedure and the polite request of authority.

She issued a whispered demand to the bemused officer and pushed him squarely in the chest with both palms.

'Out of my fuckin' way, will ya.'

Onward Bobby Jones progressed.

The winch equipment now only a few metres away.

The metallic sky-blue Audi A4 gleamed oh so perversely.

She approached the rescue unit tent with increasing vigour and determination.

A trio of police officers now pursued her down the bank in a feeble effort to intercept her mission.

The members of the retrieval team became aware of her approach.

Yet they seemed strangely content to allow her closer access.

Bobby scrutinised the water that still dripped from the car's interior as she verged on the vehicle towards the boot.

Then her attention focussed through the rear windshield and further round to the right rear passenger door. Then she positioned herself adjacent to the vacant driver's seat.

The vehicle had not been touched by any officer. The driver's door was already opened when it was pulled from the water.

There was no sign of Jim Andrews.

Her attention instinctively lifted to scan the surface of the lake.

Bobby Jones wondered if his body was perhaps out there somewhere.

She then shifted round the bonnet of the vehicle and to the nearside front passenger door which remained closed.

Peering through the glass, she studied the bloated, grey-hued features of her fiancé.

It didn't look like Martin anymore, but it was indeed him.

Death had disfigured his form. His profile now distorted beyond any semblance of the handsome man who wanted to marry her.

And yet still Bobby Jones would not allow her mind to influence her response.

Unduly aloof and officious, she completed her inspection of the car's occupants by scrutinising Jamie's starkly posed body.

His eyes were closed, as though he might have accepted fate's final decree with a prayer. In his brand-new tailored trousers and jacket.

And it was then that she noticed the brothers were holding hands.

The constables that had been assigned to give chase finally reached her, albeit too late.

The peace that accompanied their respectful arrival was interrupted by Bobby as she began to whimper.

A whimper that swiftly evolved into an outpouring so profoundly deep and troubling, she doubled up with the agony of acceptance.

On her knees beside the car, Bobby toppled forward and slammed her forehead into the glistening grass of the bank.

The torrid aftermath of what had transpired hours earlier now capably pierced her once immune barrier of resistance.

The crippling eruption of emotion ripped through her very core.

The wailing resonated for all in proximity to hear.

And as the realisation of loss shredded her heart and soul, two officers gently lifted her to her feet and escorted Bobby Jones away from the scene.

And as she departed the malevolent arena, she somehow found inner sustenance to utter a declaration under her breath.

Words that would not carry any true definition with those trying to cradle her away from the horror.

Words that only she could possibly interpret as the officers shielded her view, ignorant of the whispered sentiment that was spoken.

Emitted in earnest.

Even as the numbing evidence of the treachery that she herself had given countenance to lay in her wake.

'Hope you got out, Jim. Please God. Let him make it.'

36
FOREVER AND EVER, AMEN.

Tuesday. The sixteenth day of January.

Two Thousand and Seven.

Nearly four weeks had elapsed since the tragedy at Collinson's Reservoir.

Despite the initial police investigation leaning heavily toward suspected foul play, the trail had rapidly gone as cold as the lake itself, in identifying any strand of mitigating evidence and indeed establishing any witnesses to support the theory.

A verdict from the coroner's office had recorded that both Martin Christopher Andrews and Jamie Michael Andrews suffered death by misadventure. Specifically, through drowning.

The verdict on the whereabouts of their father, one James Ronald Andrews, could not be determined.

Because the body of the father, James Ronald Andrews, had not been located at the scene.

And despite every weighted likelihood supporting the contrary, police were adamant in their claim that after several extensive searches, the body of the suspected driver was not in the water at all.

For all intents and purposes, James Ronald Andrews remained on file as presumed deceased, along with his two sons.

*****

Friday. The twenty-sixth day of January.

Two Thousand and Seven.

Ten-twenty a.m.

The congregation huddled outside the main doors of East Park Chapel. For those present, the emotional shellshock was tangible.

It was only correct that Alex had followed with her mother and father in the Lawley's family car behind the two hearses.

Bobby Jones had chosen to follow separately and alone in a funeral car of her own.

Tears fell without restraint as the cortege pulled to a stop under the chapel veranda. It was a sight that nobody could absorb without conceding to the unavoidable onset of distress.

The caskets were carried with a cautious and fragile dignity into the service chamber.

As the mourners respectfully filed behind, their entry was accompanied by a beauteous rendition of the ballad, The Wind Beneath My Wings.

As the arena began to occupy, the gravity of the occasion began to affect everybody as though in domino effect.

John Harrison never did manage that catch-up drink with Jamie.

He gingerly seated himself three rows behind the front pews. In his trembling grasp he held the order of service, which he endeavoured to study through a swiftly moistening gaze.

The photographs on the front depicted a shot of the two brothers as youngsters. Alex had found the stills in a forgotten box of keepsakes that was still stored in her father's garage.

The picture was taken in somebody's garden.

A hot summer's day. Circa nineteen-ninety.

The exact date was unknown. Who could ever know, now?

Jamie looked to be about three. Martin about ten-years-old.

When life for those two boys was possibly so much simpler.

And possibly, hopefully, so much happier.

Even though their untold sufferance was imminent.

John Harrison conceded defeat to his bravely stemmed tide of upset, as he laid the order of service down beside him. He covered his face with his hands and silently rocked in his seat, as realisation of the tragedy swamped him entirely.

Situated in the second row, Kevin Lawley glanced helplessly along the pew to his wife and daughter. Sarah dabbed her eyes with a tissue and stared straight ahead at the vacant pulpit.

Alex was emotionally lost.

She had hardly spoken a word to her parents since news of the accident reached public attention.

She first heard it on the subsequent regional TV news bulletin.

Twenty-four hours after the event itself.

Losing Jamie was agonising enough. Yet it was the ensuing shroud of mystery surrounding matters that currently remained her biggest source of anguish.

Inescapably visualising the horrific manner of his death was impossible to erase from her conscience. To hear how the brothers had perished was unthinkable.

But only learning of the disaster a full day later, and only learning of it via the media along with everybody else in the community, was the real pinch point for Alexandra Lawley.

Unacceptable and untenable in the extreme.

Whilst her heart was now irreparably broken, she had gleaned a crumb of comfort from the bottom of her personal pit of sorrow.

She had not discussed her opinions with anybody.

But in her own mind she accepted that her previous instincts were steadily being proven correct.

She had sensed something was amiss long before the accident. She had detected an undercurrent of dishonesty well before Christmas.

A strand of deceit that she couldn't locate or decipher at the time.

Yet the interim period between the brothers' death and the build-up to the funeral had invited her to contemplate this troubling matter further.

Especially when considering her suspicions had only been given more credence because Jim Andrews' body had not been retrieved from the scene of the crash.

This smacked of something untoward, yet Alex could not yet determine how the issue might begin to manifest itself more astutely for her. But whilst she might have taken slight recompense for retaining conviction in her beliefs, Alex did not want it to overshadow the true focus of the day.

She struggled gamely to divert her attention from the two coffins that had been positioned front and centre of the auditorium.

It was inconceivable to her that Jamie - the uncontested love of her life - and his adoring older brother, could be encased inside them.

Taken in the prime of their lives.

So young.

So vibrant.

So hopeful.

So tenacious.

So helpless.

So dignified.

So mistreated.

So misled.

And despite Alex Lawley's mindset being adequately consumed by those two symbols of abominable loss, her thoughts drifted once again for a few strangely scornful, intuitive seconds.

Her private inner debate raged on akin to a lapping fire.

Was the previously obscured picture now finally beginning to attain clarity?

Or was her judgement completely fabricating the horrific possibility of purposed wrongdoings and wilful betrayal?

It was perhaps not the most appropriate time to try and analyse the quandary. But the questions were certainly present in her conscience and screamed for answers.

Yet if Alex was eventually proven to be erroneous in her conjecture, then why should she feel so compelled in that very moment to study the back of Bobby Jones' head?

She found herself helplessly transfixed by the vision of Martin's fiancée sitting in the front pew across the aisle.

She hardly knew her. They had only crossed paths once.

It was a pensive, unfeeling encounter.

But something was severely out of sync.

Alex knew it for certain.

And the crushing, perplexing fact that Bobby had opted *not* to personally make Alex immediately aware of the accident, suggested a mind guided by extremely dubious persuasion.

In the view of the Lawley family, Bobby's unethical actions were unforgivably callous.

But of course, the occasion of this day befitted tribute.

Not conflict.

Alex would quietly and determinedly uphold her personal mission to uncover the truth.

And the current garland of doubt hanging over Bobby Jones in turn alluded to Alex's ominous theory that her true intent towards the Andrews brothers had been very adeptly disguised.

How long the suspected charade had been in play was currently indeterminable.

The concerning puzzle was some way from being solved, but Alex had pledged to herself that she would reach that definitive, elusive conclusion.

One way or another. Sooner or later.

The only slightly appeasing factor of the situation was that Alex held dear the knowledge that Jamie truly loved *her*.

He foresaw the dangers transpiring around the corner and his instruction for Alex to steer clear of the situation brewing at Glenfield Avenue was indeed wise and just.

He could surely never have predicted the horrendous circumstances of his own demise that evening, but he knew enough to keep Alex protected.

The thought had crossed her mind many times over the previous weeks that should she have been involved in the scenario, then she too would have undoubtedly been placed in great peril.

It was fatiguing for Alex to keep turning events over in her head.

So many theories. So few solutions.

Her concentration resumed on the two coffins. She needed all her powers of composure to get through the imminent service.

Whilst not being directly involved with the funeral arrangements, she had been compelled to request performance of a reading.

She had been given no official notification from Bobby that her request had been approved. Only today, on looking at the order of service, did she see that her name was inserted.

Provision had been made for Alex to speak.

Yet, once again, communication from Bobby had been non-existent.

Alex glanced around at the smattering of attendees.

It was upsetting to see so much empty space in the pews. She waved courteously to fellow former St George's pupil, Clair Richards, who reciprocated the gesture and offered a sorrowful half-smile.

And then, the introductory music ceased, and the master of ceremonies came forward to his podium at the front of the chamber.

Before commencing the tributes, he walked solemnly to both coffins and touched each in turn, whilst whispering words of consolation under his breath.

Like everyone else in the room, Alex observed the appointed celebrant as he conducted his own personal conveyance of thought toward those that had perished.

And as she watched, it occurred to her that the enormity of the atrocious losses was about to slam powerfully into her conscience.

She was secretly so grateful that the officiant at the head of the room was known to Jamie.

Her throat tightened as heaving upset breached her resistance.

As all awaited the Head of Service to begin.

He turned from the caskets and appointed himself to face the tentative, melancholic throng.

Never before had response to death encroached on him so keenly.

*****

Reverend David Carroll had never been so personally affected by the undertaking of professional duty.

In a role where forbearance and impartiality are regarded as pivotal cornerstones, he had been rendered completely vulnerable to a private storm of debilitating turmoil since learning of the brothers' fate.

When the news broke, he had instantly traced Bobby via the council registry office.

He openly volunteered his services to her.

She gave her blessing and entrusted him with the wholly unenviable honour.

Yet contrarily, since committing himself to such a potentially arduous task, he had begun to question his own motives for doing so.

He had spent the previous three weeks scrutinising his will to be personally involved.

His connection to events was undeniable.

Was he too closely associated with the deceased?

Was he too familiar to offer due diligence to matters today?

Would he harbour bias against the potentially incriminated and most notable absentee that day?

The boys' father, who had been portrayed to him as nothing less than an unscrupulous and uncaring individual from the moment his wife had first walked into the parish church to beg for help several years ago.

A man who radiated sheer, unregulated menace. Not just to his blood relatives and next of kin - but also to the public at large.

And David Carroll's own torment had garnered increasing momentum in the days since the order of service had been approved.

Such was the overriding shadow of desperation, that he even considered retracting his genuine offer to be chief celebrant.

But he soon judged this to be a cowardly act on his own behalf.

And certainly, he would not disrespect the poor young men who were so deserving of his sermon.

Never had he been required to dig so deeply into his own reserves of fortitude.

Yet today was establishing itself to be the biggest test of his career.

He had observed the pallbearers and their precious loads, with hands clasped and belated admiration flooding his veins.

He had observed the sparse and grieving throng that followed inside.

Perhaps like him, hoping that this might all be a terrible dream that was to be dispersed at any moment.

But no. Such was not the case.

And now the moment was upon him, he gently nodded to Bobby Jones, who responded in kind as if to give the order for this final, harrowing procedure to begin.

Drowning in deep, slow, mournful breaths, Father Carroll engineered himself ten seconds of enforced inner calm, before climbing the six steps of the pulpit.

*****

‘Today marks a day of extreme sorrow, as we gather here to collectively mourn our loss, and bid a final goodbye to our loved ones.

This moment evokes a particular poignancy for me also, as it marks the very first occasion that I have been appointed to conduct my role, having held a personal acquaintance with the deceased.

Whilst I shall of course endeavour to uphold the dignified nature of my participation in this service of remembrance, please extend your anticipated forgiveness should I falter at any time.

Much as it is for your good selves, the emotional toll is also mighty for me personally, and has yet to truly resonate. Of this I am certain.

Rest assured one and all, that I will attempt to fully restrain my own reactions and responses during the next minutes, as far as is humanly possible.’

Father Carroll reserved some time for a sip of a water and realignment of his composure.

The room was silent, aside the inevitable sniffs and sobs.

He stared directly at the back wall of the chapel and somehow summoned the courage to continue.

'I was first introduced to Jamie Andrews when he was seventeen-years-old. He sought me out in my ordained Parish residence just north of Nottingham, asking for advice and guidance regarding the sensitivities within his domestic circumstances.

Most of you present here would never have known of the troubles that Jamie and his dear older brother, Martin, had faced in their woefully short time on God's Earth.

They had been dealt impossible odds. Trauma and upset had nigh on trivialised their lives. Yet they were determined to overcome such hurdles and pave a different path to the one fate had seemingly committed them to.

The Andrews family consisted of four individuals that were entwined in a very unorthodox, and subsequently fragmented, existence. An existence that endured for the better part of three decades. The misery and upheaval dictated unto the boys as youngsters was relentless. And despite their highest intentions, such sufferance would prove, as today offers full testimony, to be their ultimate victor.

But I wish to dwell no further on the strife that pitted their background and upbringing.

Those of you present will undoubtedly be aware of the fuller story.

And I am sure that you would agree that today should act as a marker of positivity and solidarity, regardless of any detracting historical circumstances.

The family Matriarch, Elizabeth, passed some three years before her sons, and is laid to rest here within these very grounds. Now imminently to be reunited with her offspring, we can only hope that they will be back together in an infinitely more forgiving and rewarding place.

It is perhaps fitting that Roberta has chosen this next piece of music to commemorate this sentiment. It seems so relevant on so many levels.

Even in its most basic interpretation, this song epitomises the feeling of hope that earnest faith in God might bring us.

Please be standing, for our period of reflection.

As we immerse ourselves in the messages conveyed by the classic standard, Somewhere Over the Rainbow.'

*****

The resultant outpouring of grief was not withheld.

Emotion instantly gripped the room and shook it to its foundations.

Kevin Lawley squeezed the hands of his wife and daughter as they wavered helplessly either side of him, under the omnipotent assault of their loss.

He would stay strong for his ladies, for that is the automatic duty of the husband and father. And he held acute regret in his heart that he could not have loved Jamie more than he did.

As the music endured and eventually floated away to allow the resumption of silence, the resonance of the song stayed within the chamber.

Father Carroll waited for settlement once more, lightly dabbing his own eyes with a tissue before leaving his seat and reclaiming the pulpit.

'And now, I wish to invite Roberta to take this mark and offer her words of solace.'

All eyes intuitively rested on Bobby Jones.

And Alex could not source the instinctive and arising distaste.

It was something spiritual that conveyed to her the excruciating pangs of acute wariness and blatant injustice. She always trusted her gut feelings about everything and everyone.

And she would abide by them again here.

It was most discomforting for her to have generated such contempt toward Bobby Jones without any justifiably concrete cause. Today was certainly not the day for harbouring such misgivings or promoting such disharmony. But the sense of disharmony was there, nevertheless.

Alex could not fathom why she could so resent Bobby's very presence having barely made acquaintance with the woman.

Yet her very soul writhed with trepidation as she observed Bobby departing her place in the front pew and relocating to the pulpit.

Alex found herself involuntarily scrutinising Bobby's every facial and bodily expression.

Every presumed adjustment of weight from foot to foot. Every nuance of her physical demeanour might surrender a clue.

It was a gnawing, addicting infatuation for Alex.

Bobby was a very arresting woman in looks and she had done Martin proud with her appearance today. But Alex was convinced that behind the facade of inherent beauty, something unsavoury and elusive did lurk.

The persistent, irrational belief that Bobby Jones was an actress.

That she might not be the person she had purported to be to those in her adoptive family circle. And the impending reading did very little to soften the perception.

Alex physically flinched as the husked, Gaelic tones carried around the arena.

Forced to remain and endure the seminar, Alex listened as she combatted a convulsing dread.

*****

'Thank you so much, Father Carroll, for granting me this opportunity. I first met Martin when he was around the age of twenty. He had moved up to Blackpool with his father, Jim, about the same time I had shipped over the water from Belfast.

Blackpool can be a very harsh place for the lonely, but thankfully I had made a few friends in the town, and I also found work. And it was only through finding work, that I found Martin.

That night at The Celtic Arms my breath was taken away by the mere sight of the man. I was working the kitchen and every time I was called out to a table, Martin would be the very first thing I automatically engaged attention with.

He was such a handsome specimen. Film star material, for sure. But underneath the mouth-watering looks he seemed troubled.

It was only when I was introduced to his father, that I learned of Martin's autism. Because of his condition, even though it was relatively mild and mostly undetectable to the observer, he appeared isolated quite often. Separated from the activity and the people around him.

It might have been this reserved manner that attracted me to him. After all, I've been blessed with *more* than enough gob and bluster for two. So, it was perhaps understandable that we clicked as friends.

And I quickly discovered that he loved being with *me*. And there's not too many in *that* club, I can surely vouch for! I also discovered his incredible sense of humour.

He would comment on the most obscure things that caught his eye. Things that wouldn't even occur to most of us. But he was so funny and blunt with it. He would have me howling with laughter and our bond became very close.

I found myself helplessly falling in love with him. Head over heels. The works, absolutely. His father had observed that our relationship was blooming, and very generously offered us the chance to move in together at his home. Things were fine to begin with. However, over time, Martin confessed to me that he was missing his brother and his mum, who were still back here in Nottingham.

With his father's blessing, we decided to contact Jamie with a view to moving back to the Midlands to be with him. The plan was in motion until their mother unexpectedly passed away. But Jim, being the devoted and obliging father that he was, still gave us his blessing to go and see Jamie.

I can never thank Jim enough for the support and encouragement he gave us in our quest to reunite Martin with his young brother.

We eventually resettled in Nottingham and became engaged. We had a plan to marry, and life was rosy. But when things seem too good to be true, they usually are. Jim missed his sons so badly and would regularly come down to Nottingham to treat them.

The last visit he made he wanted to take them for a spin in his new car. The boys were so excited and couldn't wait. Tragically, our presence here today is indicative of how this ride concluded. The boys had a fantastic bond with their father. They each overcame the fact that estrangement had periodically intervened in their relationship, but they entrusted each other to see it to the other side.

The very last conversation I had with Jim was when he informed me of his intention to leave Blackpool and move closer to his sons. Tragically, this fantastic gesture is never to see the light of day.

But the renewed affection Jim showed towards his two boys still warms my heart now. His sons never knew of what he had planned. It would have been a wonderful surprise. And a long overdue reinstatement of the completed family unit.

Wherever he may be now, I hope for their sakes he hurries up and finds them again, so that they might live happily ever after again in another, less intolerant place.

From the bottom of my heart, I wish to thank you all for indulging me today. We can only hope the Andrews family are back where they belong. Together and protected.'

*****

It was a complete lie. A supremely polished sham.

An entirely distorted fabrication of the highest order.

A total concoction of assuredly invented threads.

A whimsical, cruel fallacy dreamed up to fool an unwitting audience.

Alex sat with gritted teeth and the encroaching disbelief encouraged a subsequent sense of nausea. Quaking with rage at the unseen crime that had just been committed in plain sight, she covertly glared at Bobby Jones, who walked back to her seat without emitting the merest hint of guilt.

How could she contentedly stand up there and spout such untruths?

Where was her conscience guiding her?

Where was her moral compass?

Just who *was* this charlatan calling herself Roberta Jones?

Alex's inner fury burned relentlessly.

Her parents had witnessed the performance just as she had.

They too knew it was a falsified chronicle of non-existent events.

Almost an act of deposition with motives conjured from fiction.

The Lawleys knew the hard and true facts behind the breakdown and demise of the Andrews family.

They were aware of the harsh reality that those brothers had to confront and had ultimately failed to overcome.

Yet the uninitiated public had been force-fed a very different tale.

One which could not be re-appointed for debate or analysis.

Not then.

Not today.

Not ever.

For all intents and purposes, Bobby Jones had successfully created the misconception that as the bride-to-be, she was effectively the one surviving victim of this torturous chaos.

And she knew that her apparent and as-yet unquestioned credibility could never be placed under doubt or scrutiny.

Not then.

Not today.

Not ever.

There was seemingly no scope to put right such a deceptive wrong.

Alex toiled with the despicable and despairing predicament.

As Father David Carroll reclaimed his place on the pulpit as Head of Service.

In readiness to announce Alexandra Lawley as the next reader.

37
RIDING THE DECEPTION

Suffering an untimely case of fingers and thumbs, Alex unfolded the three sheets of paper on which she had handwritten her personal tribute.

Father Carroll implored her to take her time so as not to become agitated. Having spent a few seconds analysing the order of her speech, Alex finally found the wherewithal to lift her head and address the transfixed gathering.

Engaging with the pews containing only two dozen or so faces was painfully upsetting, but she was absolutely determined not to let her emotions overrun her moment.

She had not been asked to participate in organising the ceremony.

She knew this was her one and only chance to offer a contribution of authentic pertinence.

Looking to the rear wall of the room and keeping her throat taut and tense, she hoped that such measures would be enough to allow her voice clean carriage.

A few more seconds elapsed as she ensured a delicate composure.

A fleeting glance at her intensely proud parents provided the inspiration to begin speaking. They were aware that the effect of Bobby's dubious presentation would have spurred their daughter in meeting this distressing challenge head on.

Alex Lawley was in no mood to let anyone down.

*****

'Jamie and I had known each other since Year Seven at St George's. We didn't really mix in the same circles at school. For a start, he always had a queue of other female admirers to keep happy.

And being the ugly duckling that I was…well, I was never likely to be competing for his attentions, was I? We were still virtual strangers even when it came time to take our GCSEs.

But eventually, once we both enrolled in Sixth Form, he began to see what he had been missing.'

Alex briefly surveyed the reactions of the congregation.

She heard chuckles and saw smiles beneath tear smudged eyes. Nods of reassurance from her parents. Expressions of near glee blossomed from Geoff Davies, Alan Steele and Carol Thraves. The teachers that knew both Jamie and Martin, and of course Alex herself.

Martin's personal school gang - Luke, Kieran, and Daniel - wiped their cheeks clean of upset as overdue humour temporarily took centre stage.

John Harrison looked on in admiration.

Bobby Jones simply glared.

An unreadable, fixed mask of abject indifference.

Yes. Alex knew now that her personal instincts were justified.

Something about this scenario was so wrong.

So very, *very* wrong.

But Alex resumed her concentration and moved on to the next page.

'Strangely enough, I had completely given up on the idea of boys by the age of sixteen. And then, one day, as I walked down the stairs of the Sixth Form block, I caught the school heartthrob staring at me.

He was in the tennis courts, showing off with his mates.

So, I thought it only right that if he was staring at me, then I was entitled to stare back. I gave it little further thought and sat on a bench overlooking the court. Then suddenly he appeared next to me and began to try and use his charm. What can I say? It worked! From that point on we became an official couple.

I was in heaven. He was an incredible person. When he eventually went to find his brother, Martin, I stayed behind in Nottingham. He had my full blessing to follow his destiny. But I don't wish to stand here and dwell on his family troubles. It's not my business. And it's not relevant to today.

But like everyone here, I reference the two brothers now, and consider the futile tragedy of it all. Two lives taken in their prime.

Gone forever.

Yet at least they can remain together in their next life.

And of course, they will be back with their mum. For me, that is the happiest ending any of us could truly wish for. Because eventually, we are all destined to be taken from each other.

Sometimes fairly. Sometimes not.

And one day, I sincerely hope that *I* can meet Jamie again.

And it will be in a much nicer world.

Without the lies and the distress.

Without the malice and the violence.

A better place, where love can thrive instead of being trampled on and suffocated. I will forever cherish my time with him.

Our relationship was short, but all the sweeter for the fact.

Jamie my darling.

I will always love you.

Sleep soundly and we will meet again in that better place.'

*****

Alex re-joined her parents having rendered the entire attendance in a flood of appreciative outpouring. It wasn't an intention to encourage the trail of tears, but it was part and parcel of the moment.

She did not catch the eye of Bobby Jones as she walked past.

That was a determined effort on Alex's part.

Father Carroll resumed his role and waited patiently as emotion ran its course among the pews.

Sarah Lawley hugged her daughter in a gesture of immense maternal pride and overwhelming reverence. Alex had performed heroically, and even now as she sat down with the disguised fury exploding within her, she remained firmly restrained.

As the throng again settled to silence, the Master of Ceremonies stared blankly ahead, retaining a forlorn expression.

Even *he* had been dreading this moment.

Martin and Jamie had received their posthumous accolades.

It was nearly time for the ultimate, abiding, final farewell.

'Could everyone please be standing for The Lord's Prayer.'

Like everyone else, Alex rose to her feet and began to mutter those immortal lines under her breath. She had envisaged this juncture in the proceedings many times over.

And even though it now felt so very real and raw, she still held a strand of hope in her heart that it was in fact a figment of fiction.

Hoping that in truth, nobody was required to be in that chapel at East Park. And that nobody had passed.

And that she still had Jamie by her side, to hold and to protect.

She mouthed the words of the prayer soundlessly now.

As the conclusion to the service was pending.

A few seconds of quiet resumed as Father Carroll then politely requested that everyone be seated again.

'I am quite certain that Martin and Jamie would have been very humbled to view the attendance for them here today. Friends, acquaintances, and associates from their individual and collective lives. But as your grief naturally re-emerges, and believe me I feel it too, we should bear this in mind.

Those brothers would not want to see us in pain.

They would not wish to see you weep.

They would not wish to be mourned.

They would be encouraging you to see this day as a celebration.

And as we pledge to them our last parting thoughts, we should remember that we are presenting them into God's care now.

We must hold faith that they will prosper under him, and that their spirits will revive as buoyant and vigorous.

We send Martin and Jamie to our Lord, entrusting him with their futures and in turn hoping that the memories we hold dear will forever burn brighter knowing they are now in safe hands.

And now it is time, to pledge them forth unto him. And we shall carry hope that one day, we may be joined again.

The music to accompany their departure has been specifically chosen by Bobby, in tribute to her fiancée and his younger brother.'

*****

Alex put her hand to her mouth and felt her stomach cramp with excruciating agony. Disorientation was her immediate companion.

The song Bobby had chosen was not overly familiar to Alex, but Bon Jovi's 'Never Say Goodbye' was a powerful and moving ballad that touched a very vulnerable nerve with everybody present.

And unbeknown to all aside Bobby, they were Jim Andrews' favourite rock group.

The curtains began to enclose the two coffins, prior to being deposited at their final resting place.

Alex glanced to her parents, who had already succumbed to the mighty swell of their despair.

And this was the trigger point for Alex herself.

She wailed unashamedly with the wrenching agony of her loss, swaying and buckling under the mighty power of human response.

Finally, as the curtains drew fully, it hit her that she would never see the love of her life ever again.

She held her midriff and covered her eyes amid the weight of such fraught acknowledgement.

She found herself unable to observe any more of the dismal and heart-breaking spectacle.

Unlike Bobby Jones.

Who stood and stared at the curtains, as if to ensure their closure would be fully completed.

Not a flicker of emotion.

No reaction whatsoever, either to the scene at the front of the hall or to the surrounding bouts of individual release.

The music continued to provide its hauntingly glum backdrop to the untold sorrow that was in evidence behind her.

And then Father Carroll beckoned Bobby toward him to be the first of the congregation to file out of the hall.

Alex and her mother and father followed and thanked the reverend for his respectful and moving speech.

The exterior veranda of the chapel allowed the mourners to join and study the floral tributes. The crowd reconvened in that small, paved annex and attempted to stem its free-reigning desolation.

Paying their due attention to one another.

Conveying their many plaudits about the Andrews brothers.

John Harrison was to be seen in the mid distance, offering Bobby a warm and meaningful hug as some minor consolation for her loss.

Her *loss.*

Her supposed…*loss*…

And at that precise moment, despite the internal maelstrom still residing within, Alex decided to make the move.

Never mind the reputable occasion.

Never mind the ignorance of protocol.

Never mind the supposedly atrocious timing.

Appropriate or not, Alex was already weaving her way through the group toward the target. Compulsion drove her.

Compulsion that had gently simmered for several weeks.

With no one separating them, the two women engaged stares.

Mutual, nervous smiles were triggered.

Their embrace might have appeared genuine to the casual observer, but it disguised long harboured mutual suspicions between the participants.

Alex pulled away again and looked her counterpart directly in the eye. Her adopted officious tone did not diminish.

'How are you, Bobby? Your reading was interesting.'

Bobby Jones was not caught off guard.

She had secretly anticipated this contact and replied accordingly.

'So was yours, Alex. You're so brave. It packed a real punch, to be sure.'

Alex glanced around ensuring the pair were out of earshot.

Her faux expression of sincerity supplemented her next words.

'Listen, obviously there's no wake been arranged. So, I thought I'd grab you now before we go our separate ways again.'

Bobby revealed an element of surprise in her response.

'Oh really? What's up, Alex?'

This was easier than had been anticipated.

Alex didn't adjust her flow of focus.

'Can I have your phone number? I'll let the dust settle for a while. But I thought it would be nice for me and you to give the boys a proper send off at a later date. Just the two of us. What do you say?'

Alex sensed a twinge of unease in Bobby's demeanour.

Possibly for the first time that day.

'That would be lovely, Alex. What a great idea! I'm not really in the mood to booze today, anyway. So doing it another time is fine by me. We can decide what we would like to do with the ashes, too.'

With numbers promptly exchanged, Alex Lawley and Bobby Jones pledged to meet up soon enough.

They bid one another a temporary farewell.

The opportunity for Alex to unveil her misgivings was secured.

It would be the least that Jamie deserved.

And perhaps Martin too, for that matter.

*****

The congregation gradually dispersed.

Alex followed her parents into the chapel's rear yard, intermittently wiping her eyes with a tissue.

One by one, cars carrying the mourners began to exit the crematorium grounds. In truth, most of them were glad the formalities of the day were over.

But most of them had very little comprehension of the underpinning events that led to the deaths of Jamie and Martin Andrews.

Most of them would never get to learn of such terrible truths, either.

Just as most of them would not have had any cause to notice the black Lexus stationed in the far corner of the car park as they left.

The black Lexus that was not present when the congregation began to arrive some ninety minutes earlier.

The black Lexus that was parked adjacent to Kevin Lawley's silver Ford.

The black Lexus that contained a driver and two passengers.

All three of whom had stringently scrutinised the departing throng.

Alex climbed into the rear passenger seat of the silver Ford behind her mother and pulled the door closed.

Still oblivious to the vehicle parked beside her father's.

She would never have suspected that she was under the watchful eye of the occupants.

Occupants that had deliberately remained secluded for the duration of the service.

Because their particular line of business that day was not concerned with paying their respects.

Not for them was the attending of any funeral or the offer of any tribute. Their agenda was far different in motive and nature.

Alex would not have recognised the men, even if she had been given due cause to glance in their direction.

The figure behind the wheel of the black Lexus covertly observed the Lawley's silver Ford move away, before engaging the engine and following discreetly behind.

Once beyond the security barrier of the chapel property, the cars travelled in opposite directions.

The driver of the silver Ford, Kevin Lawley, was an upstanding, law-abiding citizen. A committed family man.

The driver of the black Lexus was a man of most ailing repute.

A dangerous mind that gave no concern for infringement on the lives of others. Lauded by some as the most notorious underground criminal in the north of England.

But understandably, it would only be fellow undesirables that could ever be aware of this character and his penchant for intimidation and savagery.

Because upstanding members of the community would never have had cause or misfortune to cross paths with the man named Frank McCafferty.

It stood to reason that in his line of work he would never touch the lives of the strait-laced, the law-abiding and the responsible.

However, his two accomplices sitting behind him had been asked to attend to purposely observe the trail of mourners at the chapel.

To ascertain the identities of those present.

Of particular interest to McCafferty and his discerning cohorts was the dark-haired woman from Belfast.

She was a supposedly vital link, according to his passengers.

And according to them, her ‘turn’ was definitely overdue.

They had certainly not driven to Nottingham to pay tribute to the late sons of their one-time friend and associate.

And it remained to be discovered what indeed had happened to that very same one-time friend and associate.

On the day of that very same accident where his sons were left to drown.

Because so far as they were concerned, their one-time friend and associate was still very much a wanted man.

And they believed absolutely that a certain Roberta Jones would be able to provide information as to his current whereabouts.

Frank McCafferty was a patient fellow in general.

But he had overly extended and now fully exhausted - his level of generosity to the one-time friend and associate who still owed him.

As he drove his black Lexus with both hands resting lightly on the wheel, he glanced in the rear-view mirror and addressed his companions in the back seat.

‘A little further along with the hunt today, boys. Little steps…big progress, eh? No rush, though. I wonder where our mate could be then?’

Loz Prenter and Ian Doyle smiled back at the reflection in the tiny square of glass.

Both nodded to McCafferty, as they anticipated that the active pursuit of their one-time friend and associate, would not be far away from commencement.

But for now, they would let their network of contacts do its job.

Because bad pennies *always* turn up.

Eventually.

38
LOOSE ENDS AND CONVICTION

Three weeks after the funeral of Martin and Jamie Andrews.

East Park.

The bench by the rain shelter.

A biting mid-February breeze tormented the bare branches of the nearby towering poplar trees. Yet a sliver of blue sky was occasionally allowed to peep through the layered blankets of grey cloud and the infrequent sunrays were welcome.

Alex stared straight ahead into the silent vista. From her position on the bench, she barely acknowledged the limited activity around the parkland.

Accommodating her broken heart had not deterred her from wishing to sate her curious and perplexed state of mind.

Her personal grief had no hiding place.

Pining for Jamie every single minute of the day was never how it was supposed to transpire.

Yet that is how fate had played its hand.

Strangely, the harrowing demise of the Andrews family had seemed almost a conjured misconception as opposed to a true-life drama.

Reality made its relentless presence known second by despairing second. Alex was prepared to resist its uninvited intrusion for as long as necessary.

But the constant reminders of her loss were barbed and persistent.

No one deserved to die.

No one.

Yet it seemed those brothers were always deemed to fall foul of terrible circumstance.

Perhaps this was the script written many years ago?

Would anybody have been able to interfere with or obstruct what had been ordered to take place?

Extremely doubtful.

And this somewhat cold, philosophical approach was currently much preferred to the reflective and emotional option.

But at least Alex knew that she had touched the heart of at least one of the victims. For that is what the Andrews family were.

Victims of an inflexible blueprint.

Victims of an existence that was never of their own design.

And Alex had learned to accept this harsh realisation.

The fact being, that despite the intrinsic bond she and Jamie had constructed, she would never have extricated him from the perpetual downward spiral that his life was caught up in.

Through her inherent moral fibre and common sense, she might have made his journey a little more bearable along the way, but his final destination was somehow inevitable.

Another fleeting thought occurred to her a few days after the funeral.

The observation that each of the Andrews clan had endured their entire lives as a form of penance.

Not one iota of inner contentment.

Not one moment of genuine, carefree joy.

No consideration was ever afforded to them.

No understanding was conveyed by others on their behalf.

Just a monotonous clawing through a debilitating social fog.

Finding instinctive handholds and footholds that might have offered a temporary stability, but they were never the permanent anchors that were needed for survival.

They aspired to higher things eventually, of course. Yet even as they climbed, the rockface was crumbling around them.

Any semblance of security they may have established was swiftly robbed from them.

Ultimately, they served out a futile sentence.

No reasoning attached to the atrocious conclusion they suffered.

Just a sense of utter emptiness remained.

A painful void where they once stood.

In her conscience and in person.

Amid her private analysis on that bench, Alex had not noticed the saltwater that had begun to stream from her eyes.

She let the tears fall freely.

She harboured no desire to conceal her hurt.

She had only known Jamie for a short expanse of her twenty years, yet he became integral to her emotional stability and wellbeing.

The confusing period of their estrangement only served to fuel the mutual appetite to reunite.

And how sweet it was.

So implicitly rewarding and gratifying.

She never stopped loving him.

And she knew full well that Jamie Andrews cherished the very ground she walked upon.

Her head might have argued the case at times, but her heart persistently triumphed.

Love doesn't play by the rulebook.

Their loyalty to one another was never quashed.

Camouflaged maybe, occasionally.

But never quashed.

And despite the onslaught of searing anguish that she now had to navigate every waking moment of every single day, Alex was adamant that she would not have changed a thing.

She willingly danced to destiny's tune.

Until the very end.

*****

When she contacted Bobby Jones forty-eight hours ago, Alex knew there was only one location she wished to meet up. Sitting on that bench brought warm memories flooding back, and bitter grief flooding forth.

But the request to convene was not borne out of consideration or compassion.

After all, Alex hardly knew Bobby Jones.

Their minimal communication in the build-up to the funeral was only a conduit for formalising details.

And even these exchanges were conveyed via Father Carroll.

They had never had the opportunity to develop any affinity for one another. And Alex now found herself thankful for that very fact.

Even though they had lived through the same tragedy and supposedly suffered equal loss, they were effectively still strangers.

But Alex had spent the recent weeks analysing events according to her own prior interpretation.

And she had formed judgements on what had - and indeed, what had *not* - occurred.

Supporting Jamie was always her number one point of focus. But Alex was intelligent and wily enough to see the picture beyond the one that had publicly presented itself.

And for Alex Lawley, there was an undying sense of inscrutability surrounding events. Thrown across the recent catastrophe was a veil of intrigue. Something about it all didn't add up. She felt that the common perception of those involved was somehow woefully misaligned. To a very disconcerting degree.

She never mooted her concerns to Jamie directly. He had more than enough to contend with. But In Alex's eyes, situations had developed rather too conveniently for some.

Her intuition led her to hold the view that amid the apparent unity exhibited within the walls of number thirty-two, Glenfield Avenue, earnest motives were not necessarily being employed.

She always trusted her initial responses to what she was experiencing, even if there was limited scope to act upon them. She wasn't a conspiracy theorist as such, but human nature is fallible.

And gullible.

And vulnerable.

Alex possessed cynicism in her make-up that she could not simply dismiss. She held the belief that matters were not as they appeared.

That people were not who they purported to be.

Would she go as far as to entitle her suspicions under the banner of outright deceit? The potential was there. But the jury was still out.

The plan to take breathing space after the funeral was correct and respectful to the memories of those that perished. But as the days and nights elapsed, Alex's underlying frustration only palpitated more aggressively.

Meeting with Bobby might well only serve to finally dissipate her ingrained misgivings, and allow the future to become her guide, as opposed to the past.

Similarly, it may have been far too soon to scrutinise and analyse.

But by the same token, she hoped that Bobby would be willing to engage in open discussion so both could assert clarity in some relatively muddied waters.

Yet in tandem with this hope, Alex was wary of the other side of the coin being displayed.

That being, that the playing field may prove itself not to be level.

That unscrupulous actions and plans were and indeed, *are* afoot.

For Alex, she could not grieve authentically without establishment of the truth.

She required a solid solution to her inner dilemma.

And as she pondered that very ambition, the uppermost subject in her thoughts suddenly appeared from the car park and walked steadily toward the bench where she was seated.

Alex Lawley felt nothing for the oncoming Bobby Jones.

Nothing that is, but an all-consuming prudence.

And anguish that craved respite.

39
TRUE COLOURS?

The women embraced tightly. They held one another for several seconds in a display of faux affection and obligatory consideration.

On the face of it, the moment was mutually bittersweet and yet necessarily fabricated.

Neither would have willingly elected to be convening under such circumstances.

The supposed reaction of numbness was natural.

Genuine pleasure at their re-acquaintance was highly improbable.

Yet the initial vibe ably masked over the glaring cracks of distrust.

'You're looking very stylish, Alex. Very seasonal, so you are.'

Bobby's smirking compliment was slightly disarming and unexpected, forcing Alex into immediate scrutiny of her companion's attire.

Black Denim jeans and jacket. Brown leather cowboy boots. Thick woollen pullover. Dressed for the weather, certainly. And a world away in style from the formal image Bobby had conveyed at the funeral.

'Please don't feel obliged to tell me I look nice, Alex. I look like a pile of laundry. But I just can't be bothered to make the effort at the moment. You know what I mean?'

Alex smiled politely, nodded, and gestured for them both to be seated.

'Yes, of course I know exactly what you mean. Fashion isn't top of my list lately, either.'

Both settled onto the bench and stared toward the manicured acreage of the park. Even in winter it was expertly tended by the council gardeners. Seasonal blooms and the general ambience of the area made it an idyllic setting for a potentially disconcerting exchange.

'Lovely place, this. I can see why you like it, Alex. So peaceful. I could really tap into my inner self, here.'

Alex was cautious in selecting her reply.

‘It’s just so sad we are here at all. Doesn’t seem real. Does it? The both of them. *Gone!* How can it be? Surely, they should be sitting here with us?’

Bobby crossed her legs and took tissues from her handbag.

‘Mega strange times. I’m lost with it all and that’s a fact. Like I’ve had my arms cut off.’

‘It’s understandable, Bobby. We’ve got a lot of pain to shoulder between us, haven’t we.’

Bobby gazed at Alex as though unsure how to venture forward with the conversation and avoid becoming weighed down by upset.

‘You know, I never thought of it like that. You’re right, Alex. It’s just me and you now, isn’t it? Nobody else around that gives a damn. So far as I can count.’

Alex contemplated her next statement carefully and was eventually convinced that it seemed appropriate.

Yet she also knew that the question would likely open a potentially undesirable can of worms. But she was not dissuaded to continue.

This was the reason Alex called for the meet-up.

To uncover the *truth*.

She inhaled deeply before opening her gambit.

‘Who are you *really* grieving for, Bobby?’

That was it. No backtracking now.

The words were out in the open and even Alex was taken aback by her own courage in stoking the embers of Bobby’s somewhat diminished fire.

The delicacy of the timing might have been debatable.

But the desire to learn the response was not.

Bobby’s silence endured for ten seconds or more before she turned her head at right angles to face her inquisitor.

‘*What* did you just ask me?’

Alex retained composure as she sensed her counterpart’s temper already beginning to rumble. But Alex was a slave to the compulsion she felt inside. She refused to relent in her quest.

'It's a simple enough question, Bobby. As you sit here with me now, on this bench in this park…whose absence hurts *you* most of all?'

Bobby shifted position to square up her body toward Alex.

She displayed a grimace of confusion.

'Am I hearing things, Alex…or are you going mad?'

The crystalline eyes engaged with Bobby's deep brown stare.

'No…I'm perfectly sane. I'll ask you a different way, then. Who is your heart breaking for, today?'

More soundless moments of deliberation led Bobby to turn the intrusive query on its head.

'*You* tell *me*, Alex. Did you *really* love Jamie? Or was he just another bloke in the end?'

Alex felt more than comfortable in supplying her reply.

She was also quietly amazed that the exchange had not already developed into full scale hostility.

Perhaps she had underestimated Bobby Jones after all.

Alex was prepared for absolute honesty toward her companion.

Figuring that it might give Bobby the motivation to react in kind.

'Jamie and I were soul mates. Whether that is equated to love, I don't know. But we fitted together perfectly. But life wouldn't let our relationship run its course. Shit was getting in the way all the time. I suppose you feel the same way about Martin, don't you?'

Alex observed Bobby divert her attention back across the distant parkland once again.

Looking for distractions in the scenery, perhaps.

The infrequent mothers with pushchairs and the occasional dog walkers.

The intermittent joggers and the unpredictable cyclists.

Alex was determined to peel away the top layer of the enigma that Bobby Jones portrayed herself to be.

Eventually, the thinly disguised probing received a considered retort.

Would it be construed by Alex as honest, though?

‘My relationship with Martin wasn’t ideal to say the very least. It was only when we came down to Nottingham to live with Jamie that we began to settle and find some level of happiness. Like a proper couple, you know?’

Alex’s enthusiasm for the dig was now being fuelled with each passing second. The discussion had only two partakers.

The scheme was working.

Permitting Alex to go for the throat.

‘Why did you tell lies at the funeral, Bobby?’

‘*Lies*? Lies about *what*?’

‘About Jim wanting to bring you down here. About Jim’s persona and attitude to his sons? About him wanting to be with them?’

Bobby Jones was visibly grasping for an alibi but there was no wriggle room under the glare of the spotlight.

Only now would she be discovering that Alex Lawley knew *everything*.

About *everything*.

There was no hiding place, no mitigation, and no escape.

Alex pressed further with the cross examination.

‘Have you ever wondered what might have happened if Jamie hadn’t come to get his brother? Where you might be living, right at this very moment? What life might now be like for you had you remained up in Blackpool?’

Incredibly, Bobby continued to resist the opportunity to bite back.

Her buttons were being forcibly pushed, but she held her composure admirably.

‘I dread to even think about it, Alex. I really do. But it’s all rhetoric now, isn’t it? I don’t see much point talking about it at all if I’m fair with you.’

Alex let her gaze wander to a passing gardener pushing a wheelbarrow full of topsoil. She had also noticed a convincing piece of evidence which prompted the next question.

Bobby was no longer wearing her engagement ring.

‘Do you truly think you and Martin would have got married, eventually?’

Bobby raised an eyebrow and again looked at Alex in bemusement.

The questioning was well prepared it seemed. As though Alex was conducting an enquiry of sorts.

‘We shall never know, shall we? I’d like to think so. Maybe. At some point. But like you just said…fate tended to continually fuck everyone’s plans up.’

Alex quietly considered her next tangent for a few moments.

‘*Everyone’s* plans? Or just *some* people’s plans?’

Bobby refrained from replying.

If she possibly believed that the questioning was perhaps odd or unwarranted, then the next issue to be raised was sure to spark her alertness to this fact.

‘Strange business about their father coming back to Nottingham. Don’t you think?’

Bobby began to fondle the silver locket hanging around her neck.

She had immediately been placed on the back foot by the suggestion.

Her tone was now becoming defensive.

‘I don’t get what you mean, Alex? *Strange*? In what way?’

Alex selected her phrasing cautiously.

Her combinations were forcing Bobby back to the ropes.

‘Well…for a start…as an observer I never understood why he would follow you all back here. To all intents and purposes, I was under the impression that his relationship with the three of you was dead and buried after the fight in Blackpool. There was certainly nothing to tempt him down here again. To my mind his only possible motive would be revenge. But that’s just *my* silly line of thought.’

Bobby’s stance ushered to side implicitly with Jim Andrews.

And in doing so she was exposing herself perfectly.

‘He’s not a vengeful man. He isn’t the type. It’s not in his nature to be like that at all.’

Alex wanted to laugh out loud at the preposterous remark.

Bobby was now blatantly justifying the supposed integrity of Jim Andrews' character.

Being coerced into even attempting to polish the reputation of a violent, callous, and abusive drug dealer, was exactly the tripwire Alex wanted Bobby to stumble into.

And Alex had to run with the baton now.

'Well…I have to say I'm literally stuck for words after listening to that, Bobby. He was a wild animal. Untamed and fearless. He had no qualms about hurting people that got in his way. I was told that you and Martin suffered terrible treatment. The scars on Martin's hands told a story of their own.'

Bobby was beginning to lose her previously impressive composure.

'Can we not talk about Jim in the past tense, please. He's not been found dead *or* alive.'

Alex smiled inside.

This was infinitely easier than she had anticipated.

Alex now felt rather relentless as she went through the gears of her personal investigation.

'He was a corrupt and nasty bastard, Bobby. How you can even conceive to protest otherwise is beyond me.'

'Is that what Jamie told you, is it? Is that really the picture he painted for you? Well, if not you've got a great imagination considering you never witnessed a fucking thing, Alex. Did you ever even *meet* Jim?'

The antagonism between them was building steadily.

They directly faced one another from each end of the bench.

Both exhibited expressions of dismay and anger as the atmosphere swiftly began to sour.

'Jamie told me you ended up black and blue because of Jim whilst he was with you in Blackpool.'

Bobby shook her head in fragile denial.

'That was different. Just a misunderstanding. That's all.'

'You're defending him again, Bobby. Why?'

Alex sighed as her long held suspicions were now acquiring some credibility.

The meat was forming on the bones.

Despite everything he had engineered, Jim Andrews obviously still had at least one ally remaining in Bobby Jones. But this defied logic. Surely in her position and considering what she knew about him, she should rightly be wishing him to be found at the bottom of that reservoir.

But no. The opposite appeared to be true. As though she were on some personal campaign to deflect him from criticism and even go as far as offer positive appraisal.

But Alexandra Lawley was tenacious and dogged.

She intended to force Bobby Jones into opening completely up.

'Do you hope Jim is still alive?'

Bobby's agitation was now simmering over the edge.

'What the fuck is that supposed to mean, then?'

'Exactly as it sounds. Simple question. Simple answer. Do you?'

'You've got a fucking nerve getting me here for this.'

Alex was prepared to smother Bobby Jones with her interrogation if necessary. The signals were increasingly telling.

Alex wilfully accelerated the tension of the moment.

'Do you think he came back to Nottingham knowing full well that Jamie had inherited all that money and that house? A quarter of a million pounds worth of estate? The estate you have presumably inherited as the chosen and last surviving trustee of the will Jamie wanted you to be party to. You're a very lucky girl, yes? Very lucky indeed.'

Bobby rose to her feet, snarling in retaliation.

'What the fuck has any of that got to do with *you*, lady? I can tell you what it's got to do with you. Fuck all! *That's* what!'

Alex sensed appeasement flowing through her bloodstream.

'But you're still living there. Probate won't take that long if you're in the will as the surviving beneficiary. Which is exactly what you are.'

'Mind your own fucking business you stuck up cow. For two pins I'd knock your head off here and now.'

Alex remained unruffled, now content that the authentic story was about to unfold with little further prompt.

'I was just making the point, Bobby. That Jamie's sudden wealth could possibly have been the lure that eventually drew his father back here. It's a fair assumption, isn't it? That a man as ruthless and greedy as him would not be able to resist the temptation. And I know that Jamie eventually gave him a fair wedge of cash, too.'

The spite nurtured between the two women was now sparking.

But if it got Alex to the core of the issue then the increasingly unpleasant altercation would be more than worth it.

Bobby's impatience with the exchange was now fully disclosed and on display. Her raised voice echoed along the footpath and around the treeline of the enveloping parkland.

'Stick your assumptions where the sun doesn't shine. And anyway…how do *you* know what Jamie was worth? Did he tell you himself, did he?'

'Yes, of course he did. We didn't have any secrets. We were soul mates…remember? Jay confided everything to me.'

'Well, he had no bloody right to! It was family stuff! Should have been kept private!'

Alex smirked in disgust. She was within touching distance of solving a mystery that had plagued her for so many weeks.

'You see…this is what puzzles me, Bobby. I've explained to you how *I* came to know about the inheritance. But there's no explanation as to how *Jim* came to find out about it. The boys certainly wouldn't have spilled the beans for obvious reasons. *Would* they?'

'Jim knew nothing about the money. He had no idea.'

The lies were so predictable.

Alex veritably bathed in her imminent glory.

'I beg to disagree, Bobby. I was there in the café when they first met up last year. Jamie's father knew all about the savings. That's why he wanted the meeting. I can assure you. He made out he was being chased by creditors and that he needed Jamie to help him pay them off.'

Bobby Jones simultaneously clenched her teeth and her fists.

Alex was enjoying Bobby's visible struggle to squirm free from the shackles of allegation. She persisted with the onslaught.

But the opponent was not quite ready to hit the canvas just yet.

'Okay, Sherlock. What's *your* theory. then?'

Alex now rose from the bench and moved closer to Bobby.

'It was no coincidence at all that once Jamie's inheritance cleared, his father was straight down to Nottingham sniffing out the purse.'

Bobby laughed out of despair at the disabling condemnation.

Alex was aware things might get out of hand at any moment.

'Another one of Jamie's fairy stories, yes? My god you're green as grass, Alex. Jamie was no angel, you know. You'd believe anything he said, wouldn't you?'

Bobby was clutching at straws now as she too stood up.

Her disguise was slipping.

Her initially tolerant temperament had evaporated.

'Yes, I would. Jamie was totally above board. And he made the mistake of thinking those around him were too! He would have never suspected foul play. Especially by *you*. And before you ask, no I didn't.'

'Didn't *what*?'

'I never ever discussed my opinion on this with him.'

'Oh, so this is purely your own bit of deduction work then, is it? Okay then, Columbo. If you've got all the answers, who tipped Jim off?'

Alex found Bobby's transparency to be disappointing.

It wasn't a pleasant sensation to be proved right all along.

The pair were almost nose to nose as they stared straight into one another and communicated in veritable whispers.

'Let's consider this by a process of elimination. Jamie *didn't*...Martin *wouldn't*...which leaves the only possible remaining suspect.'

'Really? Who?'

Alex carried no expression as she revealed her conclusion.

'You, Bobby. *You* told Jim about the money.'

Bobby's feigned chuckle could not hide the underlying aggression she now felt because of the charges put to her.

'*What*? Am I hearing you right, lady? Is this a bad dream? This your idea of a sick joke, is it?'

Alex now felt more assured than ever.

'It's the only possible verdict. *You* told Jim about Jamie's money. *You* encouraged him down to Nottingham. *You* betrayed Jamie and Martin.'

A cold silence befell the scene as Bobby turned away to hide her rippling guilt. But she would not crumble totally.

Now cornered, she had little option but to come out fighting.

'How…*dare* you. You don't even *know* Jim Andrews! You barely even know *me*! You call me up to meet you here. You accuse me of *this* and accuse me of *that*. You take the moral high ground about things that are nothing to do with you and that you have no knowledge of…'

Bobby squared up to Alex, whose own heart now raced with full expectation of pending physical assault.

Yet still she would persevere.

She would pursue absolute establishment of the facts.

'You're correct about one thing, Bobby. I don't know you at all. Which is why you aren't going to deceive me like you did those poor brothers. I don't buy the brash tom-boy act. I knew you were the weak link in the chain from the moment I set eyes on you. I believe Jim has moulded you into someone else than who you really are. Fed you rubbish and lies so he can get his hands on his son's cash. So, in reality, it's *you* who's the gullible one. Isn't it? And if it makes you feel any better, *neither* brother worked you out. They both thought you were the genuine article. They *both* loved you. Those poor, poor, misguided boys.'

Bobby Jones forcefully moved stance into Alex's personal space.

The blue painted nail of her right index finger moved just millimetres away from the end of Alex's chin.

'You snotty little *bitch*. We haven't even laid the brothers' ashes to ground and you're throwing your fucking weight around.'

Alex shook her head in dismissal.

'Don't come that with me, Bobby. You don't give two shits about the boys or their ashes. It didn't take you very long to take that solitaire off your finger. And whilst on the subject of their remains, *I'll* be sorting that out in due course. They belong with their mother. I don't want you anywhere near them again. Do you hear me? They've suffered more than enough because of you.'

Alex's emotions were now unexpectedly rising to the fore.

But she was not too disarmed to deflect an advancing fist away from her face. She grappled Bobby's jutting forearm with all her might.

The explosion had finally happened.

Bobby attempted to strike Alex again but the restraint on her was too strong.

Alex held firm under attack.

She was more than prepared.

'Protest all you like. My suspicions only arose because Jim was so bloody *greedy*. If he'd have been more patient, I might not have seen it coming so clearly. *You* might have even got away with it, too.'

Bobby Jones showed no contrition whatsoever.

She saw no just cause for repentance.

Her frothing anger was symptomatic of the ruse being unveiled.

'Sticking your fucking nose in where it doesn't belong. Beware, lady, I tell you. Keep sticking it in and it will get bitten off!'

'You're missing the whole point, Bobby. The boys never knew what your game was, did they? And now they never will. Your plan has *worked*. You get the full share of the spoils. Just how Jamie would have wanted it. And just how you and Jim planned it. It makes no odds to me, really. But I just wanted you to know…that I was on to you and your scheming…never forget that. I worked you out straight away…'

'Well, you can sleep soundly now can't you. Little Miss Innocent. Never done wrong in your life, have you.'

The tears again streamed down Alex's face, and she had no desire to conceal the secretion of her long-held vexation.

‘I’ve never *pretended* to love someone. I don’t know what you were cooking up with Jim and it doesn’t matter anymore. It’s too late for everyone. The sad thing is in all this, is that Martin really thought you loved *him*. All those years he was fooled by you. I only hope he never suspected the truth before the accident. I hope he can sleep soundly when I lay him down with his brother. At the very least, his final resting place should be one of peace. Don’t you agree, Bobby? At least you can give the boys that much? And you can do that for me too, can’t you? Just leave us all well alone now?’

Contemplation eclipsed Bobby’s livid defeat as she gingerly re-positioned herself on the bench.

Her world now seemingly an empty, lumbering vessel.

No foundation. No future. No direction.

She looked up to Alex who had begun to shiver under the thickening skies.

‘It wasn’t always supposed to be like this, Alex. You’ve got to believe me. This wasn’t always the plan. To think those boys’ lives ended how they did. Its unthinkable. Leaves me open and raw, so it does. Truly disastrous. Horrific.’

Alex wiped her eyes and scanned along the footpath.

‘Too late to fish for sympathy now, Bobby. The damage is done. You took two lives and chewed them up amid a blanket of lies. You should be ashamed. But the thing is…you’re *not* ashamed, are you? Not one bit. Christ…you even let Martin propose and then said *yes*! And all that time he never knew the *real* you. He had been given a chance to taste happiness and you trampled all over it. Well, it’s up to you how long you want to wallow in your victory. Just enjoy counting the money. I hope you never forget how you came by it.’

Bobby stared limply at the floor between her boots.

There seemed little point in continuing the exchange.

Alex had run out of things to say.

The game was out in the open.

It was time to depart.

'I'm going now, Bobby. Rest assured I won't be bothering you again. Ever. I just hope for your sake that God forgives your betrayal. Because I've seen first-hand what happens when he doesn't. Goodbye. And good luck. I think you'll need it, somehow.'

Bobby didn't even reply to the genuine warning.

She didn't even engage with Alex's departing vision.

She let her gaze settle to the distant naked poplar trees, as the footsteps of Alexandra Lawley gradually dispersed from earshot.

*****

An hour had passed.

Bobby Jones remained seated on the bench.

By the rain shelter.

She continued to fumble with the silver locket around her neck.

An instinctive gesture.

The locket that was a gift bestowed to her many years earlier.

Bobby took the clasp between her finger and thumb and prised open the tiny case.

Inside she had inserted a photograph.

An image of a man that she had been besotted with for a decade.

A man she had secretly hoped would be by her side forever.

And now she quietly dreamed, that if their scheme had performed to schedule, she would be reunited with him very soon.

40
HARBORING A FUTURE?

Over three months had elapsed since Bobby Jones had spoken with Alex at East Park. An exclusive joining of minds that would likely only serve to ensure their permanent estrangement.

There had been no contact between them at all since that day.

Bobby presumed that the burial of the ashes would be organised by Alex as she had requested.

In truth, it mattered little to the woman from Belfast, anyhow.

She had no allegiance to her past.

Probate been granted.

Inheritance had been assured.

Signed. Sealed. Delivered.

Once number thirty-two, Glenfield Avenue, had been established as the lawful property of one Roberta Anne Jones, it was promptly sold by her.

Relocation had been swift and relatively problem free.

The new accommodation was a temporary arrangement.

They wouldn't be there long.

To all intents and purposes, Bobby Jones had made positive steps to embrace what might lie ahead of her.

But her ties with her own history had not been completely severed.

The plan was in place and was already in motion.

She hoped to discard the typical roller coaster pattern of events that her previous existence seemed to favour.

Pillar to post. Post to pillar.

Never grounded.

Ever transposing.

Maybe now, at last, some stability could prevail.

And somehow, as instructed, she was able to retain clarity of mind.

She had been party to events that should possibly have incited insufferable guilt for the remainder of her days.

But the woman from Belfast was inducted in the school of hard knocks. Any emotional penance she would withstand.

She could accept it and accommodate it.

After all, when did feeling guilty ever achieve anything?

Regret was a human frailty that she no longer wished to associate with.

She believed she could now look to the horizon with no inhibition to bind her.

Expectant of nothing.

For her entire life she seemed to have been laid at the mercy of fate.

Like a fraying branch of a tree, vulnerable to the whim of the wind.

But as her next chapter commenced, she was convinced of its potential positive outcome.

She was there. In the moment.

And for Bobby Jones, that was enough for now.

She perched on the hearth rug next to the gas fire.

Observing the flickering TV screen.

Her considerably older companion sat in the armchair.

A man whose life policy had always been wilful detachment from any commitment or responsibility.

Now late into in his sixth decade, he cut a fatigued specimen.

Weather beaten.

World weary.

Unfriended by anyone who had happened to cross his path.

With the crossing of swords usually being the subsequent result.

Yet his relationship with the woman from Belfast had held firm despite the most testing of circumstances.

She observed his contemplation.

His pitted, battle-scarred visage conveyed very little.

Unmoving and unmoved.

She sensed the urge to speak.

But was careful to do so softly.

'You okay, my darling? Can I get you anything?'

The man's eyes eventually shifted to engage with her.

He pretended not to hear, but eventually gave up such a futile game.

'Such as?' he responded, gruffly.

'A beer? A coffee?'

'No. Nothing at all.'

The woman from Belfast moved to position herself behind him and draped her arms over his shoulders and nuzzled her cheek to his.

She whispered in his ear.

'Do you think we made it?'

More seconds of teasing silence passed as he attempted to conjure an answer she might not like to hear.

'Not cut and dried yet. Not by a long chalk.'

Her optimism would not be dented.

'But we're set up with the money. We can go anywhere and do anything we want to, now. Just like you said we would.'

He tilted his head to engage with her indulging brown eyes.

His own gaze of steel bore into her, disbelieving her naivety.

'Now we're on this road, the journey *never* ends, Roberta. We need to become different people in a different place. The status quo is tipped against us more than ever, now.'

She began to caress his neck.

She believed she loved this man.

And she was sure to profess her faith in him.

'But if we stick together, we can achieve anything.'

He studied her consistently attractive profile in the half-light.

He sighed with resignation.

'Time won't absolve us, Roberta. We can't sever ourselves from our deeds just because we've now jumped off the cliff edge together.'

Once more she exhibited her unswaying positivity.

'They won't have a clue where we are. Most of the world thinks you died in that reservoir with your sons.'

He sat up and faced her directly.

He forced her to draw back from him.

‘Listen to me. Hungry wolves don’t stop their chase. They will get to the same cliff edge and make the same jump that we did if they get the merest scent under their noses. That’s how ravenous they will be. We can’t just sit and hide. They will find us. Believe you me.’

She sensed the dream she was sold being amended slightly.

‘So, what are you saying?’

He did not disclose his agitation at her misplaced buoyancy.

‘What I’m saying is, our troubles may still be ahead of us. Not behind us.’

The woman from Belfast kissed her companion’s chafed scalp with her tender lips.

‘I know, lover. I know. But just for tonight, tell me we will be alright, will you?’

His attentions were not fully focussed on his female companion.

His thoughts were straying toward the future.

He knew that further warfare was inevitable.

Conflict was the only way he knew.

And he felt in his heart of hearts that whilst peace reigned for the time being, they could not evade their pursuers forever.

This was merely the calm before the greatest storm of them all.

The shadows of the past would loom again.

Larger than ever.

And when the day of reckoning eventually arrived, Jim Andrews knew he would need to be ready.

41
A FLEETING VISIT?

Alex Lawley exited the glass sliding doors of the college reception building.

May had been a frantic month. Exams were imminent. Four assignments were barely started. It looked like being a long evening ahead if she were to even attempt covering lost ground.

With all the distractions of the year so far, it was a minor miracle that she was still in the mix to be anywhere near ready to sit an exam.

The late afternoon sunshine warmed her face as she ambled along the tree-lined driveway. She could have caught the bus right outside the university grounds, but instead opted to walk a little way.

She checked her phone for messages before replacing it in the back pocket of her jeans and continued onward.

As she strode, her senses slowly adjusted to a familiar scent.

Feint at first but then it began carrying incredible potency.

Her mind set about identifying the potential source of the wondrous essence and why it might register as something she had experienced before.

And then the moment of acknowledgement arrived.

It was aftershave.

The fragrant balm of the man she still held in her heart as the love of her life.

Her throat constricted with the reflexive pull of rising emotion.

But she held firm and did not shed a tear.

Then, across the busy dual carriageway, something caught her eye.

Between the flashes of roaring traffic.

She squinted toward the source of her curiosity but could not decipher what it was she was attempting to visualise.

Then, a fleeting glimpse.

Amid the chaos of lorries, buses, bikes, and cars.

Was that a figure observing her from the mid distance?

She halted her march and continued to engage with the location in question, some one hundred meters away.

Squinting into the sunshine made certainty difficult.

She considered crossing the road.

Could it be?

Blinking and rubbing her eyes, she stared intently.

She was convinced she heard a voice in the air.

But when her focus settled, there was no one there.

And the fragrance had suddenly vanished.

And with it, so did the hope in her heart.

It couldn't have been him.

Not a chance on Earth.

Was there?

EPILOGUE

East Park Cemetery.

Eight months, two weeks, and three days since the tragedy at Collinson's Reservoir.

It had been a long journey with a singular purpose.

The Stranger stared intently at the three graves, as unseasonal rain pattered the scene.

Marked in black granite effect; each inscribed with gold lettering.

Indication of the final resting place of a mother and her two sons.

Three lives that had endured untenable and relentless agonies.

Whilst the lone figure paid due respects in solemn silence, it was a struggle to avoid venturing back through history and the circumstances that had evolved.

The tragic significance of the visit induced an untameable swell of sorrow and wrenching sympathy for the family's untold individual and collective plights.

The Stranger was fully aware that Elizabeth Andrews had unwittingly been subjected to a lifelong campaign of unbridled abuse, of both mind and body.

The signs were there from the very early stages of the relationship with her husband-to-be. But Elizabeth was so young. She was blinded by her feelings for that beast, and stubbornly unheeding of the warnings conveyed to her.

The foreseen legacy of torment and the ever-increasing peril was a catalyst that had influenced Elizabeth Andrews' eventual submission.

Learning of this news was shocking enough.

And to then discover that her offspring had subsequently perished, induced the severest bouts of despair.

It was always suspected that the Andrews family never stood a chance of enduring against such mighty odds.

But death was not a factor that ever featured in this prediction.

And certainly not in such a harsh, unforgiving, diabolical manner.

The heart bled for those two boys and their mother.

Two boys whose childhood was always under threat.

Whose years were never their own.

Never free to experience the orthodox rites of passage that their peers enjoyed.

And then only to meet with adulthood. A field of dreams distorted and ultimately destroyed by the imprint of their tyrannical patriarch.

Oh yes.

The Stranger at the graveside knew of these things.

The nefarious presence of Jim Andrews was always destined to render the boys vulnerable to the worst kind of danger.

But the mourner at the headstones was also in possession of unspoken knowledge.

The rumour that Jim Andrews lived on had gained gravitas.

Word of mouth here. A possible sighting there.

Despite the unofficial yet accepted line that he too had died at the bottom of that reservoir along with his children.

Public opinion had gradually become indifferent to any theory.

Interest from the Police had now waned.

Yet The Stranger held full conviction and had experienced a remarkable transition of late.

A spiritual enlightenment, perhaps.

No longer would it be tolerable to uphold the policy chosen all those years ago.

The preferable option had altered drastically, now.

No longer could they ignore.

No longer would they cower.

Pretending that the inevitable would not transpire was folly of the worst order.

The re-emergence would be timely.

And it would be brutally effective.

That much would be ensured, at least.

The natural inclination to accept that it was now too late.

Now rendered redundant considering all developments.

The flip side to this argument was gratifying to the soul.

Because *late*…was infinitely better…than *never*…

The Stranger had pledged to seek out the instigator of such tragedies.

The orchestrator of such losses.

The puppet master of a family's eternal misery would soon be found to have his seemingly untouchable reign ended.

The mysterious loner at the graveyard turned away from the holy ground where a mother and her two sons were lain.

A wry smile emerged as a potential plan was formulated.

If Jim Andrews believed that he had truly exonerated himself from his past, then all the better for it.

For the calling had come.

The hunt was now the imminent quest.

Retribution was the ultimate mission.

For Elizabeth. For Martin. For Jamie.

The Stranger had been designated for the purpose.

The sodden figure departed the graveyard and the chapel grounds.

Undetected.

Unknown.

Undaunted.

Already dispensed with any last morsel of forgiveness.

In the undertaking they were now committed to…

…TO BE CONTINUED…

ACKNOWLEDGEMENTS

I wish to thank the following people for their invaluable expertise and support in helping this book gain wings:
Samantha Thornton; Hannah Bliss; Charlotte Wilson; Robbie Wilson; Carole Thornton, Chris Bliss; Charlotte Bliss; Jeanette Taylor Ford; Sue Hayward; Ford Wood; Beverley Latimer; Yana Z and last but certainly not least, David Slaney for his superb cover design.
I couldn't have done it without any of you.
I am forever indebted.
RJT

Also Available on Amazon
by Richard John Thornton

thrillers

DELIVER US FROM EVIL
AT HELL'S GATE
THE SWANS AT CLEARLAKE
WITHIN THESE WALLS
A PRAYER FOR MARTIN
IN PLAIN SIGHT

the 80s trilogy

LAST OF THE OLD SCHOOL
NO MORE TEA AND TOAST

Printed in Great Britain
by Amazon

39340032R00199